MW00917036

Kidnapping The Princess

By

Yuriko Hime

Copyright © 2020 by Yuriko Hime

All rights reserved. No part of this book may be reproduced in any written, electronic, recording, or photocopying without written permission of the publisher or author. The exception would be in the case of brief quotations embodied in the critical articles or reviews and pages where permission is specifically granted by the publisher or author.

Although every precaution has been taken to verify the accuracy of the information contained herein, the author and publisher assume no responsibility for any errors or omissions. No liability is assumed for damages that may result from the use of information contained within.

Books may be purchased by contacting the publisher and author at:

Email: yurikohimex(a)gmail.com
Instagram: Yurikohimeko
Wattpad: Yurikohime
First Printing: 2020
Publisher: Y.H Publishing House
Editor: G.F
Creative Consultant: G.F and Tatienne

For everyone who believed in my
ability to write and for Buddy.

Table of Contents

Chapter 1

"Let go of me, you mongrel!"

I watched as the Princess struggled against the ropes that bound her ankles and wrist. She shook on the floor like a madman, her head jerking in every direction. There wasn't any question that she was searching for her captor, even while her face was covered with a black cloth. I smiled, observing it all.

"Let go of me! Unhand me at once!" she repeated. "If you come to your senses, I'll tell my mother—I'll tell my mother to spare your life!"

How lovely. I smiled again. As if the Queen could help her right now. Her mother, the Queen, wasn't there when I took her from the safety of the palace and lifted her to my shoulder. Neither was the Queen there when I brought her to this abandoned castle deep into the woods. Each one of them in that palace was doomed. That I could assure.

" I doubt Your Majesty will spare my life if I let you go," I said to the Princess. "Even if you ask her on my behalf."

"Huh?" The Princess stopped squirming. "You're a woman?"

"Last time I checked."

She tried to sit but failed miserably. How could she, when she was bound from head to toe? "What do you want from me?" she asked, tilting her head. "Why did you kidnap me? For money?

Power? Men? I can give you anything you want. Just tell me."

I stifled a third smile. It was just like the rich to search for a leverage, something I was awfully familiar with.

"I don't need your money, Princess," I said. "My bank account has more than enough to let me live as I please. Anyone can tell you that power comes with that, so it's not something I'd want either. As for men. . ." I tapped my chin. "Let's just say that I like women more."

"Then what do you want?" she asked in a small voice. The confidence she'd displayed before going here was slipping away. Not good enough for me. I wanted it squashed.

Going to the Princess to the stone floor, I took her by the arm to help her sit. She smelled of shampoo, fear, and had pulled away from my grasp. It encouraged me to lean in closer. "You asked what I want, and what I want is simple." Goosebumps marked her skin when I whispered, "Your body."

The Princess went completely still as she digested the information. A heartbeat more and she was trashing from me in disgust. "Maniac!" she screamed. "Jerk! Imbecile! You ugly son of a—"

I removed the cloth from her head and watched her mouth slack open. "Still ugly?" I asked.

It took her seconds to comprehend what she was seeing. Seconds comprised of swallowing the lump in her throat, blinking at me, and licking the dryness from her lips.

"Y-your eyes," she stuttered. "Wow. They're the strangest color."

"They're called forest green, Princess." I smirked. "Be happy I let you see them at all." I scooped her in my arms before she could say another word. Time to get this over with. Time to put her in her cell.

Traveling from the hallway to her room was not an easy feat. Not when the Princess moved with a ferocity of a bull and cursed me so many times one would wonder where she learned those words. But I did manage to open the door, bring her inside, and toss her to the bed. Afterwards, I crossed my and arms and studied her.

"Do yourself a favor and stop twitching," I said. "There's no way you'll ever get out of here. You're just making yourself look stupid."

Shock plastered on her face like an unwanted adhesive. "I do not look stupid," she said.

"Sure, you don't."

The bed creaked as she struggled to sit. "Why am I here?" she demanded. "You have no business with me. You're a low life. The lowest!"

"And you're a saint?" I gave her a patronizing look. She might have looked like one with her honey-colored hair and pinkish, plump lips. But those grey eyes must have killed me a dozen times. I shrugged at her. "You really shouldn't ask questions you'd regret knowing the answer to, Princess. That's how people get hurt."

"Are you going to kill me?"

"And she's still asking."

"Psh!" She blew the stray hair away from her face. "I'll ask whatever I want when I want to. Now answer my question, fool."

"Fine." She was too insistent. "Just to let you know, killing you would take the fun away," I said. "I'd rather keep you here for a very long time." I gestured to the almost empty room, to the blank stone walls, and the white sheet on the metal bed, complete with a single pillow. Everything had been prepared for her arrival, just as all planned. "Are you paying attention, Princess? I suggest you love the four corners of this room because they're all you'll be seeing for a while." I pointed to the windows. "Those are barred. You'll never get out even if you cut your hair and do a Rapunzel." I tilted my chin to the door. "That's been upgraded with a security code, and too bad for you, I'm the only one who knows the combination."

"Scream all you want," I went on. "This abandoned castle is located miles from any town or road. That means no one will hear you. No one will help. In this little world of ours, I'm your only friend. I will feed you, talk to you when I want, and do things that need to be done. If you're not nice to me, you'll never see the daylight again. Understand?"

"I despise you," she whispered.

"I'm sorry to hear that. But having that attitude won't help. At least not while you're here." I made a beeline for the door. Show was over.

I had done a remarkable job.

"Wait!" She sounded confused. "Aren't you going to remove my restraints first?"

I stopped on my tracks. "Only if you say please."

~ 9 ~

"Are you freaking kidding me!"

My grin was wide when I faced her, making my face hurt. "Tut-tut, Princess. I don't think Her Majesty, the Queen, will appreciate your smart mouth."

Chaos crossed her features before she closed her eyes. Did I hit a nerve?

It was a pity, though, that the mayhem had been shoved into a box when she opened her eyes again. She looked calmer when she murmured, "Please remove my restraints."

Good call. Heading back to the Princess, I leaned down to work on the knots. The rope was fastened tight, bundled around her wrist, though not enough to chafe her smooth skin. "See?" I said while untying the rope. "I know there's some manner left in you."

She pursed her lips but didn't respond. I knew she was angry with me for kidnapping her. Hell, she'd spend the rest of her days in this place cursing me. But who cares? I had my own reasons.

The Princess opened and closed her hands the moment she was untied. She took her time stretching and wriggling her fingers, simultaneously testing her feet by tapping them on the floor.

"Better?" I said.

The corners of her mouth quirked up. Pain erupted in my stomach before I realized that she elbowed me and ran to the door.

Oh no you don't!

Years of Judo training kicked in. I dashed after her even while my stomach was aching.

There wasn't much of a struggle. It was just me winning over her, pinning her hands, my heart palpitating as I brought her down and straddled her beneath me. "You shouldn't have done that!" I growled, pissed. "You're lucky I don't have a photoshoot right now! The bruise you made will be a problem."

She wrestled to free her hands from mine. "What are you saying?" she yelled. "Let go of me—let go of me now!"

I put my whole weight on her. Enough already. "I'm warning you, Princess! If you do that again, if you try to break free, I'll rip your clothes off and leave you here naked!"

That stopped her.

For a minute or so, the only sounds in the room were our harsh breaths. Both of us were sweating, face flushed, chest heaving up and down. I nudged her with my leg so she'd listen. "I'm tired of these games, so I'm going to release you. When I do, you're going to walk back to the bed, sit on the mattress, and stay still. One wrong move and you'll regret it. Clear?"

She didn't answer.

I nudged her again. "Am I clear?"

"Yes!"

Good. I finally let go of her. Once I did, we went our separate ways: her to the bed, and me to the door. The security measure beeped when I punched in the code.

"I'll see you to tomorrow." I bid my farewell.

The rooftop was my next destination. The garden to be specific. But I wouldn't go there to tend to the dahlia's, nor to survey the vast forest that surrounded the decrepit castle we were in. I would go there to rest my head. It had been pounding all night.

Sigh. . .

The Princess, as usual, had to be blamed for it. From a distance, she was a goody-goody. Anyone who'd look at her would only see composure, selflessness, like she couldn't hurt a fly. She had me fooled. Not only did her mouth run fast, her fuse run short, too. And damn, she was wild, trying to break free like that.

What a pity. With grey eyes that spoke volumes, hair that looked dipped in honey, pink plump lips, and a lean but shapely body, she was exactly my type. Too bad, she was off-limits.

The next morning, I found myself in a staring contest with her, with the same grey eyes I was fascinated with the other night. Except this time, I wasn't amused. The Princess was refusing to eat the porridge I prepared.

"I don't eat that," she insisted, head turned away. She reminded me of some of my neighbors at Kensington's. They were a challenging lot.

"Can you at least tell me why?" I asked. "Lots of children starve every day. You're lucky I'm even feeding you."

"Those children will still starve even if I eat that," she replied. "Which I won't."

Guilt flashed on her face. For a second there, she looked like she was about to apologize. Not.

"Do you even hear yourself?" I said. "You're a bloody Princess!" My lips curved down in distaste. "Oh, that's right! You talk exactly like that because you're royalty. You think you're better than us, don't you?"

"It has nothing to do with that."

"Then what?"

She rolled her eyes before standing. The Princess glared down at me, dress fluttering like a worked-up bird. "Of all the things you're going to feed me, you had to pick the one I hate most." Her nose wrinkled before she shuddered. "Porridge."

I glanced at the Styrofoam bowl in my hand. Inside was a healthy dose of grain and milk sprinkled with berries. How could she not like it? It was delicious. "What's your problem with porridge? I love porridge!"

"Then you eat it." She pushed it away.

Okay, that's it. I placed the bowl on the floor and stood from the bed. Who did she think I was? Her nanny? She wasn't in the Royal Palace anymore. She was in my domain. My prisoner.

"All right," I said. "I won't force you to eat. In fact, I don't want to be in the same room at all. I bet you'll eat the bloody porridge once you're hungry."

I left her room and came back that afternoon. The food was still untouched. Come nightfall, I was disappointed to see that the bowl was still on the floor. The Princess hadn't eaten the whole day, or to be more accurate, since yesterday. At present, she was sleeping soundly in the bed, her mouth opened a fraction. She was still wearing the blue dress from the day before. Her hair was tied in a half-crown braid. She looked like a real Princess. A beautiful one at that.

If only she wasn't so difficult.

My heart squeezed as I looked at her peaceful face. I knew I shouldn't be kind to her. I knew I shouldn't even care. But I still went to the kitchen and prepared a decent meal for her.

The Princess was already awake when I went back to her room with the plate in my hand. "What's that?" Her long lashes fluttered as she sniffed. "It smells so good."

I placed the plate on the bed in front of her. "It's steak and mashed potatoes."

The muscles in her throat bobbed as her eyes traveled to the food again. It looked like she was seconds away from drooling, but she didn't make a move to eat. "Where are the utensils?" she asked.

The mattress sagged as I sat next to her. "In the kitchen, far away for you to stab me." I motioned my hands. "You have to eat like this from now on."

"I do?" There was a second of hesitation before she pulled the plate to her. I sat there and watched. Her first bite was nothing but awkward. She was shaking from hunger and was clumsy without a fork. Still, after a moment, she turned to me while chewing. "Do you want some?"

Hmm. Was she trying to make peace?

"No, thank you," I replied, both for the food and the hidden implication. "Don't be nice to me. Don't talk to me either. I'm your kidnapper, remember?"

She ignored me and went for a second bite. Her mouth was full when she asked, "How old are you?"

~ 14 ~

Stubborn woman. But I didn't see any reason to keep that information, especially when she wouldn't kill me with that. "Twenty-two," I said. "You don't have to tell me your age. Everyone's aware that you're eighteen."

"Hmm."

"Don't *hmm* at me and eat. I know that you're hungry."

The food was gone fast. She didn't leave a single trace of it on the plate. After the last bite, she licked her fingers in a very un-Princess way and smiled widely at me.

"Any reason for that?" I asked suspiciously.

"I figured it out."

"Figured what out?"

"Why you kidnapped me." The corner of her eyes crinkled. "You said you have money and power, right? You also said you want my body. That only leads to one thing."

"Which is?"

"You have a crush on me."

Unexpected laughter burst from my mouth. Was she serious?

"Really?" I said. "You expect me to kidnap someone because of a bloody crush?"

She crossed her arms. "Uh-huh. Why else did you bring me here? You don't look poor. You don't like a hoodlum. In fact, you look like. . ."

What? Like what? Her forehead creased before she glanced away.

"Like what?" I asked aloud.

"I won't tell."

"Suit yourself." I took the empty plate and rose to my feet. "I'll come back tomorrow to bring breakfast. Go to sleep."

"Wait," she said as I started to walk away.

I turned to her. This was quickly becoming a habit. "Don't tell me you're still hungry?"

"No, that's not it." She motioned to her dress. "I want to bathe. I want to change my clothes. I've been wearing the same thing since yesterday. And I'd rather keep this to myself, but I really need to pee. Fast."

Oops. I've forgotten to tell her last night.

"Look to your left," I said. "You probably don't notice the door because it blends with the wall, but that's the bathroom. There's a tub, a shower—everything you need to clean yourself. And just in case you're thinking about it, the windows are also barred so you can't escape from there."

She looked relieved as her eyes searched for the details. "I thought you were going to make me pee in a bottle or something. I was trying to hold it in."

I flinched at that. This shouldn't happen again.

"I'll bring you something to wear," I said.

I made the mistake of coming back earlier, earlier than I should. The Princess was standing in the middle of the room when I entered, naked from head to foot.

~ 16 ~

"Woah!"

"Hey!"

A heart attack built up in my chest as we stared wide-eyed at each other. I tossed her the clothes and turned around the same time she did, but not before I saw everything. Lord!

"I-I'll change," she mumbled.

"S-sure."

Both of us were more composed when she got out of the bathroom, fully dressed. She was wearing the skinny jeans and the blue sweater I gave. And though her hair was still styled in the half-crown braid that she preferred, the casual clothes made her look different, approachable. As if a Princess like her could be that approachable.

She was fixing her top when I noticed the black choker against her neck. I've been too busy fighting her off yesterday and this morning to pay attention to it. But now that I was, my curiosity got the better of me. Did someone special give that to her? Who?

"Why didn't you remove that?" I asked.

"This?" She touched the choker for a second before her eyes darted to me. Suddenly, all the friendliness from when she was eating was gone, like I found a way to offend her without meaning to. "I don't take this off, ever."

"Mind telling me why?"

She clicked her tongue. "It's none of your business, okay? If you're not going to say why you kidnapped me, then I'm not going to give you my reasons for wearing this either."

"Fair enough. But what if I remove it from your neck? Since we're on the subject of kidnaping, I doubt you'll be able to do anything about it."

A savageness I didn't think she was capable of reflected in her eyes.

"Touch this and I'll kill you," she said. "Don't test me. I'm not the Princess that you all know."

My stomach felt hollow as what she said began to sink in. Something happened to her, something bad, and I wasn't there to protect her from it.

My hands balled into fists. Now I had to hurt her too. I had no other choice. It was our destiny.

Chapter 2

It was a sunny spring morning that day, a perfect time to sit on the grass. Flowers of varying colors were scattered between us: lilac for my dress, green for my eyes, pink for her lips. I took a flower from the ground and sniffed. The lavender smelled just like her.

"I have an idea," she said out of the blue.

"What?"

"You'll be my Prince when we grow up."

I turned and tucked the flower at the side of her ear. She was saying odd things again. Things that would often make the adults stop and stare, especially her mother.

"That sounds great," I murmured. "But there's one problem."

Her head tilted to the side.

"I'm a girl," I went on. "We both are."

"Oh." She scratched her cheek and stared into the distance. It didn't take long before she was sliding closer to me. "Do you think my handmaiden was lying then?"

"About what?" I asked.

"About Princes?"

"I'm not sure that I follow."

She took a flower from the lot and put it on my lap. "When I asked her one time, she said that you can be my Prince. And I believed her. You know why?" Her eyes sparkled when she looked at me again. "Because for some people, Prince Charming is a Princess."

A loud thud and an accompanying yell woke me with a start. Panicking, I rolled to my side, got on my feet, and put on a fighting stance at once. Pain radiated at my ribs though no one had hit me. I've fallen from the bed, again. *Crap!*

My ragged breaths filled the room as I took in my surroundings. There was no grass, no flowers, or a cute little girl sitting beside me. There was only me in a sweat-soaked shirt, inside a barely empty room.

I waited for my breaths to even. The dream was so real, too vivid, that it felt like I was still there. I was going crazy.

"Miss Kidnapper." The Princess 'voice cut through my thoughts. "Yoo-hoo! Are you there?"

I turned to the door and frowned. *Ugh.*

The Princess didn't know this, but I was sleeping in the room just across from her bedroom cell. My real bedroom was a floor below us, but I wanted to be near her just in case. Look where that got me.

"Yoo-hoo!" she called again. "Miss kidnapper. . . I know you're there!"

I hurried to the closet to grab an extra shirt to change into. She woke me from deep sleep. This better be important.

The Princess was seated on her bedroom floor when I entered, arms wrapped around her knees. She didn't smile when she saw me.

"What do you want?" I said. "You ruined my sleep."

Her scowl deepened. "You know, for someone who looks good, your attitude is foul."

"Better foul than a pushover." I leaned against the door frame and smirked. "Which brings me to the question. You think I'm pretty?"

"Give me a break." Her cheekbones looked more prominent from this angle. It was either that, or the Princess had lost weight. Not good. Especially since I've been giving in to her food request lately.

"Okay," I said. "Let's drop that topic. Why did you call me again? Is there anything wrong?"

"Aside from the fact that you're holding me hostage here?" Her eyes narrowed at me. "Miss kidnapper, if you haven't noticed, I've been inside this room for the last two weeks. I think I'm going crazy!" She threw her hands to the ceiling to emphasize her point. "You rarely talk to me. You hardly come for a visit except in mealtimes. And God knows what you're doing on the other side of that door." She groaned. "That's it! I give up. If you want to kill me, just do it."

"I told you, hadn't I?" I replied. "I'm not going to kill you."

"Then please talk to me!" she snapped. "I can't stand this! Sitting around in this room doing nothing is driving me insane!" The creases on her face softened. "Please. . . If there's an ounce of humanity left in you, please talk to me."

Damn it. No matter how hard I tried, those puppy-dog eyes got me every time. First, when she wanted ice cream the other week, then when she craved for cake. Now I found myself being dragged to her side, sitting down to honor her request.

"What do you want to talk about?" I said, simpering.

She scratched the floor with her nails. "I don't know. Tell me about you."

I crossed my legs while deciding. Maybe a teensy bit of information wouldn't hurt. She wouldn't use it against me, would she?

Not a chance.

"Okay, I grew up in England."

Her eyebrow raised. "You did? But you don't have an accent."

"I said I grew up in England," I rebuked. "I didn't say I was born there." I took her hand and placed it on her lap. She'd damage her nails if she continued scratching.

"Did your parents relocate?" she pried.

"No. My adoptive parents are British. They brought me to live with them after the adoption."

"Oh." She considered. "How about school? Did you go to any?"

"Yes. It's boring to talk about."

Besides, I didn't want to go into lengthy details about the Ivy League university I graduated from. Not today anyway.

The Princess 'nose wrinkled. She was probably contemplating the psychopath I turned out to be, not that it was any of my business. "Can I ask you another question?" she said.

"You can ask, but I can't guarantee the answer."

She ignored my lack of enthusiasm and leaned forward. A smile was beginning to form on her lips. "May I know what your name is? I can't keep calling you Miss Kidnapper. It's too long."

I gave her a long, measuring look. It didn't sound like a trick question. Didn't sound like she'd use it against me either. Had I been in her position, I'd be curious as well.

"Iris," I answered. "My adoptive parents call me Iris." I glanced away. "But my name before that was Cybele. You can call me either one."

"Cybele?" The name rolled from her tongue like a poetry. "Where did I hear that before?"

"It's a Greek name. You probably read it in a book or watched a movie with a Cybele character in it."

"Maybe. Anyway, you can call me Talia. Drop the 'princess 'already. You don't treat me like one anyhow." She offered a hand between us, a dimple appearing on her cheek. "Nice to meet you, Cybele. I like that better than Iris."

Goosebumps crawled on my skin as I focused on her face. The smile was giving me déjà vu.

"Aren't you going to shake my hand?" she inquired.

I shrugged the strange feeling away and took her hand. But instead of shaking like she wanted, I kissed her knuckles before letting go.

Her cheek was powdered with red while she tucked her hand under her leg. And then she was asking me again, "Aren't you too pretty to be a kidnapper?"

~ 23 ~

"No."

"Oh come on," she said. "Green eyes? Wavy hair? Straight nose? Perfect teeth?" She assessed me like jewelry. "And what are you, 5'10?"

"5'11."

"See?" She looked satisfied that she'd proven her point. "Last I know, kidnappers are supposed to look scary."

I snorted at her. The way she talked, you'd think she knew a kidnapper or two in her lifetime. "Flattery won't get you anywhere, Talia. I'm still your kidnapper. I won't let you go."

"I'm just telling the truth."

"Well in this case, the truth won't set you free." *Ha-ha.*

"You have a dark sense of humor. Do you know that?"

I tapped a finger on my chin. Enough about me. It was my turn to ask questions. "What's it like being the princess?" I asked. "I bet you can do what you want without any repercussions."

"If only that was true."

"Isn't it?"

Her gaze lowered to the floor. I didn't know if it was sadness or anger that flitted on her face, but whatever it was, she recovered quickly. "To be honest, it's pretty much like this," she spoke. "I wasn't allowed to leave the Palace. Not on my own. I wasn't allowed to go to a normal school either. I was homeschooled. The only difference between here and there is that I had my books and a laptop to keep me company."

"What about friends?" I asked.

"I didn't have friends. I had acquaintances." She picked on the hem of her sweater, trying to break the thread. "I know they just suck up to me because I'm going to be the queen someday. Even my fiancé is boring as crap."

Wait, what?

"You have a fiancé?"

My outburst made her look at me in surprise. "His name is Lance," she answered my question. "We are to wed on my 20th birthday. Everyone knows this."

Everyone but me. I swallowed the lemon in my throat. The thoughts of kidnapping her had consumed me for years. I didn't even know she got a fiancé. Whose name was Lance.

"When did you meet this boy?" I pressed. "Had you been together for long? Do you love him?"

"Love?" The Princess 'answering laugh echoed around the room. It just bubbled out of nowhere and surprised me. "I don't love Lance. Who would want to marry that twat? Not me!"

"Why did you agree to be wed then?" I asked. "Does Her Majesty the Queen know that you don't like him?"

She gave me an incredulous look like I've lost my mind. Maybe she was going to answer. Maybe not. But she shook her head anyhow and said, "I don't want to talk about those things right now. It's too complicated. What I really want to know is how you managed to kidnap me right under the guards noses. The head guard is especially nosey."

"They had a moment of weakness," was all I said.

The conversation had nowhere to go since none of us wanted to reveal much. We stayed silent for a while, looking at nothing in particular, until Talia got tired of playing with her sweater and asked. "Why did you do it, Cybele? You're not as bad as you make yourself sound. You wouldn't even talk to me if you were."

My breath stilled as I processed her words. At the hope beneath them. At the implications.

The Princess was still expecting my answer when I scrambled to my feet, tilted her chin to me, and whispered, "Just because we've talked doesn't mean you know me. I'm not your friend. We're not equals, Talia."

"But—"

"Shut it!" I yelled. "I'm not a good person, okay? Always remember that!"

I let her go and left the room in a hurry. My hands were shaking as I paced the hallway back and forth.

Stupid, Cybele! See what you've done? That pretty girl inside is the enemy. You know that! You're going to screw this up if you let her come close.

I yanked my shirt up so I could stare at the tattoo on my hip bone. '*Long live the Queen,* 'it said. *Remember your promise. Never forget why you must do this. Talia's not Talia anymore.*

~ 26 ~

With newfound determination, I entered the cell again and marched to where she was. Talia's mouth opened in shock as I grabbed her hand and started to pull her up. It was time for her to know her place.

She was my prisoner.

The castle where I've locked her was unique. Outside, it was decrepit, with rickety slab of stones that looked seconds from caving in. Rusted fences surrounding the area threw would-be passerby's in the other direction, if they even managed to find the castle deep in the forest in the first place. Inside was different though, because inside was a modern fanfare. Most of the rooms inside the castle had been converted to suit my contemporary style, with all the bedrooms equipped with state-of-the-art security doors. With the windows barred and everything controlled by me, no one would get in and out without my permission.

I took the Princess from her cell, through the hallway, straight to the laundry room. Only then did I let her go.

"You may be a Princess in the Palace, but here and now, you're nothing." I sounded harsh. I *should* be harsh. "Since you're so bored you'd rather die, why don't you become my servant instead, Talia? From now on, you're the one who's going to launder all your clothes. I want this whole floor cleaned. Cook thrice a day for me. Skip one meal, and I'll feed you porridge for months. Got it?"

Her gasp brought out the bigger monster in me.

"That's right, Princess." I sneered. "You're in my world now. What I say goes."

~ 27 ~

She wasn't a complete fool. She nodded to show she understood me. But then she pointed to the washing machine on the right, a quizzical look on her face. "I have no idea how to operate the machine though," she said. "Can you teach me?"

"Well aren't you an ignorant little kid?"

She put her hands against her waist. The question in her eyes was beginning to fade, to be replaced with irritation. "Well excuse me for not using those all my life," she snapped at me. "I just happen to be a Princess, you know? Do you think I've ever seen one up close?"

"A washing machine? Really?" I looked her up and down. "Princesses are supposed to be bright, right? Imagine if you become a Queen. You haven't washed your freaking clothes yet, let alone used a freaking washing machine. How can you rule a whole country?"

She pursed her lips instead of answering me and walked to the counter. I didn't think much of it when she grabbed an opened carton of laundry detergent, but when she threw the white stuff all over my face, I knew I had enough of her bratty behavior.

I bent to the floor to scoop some powder too. The look on her face was priceless when I threw it back to her.

"That does it!" She wiped her face. "Stop insulting me!"

Powder fluffed everywhere as both of us fell down following her pounce on me. She rolled us over and over, making me dizzy. Her fingers got tangled in my hair. "Ouch! Stop it!" I cried. She tried to pull her hand away and yanked, wrenching my head with it. "Stop it, Princess! Stop it! You're hurting me! You're mental!"

Talia seized the assault and giggled like a school girl. I didn't know how it ended this way, but she'd managed to straddle me while we were fighting. Already, she was on top of me.

"Why are you laughing?" I yelled. "There's nothing funny about this!"

That, and the rocking of her legs made me uncomfortable. I wish she would get off.

"There *is* something funny." She chuckled. "I'm mental?" She giggled again. "Your British accent came out."

"It did—Hahaha!" Laughter burst from my mouth. She started to tickle my tummy. "Hahaha-stop it! Hahaha!" My hands were pinned to my side. I couldn't move. She was still on top of me.

"You don't look mean and scary to me," she teased. "I know you're just trying to intimidate me, but you don't really mean it, do you? I can see through your act."

"Hahaha! Stop imagining things!"

She cupped my cheek. She was no longer tickling my sides, but this was an even bigger torture. "Do you know," she murmured, "that every time you lie, you get a sad look on your face?"

I tried to avoid the tenderness of her eyes, but I couldn't. It was all over me like smoke. It made me suffocate like so.

" I don't know the reason why you kidnapped me," she went on. "I also don't understand why you're trying to act all mean and scary. But since we're going to share this space for an indefinite period, you might as well be kind

~ 29 ~

to me. We'll burn out if we continue like this." The Princess gave a weary sigh before swinging her legs from mine. She then got to her feet, dusted herself off, and offered me a hand. "What do you say, Cybele? Truce?"

The kindness of her smile, the disregard for how silly she looked, even the way she was offering to help someone who did her wrong made me slightly proud. *You've really become a beautiful Princess, Talia.*

I took her hand and pulled myself up. "Okay," I said, "We have a truce. But let me get my revenge first."

I reached behind the Princess and pinched her butt hard.

Her eyes widened when she realized what I did, but I was already jumping away.

"What?" I said. "Can't I touch the royal butt?"

"Cybele!"

I laughed. "Sorry, Princess. You squeezed my boobs while tickling me, you know? And just to inform you, you're stuck with a lesbian."

Okay, I shouldn't have done that. But I was all for revenge. Always.

The Princess nibbled on her lip, considering what I said. Finally, she shrugged. "Well okay, you're a lesbian. But I'm not. So, stop hitting on me."

"Not even a little?"

She shook her head, all serious. "Nothing and no one can change that. I'm sorry."

~ 30 ~

Oh really? I grinned at her as I wiped the laundry powder from my forehead. If that's how she wanted it, then that's how we'll play. *Not a lesbian? Just you wait, Princess.* I smirked.

Challenge accepted.

Chapter 3

Three weeks had passed since I kidnapped the Princess. Three weeks since my country, Harland, a sovereign nation in Europe, had been thrown into chaos because of it.

People from the Palace would be freaking out by now. Soldiers would be visible in most cities as part of their feeble attempts to make everyone think that they were still in control. Nobody would know that I did it, of course. No one would suspect me. But I needed to be sure.

I left Talia that morning to investigate. The nearest town was a four-hour drive, with nothing in-between but rocky roads, groves of trees, and a stretch of desolate fields. Those were the same reasons why I chose the area for my hideout. The land itself provided me with cover.

After getting into the village and parking outside a diner, I whipped my phone out and dialed a number. There was something I must do before proceeding. Something important.

"Iris?" There was an excited answer after the first ring.

"Hi, Mum."

"Don't hi Mum me," she scolded. "Where have you been? Your father and I were so worried!"

"I'm sorry for the delay. You know I've always wanted to visit Harland. I guess I got too excited."

"Excited enough not to call us?"

"My other activities got me sidetracked. Sometimes the places I'm in have no reception."

It wasn't a lie. Not exactly. If she saw the fields where I'd just driven by, she'd think that too.

"Oh, honey. . ." She dragged the word into a sigh. "Why don't you just come back in England? You have everything you need right here. You don't have to sleep in whatever awful places."

"I'm not sleeping in awful places, Mum. Stop imagining things. And besides, we've been through this. You know I can't leave yet."

There was a pause from the other line. She must be scheming up ways to get me to go home. She wasn't as one hundred percent sure of letting me leave like Daddy was.

"Do you really have to search for your birth parents?" she asked after a while. "Aren't your father and I enough? We'll leave everything to you when we die, so if it's money you're worried about, it's not going to be an issue."

My reflection scowled at the side mirror. "Don't say those things," I reprimanded. "You're not going to die yet. And once I finish everything here, I'll come home to you and Daddy. What's the rush?"

Her disapproval radiated through the phone. Maybe it wasn't a good idea to call after all. Maybe I should have let those three weeks stretch into months with only postcards to tell her I was fine.

Mum's defeated sigh said that she thought of the same thing and didn't like it. "Okay." She resigned. "You win. But if you don't call me from time to time, I'll send the butler to check on you. Agreed?"

I didn't answer. The butler was a twat.

Mum didn't take my lack of enthusiasm as a deterrent and started again on a cheerful note. "Your father's here," she informed. "He just returned from work. I'm passing the phone to him."

There were whispers in the background. I grabbed those few seconds to look outside, to see if anyone outside the car was acting suspicious. And then Dad was speaking right to my ear. "Iris, pumpkin? Where are you?"

I moved the phone away from my ear with a flinch. Daddy's deep voice was sometimes too overbearing. Funny thing was, it often scared people away, but he was a big marshmallow once you get to know him. I took a deep breath and placed the receiver back to my ear. "Hi, Dad. I'm right where I'm supposed to be."

"Are you?" He sounded doubtful. "Your mother is worried sick. No calls. No emails. Do you want me to send the butler after you?"

Ugh, the butler again. I had enough on my plate as it was. The last thing I needed was for her to snoop on me.

"I'm fine. Really, I am."

He harrumphed. "I hope you're not doing narcotics while you're away. Your mother and I will be very disappointed."

I glanced at the phone and rolled my eyes. They were getting worked up for nothing. It wasn't liked I'd disgrace their name or anything. I might have kidnapped the Princess of Harland and be in line for death penalty once I was found. But drugs? Oh please.

"Relax," I assured. "Think of it like a vacation. Aren't you glad that you're spending more time with Mum while I'm gone?"

"I am glad, honey. But. . ." He sighed. "We miss you, too. The mansion's been empty without you here."

A pang of longing took root in my chest before I could shake it off. Unforgivable. Catching guilt or any kind of feelings at this stage in my plan was detrimental. "I miss you too," I said. "Both of you. Tell Mum I love her, okay?" I ended the call before he could answer and tossed the phone to the passenger seat. He'd forgive me for cutting him off. He always would.

"Bugger."

I settled my head on the seat-rest and glanced at the sky. It was a clear blue with no sign of rain. As bright as the day my adoptive parents took me in.

Imagine having nothing on your name and being found by two oddball billionaires when you've almost given up on life. That's what happened to me. The Prescott's took me in their home: a big mansion with its own butler and staff. They gave me the best education England could offer. They treated me as their own. So why then did I kidnap the Princess of this country? Why had I resorted to a life of crime? Because I had to, that's why. It was a mission that I should do, even if they tried and killed me for it. Even if it means that Talia would hate me. Even if I hurt myself for doing it to her.

I'd only be whole again if I carried out my plan. Until then, I'd continue being a shell of my former self, and it wouldn't be enough. Not for me.

My phone vibrated just when I was unbuckling the seatbelt. I snatched it and checked the number on the screen. No one was supposed to trace me here.

"Hello? Who is this?"

"It's me."

"Brooke?" I ran my fingers through my hair. "I told you not to call me yet."

"I know," she rushed, "But I haven't heard from you in a while. I was getting worried. Besides, your parents were difficult. They threatened to send the butler on me if I don't keep tabs on you. You know how it goes."

Those reasons were not enough, and both of us knew it. She was keeping something from me now.

"What else should I know?" I asked.

"Nothing."

"Brooke."

"It really is nothing."

"Then piss off."

"Okay, okay, I'll tell you. But please don't be mad."

"I'll make that decision myself."

Her answering groan almost got my sympathy, but I was too alarmed to speak. I waited for her to continue.

"I. . ." She gulped. "I kind of followed you."

"You what?" I jerked my head to the window, expecting her to knock at any second. The parking lot was still vacant, though it was difficult to remove the paranoia now that I knew. "You're here?"

"I'm not there, *there*," she said. "Not yet. But I need to know where you are. Your location isn't showing in my system."

"Of course it wouldn't. I'm surprised you even found this number." I checked the diner in front of the car. Only four people were inside, if the waitress was included in the count. "I'm in a town called Cluj," I disclosed. "How far are you from here?"

"Let me check." A beep sounded from her end, followed by sighing. "I'm two hours away. Can you stay there and wait for me?"

Tsk. As if I had a choice.

"Make sure you're not followed," I said.

My mood was foul when I got off the Beater. This was supposed to be a day of investigation and data gathering in Harland, not catch-ups over tea and biscuit. But now that Brooke was here, driving to me, I had no choice but to find a way to convince her to go back to England. She was too important to end up dead because of me and my schemes.

Ours was a friendship born through university days. With midnight black hair, sun-kissed skin, lips on a permanent pout, and a slender figure, only a fool wouldn't notice her. She did say that she had a thing for me weeks after freshmen year started, but I was too busy scheming to return the gesture. We became good friends instead. Her constant bugging eventually lead me to divulge my plan: me kidnapping the Princess and hiding her from everyone. At first, I thought Brooke would run for the hills after I said it, but the surprising thing was she stuck by my side and helped me. Maybe underneath that face was a psychopath, too. I really didn't know.

If there was one thing I kept from her though, it was the 'why's 'and the 'how comes. ' The reason for my scheme was my own. They'd only know at the right time. All of them. They only had to wait.

I bought a newspaper from a street vendor before heading to the diner. Talia's disappearance was still the headline even in the tabloids. How long would it take before they declared her false death, I wonder?

My nose was still buried in the paper when I entered the diner and sat by the counter. Page two had an interesting detail about how the Palace tried to conceal the truth. Talia's disappearance was only exposed when a diplomat from Asia demanded answers. Apparently, the scheduled meeting with Talia wasn't pushed through even after they've planned it for months. The Palace's excuse wasn't good enough.

"Ready to order yet?"

I glanced up to a pale waitress watching me from behind the bar. She was dressed in her pink uniform, pen poised on her notepad, waiting for me to answer. I licked my lips and watched her fall apart. "Black coffee please."

"Anything else?" She hadn't taken her eyes off me yet. Sometimes I think the word *lesbian* was glued to my forehead, and people like her, people that wanted to try a new flavor, were out to get me. I could use that to my advantage.

"Actually, there is something." I turned the newspaper to her and tapped Talia's face on the front page. "I'm a foreigner here coming from

England. Can you tell me what's going on? I'm a bit confused."

"Sure." The cleavage she flashed as she leaned to the counter didn't bother me. The smile on her face did. "The Princess is missing," she explained gleefully. "It's all over the news."

I feigned ignorance and dragged my eyes back to the article. "Did the Princess run away?"

"Nope. Rumor says the Queen's enemies took her."

"Kidnapped?"

"Yep." She didn't excuse herself as she went to the coffee maker at the back. A mug was ready for me when she returned, its steam hot on my face as the saucer was placed down.

"Tell me more about the Queen's enemies," I pressed. "Did the Princess have them too?"

"Princess Talia? No, everyone loves her." She glanced around before leaning closer to me. The woman smelled like gossip. "Between you and me, I think the Queen's too strict for her own good. I heard that some people don't agree with her laws."

"Really?"

"I'm just telling what I heard." She leaned back with a satisfied smirk. "Is the coffee good?"

"Haven't tasted it yet."

I took the mug and sipped. Yuck! Why did I even bother with this when I hated black coffee? Maybe Talia was right. Maybe I did have a dark sense of humor.

I fished money from my pocket and put it on the counter with a generous tip. The woman's eyes grew large at what she saw. "That's for the coffee and the information," I said. "Remember, I'm just a foreigner."

Brooke arrived exactly an hour later. I've found myself a nice secluded seat by the window, so I had a clear view of her walking to the door. She looked every bit a stranger here with her high boots, sunglasses, and London fashion. Unbelievable.

She slid to my booth a minute after, relief washing on her tanned face. "I missed you," she said.

I gave her a quick smile. "That's nice. Go back to England."

"But I just got here!"

"Right. And now you're going back."

She pursed her lips before bringing her bag to the table. I didn't know if she intended to get back at me by busying herself with her things while I waited, but I was about to snap at her when she handed me a bookmark. "Your Mum said you left it."

My irritation transformed to surprise as I retrieved it from her. The lilac-colored flower on the laminated paper was all that was left of that day.

"I thought I had it with me when I boarded the plane," I murmured. "Thanks."

"No problem." She glanced behind her before facing me again. Brooke could barely keep her face straight. "Is she safe?"

"Who?"

"You know who."

I covered my mouth to hide my smile. It was inevitable that she'd ask about it. That may even be one of the reasons why she was here aside from the need to see me. "Yes, she's safe."

Brooke's hands were shaking as she reached for my coffee. The warmth would be long gone by now. She wouldn't get any comfort there. "Are you going to kill her?" she asked.

"I'm not a murderer, Brooke, but Talia's mine now. I'll do what I want with her."

"Iris."

"What?"

Any trace of affection she had for me was gone as she let go of the mug and snatched her bag. She looked disgusted as she said, "If you rape that girl, I'm going to punch your face."

The cocky grin I was sporting was wiped clean. What kind of best friend was she, accusing me of that?

" Do you really think I'll do something as revolting to someone?" I said. "If I wanted to have sex, I would have done it with you, or any other female out there who kept begging me. Hell, I can even pay for that. Have you seen my bank account lately?" Big words. I know. But she was testing my patience.

Brooke rolled her eyes. "Then why the obsession with her, huh? Why go through all this? Ever since I've met you in college, she was all you could talk about. Talia this. Talia that. It's like you're in love with her!"

"Will you lower your voice?" I craned my neck to see if anyone heard. The two other customers were still busy with their breakfast. I glared back at Brooke. "I'm not in love with Talia, okay? I need her."

Brooke's jaw dropped in surprise. "What do you mean you need her? Is this some Satanic shit I should know about?"

Huh? I looked out the window and breathed in. Brooke was my ally, my friend. We shouldn't fight, much less talk like crazy people.

Ha! As if kidnapping someone wasn't crazy enough.

"Look," I said, more calmly this time. "I know how much you care for me. I also know you're worried about Talia. But believe me when I say that I'm not doing those things, or any weird cult stuff at all. I also don't rape every attractive woman I come across. You know me better than that."

She looked more reluctant than ever. "This is the first time I've heard you call anyone attractive."

"Well you heard wrong. The point is, stop worrying for me and get yourself out of this country in twenty-four hours. You don't want to be here when the next step starts."

" What next step?" She pouted. "Let me in your plans."

I shook my head. "I'm not saying anything to keep you safe. Just call me when you get back in England." I stood and tapped the bookmark on her forehead. She wouldn't get anything else out of me. "Stay safe."

It was nightfall when I reached the hideout. By then I was dog-tired from driving around. All I wanted to do was to go back to bed and entertain myself. But no such luck.

"You're back!"

The startled gasp I made wasn't from the Princess running in the hallway to welcome me. It was because of the warm hands she wrapped around my neck after she did.

"T-Talia. . . What?"

"I was lonely without you," she whispered in my ear. "You didn't say goodbye this morning."

Every inch of me protested as she pressed her chest to mine. I was having trouble breathing. It was shameful to admit, but it's been so long since I was held this way. I've forgotten how lovely it felt.

"You're shaking," she whispered.

"I'm not."

I hated that my voice sounded weak. I hated that she could easily turn me from a block of ice to this. Where did the confident Cybele from earlier go? Why did she abandon me at a time of need?

Talia broke the embrace to hold me at arms-length. Her eyes had clouded with concern. Her excitement giving way to care. "Are you sick?" she asked. "Should I prepare something for you?"

I shut my eyes and shook my head. I couldn't say that she was the reason I was reduced to this. That there was never a day when I stopped being lonely without her. What I would give so I didn't need to hurt Talia. What I would give so we wouldn't be enemies anymore.

Chapter 4

The Princess had begun to adapt to the life inside the castle. She would launder, clean, or cook depending on the schedule I've set. I wasn't doing it to punish her but to teach humility: something her mother never had.

Each night while she was tucked inside her cell, I would go to the kitchen, cut the ingredients, and prepare what she'd need for the next day. It was done on purpose so she wouldn't have access to a knife. A kidnapper could never be too careful.

"You know," Talia said one morning. "I've been here for two months, but I feel like I still don't know you. What gives?"

She was in the middle of moving clothes from the dryer to the basket as per agreed. A while ago, she was humming Harland's national anthem. Where did that question come from?

"You don't know me because you're not supposed to," I said. "Your duty is to just shut up and do what I asked."

"That still won't stop me from asking about you though." She shoved a sweater in the basket, unwary of my attitude. "Back to my inquiries. How long have you known you were lesbian again?"

I blinked at her in surprise. "You remembered?"

"How could I not? Now answer the question, or I won't stop asking."

Of course, she wouldn't. Jumping down from the counter, I folded my arms and decided whether to tell her or not. The curiosity won. "I knew I was lesbian since I was ten," I said. "How about you, Talia? How long have you known you were lesbian?"

She paused to stare at me. "I've told you, hadn't I? I'm straight as a pole. Unlike some people, I'm sure with my sexuality."

"I think you're lying."

"Why would I do that?"

I smiled. Some things were best brought out by examples. "Want to bet?"

She dumped the last shirt where it belonged and fidgeted with the ends of her hair. Talia's signature half-braid was arranged meticulously so no stray could go to her face. But she still looked annoyed for some reason. "I'll take it," she decided.

"Great. When should we begin?"

"Anytime." She flashed me a confident look. "But let's make the stakes high, shall we? I want something more challenging than guessing my sexuality. It's subjective anyway, and you look like a person who could use a good game."

"I'm listening."

Her impish smile made her gray eyes twinkle. "How about we play a game of cards? If you win, you can make me do anything."

"And if you win?"

"You'll do as I tell you."

Loud laughter echoed in the laundry room. "Why the hell would I do that?" I mocked. "I don't need a bet to make you do what I want, remember? In case you haven't noticed, you're not in the position to bargain."

"I think you're just scared." Talia grinned when my mouth snapped close. Furthermore, she went to me and poked my nose. "What?" she teased. "Cat got your tongue?"

She took an involuntary step back when I moved forward. "You'll let me do anything if I win?" I asked. "Anything at all?"

The subtle gulp she made didn't escape me. She was always like this, wanting to overcome battles she couldn't win. "Y-yes," she stammered. "Anything."

"What if I tell you to kiss me? Will you do it?"

Her eyes darted to the side. She licked her lips, thinking hard about it.

After a moment, she nodded. "Yes. I'll allow you to kiss or touch me if you win. But if I do, you'll also have to follow what I say."

I leaned back and considered her offer. What would I make her do if I win? Kissing was obviously out of the question. I only said that to make her uncomfortable.

Oh well. I'd think about it later.

"Prepare to lose, Talia. I always win."

I remembered putting a deck of cards somewhere in my room for entertainment. It took me ten minutes to search for it, go back to the third floor where her cell was located, and call her to the hallway. We sat on the stone floor and divided the cards in order.

"Just so you know," I started. "Even if you win, I can't set you free. I can't let you go out or let you harm me either. Are we clear?" I didn't wait for her to answer. "Also, I can only do what you want for a day. No more, no less."

"I didn't even think about those things," she mumbled.

I slammed the cards against the wall a few minutes later. The numbered pieces scattered around us, bitter reminders of the result.

"How did you do that!" I exclaimed. "I'm good at everything. Where did you learn to play?"

Talia shrugged and began to collect the cards. She was the only one happy with this. She won. "Whenever I was bored in the palace, I'd ask the guards to play with me," she said. "One of them was good at cards and taught me all the ropes."

I forked my fingers through my hair. I should have thought of that before accepting her challenge. Now what?

"What do you want from me?" I asked.

She tucked her hair behind her ear and beamed. "Simple. I want you to pretend that you love me."

"Pardon?"

Talia tapped the side of the cards on the floor before setting them aside. "I want to see how you love," she said. "I'm really curious. I don't think you're a bad person, just confused. If making you love me is the only way I'd know the real you, I'd go for it even if it isn't real."

"That doesn't make any sense!"

"It doesn't break your rules either." She listed with her fingers. "I'm not going to escape, it will only last for a day, and I'm not going to hurt you."

Said who?

Her eyebrow rose at me. "Should we start now?"

"B-but. . ."

"A promise is a promise."

My eyes closed as I took a deep breath. She didn't know what she was asking of me. She couldn't possibly understand the consequences of her little game.

Talia was still waiting for me to decide when my eyes fluttered open. She looked so impatient, so eager to get this on. So eager to destroy me.

Without saying anything, I lifted her from the floor into my arms. She gasped in surprise but didn't complain. I took her all the way to her cell and entered the code on the door.

Inside, the mattress of her bed was soft when I laid her down. But her skin was softer. I moved on top of her.

"C-Cybele?"

"Yes?"

"What are you doing?"

Warmth radiated from her as I leaned closer. I missed her scent, her lips, everything about her. The six-year-old child that held my hand had always been my favorite version. The her that told me that I would be her Princess was also very dear to me.

Of every stage of her, the least I liked was the version I was seeing today. She was no longer the Talia I knew. She'd become my enemy.

Don't think about that, Cybele. Not now. Not in this moment.

Steeling myself, I looked into her betraying eyes and felt the knot double in my stomach. "I love you," I whispered. "I love you, Talia. I always had."

She stiffened against me. This was an amusement for her, a prize that she'd won from her card of games. To me, the game was a twist of real life: one I had to live with for twelve bitter years while drowning with the thoughts of revenge.

I brushed a hand on her cheek. "Tell me you love me too," I murmured. "Tell me you want me." I didn't care if she heard the weakness in my voice. I'd give her a day of surrender like I promised.

"I'd be lying if I said that," she whispered.

"Then lie." My jaw hardened. "Isn't this what you want? I'm only keeping my end of the bargain. Keep yours too."

She hesitated for a split-second. The tremor that passed her face was something I didn't understand. But her gaze was tender when she finally met my eyes. "I love you too, Cybele. I'll give up everything for you. Even freedom."

I memorized her face: her straight nose that would curiously sniff at a new scent. Her lips that teased me. Her eyes that would twinkle every now and then. And her skin that would flush whenever I said something likeable. All of this was my Talia, the grown-up version of her. Maybe this wasn't so bad too, but I had yet to fully discover it.

"Come with me," I said.

"Where?"

"Just come."

The rooftop garden was warm and welcoming. Lush green Bermuda grass poked out from stone steps, while flowers were arranged in beds according to the type of plants. The fountain in the middle continuously discharged colored water, the mermaid stone on top of it watching us as if it was alive. I guided Talia further in.

"I didn't know there was a garden here." Her distracted eyes went everywhere. She stopped in front of the potted dahlias and knelt. "Are you the one who takes care of them?"

"Yes. Flowers calm me." I shoved a hand in my pocket. Was it wise to be telling her these things? Since when had I been this careless? "How about you, Princess? What's your hobby?"

"Books," she answered immediately. "I also have a blog."

" Does the Queen know?"

She stood and went to the swing chair in the corner. Only after she'd taken a sniff of the flower-perfumed air and sat down did she answer. "The Queen has certain expectations from me. She's also very. . . traditional. If she finds out that I'm blogging in secret, albeit with a different identity, she'd cut my arms off."

I wouldn't be surprised if the Queen did that. She was sick. Sicker than I'd ever be.

Then again, Talia was her daughter. A snake was venomous, but so was its children.

"Your Mum sounds fun to be with," I said.

"Ha! You don't know the half of it." Talia's forehead tilted to the stars as she frowned in remembrance. "There's this instance when she didn't allow me to leave my room for a month because I refused to learn the waltz. The maids begged her for me, but the woman was stubborn."

"How do you manage to live with her?"

"I don't have a choice." Talia's gaze lowered to me. "She's not only my mother, she's also the Queen of Harland. There's no escaping her." Talia held on to the rope above the armrest and pushed her legs back. The swing chair swayed with her when she leaned forward again. "You know," she said. "If there's one good thing about kidnapping me, it's the fact that I'm far away from the Queen. I wouldn't see her face here."

I crossed my arms and didn't say anything. Maybe Talia was lying. Maybe she was not. But what were her motives apart from torturing me?

"So what happens tomorrow?" Talia asked.

I told her the truth. At least the version she knew of. "I stop loving you."

Tomorrow, we'd go back to what we really were. Tomorrow, I'd hide these feelings again. Anyone would wonder what happened, how this all happened. It was confusing for people who weren't there from the very beginning.

For the sake of remembrance, let me go back from the start, way before I kidnapped her.

Before I was known as Iris the billionaire, or Iris the supermodel.

Back when they called me Cybele, the future Queen.

Chapter 5

Twelve years ago

"Princess Cybele, Lady Talia is here to see you."

I tore my gaze from the page I was reading and glanced at the servant. She was waiting for my answer. "Very well," I said. "Bring her to me."

The maid bowed before retreating to the pathway. Meanwhile, I closed my book and rested my head against the tree trunk. The garden was my favorite place in the Palace and maybe the whole of Harland. With hectares of land and dense trees that looked identical, anyone would wonder why it wasn't called a forest instead. My mother was to blame. She was the one who jokingly called it the garden of her youth. The name had stuck since then.

Under the aging oak tree was where I usually sat to relax. It was peaceful here, quiet. The rough bark didn't dampen my reading, but increased the experience. The Palace guards knew not to disturb me and would muffle their footsteps as they passed.

My ears twitched when a twig snapped. Looking up, I saw that Talia was standing nearby, hands on her back, the morning sunshine touching her hair. She was more like a mid-summer dream than my childhood friend.

"Cybele!" she shrieked. Her giggles bounced as she ran, until she tackled me to the grass again. "I've been begging my mother to visit for days! She finally gave in!"

Talia was heavy for a six-year-old. She pinned me down so I wouldn't move, her warm breath on my forehead.

I was enjoying the way her hair tickled my cheek when someone yanked her away. Both of us were shocked at the harshness of the voice. "Don't do that, Lady Talia! You might hurt the Princess!"

I rose to see the maid from earlier here again. "Let go of her," I ordered. "Talia's just playing."

"But, Princess. . . The Queen will get mad if she sees you like that," the maid said.

"No she won't." I grabbed Talia's hands away from her. "We're just playing. Besides, Mother was the one who told me to befriend her. I'm only doing what she asked."

The servant pursed her lips but didn't argue. She knew better than to do that to her future Queen.

"You can go," I ordered again. "Leave us."

"Yes, Princess."

Talia exhaled and collapsed by my side when the maid disappeared. "What a meanie," she murmured.

"Don't mind her." I took a piece of grass from her hair. "She's just being careful because I'm the Princess."

"And I'm going to be your bride someday."

I let the grass fall to the ground without saying anything. She always told me that.

Talia was three years old when her mother presented her to me. I was seven. I remember her running to my chair, standing on tiptoes, touching my face with her small hands. She told me there and then that I looked like a doll. Not only that, she also said she'd marry me while the adults were fawning over us.

I've been wondering about it since that day. Even now that I was ten. Was it even possible?

Surely, someday, I would be wed to a Prince. Talia, whom I've loved dearly since seeing her was only to be a support, a best friend. She would never be my bride even if we both wanted to. But I had a plan. A secret. When I become the Queen and reach the age of twenty-one, I would change the laws so I could marry her. Anyone. No one would be able to object. They'd receive the death penalty if they did.

Talia was important to me. I wouldn't let anyone take or marry her. Not if she didn't want to.

Her family came second to my own. While my father and mother were the Queen and Prince, or just King—to not make it any hard—Talia's mother, by some ancestral lineage unrelated to mine, was the Duchess. If my parents were to die, or if I did, Harland's unique law states that her mother would be the next Queen. But that would never happen. My parents were healthy. And I would be around for a long time.

"What are you reading?" Talia asked. She picked the book sitting on the grass between us and scrunched her face as she tried to make sense of the words.

"That's a book about etiquette," I explained. "As a Princess, I have to learn good manners and the right attitude to rule Harland when we grow up. I want to serve the people right."

She put the book down and rose to her feet. It fascinated me when she took the hem of her dress and curtsied. "I know etiquette too," she boasted.

"I'm sure you do. Nobles are taught about it, aren't they?" I traced a finger on the spine of the book. How do I explain to her? "But my training is different from yours or the other nobles, Talia. Mine is harder because the Governess is strict."

"She is?"

"Yes, incredibly."

Her eyes narrowed at me before she spun like a ballerina. Talia was all smiles when she landed on her feet. "That's too bad for her," she said, "The Governess. Because you are a genuine."

"A genius," I corrected. "And no, I'm not. How can you say that?"

"Well you were reading a book a month ago. I couldn't understand the words. It's for grown-ups, isn't it?"

"Kind of," I replied. "That book was Leonardo Da Vinci's biography. He's my favorite."

"I still don't understand." Talia shook her head and shrugged. "But someday I'm going to read those books with you. I promise."

"I'd love that," I said. Talia always worked hard to please me. I should return the favor.

"Enough about books." I stood and looked down at her. "What do you want us to do today?"

Talia's eyes went to the sky as she considered. The sun wasn't giving us trouble this morning. It was hiding behind the clouds. "Can we play hide-and-seek?" she asked. "Or maybe you can play me the harp. I haven't heard it in a while."

"Tell you what," I said. "Let's play hide-and-seek first, then I'm going to play you the harp after. We can also go to the pond if we have more time. Do you want that?"

She clapped her hands together. "Really? You'll do all that with me?" Her shoulders suddenly dropped. "But what about the servants? They will scold you."

"No, they won't. No one can scold me except for Father and Mother. I'm the Princess, remember?" I beckoned to her. "Come here and let me clean your dress before we begin."

It was especially hard to dust her clothes from grass when she couldn't keep still and kept jumping up and down.

"Yay!" she screamed. "I love you, Cybele! You're not allowed to marry anyone but me!"

I grabbed her shoulders and swung her to me. "Shhh! Be careful. If anyone hears that, they'll report it to our parents.

"So?"

"They may never allow you to come here again."

Water pooled on her eyes as she lowered her arms. "But why?"

"Because. . . I don't know. It's difficult to explain." That, and I've heard one or two maids gossiping about how strange my friendship with Talia was. I didn't think much of it until I've read a case of bullying in other books. Now, I was completely lost myself.

"Sorry. I'm just really excited," Talia whispered.

"I know you are, but hold it in."

"Okay! But you're IT!"

After giving Talia enough time to scurry away, I ran behind the nearest bushes to see if she was there.

She wasn't.

My feet carried me further. I wasn't too worried that Talia would stray far. She knew better, and besides, many guards roamed around for our safety. One of them would find Talia before she got lost.

Talia was lying beside the garden pond when I broke through the clearing. Her eyes were closed, her arms and feet spread apart. She'd fallen asleep while waiting for me. She could sleep anywhere.

I sat to her left and took a breath. Why was she so beautiful?

I knew that there was something different with me. I wanted her to be my Princess—the one sitting beside my throne when we grew up. But I knew it wasn't considered natural. The books I've read told me so. Girls were supposed to end up with boys. Boys should be with girls. No one said anything about two girls being together.

But what could I do? I liked Talia more than the flowers in the garden, or the lollipops some of the friendlier maids would sneak for me.

I would gladly give Talia my share if she asked. Same with my treasured books and the dresses that Mother gave me. The only thing I couldn't offer was the position of Queen. It was my birthright, my duty. I couldn't give it to anyone else, even to Talia, whom I'd offer a thousand lollipops to.

She stirred a little when I leaned down. Our faces were almost touching.

She opened her eyes and smirked. "Kiss!" she said, before pulling my head and smacking my lips to hers.

We fell and rolled on the grass. My arms were shaking as I untangled myself from her. What did she just do?

"You shouldn't have done that!" I scolded. My cheeks were getting hot.

"I'm not going to say sorry." She grinned. "Brides kiss. I saw it on TV."

"B-but!"

"Just take the kiss, Cybele. I know you like it."

"And what are you doing now?"

I knew I was blabbering, but she'd also moved closer to the pond and leaned to the water. I was curious.

"I'm checking my reflection," she answered. "I should hurry and grow up, so we'd be married already. I should also turn pretty."

~ 59 ~

"You're already pretty, Talia. You couldn't wish for more." I crawled beside her and stared at our reflection. Our hairs were toffee and honey, two flavors I liked. Our eyes were the tree and the rocks underneath it. One wasn't better without the other.

She splashed water on my face. "Let's play this game next!"

The day came to an end when Talia's mother, Esmeralda, came to retrieve her. The woman looked exactly like her daughter, but was older, not to mention stricter. Esmeralda was never rude to me since I was the Princess, but I couldn't bring myself to like her. Perhaps it was the way she looked at Talia. It bothered me for reasons I couldn't understand.

"I don't want to go home!" Talia bawled. She clung to me and refused to let go. It was always like this whenever she'd visit.

"I don't want you to go home too," I murmured. "But you have to. Your mother is waiting." I stroked her head before holding her at arm's length. Talia's pudgy cheeks were pink like watermelon. "I'll see you again next time, okay?"

"Okay." She sniffled again. The promises of next time convinced her to release me. "Next time," she said. "I'll bring you the flowers you love."

"I'm looking forward to it," I said. "I've already turned the one you gave me into a bookmark. You can see it next time."

She wiped her eyes with the back of her hand and nodded. "Don't fall in love with another girl while I'm gone."

"Of course not."

"Promise?"

"Yes."

"Then I can go home now."

I watched as her mother took her away. I stood like a prim and proper princess next to my parents even as Talia gave me her final wave. It was back to the waiting game for us. Back to days of not seeing each other. But someday, somehow, it didn't have to be. Someday, when I was Queen, I'd do everything I promised and more.

I hope someday would come soon. Until then, I'd have to read more books, study my lessons, and await Talia's return.

Chapter 6

Twelve Years Ago

The sun was still asleep when Mother guided me to the car. The dial in my wristwatch read four o'clock in the morning.

Behind us, the guards followed with rifles in their hands, the brim of their hats occluding their eyebrows, blue-buttoned uniform spotless. I stopped before going inside the Rover.

"Where are we going, Mother?" I asked.

The Queen stared at me. A while ago, she was distant, occupied, deep in thought. *Was that how I looked like when I think?* People said our eyes resembled each other's, down to the green speck.

"We're going to the countryside, Cybele," she answered. "It's been a while since the three of us visited the villa. Your father and I want to spend time with you."

That explained the travel clothes. Her dress was hidden by a heavy trench coat, her sandals replaced by boots. I squeezed inside the car next to Father. My toffee-colored hair and tall height came from him.

"My beautiful Princess," he greeted with a warm smile. "I have a surprise waiting for you."

Mother followed us in and tucked her leg, so the guard outside could close the door. "You'll like the surprise," she added.

"What is it?" My eyes widened. "Are you giving me books?"

"You and your books like a sword to a knight." Mother pinched my cheek gently. "You can have any book you want, but our surprise is different."

"Can I take a guess?"

"Sure."

The King and Queen took the time to gaze at each other while I figured out what the surprise was. There was never a moment when they didn't share an understanding that I couldn't explain. Except maybe when Talia was beside me, which brought me back to guessing.

"Is your gift Talia?" I asked with wider eyes.

Mother's warm laughter rubbed away the chilliness of the morning. "Silly girl. I don't think Esmeralda will like it if we wrap her daughter and give her to you."

My shoulders dropped. So much for wishful thinking. "If it's not her, then I'll just wait till we get to the villa to know."

Ronaldo took his place behind the wheel. From the rearview mirror, his features were hard, his face angular. It had been a familiar sight for as long as I could remember, as he'd been our head guard since I was born. "Everything is ready," he informed. "Should we proceed, Your Majesty's?"

Father waved his hand for permission. His other arm wrapped around me. "Drive carefully," he said.

Several cars fronted and tailed us throughout the journey. Riding them were the royal guards, ensuring that we'd arrive safely to our destination. Though our family didn't have enemies, it was in the Palace's best interest to proceed with caution with everything we did, funny enough, even when it came to my playmates.

Only noble children like Talia could talk to me. Mother said that when the time comes and I was ready, I'd be able to work for the unity, national pride, allegiance, and voluntary service of Harland. But until I could welcome dignitaries or perform those tough duties, I should concentrate on my lessons and study etiquette.

We arrived at the vacation home before nightfall. I was exhausted from the travel but was also excited to be there. Mother and Father were usually busy, and I was often left alone to my studies. This was an opportunity for us to spend time like Mother said.

"You look tired, Princess," Father cooed. "Would you like Daddy to carry you?" Father wriggled his eyebrows at me.

"Can we do it piggyback?" I asked.

"Of course." He pulled me off the seat like I weighted nothing, and lifted me to his back. The view was perfect from up there. It felt like I was flying. "Your father is not only the King," he said over his shoulder to me. "I'm also a strong man. That's why your mother fell in love with me."

"It's just one of the qualities I liked about you, dear," Mother said as she left the car.

Ronaldo hurried to our side. "Your Highness!" he said to father. "Please let me carry the Princess. You might hurt your back."

"Nonsense," Father scoffed. "I'm only thirty. Don't treat me like an old man." He lifted me higher. "Besides, it's not every day that I get to carry my Cybele. There will come a time when she'd be too big for me." His eyes gleamed as he glanced up. "You'll be a pretty lady by then. You'll break a lot of Prince's hearts."

"But I don't want a Prince, Father. I only like Talia."

"And so you shall have her, but only if she wants you too." He chuckled to himself as he walked us to the villa. "You're the future Queen, Cybele. Everything is yours, mostly anyway. But never forget your responsibility to this country. Rule first, and love will follow." He seemed to recall something and quickly shook his head. "What am I saying? You're years away from that. Only think about relationships when you grow up. I mean it, kiddo."

I smiled at his tone. He never should have opened the topic if he wasn't going to be comfortable with it. Adults.

Fathered lowered me to my feet only when we've entered the villa. I looked around. Aside from being constructed next to a lake, it was cozy and large, with more than ten bedrooms to spare. The wooden beams that supported the main hall was older than me, and everywhere I looked were mementos of Mother's youth—the pictures of her on top of the fireplace, the paintings of nature that my grandparents, the former King and Queen, had gifted, the piano sitting beside the big windows that overlooked the water— everything.

I noticed that snow had begun to fall outside, but my attention was quickly drawn back to the staff who welcomed us inside. "Our King." They bowed. My father was supposed to be called

Prince. But Mother had insisted. "And Princess Cybele."

"Hello," I said.

Father took my hand while the guards assumed their post. "Come, Princess," he beckoned. "Let me show you to your room."

The guest room he took me to had a four-post canopy bed, a large wooden table, a plushy couch, and a fireplace that hadn't been kindled yet. Already, I could imagine myself curled next to the fire while reading a book. Father was smiling when I swiveled to him. His handsome face looked more excited than I was. "You'll return here when it's time to sleep," he said. "In the meantime, you can stay with me and your mother."

"Cool!"

His eyebrow rose.

"I mean, yes Father. That's great."

He snorted while I tried to shake away the warmth in my face. We both knew that we could talk informally when we were alone, but I was still uneasy over it. Blame my desire to always be at my best, plus the Governess 'nagging voice repeating in my head.

A moment had passed when soft footsteps thudded on the wooden floor. A second later, Mother emerged in the room, wearing a different coat. She went to me and handed a smaller jacket. "It's snowing outside, Cybele. Wear this so you won't get cold."

"Where have you been?" I asked Mother.

"Walking by the lake." She twisted me around so she could help me put the jacket on.

"It's so beautiful here. It's a pity we don't always get to visit."

They took me to their bedroom after making sure I was warm. Seeing their fireplace already lit, I ran to it and placed my hand near the flame. I wish Talia was here to enjoy it with me.

"Have you guessed your gift yet?" Mother asked out of the blue.

I turned my back to the hearth. The gift had been long forgotten. But now that she mentioned it, I clasped my hands together. "I don't want to guess anymore. Please, please, please just tell me!"

"Nope." She wagged a finger. "You have to try first. That's how we do it in this household."

"But!"

"Try."

"Oh, come on!" Father quipped. "She's been waiting since this morning. Let's just tell her."

"You spoil her too much." Mother rolled her eyes.

"Not as much as I would want."

Mother sighed and sat on the bed. "All right. All right. I'm always the bad guy." Her eyes twinkled as she spread her arms wide. "Ready?"

"Yes!"

"I don't think you are."

"Mother!"

She smirked. "Just teasing. Our gift. . . is a horse."

"For real?" My jaw slacked.

~ 67 ~

"Yes."

I made a mad dash across the room before anyone could stop me. My own horse! I couldn't believe it! They only let me borrow Mother's before.

"Settle down, dear. It's too late to ride it now." Mother pointed to the window. "We'll show you the horse tomorrow."

"Still!" I exclaimed. "I'm going to name her Jessie after that song. Can we go here with Talia next time? I want us to ride the horse together."

"I have to talk to Esmeralda about it, but I think she'll allow her daughter to accompany you."

Three sharp knocks came from the door before I could continue rejoicing. It had to be Ronaldo, informing us that dinner was ready.

My parents and I exchanged stories while we ate, stories that were about everything. Father recounted his meeting with the noblemen, while Mother told us about her numerous charity projects. As for me, I shared about my studies and how I was learning not only etiquette but other languages too. I was comfortable in speaking about five of them now.

The three of us went back to the bedroom after dinner. The stories continued even then. Father narrated about a beheaded horseman that traveled with his lamp to eat people at night. I wasn't scared at all. I mean, why only at night and not during the days? Did it have a strict schedule like we did?

Sometime in the middle of the night, someone knocked on the door again. It was a soft rap, so low that I barely heard it. Mother and

Father exchanged surprised glances. It appeared like they weren't expecting anyone too.

"Who's there?" Father said.

"It's me, Ronaldo."

The King relaxed. "Come in."

The head guard was still dressed in his navy-blue uniform upon going in. He closed the door after entering.

"What do you want?" Father asked. "We haven't scheduled a meeting tonight. Is anything wrong?"

Mother, who was beside Father in the bed, had the same question in her eyes. I stayed by the fire watching them silently.

Ronaldo paced the length of the room without answering. Something glinted in his hand.

I only realized what it was when he stopped, gave a small smile, and drove a knife to the King's chest.

"Daddy!" I shrieked.

I left the fireplace to rush to Ronaldo— then bit his arm so hard I thought my teeth were going to fall off.

" Aargh! You brat!"

I seized his arm and sank my teeth deeper and deeper until I was grabbed and hurled away. The dizziness turned to pain as I slammed to the bedpost and fell next to Mother.

"D-dear. . ." she stammered, too busy pressing her hands on Father's wound. "D-dear, hold on. . . Hold on. . ." She gave a small gasp and turned to the door. "Help! Guards! Help your King!"

Ronaldo wiped his bleeding hand as he advanced to us. "I sent everyone away under the King's orders," he growled. "Screaming won't help you." He raised the bloody knife again, readying himself for another attack. "Nobody will come for you tonight, My Queen. You'll die with your husband and child."

Surprise flashed on Mother's face. It was like she was just remembering me. "Why are you doing this?" she said. "We trusted you!"

Ronaldo took another step forward, his wide shoulder set on a half-shrug. "Are you really asking me that question? Are you that stupid that you didn't sense it?" His head tilted. "You must have. She was bad at keeping it."

"You will be punished for this!"

"Not when Esmeralda is Queen, I won't." He nudged his chin to me. "Now choose, woman. Who will you try to save?"

It didn't take long for Mother to make the decision. Her duty as a mother came first. The Queen ran in front of me, took a stance, and stared Ronaldo straight in the eyes. "Don't do this," she pleaded one more time. "Cybele is just an innocent child! She doesn't—none of us deserves this!"

I didn't recognize the man who shook his head. He was Satan himself. "This is for Esmeralda." He raised the knife higher. "Prepare to die!"

Mother kicked him in the stomach before he could swing the knife down. Both were well-trained for fighting, me included.

But it wasn't like that was important now. The King was dying.

I pushed myself up and crawled to the bed. "Father!" I gasped. "Father, I love you!"

"P-Princess. . ." Blood sputtered from Father's mouth. He was drowning with it. "M-My Queen. . ."

"Don't leave us!" I cried. "I beg you!"

Father gasped and coughed. He wheezed for the last time before laying still. He couldn't even say he loved me back.

My eyes burned with tears. My chest was set on fire. I couldn't look at him anymore. He was gone.

I stared from one tragedy to the next. Ronaldo had won over Mother and was pinning her to the floor.

"Cybele!" Mother gasped, raising a shaking hand. "Run!"

For a few seconds, all I could do was stare at the redness beginning to spread on her dress. To watch as her lovely green eyes began to dull. To see her lips moving to whisper my name. And then I was running to the hallway, panting, aching, afraid.

But small feet were no match for Ronaldo's powerful ones. "Come back here, sneak!" Big hands clamped over my collar, pulled me, and dragged me back to the room were the dead King and Queen remained.

"Get off me!" I yelled.

"Only when you're dead!"

I swiveled around and kicked him between the legs. It caused the knife to fall from his hand.

Seizing it from the floor, I stabbed him with all I've got. Again. And again. And again. Until his screams echoed in the room. "Bitch, I'll kill you!" Ronaldo punched me, retrieved his weapon, and dug it in my back before I could escape. "Talia's better than you, Cybele! Let those words be the last thing you hear!"

He pushed me away and turned around. He didn't even look while I collapsed to the ground.

Everything was red the next time my eyes opened—the curtains, the bed, the door. The villa was burning!

Every muscle in my body screamed when I began to crawl to the window. My eyes were so blurry from the smoke, I could barely keep them open. But even while my lungs were working double time, and I was bleeding inside and out, I was alive. That was what mattered now.

I glanced at my parents after I flung the window open—at my father's open eyes, and my mother's bloody dress. It was still the picture in my head as I started climbing out.

There was no one in sight as I walked away, barefoot, freezing, bleeding.

My feet dug in the cold snow, but I didn't mind the biting pain. It was nothing compared to seeing my mother and father dead on the floor. It was nothing compared to the betrayal that Talia and her family did to me.

One step after another, my foot carried me to God knows where.

Revenge. Revenge. Revenge. It kept repeating in my head.

Run, Cybele! My mother's voice shouted in my mind.

Yes, I would, Mother. But trust me. Someday, somehow, I'd come back to claim what was mine. Even if I hurt Talia. Even if I hurt myself.

Chapter 7

An elderly woman and her female associate hovered over me. ID's dangled from the strap on their necks; *Augustine Center,* it said in plain black letters.

"Can you tell us your name?" the woman asked. "Do you remember where you lived?"

I crawled to the corner of the bed until my back touched the wall. It was cold, hard—just like the rest of this place. I didn't like it.

The woman sighed at her associate. "A month, and still no progress. She doesn't eat much either."

The associate removed her eyeglasses and began to wipe it in circular motion against her cardigan. She then took the elderly woman by the arm, and swung them around so they were both facing away from me. "The kid was bloody and almost dying when we found her. No child should have gone through that." Her voice was low, but I still heard every single word. "I hope we can do something. The counsellor said that trauma is what's keeping her from talking."

They snuck glances at me.

"We'll try again later," the old woman said. "We should prepare for now. The Prescott's are arriving from England."

I hugged my knees after they gave me reassuring smiles and walked away. The room was empty again except for me. Three other beds were fixed, their owners in the dining room a floor below. They could be eating, or playing, or laughing. Doing things without me.

On the first night that I got here, I told the kids that I was the Princess. But did they help me? No. They said something was wrong in my head. They said they didn't believe me, even if I had insisted.

How could they believe me, though? I wouldn't believe me either. People outside the Palace had never seen me. The commoners were aware of my existence, but my parents kept my face a mystery to give me privacy for as long as possible.

Now, I'm wishing they didn't.

Something moved from the corner of my eye. Something big. Henrietta was sneering at me when I looked up. She was this mean kid who was taller, slower, and dumber than any ten-year-old I've met before. She was the troll in my fairytale books.

"Hello, Princess." She snickered.

I didn't respond and stared at the floor. The kids from the other rooms somehow found out about the princess bit I had said and thought it was funny. It attracted flies like Henrietta.

"Why don't you talk to me, Princess? Are you scared?" She grasped the end of my bedsheet and pulled. I didn't do anything to stop her. "Are you mute?" she asked again.

My pillow fell to the floor. I moved an inch closer to the middle of the mattress every time she pulled. Couldn't she leave me alone?

"Maybe you're not a mute after all. Maybe you're just shy. But you know what I think?"

Henrietta's grin was evil. "I think the King and Queen forbade you to speak."

"Shut up," I whispered.

"I heard what happened to your parents," she continued in a mean voice. "Did you hear what happened to your parents?"

"Shut up."

"They said that the King and Queen are dead—"

"SHUT UP!"

I didn't know how I managed to reach her. But the smile on my lips was wide when I twisted her arm. The sound of her cries made me happy.

"I'll break your arm if you say that again," I whispered. "I'm your Princess. The throne is mine. And when I get it back someday, you'll all bow down to me. Do you understand?"

Her eyes searched for the exit while she squirmed against my grip. "Let go of me!" she squeaked.

"Apologize!"

"No!"

I twisted her arm tighter. Any moment now, a popping would sound.

"Okay!" she yelled. "I'm sorry!"

She stumbled back when I let her go. Henrietta grabbed the over-sized shoe that had slipped from her foot, and ran faster that anyone I'd seen before.

Nobody bothered me for hours after that. Maybe Henrietta told the other kids what happened. Maybe she told them not to go near me. Fine with me. I used the isolation by catching up on sleep. I couldn't get enough of it because of the nightmares.

The smoke. The fire. The blood that kept oozing everywhere I looked.

Someone nudged me awake sometime in the afternoon. It was just a gentle pat on the head, but my eyes still opened to check who it was.

"I'm sorry, I didn't mean to wake you." A woman with cascading brunette hair and eyes that almost had the same color as the diamond on her neck was beside my bed. The jewelry glimmered to life as she knelt on the dusty floor to me. "Won't you hurt yourself sleeping like that?" she asked.

I didn't remove my back from the wall or lie down on the bed like what she must have wanted. Who was she anyway? What did she want from me?

The woman didn't leave. She kept kneeling there, looking at my face like I casted a spell on her. "You're a pretty girl," she commented. "The prettiest I've seen in my life. Would you like to come with me and my husband?"

What a strange question. Weren't the adults informed that children were taught not to trust anyone? Even for a candy?

"Come where?" I couldn't help but ask anyhow.

Her smile vanished after hearing the scratchiness of my voice. I haven't been using it that much. But she was back to a smile as she offered a hand to me. Her finger had a diamond ring on it, so had her wrist. "We're looking for someone to adopt," she explained, patiently. "I know they don't let us choose, but I'll fight for you if you want to come with me."

A moment passed without me speaking or moving.

The woman didn't give up. "I think the two of us will get along. What do you say to becoming my daughter?"

"I can't."

"Why?"

She wasn't going to let this go. The truth needed to be said.

"I can't call you Mother," I admitted. No matter who she was or how kind she appeared to be, no one would replace the Queen, ever.

The confusion on her fell off like washed mud. Somehow, she understood what I was trying to say. "Oh, Pumpkin, I'm not here to replace your mother," she whispered. "My husband and I just want someone to love. We weren't given any children."

"Are you there, dear?" a man's voice called out.

The woman glanced over her shoulder. "Yes, dearest. I'm here with her."

Heavy footsteps approached the room. In a while, a man in a gray suit and a trilby hat over his black hair appeared. His tie was straight, but his smile was crooked. Behind the circular spectacles were kind eyes that resembled his wife's.

"This is Larry, my husband," the woman introduced. Surprise flashed on her face. "Great

Scott! Here I am telling you his name when I haven't properly given you mine. I'm Samantha."

Larry and Samantha. They looked like decent people. But looks, I've learned, were not good enough. Never.

Samantha didn't get up as her husband went into the room. She continued studying me. "You've been sleeping in that corner since we arrived, so we couldn't help but ask the people here about you." She exchanged worried looks with Larry. "We heard you've been through some rough stuff. The staff also said you didn't want to talk to them. If you let us, we can take you far away from here where you'll feel loved and cared for. We'll protect you as best as we can."

Larry knelt beside her and added, "We'll give you all the toys you want too." He tried to keep his voice gentle, but it still came out deep and strong. A wound opened in my chest because of it. He reminded me of Father. "You'll have a large room and pretty dresses. You can be a ballerina, a musician—anything you want to be."

My hands grasped the bed sheet. "What if I want to be a Princess?" I murmured.

"You'll be a Princess, then. We have all the resources to make you feel like one," Larry said. "That, I promise."

No one would believe me if I say that I was the future ruler of this country. The news told everyone that I died with the King and Queen. Besides, who could I trust? If my mother's best friend had plotted to have us killed; the staff, the nobles, anyone who knew my real identity could be dangerous. But if I go with Larry and Samantha now, I'd have the chance to live a good life. I could wait until the right time to get my crown back. It was the best decision.

"Okay," I said. "I'll be your daughter."

The Prescott's visited me often while the paper works for my adoption were being fixed.

During those days, I learned that they were a rich and influential family in England who'd won awards for their contribution to the scientific community. But even if they had a lot of connections, the two were nothing but humble. The staff from the adoption home sometimes even called them odd.

Larry and Samantha would often crack jokes about science. They took pleasure in discussing Physics, Chemistry, and hypothesis, instead of gossiping like the other adults. They were two geniuses who fell in love with each other and were happy enough.

I hated to use them for my own selfish reasons, but what could I do? I was a child, a lost one, no match for the world. Beggars couldn't be choosers, and I, as mean as this sounded, had struck gold.

The day of our departure to England finally arrived. I was passed around for goodbyes in the adoption home, sent straight to the car, then walked to a private jet. But even if it was a busy day, I didn't forget to do one thing.

Kneeling on the ground, I kissed the pavement and murmured, "Wait for your Queen. I swear I'll be back."

"Are you all right back there, Iris?"

Samantha had noticed that I wasn't behind her anymore. She stopped boarding the jet to look for me.

I jumped up and waved to her. "I'm okay, Mum. Don't worry."

The bookmark that Talia gave was clutched around my fingers as I scampered to the plane after my new parents. I found it in the pocket of the jacket I was wearing when I escaped the villa. It was all that was left of my previous life. I'd make sure to give it back with revenge.

The Prescott's home in England was a mansion. Not as big as the Palace, of course, but beautiful too. A stone fountain of a woman holding a jar was placed near the gate to greet the guests. And from what I could see through the car window while we slowed down the circular driveway, there was no shortage of trees and flowers everywhere.

Mum and Dad took their time introducing me to the staff. They were polite and friendly, all that is, except for Chandra, our butler. Something was off about her. I could feel it.

On the first night of my stay in the mansion, I woke up because of a strange shaking of the bed. Opening my eyes, I saw the butler holding a magnifying glass near my face.

"W-what are you doing!" I cried.

"Nothing much." Chandra lowered the magnifying glass and leaned back. "I'm just looking for an imperfection. That's all."

She'd never see one. I was careful not to mess around my parents or people in the mansion. I had a goal. A mission. I couldn't afford to make a mistake.

Years passed like that: me keeping to myself, studying, being perfect. Before I knew it, college was already knocking on my door. That's when I met Brooke.

"Miss Iris, you have a visitor," a voice informed outside my bedroom.

I removed my glasses and placed it on the table, to be quickly followed by the book I was reading. "Who is it?" I called.

"It's Miss Brooke. Should I let her in?"

"Go ahead."

I waited for a few more minutes before a soft rap sounded again. When the door opened, Brooke, in her jean shorts, a cropped top, and sneakers came in. How was she able to pull that off in a chilly day? In England too?

" Iris," she greeted.

"Brooke."

"How are you?"

I shrugged. "Not much has changed since we saw each other yesterday, I guess. I'm still the same old boring college classmate you have."

She touched my shoulder upon reaching my side. The woman smelled strongly of vanilla. "Don't say that," Brooke dismissed. "You're not boring at all. You're just a little. . ."

"Weird?"

"Antisocial." Brooke gestured to the bedside table. "You're always with your books. You never go to parties. Is your boyfriend keeping you busy?"

"Absolutely not."

She gave me a quizzical look.

"I'm not the type to have boyfriends," I explained.

A slow smile spread on her lips. One of the good things about her was she never hid her feelings. Her expression always gave it away. "So you're the type to have girlfriends instead?"

"I don't do girlfriends either."

I reached for my eyeglasses and textbook. If she wanted to talk about those things, then I'd rather go back to Dunham.

"I don't get you," she grumbled. "Everyone wants to hang out with you, yet you'd rather read those." She stole the book from my hand and examined the cover. "Journey Through Genius." She frowned. "We're all studying in an Ivy League school, but man, your choices of books are mental. Who reads about math in their spare time?"

"I do. My parents do." I snatched the book from her again and kept it by my side. The poor thing had been going back and forth like a ball. "Math is a universal language, Brooke. Learning it will help you with logic, and logic will help you with hacking."

"Hacking?" Her eyebrows rose at me. "What are you going to hack?"

"Nothing. It's just a theory I'm working on."

A theory that involved hacking the main security server of Harland's Palace. It was the only way I could kidnap the Princess without outside help. Bwahaha!

Brooke shooed me away to get into the bed. "Told you, you're strange."

"That's me. Iris Strange Prescott."

She glanced around my room. Like any other person entering another human's domain, she must be looking for traces of my personality through my things. And like the butler wouldn't see an imperfection in me, Brooke would get nothing but studiousness in this clean, spotless room. Everything I am was locked up in my brain. The outside appearance was different from the chaos building inside.

Her eyes went to me once more. She leaned a little bit closer. "Isn't it mad," she said, "that even if you're a loner, I still find you interesting? You're a combination of beauty and brains, Iris. That's hard to find."

Her hand slid from my arms to my neck, all the way to my face. Brooke removed my glasses a second time and made it disappear like magic.

"What are you doing?" I asked.

She cupped my cheek and moved closer still. "I'm going to show you how amazing having a girlfriend is, Iris. Just let me kiss you."

I gasped. Brooke's face wasn't there anymore when I blinked, Talia's was. But the Princess was older, like the pictures I saw in magazines when she had an interview a few months back. Was I hallucinating?

"Relax," she said, drawing my lips to her. Our mouths touched. And then we were kissing, making each other moan, touching each other, until I pushed her to the bed and climbed on top of her.

God, she was so beautiful.

"Talia," I whispered, seconds before I started to ravish her.

Chapter 8

Revenge: a single, simple, powerful word resulting from hate. It's been on my mind since that forsaken day in the villa.

I've wanted nothing more than to kill the person who ended my parents life, to show Talia's family no mercy for stripping me of everything. It kept me awake at night. It ate away at my soul like a sickness.

Because of it, I thought I was strong enough to resist temptation. I thought revenge was all that mattered, nothing else. But sometimes, even when that's all you could think about, a momentary lapse of judgment could happen, especially when what you've wanted most was dangled right in front of you.

"You're so sexy," Talia purred against my ear at present and smiled. The sound sent a chasm in my chest. It was surprisingly stronger after all these years.

I buried my face in the hollow of her neck. She'd always smelled like the lavenders in the Palace garden. I've tried to get rid of the thought of it, but it followed me like a shadow everywhere I went.

"You're sexier," I murmured.

The hum in her throat as I nipped her jaw was a sign to continue. I moved up to her lips.

Talia removed my shirt one tantalizing button at a time as a result. Her fingers trailed against my chest as she moved along: hot, shaking, ready for me.

My turn.

She raised her arms as I lifted her top. The blue lace that cupped her breasts was begging to be removed. But she wasn't willing to play there yet. She pressed a finger on my lips and smiled. "Let's take off those jeans first, shall we?" Her other hand tugged my jean button loose. I moved us to our side so she could work her way down. My legs were weak as she slipped me out of my jeans.

My underwear was being tugged free when she paused. "I didn't know you had a tattoo."

My gaze was pulled to the writing on my hipbone. *Long live the Queen,* it said.

Seeing it, a violent shiver erupted in my spine.

How could I forget? The abomination. The loss of trust. The betrayal to my family? And for what? A moment of carelessness?

The girl I'd been pining for was no longer there when I looked back. She was another woman I'd nearly screwed for lust. Yet another mistake.

The hurt on Brooke's face as I left the bed was a slap on my own. Why was I so callous? So hateful? She had nothing to do with this.

"Is it another woman?" she asked in a small voice. I hated how weak she sounded. None of this was her fault.

I could barely look at her as I nodded. The wildfire in my chest was overwhelming, threatening to burn me into cinders. "It's not only that, I. . ." My hands clumped into fists. "There is something wrong with me."

"You mean aside from not wanting this perfection?"

Her statement made me frown. I couldn't argue with the fact that she was pure temptation in that skimpy lace. She deserved to be unwrapped like a gift and worshiped like a Goddess. Not turned away like what I did. Something was clearly wrong with me if I didn't take that offer.

Brooke's eyes didn't waver as I took a seat. It was an admirable trait, lovable even. "You're one of the sexiest women I've ever seen," I admitted. "Whoever doesn't see that is a fool."

"Like you?"

"I don't have time for love."

"Or sex," she remarked with a scowl.

"I can give you that," I confessed. "We can do it anytime you want. Anywhere. No strings attached. Just good old-fashioned sex." My shoulders sagged. "But there's always the risk of you falling in love with me, and I can't let that happen."

"That's so cheeky of you."

"Not cheeky: the truth." I reached for her long hair. It was midnight black, straight, beautiful. Touching it was more than enough. Owning it was too much. "I'm messed up," I murmured. "There's only darkness in my heart. And if you make the mistake of falling for me, you'll end up broken too. Love isn't something I can afford right now. Not until I get my goals."

"Which are?"

"You can't handle it."

Brooke snorted.

Was that what she really wanted? Her eyes said so. They challenged me.

She cried in surprise as I twisted her hair around my hand and tugged. I needed to test her.

"I want to kidnap a Princess," I said.

Brooke had avoided me for a week. No calls, no excuses to visit my house like she'd been doing since class started, no nothing. I wasn't complaining though. It was better for me to be alone. She wouldn't understand what I was.

My usual routine continued without her. University in the morning, study during free periods, go home after classes, and learn about hacking at night. The first step to kidnapping Talia would involve bypassing the server in the Palace to search for vulnerabilities. I've heard that they'd installed cameras last year. Through there, I'd know how many guards there were, how they handled security, what time they changed shifts, and what Talia was up to.

I've also learned through my adoptive parents 'connections that her room was equipped with a camera too. It wasn't open to maintain Talia's privacy, but it was installed in case of an emergency. I'd use that to stalk her.

Brooke had taken a backseat in my mind because of the busy schedule. That's why it was surprising to see her walking towards me in the school grounds one sunny morning. Her hips sashayed with every bounce of her feet; the sunlight fixed on her face. She didn't look scared as she went to the grass where I was sitting, took my hand, and pulled me up.

"What?" I asked.

A punt with two passengers passed the river not far from where I sat, but they didn't notice the harassment Brooke was doing. She'd collected my books, pens, satchel, and pushed them to my chest. "We're going to my room," she declared.

"We are?"

"Yes. But we may need to take a detour to Greggs first. I'm starving."

"I'm busy," I said.

"Trust me." She smirked. "You need to hear what I'll say."

My curiosity was piqued, so I went along with her plans. We headed to Greggs—one of the popular pastry shops in the vicinity— and ate a bagel as we walked the stone path leading to her dorm.

The room we entered made me blink rapidly. Compared to the boring, neutral tones of mine, Brooke's was finished with bold pink and purple. There were pictures everywhere too, from the walls, to the bulletin board above her bed, to the frames adorning her desk. The beanbags on the floor were a nice touch. They looked soft and comfortable to rest on.

Brooke took the things from my hands, dumped them on the bed, and motioned for me to follow. The mattress sagged under our combined weights.

"Why do you stay in the dorms?" I asked.

"Why don't you? People usually live here for college, you know?"

"I have my reasons."

The Prescott's mansion was simply safer.

~ 89 ~

Brooke gave me an inquiring stare. "By the way, this is totally irrelevant to our previous conversation, but do you travel often?"

"Not as much as the average student here," I said. "Why?"

She shrugged. "You have this accent."

"So do you."

She looked impressed. "How did you catch that? People usually can't." Her hands moved while she explained. "Mom's Aussie, so I kind of picked up on how she talks. How about you?"

"I wasn't born here." The pictures on her walls were suddenly interesting. I looked at them as I continued. "I was adopted."

"Really?"

I nodded. It was refreshing to tell someone after a long time. No one had asked me before either, so it wasn't brought up.

Brooke didn't look as shocked as I thought she'd be. She just gave me a thumbs up, took the laptop perched on her pillow, then placed it on her knees. "You must be wondering why I brought you here by now," she said, her fingers working on the keyboard. "About the other week. . . Were you serious about kidnapping a Princess?"

"Do you think I'd joke about something like that?"

The typing stopped.

I gauged her reaction while waiting for a response. One hint of going to the police and I'd take it all back.

"Well then." She cracked her knuckles and nodded to herself. "I've been thinking about it over the week."

"And?"

"If I put kidnapping and hacking together, my guess is you're going to break into a server." A wide smile crept on her face as she glanced at me. "Count me in."

"Count you in?" I shifted in my seat. "But you don't even know what's going on."

Her shoulders lifted in a half-shrug. "So? I like you, Iris. I want to win your heart."

"Brooke—"

"Or at least your friendship," she added tersely. "What do you think?"

Her eyes were hopeful as she anticipated my reply. She hadn't proven herself to me yet. I didn't know if I could trust her a hundred percent, but I guess I'd have to wait and see. If things go bad, I could always threaten her family.

"How will you help me?" I asked.

She pointed to her laptop where a command prompt was open in the middle of the screen. "My mom is an ace programmer. I learned all sort of things from her."

"But do you know how to hack?"

"I'm glad you asked." Brooke's fingers were lightning-fast as she typed again. She looked like a pianist playing for the concerto. "How do you think I knew all the answers to the entrance exam?"

"Did you steal it?"

She winked at me. "Nope. I did get in the Uni with my own efforts, but I enjoy hacking the government's server when I'm bored."

"Good for you."

She faced the laptop to me. The command prompt was gone, replaced by a website. "Prepare to be amazed."

The rest of the day was spent trying things out. She wasn't kidding. The girl knew her stuff. By the end of the night, I'd already learned the basics of getting into the Palace server, protecting myself from being found, and destroying evidence when push comes to shove. She was a miracle worker.

"Thanks for everything," I said. My things have been collected, and her roommate was about to go back. It was time for me to go home.

Brooke and I went to the door together. I was about to reach for the knob when she stopped my hand. "Nah-uh. Don't I get a reward?"

I turned to her. "How much do you want?"

Her giggles echoed in the room. What did she find so funny?

Brooke wiped the imaginary tears at the edge of her eyes and curled a finger to me. "I want something money can't buy," she said. "A kiss."

A kiss? It was just a thank you. Nothing more.

I moved closer and stopped inches from her face. She still smelled sweet, almost like candy. My hand found the small of her back. "Don't fall in love with me," I murmured. "I mean it."

Her lips were minty, soft. I stepped back when she tried to lure me with her tongue.

"Iris," she whispered. Her hands were still raised as if she was holding my face. Her breath was fast and shallow.

"Goodnight, Brooke."

She was still panting when I swiveled around and left.

The travel back to the mansion was a blur. Everything happened so fast, I didn't know what to make of it. Before I knew it, a staff was greeting me by the door, looking glad that I was home. "Good evening, Miss Iris. Do you want to eat your dinner now?"

I handed her my coat. "No, thank you. Are my parents here?"

"Not yet, Miss. They haven't arrived from their trip."

"Okay. I'll be in my room."

My footsteps rang on the marble floor as I headed to the grand staircase. The other staff were absent. They were probably in their rooms.

Halfway through the stairs, something pulled my foot. "What the hell!" My heart blasted like an explosion as I held onto the railing for dear life. The butler let go of me when I glanced back. "Chandra!" I snarled at her. "I could have fallen and broken my neck! What's the matter with you?"

"You have to eat dinner."

The forty-something woman had an unusually nasally voice. If one was to look at her, she'd appear like a nice, normal lady whose hair was pulled away in a bun, and whose uniform was always put-together. But she wasn't. She was cuckoo. No explanations needed.

"God, you scared me!" My heartbeat was still fast. "I've already eaten with Brooke."

"Your friend from school?"

"Yes, yes. I'm going to my room. Please don't disturb me."

I ran the rest of the way up without looking back at her. Bloody hell, she was strange. Where did Mum and Dad get her?

I made sure to lock the doors as I got inside my room. Tonight was extra special. I didn't want anyone getting in my way, especially Chandra.

The laptop was waiting for me on the desk. I took it with me to bed and ran the program that Brooke recommended. Time to practice what I've learned.

It wasn't easy to break down the security protocols and take over the main server of Harland's Palace. It took patience. Skills. But it was only a matter of time before I got in. Soon, I was looking at the guards through my monitor as if I was watching a television series. They were miles away in my home country, but the way I saw it, distance wasn't important when technology was there to help.

Around midnight and numerous searches, I finally found the control for Talia's camera. A single keystroke allowed me to activate it. A live feed of her appeared on my screen.

My breaths waned as I concentrated on the image. Talia was sitting in my bed, or at least what used to be mine before she and her mother stole it. I zoomed the camera to check the book wrapped around her fingers. How ironic. She was reading The Count of Monte Cristo. A story about revenge.

I stared at her for a long time. I stared at her until my eyes were so strained that I thought they would bleed. She was sixteen now, so different from when she was six. Talia had grown up to be lovely like she wished.

My nails dug on the mattress. What was I thinking? Lovely or not, she shouldn't be reading in my room, pouring over books that I loved. Her mother should have been dead instead of mine.

Still, I tortured myself by keeping my eyes on the screen. It was a bittersweet sensation, one that took the air from my lungs. The good and bad memories of her were like tattoos etched in my soul. I couldn't get rid of them.

Sometime in the wee hours of the morning, Talia decided to go to sleep. She got up from the Queen-sized bed, tossed the book to the bedside table, and stretched her arms.

I was about to close the screen when her dress fell to the floor. Talia, in all her splendid beauty, unknowingly gave me a view.

I knew what would happen next when her hands went behind her bra. I slammed the laptop shut before I saw what was peeking underneath. It was an image I wouldn't erase no matter how hard I tried.

"Crap!"

An avalanche in my chest threatened to crush me alive. I was supposed to hate her, wished badly of her, want her to suffer like I'd suffered. And yet for all my dark expectations, a question begged to be answered. If I hated her so much, why did I want to hold her?

Chapter 9

"It's unusual for you to take us somewhere like this. Where are we going?"

Mum's voice was startlingly loud inside the car. From the rearview mirror, I saw her play with the diamond ring on her finger—the same one she wore years ago at the adoption center. It brought back certain memories, good and bad.

"It's a secret," I said. "We don't want to ruin the surprise."

"Can't you give us a hint?"

"No."

"Just a teensy bit, Pumpkin?"

"Just let her be, Samantha." Dad, who was sitting beside Mum at the back, squeezed her hand. "I'm sure our daughter has a good reason for kidnapping us tonight. You know it's serious when the chauffeur is given a day off."

I struggled not to laugh like a maniac. He was right in a way. I'd kidnap someone all right. Soon.

The restaurant by the lake was vacant of other customers 'chatter when we got there. What waited for us instead was calm water, a windy atmosphere that blew Dad's hat away, and a table full of seafood. I'd made the reservation weeks before for privacy. It was just one of the many steps to my success.

After the maître 'D had come and gone to have us seated, I turned to my parents with an easy smile. Time to put the plan into motion. "So," I started. "I just turned twenty-two last month. The degree you wanted for me is finished too. . ."

The Pinot Noir in Mum's wine glass formed a small tornado when she swished it around. "We know that perfectly well, Iris, dear," she spoke.

"I'm glad we're on the same page then." I took a breath. "I want to—"

"We think it's time for you to take over the family business," she interrupted.

An awkward silence hung in the air.

Taking my glass from the table, I drank until every last drop was gone. The rich taste of the wine didn't erase the bitterness in my tongue, but it did give me confidence.

"I don't think being a scientist is for me, Mum," I started. "Neither does being a professor, a philosopher, or whatever it is both of you do on your spare time. No offense."

"Are you saying you want to be a model forever?" Dad was talking about the campaigns that Brooke forced me into shortly after graduation. It was one of the payments she asked for helping me out, and I must admit, it was handy too.

Through those modeling gigs, I earned connections that I wouldn't have gotten if I stayed in my room. They taught me how to smile, to engage, to disarm with simple body language. I was still the lone wolf, but a wolf who knew how to hook a prey.

Mum twisted the napkin she'd grabbed. If Dad had looked bothered, she was beside herself with worry. "Don't feel bad about what your Father said," she reasoned. "We only want the best for you."

"I know," I acknowledged with a smile. "And I'm thankful for it every day, believe me." My nails clawed on the side of the chair. Now was the best time to tell them. I shouldn't linger. "The truth is, Mum and Dad, I brought you here to say that I want to go back to Harland and find myself."

"Find yourself?" Mum asked again.

"Alone," I added.

Shock spread on their faces. This confession had been a long time coming, but in all those years I hadn't given them a clue.

Mum clasped Dad's sleeves for support. "L-Larry," she stammered. "Our baby doesn't want us anymore."

"You don't?" Dad had the same crestfallen expression.

Goodness.

"Do you know how silly this sounds?" I said. "Of course I love you. I do! But some part of me is back in Harland, waiting to be discovered. I can't sit around just driving an expensive car, or strutting my stuff at the catwalk until I've figured it out." I reached out to them. "Will you help me?"

Dad took the handkerchief from his front pocket and dabbed his forehead. Of the two he was more rational, though at the moment his skin was also pale. "Can you give me a moment to talk to your mother?"

The lake was calm and quiet when I reached the dock. The sky was a midnight blue, enhanced by the small number of stars that weren't covered by the clouds. Mum and Dad were still by the table in the restaurant, too far to hear. They would have a long discussion that I didn't want to be anywhere near to.

Fishing the phone from my pocket, I dialed Brooke's number and gave her a ring. "Let me guess," she answered. "You found out you're in love with me, so you're calling to ask for sex?"

I rolled my eyes. Typical Brooke.

"Friends don't fuck friends."

"Friends with benefits do."

I sighed. "You know I don't have time for those, so stop being horny and talk to me like a normal person. Seriously, you and your sex talks."

She grumbled. "Okay, party pooper. What did you want to talk about?"

I bent over and took a pebble. A few of them had mysteriously found their way to the dock. "I've told my parents my plan to go home."

"You didn't! What did they say?"

"They're still talking about it."

She snorted. "Maybe they're creating a mathematical equation to make you stay."

"Probably."

I glanced over my shoulder to see whose shoes were making the thudding noise on the dock. The footsteps belonged to my parents. I covered my mouth. "They're heading this way, Brooke. Catch you later."

I'd ended the call when they got to me. Dad spoke before I could. "We've always treated you as our own." He wiped the edge of his eyes with the handkerchief. Beside him, Mum was sniffing, trying to hold herself together. "It pains us to see you go," he continued. "But you're an adult now. You should try to find your own way."

The pebble fell from my hand. Even if I wasn't a big hugger, I looped my arms around them both, elated that they've given me permission.

Mum released the tears she'd been holding back, while Dad patted my head. "Promise us you'll come home soon."

"I promise," I lied.

The road I was taking had only two endings: to get the crown back or to end up dead. I might never see them again.

The first thing I did after stepping foot in Harland was to kiss the ground. I was finally home.

It didn't matter if people looked at me strangely. It didn't matter if they thought I was crazy. Running through my veins was a certain kind of ecstasy, a joy that could only be brought by knowing that what I'd been longing for was within reach. I was unstoppable.

One of the best things about Europe was how castles were sold like any other properties. You could contact an agent, find the match for you, pay a King's ransom, and voila! The Queen of your own fortress.

As it was, I'd been eyeing a particular castle for some time. It was located deep in the forest, hours from any town, unsold because of its seclusion. I bought it.

"Make the doors unbreakable," I told the engineer. "Seal the windows. Modernize the interior if you can, but make sure it still looks abandoned from outside. It adds a certain charm."

The engineer, a striking man with blonde hair, rolled the blueprint I'd given him. He was recommended to me by a contact, and as I was told, not only adept at his job but could also keep his mouth shut. "Before we begin, Miss Prescott," he said. "May I ask what you're going to need this place for?" He tucked the blueprint in a tube before looking back at me. "Call it curiosity. I've worked for hundreds of clients but had never encountered these kinds of specifications. Much more for a castle."

"Understandable." I clapped a hand on his broad shoulder. "My demands are peculiar."

"They are."

I sniffed and checked the castle in front of us. People were too nosey for their own good. "To be honest, I'm going to use this magnificent structure as a hideout."

"A hideout?"

"For killing women," I went on. "I like to tie them up while they scream, then drag a knife over their stomach like you would with a pig. Didn't you see the papers? I'm a serial killer on the loose."

The engineer stared at me with his mouth open. He snapped it close. "You almost got me there." His chuckles were light. "You're good."

" So they say. But do the job right, and you'll never have to work a day in your life again. Keep that in mind."

The outcome of the construction was everything I wanted. The security was tight. The doors were unbreakable. And I could live without the fear of anyone finding it out. One of the rooms had been converted into a control center where I could see and manipulate everything with computers. Technology: helping kidnappers since its conception.

After paying the team for a job well done, as well as keeping their silence, I moved into one of the chambers in the castle. There, I was allowed breathing space to be myself. To not be constantly on my guard like I was in the Prescott's mansion.

Books, gaming consoles, and small trinkets that fascinated me were everywhere. I didn't have to hide the dark novels that were always about revenge. Neither do I have to conceal the strategy games that allowed me to pulverize made-up enemies. I could pine over lovely mares that reminded me of the King and Queen's last gift to me: Jessie.

Speaking of my real parents, abduction day has arrived after months.

The Royal Palace that should have been mine had acres of land. It covered a forest, the Palace itself, and an impressive yard that tourists could see from outside the gate in the distance. People normally wouldn't have access to its blueprint, but I wasn't just any other person. I was its Queen. Add to that, my developed expertise over the years of bribing and scaring people, and soon, the Palace's blueprint was mine.

Esmeralda, the snake who dethroned me, might have made improvements to the Palace here and there over the years. She might have tightened the security, or built defenses of her own. But every problem had a solution.

Aside from memorizing the blueprint and taking notes of the guard shifts through the hacked security cameras, I had a winning card that only I was aware of. All over the Palace grounds were secret passageways and tunnels, constructed to protect the royal family since time immemorial. Only heirs to the throne, the true owners of the seat, were told of it in each generation. I'd use that tonight.

Come midnight, I parted the bushes where the opening of the secret tunnel was located. It was several kilometers outside the Royal Palace, snaked underneath the ground, and ended in the garden, near the pond where Talia and I used to play as children.

My muscles worked overtime so I could roll away the stone obstructing my path. Once it was clear, I knelt on the ground, took a glow stick from my backpack, and snapped it open. Cold breeze from the tunnel whipped on my face. Here I go.

The guards were about to change shifts when I re-emerged on the other side of the tunnel. I had a window of ten minutes to do my plan and escape. It was best to begin.

I stuck to the shadows while walking, careful of every footfalls and breaths. The back entrance dedicated to the servants of the Palace was eerily quiet as I crept inside. Everyone should be asleep.

I found the secret passage near the stairs, went in, and reappeared behind the wall; a stone's throw away from Talia's room. *My* room. Victory was almost mine.

Tok. Tok. Tok.

What was that?

Tok. Tok. Tok.

I strained my ear.

Footsteps! To my left.

The martial arts training I'd continued under the Prescott's care proved to be beneficial. I was silent as a cat as I tiptoed to a medieval armor in the corner, and ducked behind it before the person walking in the hallway could spot me.

The footsteps stopped right in front of the armor. Whoever it was breathed loud, cleared his throat, then continued walking. He was long gone when I stepped out.

Talia was asleep when I made it into her bedroom. After locking the door behind me, I edged to the bed, guided by the moonlight streaming through the window. My breaths stopped the moment I caught sight of her face.

The Princess 'lashes were long and curled. Her cheeks were naturally flushed with pink. She was eighteen now: ripe, beautiful, a heartbreaker. Her wish by the pond had come true.

Slowly, slowly, I leaned to her sleeping form. Her mouth was like gravity, pulling me against my wishes.

Wait a minute! I stopped. What the hell was I doing?

Ignoring the pounding of my heart, I straightened away from the Princess and scowled. *Concentrate!*

I shrugged off my backpack as quickly as possible. There were dozens of ways to restrain her. I could even use chemicals to knock her out temporarily. But those were too easy. I didn't want her to be asleep when I did the kidnapping. I wanted Talia to be awake, aware, terrified, just as I'd been when the King and Queen were murdered.

The Princess 'eyes snapped open the instance I taped her mouth. Those split-seconds of us gazing at each other knocked the wind off my chest.

She'd seen me. She looked right at my eyes. Could she have recognized me?

No, probably not. She was too young the last time I'd seen her. She'd have forgotten everything about us, and besides, everyone thought I was dead.

I shoved a black cloth over her head. Talia couldn't scare me anymore.

"Mffff! Mffff!"

She struggled against me as I looped a rope over her wrist.

"Mffffffffffffff!"

I avoided a kick to the stomach and tied her legs next. The guards would be getting back soon. I needed to hurry.

It was a challenge to subdue the Princess while I fished the cellphone from my pocket. Using the program I created, everything in the security cameras were wiped clean with a touch of a button. Once the guards get back from their ten-minute shifting, all they'd see was static. Good luck finding out who took the Princess.

I tucked the phone back in my pocket, lifted Talia over my shoulder, grabbed my bag, and made my escape.

I was closing the tunnel that would lead us to total escape when voices broke into the garden. Did they find out already? Were they following? I shifted Talia close to me and strained my ears to listen.

"What are you doing up? Can't sleep?"

"Yeah. There's something about tonight."

"Too hot for ya, boss?"

"Nah. Just this itchy feeling I get sometimes. How about you?"

My eyes closed on their own. One of the men speaking was familiar. So familiar that I didn't have to imagine how he'd look like with a bloody knife in his hand. He was my nightmare. My enemy. The time would come when I'd behead Ronaldo myself. I swear on the King and Queen's name.

But first, I'd make their lives a living hell. The Princess was mine now. The throne was mine. Now it was time to play a little game of chess.

Chapter 10
Talia

Twelve Years Ago

Mommy Esmeralda looked happy today. She had a bright smile on her face. She even smiled at the men in uniform as she dragged me to the car this morning. Lots of them were waiting for us outside my house. They had long rifles and shiny boots.

"Are we visiting Cybele in the Palace today, Mommy?" I asked.

My question was ignored as we entered the Rover. Earlier, the maids packed my toys and clothes. Why would they do that?

"We can proceed," Mommy said to the driver. The smile on her face was back as she leaned on the seat. Maybe she was just happy to see the Queen. They've been besties for a long time, they said.

The sun was almost gone when we arrived at the Royal Palace. I yawned as I jumped off the car, feeling like a zombie beside the adults who welcomed us. Their eyes were more awake than mine, but they were whispering.

"The family was forsaken," one of them said. I didn't know who, but he sounded scared.

" Their bodies were found in the bed, but the child's corpse was missing."

"Maybe she was burned into ashes."

"Maybe she was stuck under the pile of rubble in the villa."

"Mommy, what's going on?"

The adults turned to me. Most of them looked frightened at what I said, but Mommy's expression remained the same. "This is grown-up talk, Talia. What did I tell you about that?"

My cheeks heated as I lowered my eyes. "Don't interrupt when the grown-ups are talking," I mumbled.

"Exactly." A maid came forward when Mommy Motioned to the staff. We were almost to the big doors leading inside the Palace. "Show Talia inside and make sure she stays there," Mommy instructed. "We haven't gotten a chance to talk."

I was passed from Mommy to the maid, and pretty soon, the big doors were groaning to let us in.

The strange feeling at the back of my throat was gone when I saw the suit of armors in the hallway. They've always been huge, shiny, and a good place to hide when Cybele and I would play. The paintings on the ceiling had always been my favorite, too. Cybele and I would sometimes lie down on the carpet, point to the art, and imagine the people from the scenes reaching down to us.

"Is Cybele in the garden?" I asked the maid. I hadn't seen Cybele since we came in. The staff were different too. The ones who'd always scolded me were not around.

"The garden is not a good place to be right now," the maid whispered.

We went directly to Cybele's room after, which made me glad. But why didn't they just say so? I wouldn't have asked if I knew we were coming here.

The maid opened the door and motioned for me to walk in first, so I skipped inside and glanced around. It was quiet here, empty. The sheets on the Queen-sized bed were changed. The big, fluffy pillows that Cybele loved were missing too, but what bothered me most were the bookshelves. They were blank and clean, and Cybele always preferred them full.

"Where's Cybele?" I asked in a small voice. She'd be mad if she sees her favorite books removed. She'd cry. And then I'd cry too.

The maid's eyes were red and watery when I turned to her. Did I say something bad?

"What's wrong?" I asked. "Where's Cybele?"

"She's. . . I'm sorry. I-I need to go to the kitchen. Stay here." She rushed out of the room before I could say anything else.

No one came for me for a long time. No one entered the room even when my tummy began to hurt. I missed Cybele. She was always the one who took care of me, made me laugh, hugged me. If she was here, she wouldn't leave me alone. If she was here, she'd tell me stories about the books she'd read until I fall asleep on her chest. If she was here. . .

"Are you awake?" Mommy said. I didn't hear the door open.

She let herself in, went to the bed, and patted the space beside her. I left the window before she got mad and sat on the mattress.

Mommy was quick-tempered, as a maid had told me once. It was better to follow than be scolded.

"Listen to me, Talia." She shifted in her seat to take a better look at me. "This room is yours from now on."

"It is?" I fiddled my thumbs and tried not to move too much. Mommy didn't like that. "What about Cybele?"

"You'll be the Princess." Mommy acted like she didn't hear me. "Someday when I'm gone, you'll replace me as the Queen."

"But isn't Cybele the princess?"

Why was she saying these things? It was weird.

Mommy's eyes were stern when she shook her head. They were grey like mine. I was a small version of her, they said, but Cybele always disagreed. She said I had kinder eyes, and I believed her. I always believed her.

Mommy dusted something from my shoulders. "Cybele is never coming back," she whispered. "Don't wait for her anymore."

"Huh?"

"I said she's never coming back."

"B-but. . . That's mean, Mommy."

"What is? Everything I said is true, Talia. Cybele and her parents are gone."

"No. . ."

"But they are." Mommy tucked a lock of hair behind my ear. "I'm the Queen. You're the Princess now. How hard is that for you?"

Was she playing with me? Was this a trick? Whatever it was, I slapped her hand away and screamed. "Stop lying to me, Mommy! Stop lying!"

Mommy's hand struck my face like a belt. She stood when I fell. She glared when I cowered. "Cybele is dead!" she hissed. "You're the princess now! Put that in your head!" She was making her way to the door when she glanced at me over her shoulder. Her eyes were colder than the snow. It made my heart freeze. "Your lessons start tomorrow."

The days fell off like the shedding of skin. But I didn't let it grow on me again. I picked on it like a scab. And though all I wanted to do was continue to peel it off, everything around me kept progressing at a constant speed. Before I knew it, my thirteenth birthday had arrived. *They* were wrong if they thought I was going to regenerate.

"There you are, Talia," Mother said. "I'd been looking all over for you."

I closed the novel on my lap and sighed. To think that she'd manage to find me next to the window of all places. The party was in fully swing too. "Don't you have guests to please?" I said.

"So do you. It's your birthday party."

"They came here for you, Mother. Not for me."

I fought the urge to roll my eyes. She was the type of parent to scold her daughter while guests were around. I was the type of daughter not to listen. That part of me ended when she lied about Cybele. How could she?

Mother looked behind her to check if anyone heard. Satisfied that none did, she turned to me with a grim smile on her lips. The usual, really. "Stand up straight and get rid of that annoying pout, Talia. I have someone to introduce to you."

At a gesture of her hand, a guy close to my age approached us. His bow was exaggeratingly low. His suit was as expensive as his smile, his brown hair a curly mop on his head. His eyes were the color of the sky, but they hinted of a storm. Of trouble.

"His name is Lance," Mother introduced. "Your future husband."

My what?

"Get acquainted with each other as early as today. When the time comes. . ."

Mother's voice was getting smaller, distant, insignificant.

"Are you listening to me, girl?"

My eyes snapped to her. Didn't she care how I felt? A husband? Didn't she want me to be with someone I loved?

"As I was saying," she continued. "The two of you will be wedded on your twentieth birthday. The celebration will be grand. It's going to be the wedding of the—"

"There's no way I'm going to marry him!" I spat.

She scowled at my tone. "You have a responsibility to this country, Princess."

"Princess?" I sneered. "Since when? You're deluding yourself, Mother!"

~ 113 ~

I turned around and escaped, drowning my ears from her cries, blind to the ghastly expression the guests were making. They weren't more important than Cybele. She was all I could think of.

The garden was expectedly empty when I reached the oak tree. The bark was rough against my palm, the leaves blowing like they felt my presence. I needed their comfort more than ever. Forget that. All I needed was Cybele.

"Please come home!" I pleaded. "Help me! Save me, Cybele! I beg you!"

" Whose name are you mumbling in the dark?" someone asked.

Lance was standing there when I swiveled around, his hair blown back by the breeze. He glanced around like he was searching for someone. Perhaps he was expecting another guest to be speaking to me.

"It's none of your business what name I mutter," I said. "Why are you here?"

"I wanted to talk to you."

"The feeling's not mutual."

He scratched his head with the impression of someone trying to figure out what to say next. Eventually, he lowered his hand and mustered a smile. It made me want to punch his mouth. "The Queen and my parents were the ones who came up with the agreement to let us marry," he said. "Are you saying your mother is wrong?"

I crossed my arms and looked at him from head to foot. He was just like the rest of them. "You know what, Lance? If you admire my mother so much, why don't you marry her?"

His mouth opened a fraction. "I was just saying—"

"Save it for someone who cares. I'm going back to my room. Stop following me."

The next couple of hours were spent busying myself with a book. They've been my escape these past few years and had opened me to adventures even while my own doors were always closed. They also reminded me of Cybele. Anything that would keep me close to her was important.

Unfortunately for me, Mother had other ideas. She barged into my room without knocking, eyes burning like charcoal, veins popping in her neck. Here we go again.

"How dare you act like a brat in front of the guests!" she yelled.

I closed the book and moved it from arm's reach. She had every right to get mad at me, and I had every right to make sure that she wouldn't wreck my things while returning the favor.

"Look at me while I'm talking to you!" she shouted. "I'm the Queen!"

"And I'm your daughter!" I shouted back. "Why are you doing this to me? It's like you don't even love me!"

Something in her eyes changed. Something wild, feral, suddenly coated in honey. The next time she spoke, she was calmer than before. "You're such an arrogant child. Everything I did, I did for you."

"You think I care?" I stood from the bed, trembling from head to toe. It was time I said these things. It was time I let go. "You told me that

~ 115 ~

Cybele is dead! I can't believe that! You lied to me!"

"I never lied to you."

"You did! About every single fucking thing!"

"Princess!"

"She'd never leave me like this!" I rambled. "She'd never just disappear without a goodbye! How did you become Queen anyway? It's time people tell me the truth!"

The slap came from nowhere. It was hard, fast, but didn't sting as much as the next words she spoke. "Do you know why she died?"

I covered my ears.

"Do you know why she's not here?"

"I beg you!"

"She died because of her own selfishness!" Mother grabbed my shoulders. Her nails dug into my skin, rough and painful. "Cybele never cared for you, Talia. She only got close so she could destroy you later. That's how her family works. We were spared from it."

There was bile in my mouth. To hear such lies—to have them rip the wound that never healed—was killing me.

"You're lying," I whispered.

"Her parents hated us," she insisted. "They were threatened and bitter because people loved us more. Cybele wanted you dead to preserve her throne."

"Please. . ."

"It was them or you," she finalized. "What happened, happened for a reason. Accept that fact and move on."

It was easy for her to say because she wasn't in my situation. It was easy for her to pretend that nothing was wrong. But I wasn't her, nor did I aspire to be.

Days after our talk, I've decided to end it all. If I wasn't with Cybele, there was no point in living. Under a moonlit sky, I took the dagger out. To the garden I went, the most appropriate place to die.

I closed my eyes and thought of Cybele. Her smile. Her lips. How safe I felt when she hugged me. Those little things kept me through everything. Now they'd accompany me to where I was going.

My hands didn't tremble as I unsheathed the dagger. There was only calm in my chest, an assurance that it was going to be worth it.

"See you soon," I whispered.

Chapter 11
Talia

What would happen to a bird if its wings got cut off? Would it weaken? Would the predators harass it? Would someone take it, lock it in a cage, to the point where it was wishing it was dead because it could never touch the sky again? Maybe all those things could happen.

"You should have let me die." I leaned my head against the window next to me. The warmth that had been there throughout the morning was slowly making its farewell. Soon, it would be dark, and I wouldn't see outside again. But I wasn't worried about the night anymore. The bad thoughts didn't come because of it; they rarely ever left.

The pierce of Mother's glare reached me from the other side of the room. She was in my bed, watching me, probably thinking of ways she could escalate the torture. "I can't let you die, Talia," she said. "You're my successor to the throne, remember?"

"Is that all I am to you, Mother? A successor?"

The mattress shifted when she stood. Her footsteps echoed on the stone floor, only stopping when she'd reached me. "I do love you," she said. "You're my only daughter."

I flinched when she tried to hold my arm. She didn't have a right to touch me. Mother sighed and buried her hand in her coat pocket. A strip of black cloth was offered to me the next time she took it out.

"What's that for?" I asked.

She dropped the cloth on my lap, then gazed at the bandage on my neck. "Your wound will turn into a scar in a few days, child. You have to wear the choker from now on to avoid rumors."

I hurled the damn thing across the room. "Let them see the scar on my neck!" I yelled. "I'm not ashamed!"

Mother's nostrils flared as she raised her hands to slap me. But she couldn't, could she? Maybe some other day when I wasn't recovering— when I hadn't just tried to slit my throat a few days ago before a roving Palace guard found me. "How many times do I need to repeat it, Talia?" Her jaw hardened. "Cybele never cared for you. Cybele wanted you to die."

I met Moter's cold stare. Nothing scared me anymore, not even her. "So do I, Mother. So do I."

Present Day

A sobbing near my ear made me open my eyes. It was low, disturbing, rocking my chest like an earthquake. Only when I tasted the tears on my tongue did I realize that I was the one doing the sound.

The past had always been too painful, even in the form of my dreams.

"Talia?" Cybele dropped what she was doing and rushed to my side. She took me in her arms then started rocking me back and forth. "What's wrong, Princess?"

Her gentleness only made me cry harder. "I—" I gasped for breath. "I had a dream."

"Is it awful?"

"Y-yes." I stared at Cybele. "I think I miss someone. The problem is I don't remember who."

Cybele froze for a second. The second came and went, and then she was rubbing my back.

When the pain in my chest subsided to a dull throb, I wiped my eyes with my sleeves, sat straighter, and gave Cybele a smile that would warrant for an award. If I wasn't a Princess, I'd probably be an actress. That's how good I was.

"You're a kind kidnapper, Cybele," I said. "Do you know that?"

Her concerned features rearranged into a scowl. "No, I'm not." She followed it by standing and moving away from me. She paused upon reaching the clothes she dropped on the floor, considered, then grabbed and tossed them to my bed. "I brought those for you, by the way. Take a shower."

The warm water was a relief to my soul as much as it was for my body upon opening the shower. It felt nice, I'd have to admit. If only it was nice enough to help me get through.

I'd been inside this castle for four months. Four months of not knowing what my kidnapper wanted from me, what would happen, and whether she'd keep me alive.

I thought it was over when she took me that day from the Palace. She was menacing when the cover was removed from my head. But as I looked at her more, the realization hit me like a truck. *It was her.*

I mean, it could be *her*. I wasn't too sure. They said she was dead.

She acted like she didn't care for me either, and that we didn't have a past. She was mean, hurtful, and even though she wanted to be called *Cybele*, she displayed none of the traits that I remembered.

I put an act from then on, to make as if I hadn't recognized her. I pretended like all those years were forgotten and left in the memories of my youth. I had to protect myself from this madness, hadn't I? How could I trust anyone apart from myself?

I turned the shower off and reached for the towel. After drying myself and wearing the clothes for today, I clasped the choker against my neck. Cybele could never find out what was underneath it. She'd only laugh and ridicule me for trying to kill myself because of her. I wouldn't give her the satisfaction.

The metal doors activated minutes later. Cybele, looking at my wet hair, signaled for me to follow.

I was given more freedom to roam her castle lately. Not only could I stay in my room, I could go to kitchen, laundry room, and visit the hallway too. But I wasn't allowed to leave the floor just yet. The only time that would happen was when she'd take me to the garden.

~ 121 ~

That was my favorite spot here so far. Though not as large as the one in the Palace, the dahlia's and roses were beautiful and well-cared for. I'd have second thoughts about Cybele whenever I looked at them, but I was afraid to ask.

"What are we doing today?" I said. One day it was laundry. Another day it was cleaning.

"We're cooking," she answered. Cybele continued down the hallway putting as much space between us. I wasn't bitter though. The view from behind wasn't bad.

Today, she'd worn jean-shorts that exposed her legs, and a white buttoned shirt that placed bad thoughts in my mind. It wasn't like I was jealous of her, but times like this, I wish she wasn't as tempting. The woman dwarfed my height, was beautiful as a living doll. She was rough on the edges because of her attitude, but that only made her more irresistible.

To think I dreamt of her every night since getting here, too. Dreams that revealed that I wanted her, that I hoped we weren't like this. Dreams that weren't all innocent. Dreams that made me grasp the bedsheet and moan her name.

We entered the kitchen together and took our respective places. The ingredients, pots, and everything else were prepared on the countertop. They always were whenever she wanted me to cook. Maybe she thought I'd stab her with a knife if I got my hands on one. What a joke.

"What dish do you want me to make?" I said.

"Doro wat."

~ 122 ~

"Doro *what*?"

Her lips quirked up. "No, we'll start you with something simpler." Cybele pointed to the poultry on the table. It wasn't marinated, but I had a feeling we'd be dipping it in sauce. There were a couple of them divided in saucers.

"It's not fried chicken today, is it?"

"Nope."

I followed her with my eyes as she went closer to the table. Every move she made was graceful, dignified, royal. I've been taught to do the same but it just wasn't quite like hers.

Sad thing was I couldn't clarify anything without getting hurt. To do that I'd have to ask questions, questions she wouldn't answer and would slap back at me with something nasty. That was the kind of relationship we had now.

Cybele gestured to the ingredients. "One time while modeling in Asia with Brooke, we were offered a dish coated in salt, garlic, vinegar, and soy sauce. I'm going to teach you how to make it. It's called Adobo."

Of all the things she said, only one word registered in my head. "Who's Brooke?" I asked. "Is she your girlfriend?"

Cybele rolled her eyes. "Why do people keep asking me that?"

"Maybe you don't answer them enough."

"Or maybe they should mind their own business more." She sighed and looked at me through tired lids. She didn't look too eager to answer. "I don't do girlfriends, okay? I don't even remember what love feels like."

I gnawed on my inner cheek as I turned to the table. Talks like this always made me anxious. "Where should we start?"

Cybele tried her best to explain the recipe to me. I might have listened, but I think I spent more time staring at her lips.

I had no idea where to begin when it was time to cook, so I just mixed ingredients here and there, hoping I somehow manage to get things right. Twenty minutes later, the pot was boiling with brown liquid, steam rising in the air, the kitchen smelling of vinegar. I placed the spoon down and called Cybele to me. "Can you try it?" I asked. "I don't know how it should taste like."

She jumped down from the countertop, placed her Rubik's cube on the surface, and strode to the stove where I was waiting. A dip of the spoon in the dish, a lick, and her face was wrinkling like a prune. "Ugh!"

"What did I do?"

"Too sour. Remedy that, or else."

"Or else what?" I put my hands on my waist. Weren't all those months fighting like animals enough for her? Why did she have to threaten me every chance she got?

"Remedy that or I'm going to feed you porridge," Cybele said.

"Oh really?" I took another spoon from the counter and dipped it in the pot. She shouldn't have said that. Really. "Maybe you should taste it again." I had my revenge by flinging the spoon's content to her.

Cybele glanced down at her shirt in shock. The sauce dirtied everything it touched.

~ 124 ~

"Whoops." I did it again. The sauce landed on her neck this time.

I was too busy laughing that I didn't notice how she was readying for retaliation. The sauce was rubbed all over my face before I realized what hit me.

She. Did. Not.

"I know that face," she warned. Her hands have gone in front of her. "Don't think about it, Talia."

But I was, and I did. We tumbled on the floor as I leaped forward, knowing damn well that she'd catch me. If only she'd do it with other things too.

After things have calmed down, Cybele and I sat on the floor hugging our knees, covered in brown sauce. Both of us smelled sour, yet that didn't stop the smiles from emerging. It was kind of our thing in this castle. I wish it wouldn't stop.

"Why don't you do girlfriends?" I said again.

Her eyes flickered to me. "Do you really want to know?"

"I wouldn't 'have asked if I didn't."

Her shoulders hunched as she considered. Curled in that ball, she suddenly seemed small. "My first love betrayed me," she whispered.

I swallowed the lemon in my throat. Was she talking about me or some other girl?

"What's her name?" I asked.

"Talia."

Me? Now wait a minute. I didn't betray anyone!

"Stop joking," I said. "I'm straight, remember? How can I betray you?"

How many times did I have to deny? How many times did she have to taunt me for her sick games?

"No you're not," Cybele said. "We both like women."

My fingers found their way through her hair. It was only fair that I played her game too, whatever it was that made her kidnap me, be mean to me, egg me whenever she wanted. I smiled through my teeth. "I don't get why you keep pushing your gay agendas on me, Cybele, but I'm willing to change my mind if you show me."

"Show you what?" Her eyes narrowed.

I leaned a little closer and whispered. "How women love."

Chapter 12
Talia

Life inside the castle with Cybele had its pros and cons. Let me start with the negative. There was no TV, internet, radio, and any communication devices that would let me send messages outside. She wouldn't let me go to the forest either. I spotted it from the rooftop garden one time, and I really wanted to explore, but she said that wasn't how being kidnapped worked. Yeah, sure.

On a positive note, the good outweighs the bad; I was with Cybele. I got to see her every day. And though she wasn't the person I used to know, having her by my side, however mean or secretive she was would be better than not at all.

Moving on to the castle. It wasn't as dreary as I first thought, with the structure being a constant source of wonder. Every nook and cranny demanded an investigation from me. How old were those walls? Who lived there before? What happened to them?

And if we talked about being contained in a bedroom cell, though Cybele would lock my door before going to sleep, it would be open each time I've awakened. She'd then lead me to the kitchen or laundry room to do the chores. It wasn't that bad. There was something reassuring in doing menial things without the maids, staff, and guards constantly breathing down my neck. It was a prison I'd happily live in forever.

The cell door groaned as it opened that morning. Cybele, hair still wet from a shower, went inside my room sporting her usual poker face. "I'm going outside to take care of things," she said. "The door will be left open so you can walk around. There's also food in the fridge in case you get hungry." Hesitation flashed on her face before the lines on her forehead smoothed again.

"Is anything wrong?" I asked.

She blinked and stared at me. "No, everything's fine. I just wanted to say that my handheld console is on top of the kitchen table. There's no wifi anyway, so feel free to use it when you're bored."

"Oh, all right." I leaned forward in the bed. "Can you do me a favor though? I mean, while you're out?"

"It depends." She crossed her arms. "What is it?"

"It's not that much. I just want to have books to read. Any genre is fine, as long as it's engaging."

"I'll see what I can do. Anything else?"

Can you kiss me?

I smiled at her. "No. That's about it."

I went to the kitchen and made myself a salad after she was gone. The food didn't taste as good without her, but I knew she'd scold me if I failed to eat. That was another strange thing about this new kidnapper Cybele. She acted like she didn't care, but few occasions told me she did.

On my way out of the kitchen, I noticed a shiny gadget on the table. It must be the toy she was talking about. I took it and headed to the living room near my cell. Maybe I'd check what the fuss was all about.

Cybele returned hours later with a duffle bag. I didn't have to look at her to know that she was staring at me like I was crazy. Her tone was enough validation. "Why are you giggling like that?" she asked.

I giggled some more. She sounded snobby with that British accent. Pity it didn't come out more often.

"Don't mind me," I said. "I'm just happy to beat the boss in the game. Take that, sucker!"

She sat in the sofa beside me and stared at the screen. "That's only the first boss," she said. "There's like a dozen more."

"Shut the—Really? I've been playing this game for hours. I thought I've already won." I dropped the handheld beside me in disgust. Did the developers want us to play this forever?

"Is this your first time trying that?" Cybele asked. "After defeating the first boss, he'll just run off with the Princess to another castle."

"He's cheating!"

"He's a good kidnapper. Give him some credit."

"Hmph!" I nudged my chin to the duffel bag on her lap. It intrigued me more than the game at this point. "Did you bring the books I requested?"

"Nope."

"Why?" I pouted at her. It was a simple request.

Cybele's eyes twinkled as her fingers worked to unzip the bag. Soon afterward, a bouquet of roses was handed to me. "Saw those in a shop on my way home," she murmured. "It reminded me of something, so I bought it."

I pressed the flowers to my nose and took a deep sniff. Just like that, I was in the Palace garden again, young, carefree, innocent. And Cybele? She was still her. Not the girl Mother was talking about. Not the kidnapper. Not the person who hides secrets.

If only that was true.

"Thank you," I said.

"Anytime." But she wasn't done talking yet. There were more to those lips. A continuation waiting to be spilled. "I can show you now if you want, Talia."

"Show me what?"

Cybele cleared her throat. Was she nervous? Or did that slight tremble of her hands mean nothing? "Let me show you how women love," she whispered. "It will all be pretend, of course, but since you're the one who suggested it yesterday, I'd like to think you're still interested. Are you?"

Her smoldering gaze made me shift in my seat. I've almost forgotten about that. "Of course I'm still interested," I said. "When should we begin?"

"Right now." She stood and placed the bag in the couch before offering a hand to me. "But let's go to my room. It's more appropriate to do it there."

"Wait. . . We're not going to have. . ."

"No." She rolled her shoulders and relaxed. "Just trust me, okay?"

Following our brief but meaningful exchange, Cybele guided me to the hallway, then to the main door of the floor. We always went

~ 130 ~

through there when we were headed to the garden, but not until she'd entered a series of codes that were too long to memorize. She must have known them by heart.

We went down the stairs and entered another door afterwards. I have never been to that floor before, but it was different from the place I was staying in. Somewhat homier.

The doors in the hallway were still locked with security codes, but there were paintings on the wall and décors here and there. Cybele steered me to a room before I could inspect them one by one.

"In here, Talia."

I stopped dead on my tracks. The room was hers. It had to be.

Not only did it smell of green tea like her, books were also everywhere—in the shelf, her bedside table, stacked against the corner. She was still a voracious reader, and judging from how spotless and orderly the contents of the room were, also a neat freak.

I pinched my arm to check if I was dreaming, then looked back to her. She was watching me silently. "How exactly do you plan to go with this?" I asked. I was amazed that I could keep my voice from wavering when all it wanted to do was crack.

She gestured to the bed. "After you."

The bed didn't creak as I crawled to the satin-covered mattress, but my heart was making a lot of movement. It doubled in intensity when Cybele followed me in it, then pulled me by her side so we lay facing each other.

"Close your eyes," she whispered.

The room vanished, and she took my hand.

I stifled a gasp when my fingers were trailed to her skin. I could make out her cheek. Her nose. Her lips. "They're so soft," I murmured.

She smiled against my hands. "That's the difference of women. We're softer. Gentler. Don't open your eyes." Her warmth disappeared from my side, but soon after, relaxing music began to stream inside the room.

"Where are you?"

"Miss me?" My stomach flipped when the mattress sagged under her weight. She was here again, warm, taking my hand and leading it to the curve of her hips. "Feel this, Talia? I'm smoother than any boy you'll date." Her breath tickled my ear. "Sexier too."

"Cybele. . ."

"Yes, Princess?"

My hand was guided to her flat abdomen, upward, and by the time I'd realized that she wasn't wearing a bra, I was already aroused.

"Here is where it really differs." She guided my fingers to her chest where something began to stiffen, to respond to my touch, and we were both gasping. "It's perfect, yes?"

My head was lost in a sea of sensations. I could barely hear my own reply.

But Cybele continued to speak. "And if you're wondering how women make love, like we were talking about, we make love using our heart. Our mouth speaks the words while our tongue provides the excitement. As for our hands. . ." She tightened mine so they were squeezing her breast. "It does everything else."

I couldn't take it anymore. My eyes snapped open. Cybele was looking at me tenderly, unguarded, like the way she used to when we were young. A part of my heart caved in. I would tell her I loved her.

Always had.

~ 132 ~

But then an alarm rang, and the room turned blood red before I could say anything. I covered my ears. "What's happening?" My cries sounded small compared to the wailing noise. It was deafening.

Cybele pushed me aside so she could leap from the bed and run to the door. "Someone broke into the castle!" she shouted.

Chapter 13
Talia

The intruder wasn't a Palace guard like I originally thought. She was a tall woman with midnight black hair and eyes that looked like granite. True to the manner of breaking in, she wore figure complementing black jeans, and a long-sleeved shirt that didn't do much of a job in hiding her sexiness. Adding insult to injury, Cybele seemed to know her.

"I told you to go back to England, didn't I?" Cybele paced the living room, hands going through her hair, white shirt wrinkled. It was a reminder of what we've been doing before we were interrupted. She stopped mid-pace and glared at the woman. "We need to talk."

The intruder smirked. "As much as I'd like that, aren't you going to introduce us first?" She nudged her chin to me.

Cybele only seemed to register my existence again at that point. Her nose wrinkled. "Talia, this is Brooke. Brooke, she's Talia." She hadn't gotten the last word out when she rushed to my side and took my hand. "Let's go to your room, Princess."

I didn't have much of a choice but to follow her to the main door, then back to my own floor. But my mind was not at ease when we reached my cell. I had to confirm. "I thought she wasn't your girlfriend?" I said.

"Who?"

"Brooke." I pointed my thumb to the door. "That girl in the living room. You mentioned her to me once when we were cooking."

Cybele dropped my hand. "So?"

"Why is she here?"

"I don't know."

"You don't know?" My tone was mild as I checked Cybele out. "How can you not know?"

"Because. . ." Her forehead creased, followed by a scowl. She seemed angry for some reason. "Look, I don't get why I should be explaining this to you. It's none of your bloody business." Cybele was nothing like the woman I was flirting with when she stepped back. Her walls were fortified.

"Where are you going?" I asked. She'd turned around and was heading to the door.

The corner of her mouth moved. "Like I said, Princess. None of your bloody business."

She didn't come back after an hour or two, not even three of waiting. I was angsty, frustrated. How could she act like this when we were sweet just a few hours ago? I went to the kitchen to release my aggression. It didn't fare well.

"What's that supposed to be?" Cybele walked in just when I was getting rid of the evidence. What awful timing.

"Nothing." I quickly tossed the burnt chicken to the trash bin. It wasn't my fault, really. Well, maybe it was, but just a little.

Cybele yanked the trashcan lid from my hand before I could bury everything behind me. Her lips pursed when she looked in. "Tsk!" Her eyes flared. "You've wasted food again, Talia. What the hell is wrong with you?"

"Nothing's wrong with me. If you were here fifteen minutes ago, maybe you could have guided me. But you weren't, and it's burnt, and I'm sorry."

She scowled and placed the lid on the trashcan. "You don't look sorry enough, Princess."

I stared daggers at her. "Neither do you, Cybele."

"Looks like I'm cooking," a third voice added. My eyebrow rose when Brooke came into the kitchen, went to the stove, and took the spatula from the pan. She'd changed into the shortest shorts I've seen, and Cybele, like any other hot-blooded lesbian, followed my eyes and smirked.

I gritted my teeth. "I thought your friend went home, Cybele. What is she still doing here?"

"She's staying."

"Sorry for the intrusion." Brooke threw me an apologetic look. "I hope we make this work." She'd said it like we were on vacation. She even went to the fridge as if everything was normal, grabbed a fresh batch of poultry, and closed the door with her leg. I didn't know what to make of it, so I marched to a stool and watched the two of them quietly. Cybele didn't cower under my stare. She turned her back to me and pretended to look at the blank wall. How convenient.

The chicken was browning in the pan when Brooke glanced at me over her shoulder with a smile. "You're Talia," she said.

"I know." I fought the urge to roll my eyes. "You don't have to tell me my name."

Brooke's ears were pink when she tended to the pan again. I guess she wasn't in the mood to talk after all.

But wait! There was more. She had taken a deep breath, which meant she would ask again against all odds, and she did. "By the way, Princess, I've been meaning to ask. How's life in the Palace these days?"

"How would I know?" I sighed. "I was kidnapped by your friend, remember?"

Cybele left whatever interest she had with the wall to swivel to me. Her arms were crossed when she mouthed, *'What's your problem?"*

What's my problem? Was she seriously asking me that? Phooey! Let me draw a picture. I've spent all those years alone, waiting, miserable in the Royal Palace thinking she was dead, but she wasn't. She was here, confusing me, and to take the crazy level up a notch her, quote and quote, friend—slash sexy vixen stalker— who broke into this castle was staying with us. The hell?

"Talia, love, smoke is coming from your nose." Cybele had said it so calmly that I wanted to smack the chicken on her face. Maybe I would. But before I could, Brooke finished cooking and delivered the plateful of chicken at the table.

"Dinner!" she chirped.

The three of us took our respective seats, but I was the only one who grabbed a drumstick. Really, now? I checked out their model-fit figures. Well they could suck up to their diet all they want. I took a big bite and chewed.

"Slow down," Cybele warned. "You might choke on that."

I ignored her and continued eating.

Five minutes into the meal, Brooke began to start yet another conversation with me. Hadn't she learned her lesson yet?

"I know it's none of my business," she began. "But I'm curious about royalty, as I'm sure you get a lot." She fidgeted in her seat. "So, uhm, do you have a boyfriend, Princess?"

I swallowed the large bit of chicken before it killed me. She was right. It was none of her business. But I hadn't eaten food this good since. . . Well since I'd been making them. So it called for a reward, no matter how bitter I was.

"I have a fiancé," I grumbled.

"Really?" Brooke leaned forward, interested. "Mind telling me where you met?"

"Let me see." I pretended to recall the information that had never really left my mind. "I met him at my thirteenth birthday. . ." I trailed. "Right after the Queen told me that he's going to be my husband."

Brooke's lashes fluttered as she blinked fast. "You're not talking about arranged marriage, are you?"

"Yes, I am."

Brooke exchanged glances with Cybele before staring back at me. She looked like a concerned parent. "But don't you have someone you like?" she said. "I mean, I'm not implying that you don't love your fiancé, but your tone suggests—" She waved her hands in the air. "Never mind. I don't want to pry."

"You're not prying," I assured. "Everybody in this room knows that I don't like Lance. It's no big secret." I tossed the leftover drumstick to the plate and stood. My appetite was gone. "Regarding your second question. Do you still want me to answer?"

I caught sight of Brooke's reluctant nod while I carried the plate to the sink. "Only if you want." But she sounded unsure.

I trashed the chicken bones before opening the faucet. The splash of water almost drowned my voice. "I do like someone," I confessed. "But it's impossible for us, so I gave it up."

" Who?" It was Cybele who asked. The tremble in her voice carried to me like the sound of a guitar string: lovely and collected, but underneath was a violence waiting to be unleashed. All it needed were the right hands to pluck it. Mine.

I smiled and twisted to them. "I'm in love with you, Cybele. Who else?"

The muscles in her jaw tightened. "That's not a good joke," she said.

I shrugged. "It isn't one."

Her lips pressed into a line. It opened again to say something, but before I knew it she was standing from her seat, escaping from the kitchen, disappearing through the door. Brooke winced a few seconds later when a door was slammed close. "I'm sorry," she murmured.

I turned back to the sink, the ribs in my chest constricting me. God, what had I done?

"Don't be sorry," I said, as if it didn't matter to me. "You didn't act like a jerk, your friend did." The plates called my attention. They were still dirty even though they were washed, at least they were to me. Or maybe it was my imagination.

"Iris is not a bad person." Brooke added to my regrets.

My hands tightened by my side. "How would you know?" I asked. "Is she your girlfriend? Is that why you're here?"

"I was concerned about her decisions."

"You didn't answer my question, Brooke."

Silence permeated the kitchen. Brooke didn't leave. She didn't dare. But it took her a minute to come up with the truth. "Iris is not my girlfriend, all right? But she's my friend. And friends look out for friends. That's why I'm here even if I don't condone her actions."

My irritation melted like snow. When she put it like that, when she placed Cybele's welfare above everything, it felt like I was the bad person. The kidnapper, not the other way around. But that didn't mean that we would be best friends or anything. Because even if she didn't admit it, even if she tried her best to hide, I heard the undertone there. She wasn't Cybele's girlfriend, but she wanted to.

I said what needed to be said. "I have nothing against you, okay, Brooke? Just stay out of my way."

Somewhere between twisting in my bed and hating Cybele's guts, I must have fallen asleep. I came about when someone entered my cell, took me from the bed, and carried me to the hallway.

My eyes squinted at the lean figure. "Cybele?"

Gentle fingers curled on my back. "It's me. Don't worry."

"Where are we going?"

~ 140 ~

"It's not important." A hand was brushed over my eyes. "Go back to sleep, Talia."

I didn't. I snuggled to her chest, savoring her warmth.

How was it that a simple gesture, a few simple words could make me forget the awful things she did? How was it that even though she kidnapped me, I was still drawn to her? She was the candle and I was a moth. She'd burnt me more times than necessary, but I always found myself flying back to her. It was dangerous.

"Here we are," she murmured as she placed me in the bed. From one room to another, we were surprisingly back in hers.

I grabbed her hand when she turned to leave. "Where are you going?" I asked. "We just got here."

She looked at me over her shoulder and shook her head. "I can't stay here. Not while you're inside."

"Why?" I scrambled to sit. "Why take me here when you're just going to leave?"

Her eyes flickered. "Because I have to, Talia. You will never understand."

"Try me."

"Go back to sleep."

"I said try me." I clung to her fingers. "Try me, I—"

"No."

"Please!" Desperation crept in my voice. "Let's not be like this anymore, Cybele, we. . ." My hands slipped from hers. She was going away with all the things unsaid between us again. It was maddening. "I know you!" I blurted.

She froze.

"I know you." My voice was a whisper. The secret was out. There was nowhere to run. What more was left to say than, "And I love you." I reached for her again. "I always had, since were children. Give us a chance."

The calm mask she'd been wearing crumbled to pieces. She tilted her head to me. "Love?" Her brows knitted together. "What do you know about love, Princess?"

"E-everything. If you just listen to me first—"

Laughter barked from her. "Listen? Listen!" She gave me a once-over. "Why should I? You disgust me!"

There was a rush in my ears. I couldn't understand her hatred, her repulsion. All I knew was I needed to be with her, to love me, to pretend. I clutched the hem of her shirt like a pathetic woman. "Don't do this to me," I begged. "I've been waiting for you for many years." She pushed me away, but I wasn't going to give up. "Stay with me for the night."

Cybele gave me an incredulous stare. "You're out of your freaking mind!"

"I am!" My hands couldn't let go. I embraced her. "Stay," I repeated. "This will be the first and last. You can hate me all you want after. I don't care."

It looked like she was about to hit something, kill something, but I was surprised to see her close her eyes, the muscles in her throat moving. Her hands then wrapped on mine so tight she could crush my fingers. "This will be the last time," she hissed. "You will never do this to me again, Talia. You will never use my weakness against me."

The satin sheets ruffled as we draped it over us. Cybele had climbed in the bed beside me. I had no idea what possessed her to say yes, or what her motivations were, but I couldn't complain as my hands found the contour of her waist, my chest the warmth of her embrace. I wanted to cry.

How would she react once morning comes? How would I? Why were we brought together only to be always pulled apart?

The soft beating of her heart, plus the gentle breaths she took, soon lulled me to sleep. When light began to stream inside the room, I woke up to reality.

Cybele was sitting at the edge of the bed when I got up, lost in her thoughts. And me, still groggy from sleep, crawled to her, circled my arms around her waist, and leaned my head against her back. "Good morning," I whispered.

Her eyes were vacant as she got up. "What's so good about it?" she said.

"Huh? I was just. . ."

"Just what? Pretending we're close?" Dark circles bruised her eyes as she scrutinized me. "You don't know me, Talia. Not anymore. And just so you understand, I despise you, your family, especially your mother."

The temporary happiness I felt from waking up next to her burst like a bubble. How could she say that? Was Mother right all along, that Cybele and her family wanted us dead?

The need to protect myself prevailed. I said the most stupid thing I could come up with at such short notice, and I did it with a smile. "It's a prank." I laughed when her eyes widened. My words caught her by surprise. "Yeah, I don't know you. But you seem to know me, so I used that to shut you up last night. It's pathetic."

"Talia." She growled.

I lifted my chin up as I jumped out of the bed. I had never been so mad at anyone. "Also, if you despise me, Cybele, then I hate you more. I did nothing to you to warrant such treatment."

"Nothing?" Her eyes flashed. "I'm a fucked-up person because of you and your family!"

"I think you got this all messed up," I argued. "You screwed me, not the other way around. You reap what you sow."

She headed to the door, looking like she'd rip it loose as she flung it open. "No," she said. "You broke me, so I'm going to break you too."

Before she completely left the room, I yelled to her, "You can't break what's already broken. Remember that!"

Chapter 14
Talia

The scraping of utensils against the plates were the only sounds in the kitchen. I glared at Brooke while she was mid-bite. I wasn't allowed a fork but she was. She noticed me looking and lowered her broccoli. "Is there something on my face?" she asked.

I didn't answer and continued munching on the pasta. Figure that out.

Brooke didn't go back to eating. Instead, she sat there for minutes watching me and Cybele, exhaling for what seemed like the hundredth time today. "Can the two of you please start talking again?" Her question came out of nowhere.

"No," Cybele and I said in unison.

I glared at her. She glared at me. We went back to eating lunch.

"But. . ." Brooke sounded helpless, but none of us wanted to glance at her again. Too bad. "You haven't spoken to each other for a week," she reasoned. "What caused this? Can't someone apologize already?"

Cybele rolled her eyes. "If someone should apologize in this room, it's her." A fork was pointed to me. "This is all her fault. She and her mother."

"Excuse me?" I snatched the table napkin and started wiping my hands. This woman needed to be put in her place. "Why should I apologize when I did nothing to you?" I said. "If I recall correctly, you were the one who kidnapped me. You were the one who forced me to eat porridge.

~ 145 ~

YOU were the one who kept insisting I was lesbian."

"Because you are!" Cybele snarled.

"In your dreams!" I threw the napkin down in protest. "I was just riding along."

"No, you weren't!"

"Yes, I was! What else could I have done? You were unreasonable!"

Brooke raised her hands to stop us from fighting. We both ignored her. Cybele and I hadn't spoken for days: a week. The pressure built up like a balloon, and exploded when it was triggered. So no, Brooke, we weren't going to shut up.

"You know what, Talia?" A vein became visible on Cybele's neck. "I've expected this from the start. You're a snake like your mother." She slammed her hand on the table. "And to tell you frankly, you were always lesbian. You've been since you were a baby. You will be until you die. So don't deny it to other people, especially to my face."

"If I were a snake then what are you?" I sneered at her. "Oh, I know! You're a she-wolf who kills her victims when they think they're safe. I should know, because that's what you did to me."

I stood and went to Brooke's side. The woman's mouth opened in fright when I grabbed her arm.

"Lesbian, am I? Fine! Let's see how much of a lesbian I am when your girlfriend falls in love with me."

Cybele's chair toppled back when she stood too. But the sound was masked by her footsteps as she came to Brooke's other side and grabbed the woman's right arm. "First of all, Talia, she's not my girlfriend. Second, you can't make her fall for you."

"Why not? You think I'm lacking on the charm department?" I tugged Brooke's arm again, trying to shake Cybele away. She remained steadfast. "For your information, Miss Kidnapper, people find me beautiful too."

"Who? Your mother?"

"No, my fiancé."

My stomach lurched at my own retort. Ugh! Truth was, Lance and I had never been like that. We barely even talked. But seeing Cybele's reaction? I'd vomit this disgust later.

" You're really like your mother, aren't you?" Cybele looked at me from head to foot in disdain. "It's obvious where you got that attitude. Pathetic."

"Oh yeah?" I reached for Brooke's face. "Well I won't be so pathetic in a while." She'd see.

I licked my lips and began to make my move. Brooke, frozen in her seat, watched me with wild eyes while I leaned closer. My mouth opened to do the unspeakable, but before I could finish it, the wind was knocked from my chest and I was staring at Cybele from the floor. What the hell just happened?

"How dare you try to kiss another girl!" Cybele raged.

I tried to push her away. She was on top of me. "Why do you care?"

"Because I do! Stop squirming!"

"*You* stop squirming!"

We rolled over and over, knocking things, bumping on walls. She was furious when I ended on top. Cybele wasn't as good with her legs like I was, and realizing this, she wriggled underneath me and cheated.

I froze when her tongue glided on my neck.

"Talia." My name came out like a beg from her lips. She looked suddenly scared, and I knew why. It was her fault, always her fault.

~ 147 ~

I pushed her down and leaned to her ear. I couldn't think of anything anymore. My control was gone. "Kiss me," I whispered. "Kiss me hard, now."

She trembled. "This isn't. . ."

I tightened my hold on her shoulder. "Don't think. Just do it."

One last roll did the trick. Before I knew it, she was on top of me again, lips plump, eyes searching mine. She swallowed when I nodded my consent and began to lower her head. I closed my eyes and waited.

Before something cold splashed on me.

"What did you do!" Cybele sounded like she'd kill someone. My eyes opened to see her hair and clothes dripping.

The culprit was standing by the doorway, holding a bucket in her hand. Brooke's gulp was loud. "Y-you were fighting," she stammered. "Seeing you on the floor, I thought. You were. . ." She lowered the bucket. "I had to stop you from killing each other. I did what I could."

"Leave us!" Cybele snapped.

"A-are you sure?"

Cybele stared pointedly at her and moved away from me. "I'm sure," she repeated. "You've caused enough trouble, Brooke. Get out of here before I do something I'll regret."

I scrambled to my feet when the woman vacated the kitchen. That sounded so wrong. "You don't have to be harsh to her, you know," I said.

Cybele gave me a side glance. "You're on her side now?"

"Well no, but her intentions were good." I snatched the ends of my hair and squeezed. Blackish liquid dripped on the floor. "Gosh, what did she put in that water?" I turned to Cybele and raised a brow. Her eyes were not on my face anymore. It was on my white V-neck. Specifically, the things underneath that had peeked because of the water. A smile crept on my face. "Like what you see?"

She blinked a few times before her gaze rose to mine. "W-what?"

I bit my lip to stop myself from laughing. One minute she was mad, and now she was blushing. How could I stay mad at this woman? More importantly, how could I not love her?

Flipping my hair back over my shoulder, I walked slowly to Cybele. She took a step back. "Why are you going backwards?" I murmured.

Her face flushed a deeper shade of red. "Why are you heading to me?" she asked.

I shrugged and stepped forward again. "Because I can. Because you're letting me." Cybele's lower back hit the table. Lucky for me, she had nowhere to run. I grinned. "I just realized something."

Her eyes flickered to the door. "What?"

I licked my lips and stared pointedly at her chest. "Everything we've been doing is foreplay. Isn't that fun?"

My raunchy statement made her gasp in surprise. She leaned back on the table until she was almost touching the plates, so I did what I could to help her. I swept everything to the floor, barely noticing the mess they made.

Cybele's eyes were still locked on mine. Her mouth was agape. Her chest moved up and down in quick succession. She was excited, but so was I.

Taking advantage of the situation, I got on the table and put my legs on either side of her. She swallowed. "Whatever you're doing, you need to stop it," she said.

I stroked her face and bent closer. "Make me," I teased.

Her hands came up as if to push me away, but they fell to her side before they did. "I can't." She gave up. "No matter how mad I am, no matter what you do, I just can't let you go." Her eyes were pained as she inhaled. "You're my Achilles heel, Princess. You've always been. I hate you for it."

My eyes squeezed shut. "Don't say that. It hurts." I shook my head. "I'm not your weakness. I refuse to be."

"But what am I going to do with you?" Her hands traveled to my cheek. "I'm so torn."

"AHEM."

Cybele and I turned to the sound. Brooke was by the door again, one foot out, another foot in. She looked hesitant as she said, "Are you guys trying to kill each other again?"

I didn't want to be caught in the middle of their argument. Another one was brewing. I was sure of it. Squirming away from Cybele, I excused myself and went back to the room. We've miraculously stayed in hers even though we weren't on speaking terms. We were two strange creatures, she and I.

Cybele took her time doing what she did when she wasn't with me, while I showered and dressed and kept to her bedroom all day. It was filled with books, so I kept myself busy reading. When she returned at nightfall, she crawled into the bed next to me.

"What's that?" she asked, pertaining to the book on my lap.

I turned the page and continued reading. "The Secret Garden," I murmured. "I'm sure you've read it."

"I had." Her head rested on the pillow beside me. I thought she was going to sleep, but that was before she snatched the book, closed it with a snap, and put it on the bedside table. "Can we go to the garden?" she said. "The real garden?"

I stared at her in mild surprise. She'd never acted more eager. "Now?"

"Yes. Now. Come with me."

The lights in the garden weren't on, but the shimmer from the moon and stars illuminated our way. It was enchanting.

On the way to the swing chair, I stopped beside the dahlia's and turned to Cybele. She'd been looking at me before I did. It brought a smile to my face. "I love the flowers," I said. "You've done a great job taking care of them." She didn't reply as we continued to the seat.

The wind was extra chilly tonight, and adding Cybele's silence while we shared a seat, I couldn't help but fiddle with my choker, trying to come up with something. That drew her attention. "What's that for?" she said, eyes going to my neck.

I dropped my hand. "I told you. It's nothing."

"If it's nothing, you wouldn't wear it all the time."

I bit my lip when she touched my jawline. She was so tender, so sweet: the Cybele I knew.

"Take it off," I said, looking at anything but her. My legs were shaking. "Hurry before I change my mind."

Cybele shifted so she could snake her arms around my neck. Her lips were dry, her eyes questioning. Nevertheless, she removed the choker, then took a sharp breath upon seeing what was waiting beneath the cloth. "What happened to you?"

My smile was bitter. "Do you think it's ugly?"

She remained quiet for a while. Then she tilted my face to her. "We were both young when we first saw each other," she whispered. "Looking back, I thought to myself, how could anyone be so perfect? You were flawless, gorgeous, mine." She shook her head. "But I was wrong, Talia. Your scar proves that. You're not perfect, and I love you more for it."

My eyes blurred with unshed tears as I locked gaze with her. "You knew that I just pretended not to remember you again?"

She wiped the first drop of my tears and nodded. "I figured it out today after our shouting match in the kitchen."

"I'm sorry!" I hugged her. "I'm sorry! I had to!"

She burrowed my face in her neck and kissed my head. "Princess," she choked. "My Talia. . . My heart was always with you."

I pressed myself to her: the warmth, the firmness, the safety. The person I'd been waiting for.

"Don't break the embrace," I begged. "I need this. I need you."

"Okay," she whispered. "I'm right here. I'll always be."

It was morning when I woke up inside her bedroom. Cybele was nowhere in sight. Turning to my left, I saw a note with her neat script handwriting. I snatched it from the table and read.

Talia, you fell asleep last night out of exhaustion, so I carried you back here. Brooke and I are going to town to get supplies. I didn't want to wake you, so here's a note instead. We'll talk about things when I come back. Love, your Princess Charming. '

I grinned from ear-to-ear, seeing the parting words of the letter. She was adorably romantic. God, I needed to prepare.

Afternoon couldn't come soon enough, and I've busied myself while waiting for them. Clean the house, done. Prepare the snacks from when they return home, done. Borrow something passable to wear from her closet, done and done.

Cybele and Brooke still hadn't come home by dinner, but I wasn't that worried since Cybele always took time when going on errands outside. So, what I did to cover the hours was to read, play her handheld console, and read some more.

I was just beginning to doze off when chaos came. Literally. In the form of buzzing alarms and red-streaked lights. "What the!" I looked about. The last time it happened, Brooke came in. Was there another friend? Another intruder? What was going on?

I jumped from the bed and sneaked to the hallway to investigate. The main door broke open just then, and to my terror, four people came in, all wearing ski masks. Oh God!

Fearing for my safety, I ran back to the bedroom and closed the door quietly behind me. Where should I hide? What should I do? There were neither weapons nor means to escape. Who were those people?

I locked the door before hurrying to the bathroom. Inside, I curled up in the jacuzzi, waiting, praying they get what they wanted and leave. But the sound of rooms being searched were too loud. It was only a matter of time before they got to where I was, stood over the jacuzzi, and leered at me through their masks.

One of them, a woman, spoke. "We got ourselves a good haul for tonight."

A bigger man with muscled arms could have smiled. At least his voice was. "Told you, it's worth it." He gestured to a third guy behind him. "Hurry up. Cover her face."

His maniacal eyes were the last thing I saw before someone placed a sack over my head.

"Not again," I whispered, as someone hauled me upward, away from the castle. Away from Cybele.

Chapter 15
Talia

The miserable fools who kidnapped me used a cloth to gag my mouth, a rope to tie my hands, and a sack to cover my face. I struggled and bit on the gag until it loosened. The new kidnappers weren't as efficient as Cybele.

"Where are you taking me?" My voice was hoarse, scratchy. I was in bad need of a drink, and it didn't help that the floor underneath me was vibrating and making me dizzy. We could be in a car. I wasn't so sure.

No one answered my question. "Hey!" I said, then swallowed. "I know you're there. Hey!" God, I could hear them breathing. Someone close by stank of sweat too. I've never had body odor issues with Cybele. "Has anyone forgotten to shower?" I jerked and kicked. There was nothing around me. "You stink! You stink so much, it burns my lungs!"

"Make her shut up. She's so irritating!"

I stilled. Finally! A response! But then the floor creaked and groaned. Someone was coming.

I started to trash about. "Get away from me!" There was a cracking of knuckles. "Get away!" Before someone punched me in the stomach, making me lose my breath, making my eyes roll back. Then nothing.

"Rise and shine, sweetheart!" Something cold, wet, and slimy splashed on me. I sputtered water out of my mouth and coughed.

"What the hell? That was so rude!"

Cybele is going to get it when I roll out of bed. I'm going to punish her and torture her and. . . My eyes snapped open. Shit!

A man with a toothy grin studied me a few paces ahead, a grimy but empty bucket in his hands. I gulped. He wasn't Cybele. That much was clear. Except maybe if the woman gained weight, turned into a man, looked paler, had a dirty t-shirt on, and smelled like expired peanut butter if I've ever encountered one. Yuck!

"You're pretty." That was the first thing the man said. I was pretty. He was, too: pretty dumb. He sounded like one.

"I'm not pretty," I rasped. "I'm normal-looking. If you want to kidnap someone beautiful, go for an actress, not me."

Toothy dropped his bucket to scratch his balding head. Dumb just got dumber. But it was my opportunity, wasn't it? I glanced down at myself to check the damage.

Okay, I was tied to a chair. That was expected. But nothing seemed to be broken, if I didn't count my stomach. It ached every time I breathed.

My gaze went to the room next. We were in an old, shabby house that was probably more than fifty years old, its wooden ceiling rotten with decay. I gagged at the smell. Aside from being situated in a messy living room with a floor that looked like it hadn't been cleaned in a while, it smelled like. . . like. . . What was that smell?

I bit my tongue when a rat the size of a cat ran past me. It was humongous!

Toothy began to walk to me, too. My attention went back to him. "What are you doing?" I said.

He stopped inches from my knees. "Eat," he said, grinning.

My eyes narrowed. "Excuse me?"

He pointed to himself. "I eat." His finger and all its dirty glory aimed at my face. "You." He guffawed like a sick dog. "Eat your foot. Eat your tummy." Toothy licked his lips. "Eat your brains. Yummy!"

I bucked against the chair, screaming, "No!" What had I gotten myself into? Why cannibals? Why!

Toothy's laughter followed in the wake of his heavy footsteps as he headed to a door on the right. He didn't tell me where he was going, or if he would start eating me as soon as he came back. But I needed to save myself. I had to get out of there. I searched the room the instant he was gone.

Broken sofa in the corner. No! Old and damaged TV? Not! I glanced a bit ahead and saw a cabinet. Bingo!

It was cruel how most people underestimated their own weight, me included. As I tried to move the chair with me in it, my respect for Cybele grew more with each budge. She could carry me with one arm, maybe while smelling a dahlia while at it. Me? I could barely shift the chair, let alone reach the cabinet without breaking pools of sweat.

Toothy walked in while I was halfway to my target. And not only that, he was—gulp—holding a knife. A big, big, butcher knife.

"You silly girl," he muttered to himself upon reaching me. An alarm rang in my mind when the knife was raised, glinted in the light, and moved on top of my head.

If I had known that it would end this way, I would have seduced Cybele earlier, no questions asked. But it was too late. I would never see her face again. I squeezed my eyes shut and said a silent prayer.

"What do you think you're doing?"

Another guy wearing a black muscle-shirt had entered the room when I opened my eyes. He was younger than Toothy, maybe around my age. His unblemished face was set on a frown, but worse than that. . . The subtle flexing of biceps didn't escape me. Ugh, he was full of himself.

"I told you not to frighten the guest." He motioned to me.

Toothy lowered the knife. "Sorry." He looked shameful. "The girl was gullible and stupid, so I wanted to tease her."

Sorry, what? My lips drew in a snarl.

"Who are you calling gullible and stupid?" I protested. "You're the one who looked like a troll! You're the one who kept saying, eat! Eat! I'm neither gullible nor stupid, you mongrel! Go to hell!"

There was silence, a stretch of quietness. Uh-oh. Me and my big mouth.

Muscle-guy was the first one to react. He looked like the smarter one between the two. If only he didn't reach for my chin and squeezed. "I hate girls like you." He stared me up and down. "You think you're so pretty, but you're not. Truth is, you're just a basic bitch."

My stare was defiant. Look who was talking? "If you hate girls so much, then get yourself a boyfriend, sicko!" I gasped when a slap was awarded to me. How dare he?

Muscles was pleased with himself as his hand lowered to his side. "I do have a boyfriend." He motioned to Toothy. "We're engaged."

I sneered through the sting on my face. "You can do better."

His eyes flashed. "You little bitch!"

He was about to do something stupid and horrible but was stopped at the last second by yet another woman who entered the room. "Don't hurt the Princess," she spoke. I followed everyone's eyes. She must be the leader.

The woman carried herself in a self-assured manner that only the leader of a cannibal, or whatever this group was called, could pull off. A bit older than the two men, a t-shirt that looked like it had been snipped with scissors on the sleeves, and a few missing teeth in her mouth, she must have been in one too many fights.

Yet I wasn't thinking too much about it. I had other questions on my mind. "What did you call me again?" I said.

"You're the Princess."

"I'm not," I denied.

She smirked. "We're going to get a huge amount of money once we trade you with the Royal Palace. Or we can always sell you to the highest bidder. Think about it." Her gaze went to my chest. "Can you imagine how many rich old fools will want to taste that young body of yours? We'll be rich!"

"You're cannibals!" I yelled.

Her brows furrowed. "What?" She snapped her fingers at Toothy and Muscles. "What is she talking about?"

Toothy shrugged. "I don't know. She's dumb."

"I'm not dumb!" I rocked back and forth in my chair. Why were they pretending?

The leader shrugged and shook her head. "It doesn't matter," she said. "Take the Princess to her room."

I screamed when Muscles and Toothy lifted my chair, and brought me from the living room, to a dark hallway. I was wasting my strength. It was stupid of me. But it felt so good, and they were annoyed about it, so I continued until they got me into another room.

The two only removed the rope and took the chair before shutting the door and bolting it from outside. I was left alone again, trapped.

I stared at the cracked floor and peeling walls. Why did people always kidnap me? What had I done to them? Dust clouded around me as I collapsed on the springy bed. What was left to do than sleep?

A scratching sound in the middle of the night woke me up. I just guessed the time. There was no window in the almost empty room. Didn't rats come out mostly at night too?

" Come here, rat," I whispered to myself. "Come here, ratty, ratty."

"Are you awake?" someone whispered back.

"Oh my God, it talked!" I covered my mouth. "Is that you, Mr. Rat?"

"I'm not called Mr. Rat."

"Then what are you called?"

The faceless voice didn't answer for a few seconds. When it did, it sounded more like a woman than the creature in my head. "They call me Van," she said.

I went to the door and tried to find cracks that would let me see the person on the other side. There was none, so I slid to the floor. "Is that short for Vanessa?"

"No, it's just Van. It means friend," she answered.

"Are you?" I fiddled my hands. "A friend, I mean? If you're here then it must mean that you're one of the kidnappers."

A sigh from the other side. "I didn't know this would happen. The original plan was to break inside the castle, take whatever valuables we could, and go. Unfortunately, my crew recognized you. I'm so sorry this happened."

"I'm sorry too. You hang out with the wrong crowd, Van." I rested my chin on my knee. She sounded friendly, but I wasn't too sure. "How did you break in the castle anyway?" I asked. "I think it's highly secured."

Van cleared her throat. "My father was one of the people who worked on that. He installed all the security measures there, and since he trained me growing up, I knew how to disarm the system. Muscles found about it somehow, so they kind of blackmailed me into the whole thing."

"No way. . . The muscled guy's name is really Muscles?"

"Yes." She made an embarrassed laugh. "Believe me, Princess. You wouldn't be here if I had a choice."

"I forgive you."

"You do?" She was astonished.

I nodded to myself. "Yes. You said you were blackmailed, but. . ."

"What is it?"

"Will you help me escape?" I turned to the door imagining the woman on the other side, and furthermore, the woman who was waiting for me at the castle. I could only guess the look on Cybele's face when she came home and saw me missing. She'd be devastated. "I can't be here," I continued. "There's a woman, she—" I bit my lip. "I need to be with her."

There was a pause, a consideration, and then a sigh of defeat. "Okay, Princess."

My hope surged. "Okay? You mean. . ."

"Yes, I promise to help you. But I can't do it today." A breath, a whisper, like she'd gotten closer to the door but lowered her voice. "Everyone is guarding the house. Let me think of a plan so we won't get caught. Deal?"

"Deal!" I tried not to skip back to the bed.

"I need to go before they catch me," she said. "I'll make sure you get fed properly tomorrow so you'll have strength. Goodbye, Princess. And goodnight." Van's retreating footsteps sounded before I could say my own farewells. My lips stretched into a smile for the first time since being kidnapped again. There might be hope yet.

The next morning, a tray filled with food was waiting for me on the floor when I woke up. There was a sandwich on it, an apple, a bottle of water, and a note. *Prepare for tonight, it said. I have a plan. '*

Evening couldn't come soon enough after I've read the message, but when it did, Van pulled through. In a very strange way.

It started with the door opening: a creak, a subtle swing, yet when it was fully unlatched, no one was standing on the other side.

"Van?" I whispered.

No reply.

Curious, I went to the door. The hallway was bare when my head poked out to investigate. No Muscles, no Toothy, and hell, even the rat was missing. I checked left and right.

Why would they do this? Why should I care? The door was open, and I had the chance to go out. I'd be stupid not to take it.

My steps were silent as I crept to the hallway, through the kitchen, and finally, the living room. To my surprise, the door leading outside was wide open. I didn't stop to think if it was a trap. I'd cross the bridge when I get there.

A black truck was waiting for me outside, along with it, a woman who signaled for me to ride in front. I only asked questions when I was buckling the seatbelt. "Are you Van?" My eyes flickered to the house. No one had followed me.

"That's me." She started the truck and sped to the dirt road. I only began to notice the trees. We were somewhere secluded.

"That was close." I breathed a sigh of relief and concentrated on her for the first time. My eyebrows rose.

She didn't resemble any of the lunatics we'd escaped from. Her ash-blonde hair looked shiny even in the darkness of the night. It fluttered from the wind coming through the window. She was also wearing a flannel that looked remarkably clean, and her smile, genuine and comfortable, flitted to me as her eyes met mine. I saw the faintest color of blue before it went back to the road.

"Nice to finally meet you," she murmured. "I'd shake your hands, but I don't want to crash." She had an accent that I couldn't place. Russian, maybe?

I leaned my head on the seat. "Don't mind me. I'm just happy that you got me out of that hell-hole." I stared at her. "How did you even do that without being caught? Where are the others?"

Van's lips spread into a smile. She had one of those disarming grins. "I'd rather keep it a secret for now, Princess. Let's leave a bit of mystery between us."

Chapter 16
Talia

The same scenery stuck with us for hours: groves of trees, tall grass, a rocky road, and the moonlight shining through the thick branches of the forest. Beside me, Van was concentrated on the path, careful to follow the trail marked by the uneven soil. There were no other tire tracks aside from ours.

I sighed for the hundredth time. "Are you sure you know where we're going?"

A nod. Earlier, she'd switched off the light inside our truck, sticking to the glow of the dashboard. It made her face look blue and mine red. I blinked against it. "Muscles was the one driving us before," she said. "But I'm sure this road leads somewhere." Van gave me a quick smile. "Wherever it is, it's better than where we came from, right?"

" Right," I agreed.

"Take a nap instead, Princess. I'll wake you up when there's any development."

It was strange to sleep in the presence of someone I barely knew, in a car going to a place I had no clue of, but I was tired. It's been a long day. Soon, I was fighting against heavy lids, until my eyes could no longer support it. I drifted off into an uncomfortable sleep.

"Princess." Van was looking at me strangely when my eyes squinted at her. She was blurry and out of focus. I wiped my mouth and swallowed.

"Yes?"

"What were you mumbling in your sleep?"

"Nothing." I was dreaming of Cybele. She must be crushed to find me missing. I glanced around to push away my own fears. "We've stopped?"

"We had to." Van pointed outside the windshield where something large, a cabin, was waiting. "I'm going to ask for directions," she said. "I hate to admit it, but I think we're lost."

I stopped her from reaching the seatbelt. "Is this a good idea?" I asked. It was dark here, secluded. What if bad people were in there? We might run into even more trouble.

Van must have understood what I was communicating with my eyes because she touched my hand gently and nodded. I withdrew from her and flashed a polite smile. She got that too. "You don't trust me a hundred percent yet," she said. "I get that. I should have explained earlier instead of brushing you off." She sniffed. "We escaped from Muscles and the others when I sent them on a job elsewhere. I'm their unwilling informant."

I crossed my arms. She sounded genuine. "All right, ask the owner of the cabin where we're supposed to go," I said. "But I'll stay here."

She winked. "Just in case I try to lock you inside the cabin?"

My smile was like Cybele's: cynical but self-assured. "Just in case someone comes out with a shotgun and I need to ram the truck to him." I nudged my chin to the house. "Go."

Van made a small salute after she'd unbuckled her seatbelt and opened the truck's door. If Cybele looked like a proper royal with a hidden bad girl side while she walked, and Brooke simply exuded the word *model* with her strides, Van's walk was much like watching a hyena in the wild. There was barely held excitement in her steps, but from the swing of her arms and the confidence she had, the woman was ready for anything.

I didn't take my eyes off her as she knocked on the cabin door, went to the window, strolled back to the door again, and turned the knob. *What was she doing?*

Van held up two fingers before she went inside. Two minutes.

I waited that long, but she didn't come back.

"Damn it." I craned my neck. Where was she? Did she get into an argument for entering without permission?

Van came out just when I was unbuckling my own seatbelt and knocked on the car's window. I opened the door for her. "There's no one inside," she said, thumb pointed back to the cabin. "It's empty."

"Let's go then," I urged. "There's no use sticking around here. Muscles might catch up to us."

"Okay."

I brushed the goosebumps from my arms while Van settled back into her seat. She brought the chilly air with her. It made my stomach hollow.

She twisted the key but nothing happened. Twisted it again to get the same results. "This is an old truck," she murmured. "Sometimes I have trouble getting it to start." The engine whined and groaned at the third try, until something, perhaps a fuse, cried its painful death. "Shit."

My hands tightened on the seat. Could this day get any more worse?

Van took a deep breath and stared at me. "Will it be okay if we spend the night here?" she said.

I deflated. "Can't you fix it?

"Not until tomorrow. It's too dark. We might need to score a few materials too."

I threw a second glance at the cabin. "What if Muscles finds us? It's not impossible. We're just a few hours away from them." And every second I spent away from Cybele made everything hurt. Why did it have to be like this?

It was obvious that Van wanted to help but couldn't as she shook her head. We were stuck. "The cabin is secure," she said. "We can push the truck somewhere covered, and when Muscles and the others come knocking, we just hide. They're not the smartest bunch. They're going to think we're already in town."

I wrinkled my nose. "It figures. Okay, you push, I steer."

"Sounds like a plan."

Van did all the heavy work while I directed the truck to a bushy spot. Sweat was dripping from her forehead when she came to my side, but the woman was still smiling when she assisted me out.

"You don't have to do this," I said. "You're not my servant."

"But you're still my Princess." She shut the door. "A Princess who was declared missing a few months ago, who turned up in an abandoned-looking castle. But you don't seem to want to talk about it, so my lips are zipped."

I turned my face away. Maybe she was more trustworthy than I was giving her credit for. "Thank you," I murmured.

The cabin was darker compared to outside. I jumped when light flooded the room suddenly. "Scared you?" Van lowered her hand from the switch on the wall with a grin. I rolled my eyes at her and assessed the place.

It was nicer than the house we've escaped from, with no falling ceiling and ragged couch. But everything was simple. There were no decors on the walls to tell us what kind of person lived there, or if someone lived there at all. There were just wooden furnitures. "Maybe this cabin is used for vacations," I said aloud.

"Possibly." Van trailed further into the living room and dragged her finger on the windowsill. She scowled at the dust she collected and wiped her hand on her jeans. "I saw several doors on the corridor when I came in. Maybe they're bedrooms." She continued to another part of the house before I could ask where. I locked the door behind me and followed.

The corridor mentioned was short and narrow, with two doors on either side. Standing between them, Van twisted to me with a sparkle in her eyes. "I think it's better if we sleep together," she said.

I shook my head before considering it. "No offense, but I'd be more comfortable sleeping alone." That, and Cybele would kill me when I get back. It was best to get on her good side. We hadn't really established what we could or could not do. Hopefully, we get that chance, if ever.

"Are you sure?" Van's gaze bore onto me. "It will be more convenient to stay in the same room."

"I'd really want to sleep alone. Thanks for the offer though."

"Okey dokey." She chose a door to her right. I turned to the left. We opened each door simultaneously. "It is a bedroom," she confirmed.

I stepped into mine and turned around. Van had already entered hers and was studying me from across the hall.

"Are you sure you don't want to share?" Her door opened wider.

I shook my head. "No thank you."

"If that's your decision. . ." She bowed. "Goodnight, Princess."

"You too." I breathed a sigh of relief when my door was closed. That was awkward.

With so many things happening in a span of a few days, no sooner had I hit the dusty bed in the corner did I fall asleep. My dream was about Cybele. She was warning me about something, as always. I jolted from the bed, sweating from the dream. Someone was knocking on my door.

"Wha—"

"Princess! Princess!" Van sounded panicked. "Open up! Please!"

My feet were cold against the floor, but I didn't bother wearing my shoes. Looking at the window, I saw that it was still dark. I opened the door a crack. "Is something wrong?"

Van's wild eyes darted to the corridor before going to me. Sweat soaked the front of her flannel like she'd been running. "Someone came inside the cabin!"

My eyes widened. "Muscles?"

"I didn't see the face. He was wearing a mask." Van grasped my arms, realized what she did, then let go. The terror hadn't left her face, though, when she stepped back. "He might be dangerous. Let's hunt him down."

"Hell no!" I shook my head fiercely. "What if he has a gun?"

"He would have shot me already." Van's jaw clenched. She didn't look scared anymore, just frustrated. Realizing that the intruder didn't have much of an advantage over us did the job. "I'm going after him."

"With what? Your bare hands?"

"It's better than waiting here like sitting ducks." Her boots thudded on the floor. "Lock the door behind me."

I rushed to my shoes when she disappeared through the hall. The woman was stubborn as Cybele, though much more irrational. If Cybele was here, she wouldn't go out without a plan. She'd make a trap and set things in motion without getting hurt. She did get in the Palace undetected. This would be child's play for her.

Problem was Cybele wasn't here, and I was left alone with a woman who went in search for a mysterious man. I cursed under my breath as I wore the shoes and ran to the living room. The door leading outside was still closed, but Van was nowhere to be found.

"She should have waited for me!" I scanned the room for weapons, a broken chair maybe, but there was nothing to be used, even a large vase. I turned the light off and peered through the window. The truck was still there, yet it was too dangerous to go outside and search for a rod. My breath caught in my throat when something creaked.

"Van?" My voice came out in a whisper. Something breathed behind me.

I slapped the monster and ran. It ran after me.

"Help! Van!"

Whatever, or whoever it was preyed on me like a loose animal in a zoo. I stumbled on the couch. It sprinted after me.

The demon gave chase in the living room, then the corridor, where I tried to enter a room but couldn't because it was in hot pursuit. After that was the kitchen. But it was a little too late when I realized it. The man had gotten me cornered.

From what little light coming from the window, I could see its menacing form approaching from the north. I stepped backward, panting. "What do you want? I have money!" It was a shame that cash was the determinant for safety these days, but with a world full of crazy people, what could you do? I wanted to tell him that I was the Princess, but look where that got me. I took another step back. He was still advancing.

"Better this than a cannibal." I gulped. A third step back. Then another, and another.

He lunged.

My hands grabbed at his neck, his face, his mask, before I lurched backward and tripped on a chair. The last thing I saw before I hit my head on the floor was Van, smirking at me.

Chapter 17
Talia

"Wake up, Princess! You are having a bad dream." Someone nudged my shoulder hard.

Throbbing pain radiated in my skull when I turned to the right. The urge to vomit was strong as I opened my eyes. Everything in the room was spinning, including Van—in the bed. My bed. Crap!

I was wide awake when I sat up, scampered from the mattress, and glared at her. But my arms were leaden, and I couldn't raise them for self-defense without getting off-balanced, so I settled for an insult. "You're a maniac!"

A bemused expression flitted on Van's face before she lifted both hands in surrender. "I am," she said, "but only to women."

My mouth fell open. "So you wore a mask and chased me because of that?"

It was her turn to look confused. "Woah! That's a bit extra. I was talking about staring at you while you were asleep. You're beautiful. I'm a lesbian. Well, bi. That may sound stalkerish, but I promise you, it's not."

I stepped back when she arose. Her hand went to her hair as if she was upset, but how could she be when I was the one who was traumatized?

By her.

"Get away from me," I said. "Put your hands where I can see them."

"Inside or outside?"

"I'm not kidding!"

"Okay! Okay!" She wriggled her fingers to the ceiling. "What else do you want me to do, Princess?" I ignored the suggestive remark and went to her. Van grinned while I frisked her shoulders, then her waist. "Lower is so much better," she murmured.

"Quiet."

"Just saying."

My search ended, but I wasn't contented yet. There were things we should both be clear about. Starting with this. "I have a girlfriend." I gave Van a stern look. "Right now, she's searching for me, and knowing her, she won't stop until every hay is turned. If you hurt me—"

"I won't hurt you."

"If you hurt me," I hissed, "she will gut you, and then kill you. Now where's your mask?"

"I don't have a mask."

"Just give it to me."

Van's sigh was weary. "I told you, you were having a bad dream. You fell on the floor, and I was awesome enough to carry you back to bed. And look." She pointed to the window. Only then did I notice the rays of sunshine beaming inside the room, covering almost every surface, warming the side of my face. I blinked and scowled. Van shifted her weight. "If I wanted to hurt you, I wouldn't have let you live through the night. I wouldn't have rescued you from Muscles. What do I get from that?"

I looked at her doubtfully. "What do you have to gain by helping me?"

"Nothing," she admitted. "But at least that's one less thing on my conscience." She left my side to go to the door. Pausing there, she scratched at her blonde hair, considered, then glanced at me over her shoulder. "I found a knife at the back while you were sleeping. You can hold onto it if it makes you feel better, but I suggest we hunt for food first before I fix the truck."

Van was checking the truck's engine when I made it outside. It was still covered by the bushes, so if not inspected thoroughly, an unsuspecting visitor wouldn't see it at once. The door to the passenger seat was open, with the knife resting on the seat. I hurried there and snatched it clean from the chair before going to Van. She was shaking her head when she lowered the hood. "That will take a while to fix."

"How long?"

"No estimate." Her eyes flitted to the knife, then to me. "I see you've found my gift. Do you trust me now?"

My hands tightened on the handle. "I won't hesitate to stab you," I cleared.

She walked backwards. "Just make sure to do it in the right hole, Princess. That way, we both enjoy it." A flirty wink, then she twisted to the woods. "Hunting time."

I couldn't count the number of books I've read about the forest, yet somehow, all the tales about survival were conveniently wiped out from my mind. Perhaps it was thirst. I haven't drank since yesterday. Or perhaps it was just the hunger and the combined heat in the woods. I expected it

~ 175 ~

to be cool and shady, but the streaks of sunlight against my skin were like needless pricking. I tried to avoid them while walking.

Meanwhile, Van continued in front of me, footsteps silent as Cybele's, head facing random directions whenever there was a sound. I didn't want to talk in fear of distracting her. She was the more skilled hunter. I had to admit as much.

Minutes into doing nothing but hiking, Van stopped, raised a fist, and slowly, as if anticipating something, turned to me. "Give me the knife," she whispered, eyes sparkling with excitement.

I clutched the weapon to my chest. "No way!"

"Shh!" She pressed two fingers on her lips and pointed to the trees. I caught a subtle movement before looking back at Van. She was happier now. More confident. "There's a rabbit there," she whispered again. "It will take a while before I make a trap, which means if you don't give me the knife, we'll lose it. And if that happens, I won't get the strength I need to fix the truck. You feel me?"

She didn't need to say the rest because I understood it perfectly. No truck, no Cybele. I handed her the knife reluctantly. "I have my eyes on you."

"I thought you have a girlfriend." She stuck her tongue at me before proceeding with care. "Just teasing," she murmured.

If Van made little to no noise before, now it was as if she was gliding even though dried leaves and twigs were everywhere. She had almost made it to the rabbit when two white ears pointed from the grass, followed by the curious wiggle of chubby cheeks. Van inched closer, and raised the knife.

"It's running away!" she yelled.

"Wait!"

Van, like last night, had decided to leave me scampering. I dashed after them, a meter or so away, relying solely on her back for directions. The meter between us became two, then three, until I was turning, twisting, trying to recall where she'd disappeared to. Every tree looked the same. Every bend was identical. Maybe except for one thing.

Muscles 'grin widened when I stopped and noticed him. He didn't look as menacing under the sunlight, but maybe the brightness and the distance were nothing to him. His biceps flexed when he crossed his arms. "Get her," he said.

Aside from my throbbing head, my arms ached from trying to fight Toothy. He came out of nowhere in the forest and jumped me.

Once more, I tried to free my hands, but his grip was too strong, too tight. "Let go!" My cries had weakened. Absent of food and water, I was useless as bent fork. But I wasn't giving up. "Someone will rescue me! Don't think for a second that you're getting away with this!"

Toothy's laughter was deep and loud. He pushed me forward roughly. "Who will rescue you, girl? There's no one here." The cabin came into view. It brought me no relief, though, and I was more interested on the idle truck in front of it. Different color but the same model—someone was already sitting at the back. "There's your rescue." Toothy pinched my wrists. "Stupid, Princess."

I tried not to let the shock reflect on my face as I was forced to climb the truck and sit still while he gagged my mouth and subdued me for the umpteenth time. It was only when Toothy and Muscles went in front and buckled up did I meet Van's eyes. Captured and detained, she looked as scared beside me, maybe even more.

Their hideout was just as shabby upon our return. Underneath the cabinet, I could spy glowing eyes staring at me, following us as Toothy and Muscles shoved me to the hallway. The rat must be pleased to see me again.

"One more try for escape and we're going to make you bald," Muscles threatened. He seemed most irritated with me among their circle. My comment about Toothy must have really gotten to him. "Snip! Snip! You hear me, Princess? Snip!" He motioned to my old room once the door was opened. Beside me, Toothy was removing Van's gag and rope. "Both of you. In." I looked at Van reluctantly before stepping inside. Once we were both in the middle of the room, the door slammed close.

"I'm an idiot!" Van rushed to my side and began undoing the restraint over my mouth. My jaw relaxed once it was free. She worked on my hands next. "If I didn't run away, if I stayed by your side—"

"There's no use arguing now," I said. "We're here. No one will help us from outside."

I massaged my wrist when it was untied. Van walked to the bed, sank down on the mattress, and groaned. "It's still my fault. You have no idea what the gang will do to you. They're planning to sell you to Mr. Wang."

~ 178 ~

"Wang?" My eyes searched for an exit. I didn't miss any window, did I?

Van rolled out of the way when I jumped on the bed. "Have you lost your mind, Princess?"

"No." I signaled to her. "Come on. Lift me up."

Understanding flashed on her face before she leaned back on the headboard. "That won't do," she refused. "The woman is upstairs. She'll see us and alert the others even if we're able to wreck the ceiling."

I collapsed in the mattress. "What are we supposed to do now?"

"I don't know," Van admitted. "You can try begging Mr. Wang to be gentle, I suppose, but he'll probably feed you to his pet lion or something."

Just thinking about it made me wince. "Cybele won't like that."

"Who?" Van gave me a curious stare.

I frowned and looked away. I've said too much.

The two of us continued sitting in the bed for minutes, most probably thinking of a way to escape. It could have been my imagination, but the room seemed to grow colder with every second. A chill erupted across my skin.

Van slid closer to me. "A-are y-you f-feeling that t-too?" Her teeth chattered, a cloud of fog hovering over her face. She rubbed her arms. "It's suddenly freezing in here."

The goosebumps in my spine had turned to a full shiver as the chill intensified, but I recoiled from Van when she tried to put an arm around me. "Don't."

"It's for Cybele." The statement caught me by surprise that I could do nothing but allow Van to embrace me. "She's the girlfriend you were talking about, isn't she?" she asked. "If you want her to find you alive, you'll try harder."

The rest of me had numbed, but I was still able to give a nod. This wasn't the time to be sensitive. I had to be stronger. "T-thanks," I whispered. "You're. . . bleeding?" I held onto her when she tried to remove her hold. Her left arm was startlingly turning red. "How long has that been there? Did they hurt you? Why didn't you tell me, Van?"

I must have squeezed too hard because she winced. I let go in an instant. "It's Muscles," she said. "He gets too violent sometimes."

"It might get infected." I pushed myself from the bed, ignoring the panicked looks she was giving me. Van was the reason Muscles got me back, but she did her best to save me. I went to the door and banged it with my fist. "Anybody there? I have an injured woman in here! Hey!"

"Princess!" Van followed me. "Princess, you'll upset them."

"I don't care!" I banged on the door again. "Hey! I know you're listening! If you don't give Van proper treatment, I will sing all night until you're deaf. You won't like me when I sing. Even my mother once said that I have the most awful—"

The door swung open before I could finish the sentence, and Toothy, scratching his stomach, beckoned to Van. She shook her head. "I'm not leaving the Princess."

"You have to." I pulled at her good arm. "Please, Van! I would feel so much better."

"But. . ."

"Don't worry about me." My smile was fake, but so what? "Just make sure you're treated." I glanced at Toothy. "Properly, or else."

My warnings were disregarded as Van was called to the door, then outside. "I'll come back for you," she promised, before the door was sealed off once again.

She didn't come back—not minutes or hours later. I was left alone in the room, wondering where they've taken her, anxious for both of us. I scrambled up when I heard noises from the hallway. Someone was opening the door.

"Van, is that you?" A creak, a swoosh, a tray was pushed inside the room before the door banged shut. They didn't bring her back. Something awful could have happened to her.

I forced myself to kneel on the floor despite the bad scenarios playing in my head and devoured the sandwich. It was the only thing I could do to help myself. I had to prepare.

Come evening, I perked up when footfalls sounded in the corridor again. It was lighter, faster, could be a woman, but I wasn't too positive. The door cracked open, and instead of waiting for other people to decide my fate, I yanked the wood wider, slammed the tray on whoever was delivering dinner, and watched with satisfaction as the group's leader, the older woman from before, slacked on the ground.

~ 181 ~

"Say hi to Mr. Wang for me." I put the tray down so I could drag her inside the room. She might wake up any second. I should hurry.

Once our position was reversed, I bolted the door behind me, grabbed the tray, and made my way to the hallway. A loud sound halted me in place. Realizing it was only Toothy's snores from upstairs, I continued to the living room.

Every place was bare of Van, even the kitchen and the nearby rooms I passed. What if I didn't see her on the way out? What if she was already—no don't think of that. I've made it to the front door when I turned around. Would she hate me if I met with Cybele first and just come back to rescue her? But I had no choice. I'd save her later.

Outside, I was met with nippy wind and the blackness of the night. The truck was missing, but I'd expected that when planning for my escape. I'd have to take the rest of the way to town by foot and just hope for the best.

I was a foot away from the door when a flashlight flicked open. The light blinded my eyes, traveled down the grass, until it focused on another face set on a grotesque smile. "Going somewhere?" Van said.

Chapter 18
Cybele

Brooke and I went to town to get additional supplies. I didn't want to leave Talia's side this morning, not after we've made a lot of progress last night. But the pantry was bare and I wanted to cook for her. It was my way of apology for treating her the way I did. Perhaps it was time to have a talk and make amends, though we had a lot to discuss and I didn't know where, or how to begin.

"You're in a good mood today." Brooke broke through my thoughts. Her hair fluttered with the wind from the open window. It carried the chilly air of the night, and the scent of grass and possibilities.

I concentrated back on the dirt-path. We were minutes away from the abandoned castle. I'd see Talia soon. "How can you tell?" I said.

Brooke toyed with her dagger, the one I gifted her years ago when we enrolled in weapons training together. She shifted it to one hand, then back to another. The letter B on the hilt was engraved for her. She wanted to add another letter for my name, but I refused. "I don't know," she admitted. "Your aura is different. Did something happen between you and Talia last night?"

"Like what?"

"You tell me."

The statement was wrapped with suggestions. I rolled my own window down, feeling my cheek heat up, and by the time it was fully opened, the car had hit the bumpy path that said we were entering an even isolated territory. My hands tightened on the wheel. "Nothing happened," I said, the answer coming out as shaky as the road. "Let's not talk. I need to focus."

" Way to avoid the question as always, Iris," Brooke grumbled under her breath.

The workers who handled the restoration of the castle installed a garage for me by the east entrance. The main door on the front was a decoy. It was through the garage that one would be able to access the rest of the grounds. I parked the car there, tossed the key to Brooke before getting out, then headed to the worn-looking double doors. It had to match the abandoned façade of the rest of the castle, so at a glance you wouldn't think that it was highly secured.

I stopped by the entrance. "Brooke?"

"Yeah?" She closed the passenger door of the car and bounced to the trunk. Maybe she didn't hear the anxiousness in my voice, or I was just good at hiding my feelings.

My hands fisted by my side. "Did you leave this open?"

Her head poked out. I knew without looking that she must be wearing that worried face she'd get whenever I'd say something ridiculously dangerous: like hacking a server or asking for an access to the dark web to get my own connections. Brooke hurried to my side. "You're the last one to get out," she reminded. "Why?"

Why?

WHY?

I kicked the useless door and rushed inside. Cold sweat broke on my neck when I reached the landing on the second floor. The door leading up was ajar too.

"Talia!" My screams echoed and bounced back to me. "Talia, please!"

"What's going on?" Brooke's voice trailed on my back as she followed me up the stairs to the second floor. Every door, every room was empty of the Princess.

I was panting when we finally reached my bedroom. Silent as a tomb, it was bare, cold. Talia was missing. My teeth chattered. "Whoever took her is going to pay!"

Brooke walked behind me while I marched to the control room. My hands were shaking as I punched in the code to the computer, rewound the tapes, and reviewed the monitors. It didn't take long before I saw something that shouldn't have been there: four people breaking in, all wearing ski masks like the proper criminals they were.

"Oh God!" Brooke covered her mouth. I kept my eyes on the screen, watching, seething, as I saw Talia being carried away. One of the intruders had almost made it out the door when she backtracked to the hallway and turned to the camera. My mouth opened when she removed her mask. A cascading blonde hair, a twinkle in her blue eyes, a mischievous grin that I wanted to butcher. She was mocking me.

I paused the video on her face and began to make my way to the door. "Find out everything about that woman," I growled. "I want her name, her address, how she thinks, who she loves, even the breakfast she ate this morning."

~ 185 ~

Brooke made an uncomfortable-sound behind her throat. "Where are you going?"

"Making some calls. We need to leave this place. It's not safe."

The rooftop that had always given me solitude in the castle was forlorn and empty-feeling when I made it there. I avoided looking at the swing chair altogether, afraid to get ripped by the memories I'd see there. How could everything change so fast overnight?

Mum picked up my call on the third ring. I forced myself to perk up. "Hey, Mum. Are you all right?"

Some of my fears ebbed away when laughter rang in the background. She was with Dad. They were probably with colleagues. "I'm marvelous," she answered, sounding both happy with friends and hearing my voice. "Why hadn't you called sooner, Iris? It's been donkey years."

I walked closer to the flower beds. If she knew the real reason, she'd send the cops. "I was busy. Still am. This is going to be a quick call, Mum, so tell Dad I miss him too. Be safe."

Anxiousness must have wormed into my tone because she didn't argue much when I told her I'd end the call. The next person I contacted was not for family matters. It was the last choice, the call-a-friend button in times of dire need. Only, Viper wasn't a friend. He was an assassin I've met through the dark web.

A mechanical voice of a man answered the call. "Code?"

I covered my mouth by habit. "7292014."

"Phoenix," he greeted. "I thought you'd never call."

I paced the rooftop. Viper and I had spoken by chat maybe one or two times, but never like this. Not when it involved killing. My eyes darted to the swing chair. "How soon can you get to Europe, at a country called Harland?"

"Seconds," he answered, as if I shouldn't have asked in the first place. "My network has no limit. You just have to specify."

I nodded to myself. This was why I wanted him by my side. "I'm sending you a picture and a location to scout in the next few minutes," I said. "If you find the target, don't hesitate to eliminate. I'll wire the funds after."

"Copy."

Brooke was tinkering with the monitors when I came back to the control room. Taking a picture of the blonde girl in the video, I sent the file to Viper before tapping my best friend's shoulder. "Do you have your laptop with you?" I asked.

She spared me a glance. "What's a hacker without tools? Do you want me to trace anything?"

"No." I motioned to the CPU. "But I need you to copy all the files from this drive to yours. We'll search for Talia while on the move."

With a nod of agreement, Brooke jogged from the room, returned with her pink laptop, and set out to do her task. It took her a total of ten minutes to get everything. Afterwards, she gave me an ok signal. "It's done. I'll wipe out the rest of the data you've stored here. Do I have your consent?"

"I'll get the gasoline while you're at it."

Another fifteen minutes went by before everything we'd need was packed in the car. It wasn't much—just the food we'd brought and Brooke's beloved laptop. The bookmark that I valued was safe in my pocket, close to my skin, never leaving my side. The rest wouldn't be missed.

"Help me with this." I gave Brooke her own can of gasoline and started pouring some of mine on the intricate control system. I've spent days, hours, weeks planning for this hideout, but now I wanted to see it burn to the ground. "By the time people realize that someone was here, we'd be long gone," I murmured. "Are you done?"

Brooke tossed her can to the side. It made a clanging noise as it rolled to the computer chair. "What about the rest of the castle?" she said.

The lighter on my right hand flickered open. "I've taken cared of it."

The castle was a gruesome sight of orange when I checked the rearview mirror later on. Beside me, half of Brooke's body was leaning out the window, bouncing every now and then as the car sped through the bumpy trail. Unease was dominant on her face when she sat properly. She blew out a breath and rubbed her arms. "I guess there's that," she murmured.

I kept my eyes on the road. It was too dark; wherever there was no Talia was too dark. "How soon can you find that woman in the video?" My voice was startlingly loud against my own ears.

I was glad for the distraction. The fire we've created was making me think of things.

Brooke reached for her laptop on the dashboard and snapped it open. "Give me a day or two," she said.

My knuckles turned white against the steering wheel. "I don't have a day or two. Every second, every moment she's away from me could endanger her life! Do you even know what they'll. . ." I stepped on the brakes. My hand was too clammy. My voice was too shaky. I forced myself to breathe and look at Brooke. She was scared. But then so was my Princess. "I need her back," I whispered. "Do you understand?"

Brooke's eyes were unreadable as she reached over and squeezed my arm. "I know that," she said. "But all we have is a face. It doesn't work that way with hacking. A face tells us nothing."

I shrugged her off to work on the gear stick. "A face tells us everything," I said. "It tells me who I have to kill."

The scenery barely changed in the next few hours until the grove of trees widened in favor of a wider road and spacious field. Brooke glanced away from her laptop for the first time and squinted at the building waiting for us. "Is that a farmhouse?"

The car slowed to a stop next to the old structure. On the horizon, streaks of dawn were peeking behind the clouds. I unbuckled my seatbelt and gave Brooke an exasperated sigh. "Let's get settled in."

The farmhouse was right beside a barn. Both were rickety, looked like they had seen their fair share of bad and good crop seasons, and had slanted roofs that were fading in color. Brooke wrinkled her nose upon stepping outside the car. "It smells like the loo."

I paid no attention to her small complaints and continued to the entrance. Like the castle, the farmhouse had a sophisticated security system that would only reveal itself to knowing eyes. I input the code hidden in the wall by the side, then waited for the bolt to sound before turning to the door itself. Everything changed when I stepped inside.

"Well, I'll be gob smacked! Everything's modern!" Brooke closed the door behind her, making the locking mechanism fall into place with a beep. She stood beside me, raised her head, then stared around.

The large, white sofas adorning the living room were armed with cushy pillows. Sitting at the head of the space was a fireplace. Other details like the wooden beams, the high ceiling, and the painted landscapes on the wall complemented it. Always have a back-up plan when kidnapping someone.

"You can pick any room," I said, "but the one furthest to the right is mine." *And Talia's.* I ground my teeth together. "Meet me here after ten."

I shuffled to my bedroom while Brooke remained standing in place admiring the decor. My door was the only one with a code aside from the main entrance. And once it was opened, I immediately went to the walk-in closet, changed into an all-black ensemble, then backtracked to the living room. Brooke came in ten minutes later, wearing almost the same outfit, down to the black boots. She wasn't wearing a jacket though, just a body-hugging top.

I sighed as we both headed for the same sofa. Her laptop went to the coffee table, while I settled my back in the couch. "Why don't you sleep first?" she said. Brooke was continuing whatever she had started in the car. The fast typing was too rhythmic for my taste, too relaxing. But I couldn't afford that.

"Not while Talia is missing," I said.

Brooke nodded. "Suit yourself."

Having nothing else to do, I paced the living room, going over and over with the same awkward steps, feeling like the ground under me wasn't leveled. It went on for minutes until Brooke was slamming her laptop close. I paused to look at her. "Any developments?"

"No, Iris." She sounded irritated. "There won't be any developments if you continue that. You're making me dizzy."

I rubbed my neck and mumbled an apology before going beside her. All this energy had to go somewhere. Maybe I should get a horse from the stable and let it gallop on the fields. On that note, I still had to tell the farmer I'd hired to feed the animals not to come here in the meantime.

I raised my eyes to see Brooke glaring at me. "Go to sleep," she scolded.

I must have dozed off on my own. I wasn't too sure. Because the next time I came to, Brooke was nudging my arm and pointing to her laptop screen, saying something lost in translation under the drunkenness of sleepiness. I shook it away and tried to focus on my wrist. My eyes widened when I saw the time.

"Six in the evening! Why didn't you wake me up? How did I sleep that long?"

Brooke raised a hand to calm me, but the guilty expression on her face didn't slip away. "I made you swallow a sleeping pill while you were zonked out," she confessed. "I couldn't deal with the tension. It was the only way I could search quickly until—"

"Until what?" I snapped. She had stepped the line. Talia was out there cold and miserable, and I was what? Sleeping?

Brooke placed the laptop between us before I could bludgeon her and pointed to the screen. "Listen first," she begged. "I found her, okay? The girl in the video."

My mouth closed, then opened. "You did?"

She nodded meekly. "I figured that only the crew you've hired to renovate the castle could probably know about it, so I did a little digging." Brooke scrolled through a page and had me squinting my eyes. The man in the picture looked familiar. "This is Gerard Krieger," she explained. "Head of the project, wife deceased, and see here." She opened another tab. "His daughter is Vanessa Krieger. Nineteen years old. Location unknown. She was studying in the university when her mother died in an accident. A few months after that and the father's death followed. After that, no one knew where Vanessa went."

My eyes burned at the picture of the woman. Blonde, blue-eyed, and a smile that laughed at me even behind the monitor. I gripped the sofa. "Where did you say was her last known location?"

"The dorm room of the university," Brooke answered. "But their real house is a three-hour drive away from here. Do you want to investigate?"

I fished the phone from my pocket and tossed it to Brooke after getting up. "Send every detail you've told me to one of my contacts. His codename is Viper. I'll get our tools."

Her eyebrow raised. "What tools?" I heard her saying, but I was already on my way to one of the rooms.

Going back, Brooke shifted in her seat when she saw me carrying a black rectangular box the length of a guitar case. I put it on the table and unlocked it with a click. She gasped when she saw the guns and ammo.

"What's that for?"

I took one of the weapons, attached the silencer to the barrel, and loaded it with magazine before handing it to her. "This is for taking my Princess back."

Chapter 19
Cybele

When she wasn't looking at the road to drive, Brooke was staring at my hand and sighing. I didn't see what the big deal was. It was just a gun.

"Are you even going to use that?" she finally asked.

I nodded while trying to control the volcanic eruption in my chest. Locked in the car, not even the one in the driver seat, my pent-up emotions were making me edgy. "That's kind of the point of bringing weapons, Brooke. You use them eventually." I jutted my thumb behind. "There's more where that came from. How far are we from our destination?"

She took the computer resting on her knee and pulled the lid up. The woman was joined to the hip with her technology. "We've passed this sign a few kilometers ago," she murmured to herself. Brooke's eyes were remarkably awake when she shut the laptop again. "Thirty minutes."

I studied the lonely road while she continued to drive. Though groomed to take over my late parent's throne, I've yet to memorize each blade of grass, each region of Harland. But there would be a time and place for all of that. Retrieving Talia was top priority for now.

Brooke's prediction came into reality when after thirty minutes we came into a town. Situated in the countryside, it was normal to see that the shops were closed, the signs were out, and the only light aside from ours were the street lamps evenly spread apart. The car crunched on gravel as Brooke steered us to the side street. "There it is." She nudged her head to the moderate-sized house paces away. "Do you think she's hiding Talia there?"

I cocked the gun and unbuckled my seatbelt. "Only one way to find out."

My breath was foggy when I stepped out of the car and ducked behind the vehicle. In addition to Brooke's favorite dagger, she was holding a machete when she came to my side. I gave the weapon a weary glance before looking at her. "The hell is that?"

"What?"

"That." I pointed to the blade. "You need a gun, not a hacking tool."

She pursed her lips and flipped her long black hair behind her back. She didn't tie it into a ponytail like I did with mine, and she accused me of being cheeky. "You know I don't like guns," Brooke whispered. "Leave my babies alone."

I rolled my eyes. "Fine. Fine. As long as you can handle yourself." I peeked from behind the vehicle and circled my pointer finger. "Here's the plan. You go right, I take the left side. Let's meet at the back. Clear?"

"Roger."

Brooke was about to leave when I caught her hand. There was one more thing. "Be careful," I warned. "Okay?"

Instead of nodding, an amused grin began to spread on her face. "I knew you cared for me too," she gushed.

~ 195 ~

"Of course I care. You're my best friend."

Brooke didn't look convinced as she darted to the side, the machete gleaming dangerously under the streetlamp. Following her example, I slipped from the car and moved stealthily to the house. Nobody was in the street with us, but we were dealing with criminals, and criminals had precautions of their own. Vanessa would be waiting.

My senses were at an all-time high as I went to the side of the house and checked for perimeter guards. No one took a shot at me when I made to the back. Then again, Brooke wasn't at the rendezvous point either.

Worried, I started to take the side of the house she was covering, only to bump into a black figure. I lifted the gun to defend myself. "It would be nice if you don't kill me." Brooke's gaze went to the bridge of her nose where my barrel was pointed. She exhaled when I lowered the weapon. "Bloody hell, you're making me nervous with that thing." She straightened and sheathed her machete, then motioned to a nearby window. "I checked the house but nobody was there."

"What do you mean nobody?" It was like she was speaking a different language from mine as I hurried to a window and looked inside myself. My heart sank to the ground. It was dark inside but no one was moving. And if it were a trap, my head would have been blown to pieces by now. I smashed the glass using the handle of the gun.

"We're breaking?" Brooke's voice was high.

I reached through the broken shards of glass and twisted the lock from the other side. "Entering too."

~ 196 ~

The house was musty with most furnitures covered with white sheets. Third round wasn't a charm for us, because even though we've searched every room and practically every closet, Talia wasn't there.

I kicked a chair out of the way. "Where did they take her? Where!" It wasn't like me to lose composure. I've always kept my anger at bay.

Brooke came beside me and gently took the gun from my hand. "We'll find her."

But what if we didn't? What if Talia was forever lost? I would never forgive myself for leaving her defenseless.

A vibrating sound pulled me away from the dark thoughts. My eyes flickered to Brooke who was reaching to her back pocket. My cellphone was retrieved and given to me. "I forgot I had it," she said.

The call continued until I pressed the answer button and listened to the line. A deep voice on the other side made my skin crawl. "Phoenix."

"Viper," I said. "How's the search going?"

"Some good and bad news. I've searched the location but didn't find the target."

I switched the phone to my other ear. "And the good news?"

Viper cleared his throat. "After talking to some of my sources, it appears that a Princess-apparent is being auctioned and sold to a Mr. Wang, a Chinese tycoon. It was done through the black market, so the authorities don't know a thing. If what they say is true, the Princess would be ready for shipment tomorrow night."

~ 197 ~

"Shipment?" It felt like I've swallowed something nasty.

" It means the Princess would be delivered to Mr. Wang," he explained. "I'll send the coordinates where they'll pass. My contact person is far from the location, so you might want to intercept it yourself."

"I have one more question before you go, Viper."

"Yes?"

My eyes went to Brooke. She only heard one side of the conversation, but she'd get it when I ask. "How did you know I was also looking for a Princess?" I said. "I never told anyone about that."

There was silence on the other line, followed quickly by a low chuckle. "Don't worry, Phoenix. I'm not your enemy." I pulled the phone away from my ear when the dial tone sounded. It vibrated one more time before coordinates flashed on the screen.

My brows furrowed to Brooke. "Do you think it's a trap?"

"Do you want me to research him?"

I shook my head as I tucked the phone in my back pocket. An assassin wouldn't leave records of himself, both hidden and legal. No matter how good Brooke was with hacking, I didn't doubt for a second that Viper had a few tricks up his sleeve.

"Iris?" Brooke wrapped her arms around herself. "Before we rescue the Princess, can you clear one thing for me?" Her eyes searched mine. "Are you in love with her?"

The question hovered over us like a dark cloud. I've avoided answering it for years, but at this point it might as well be a flashing sign on my head.

"Brooke. . ."

"Don't." Her hair spread over her face to protect her from me. But I didn't want to hurt her. I've been clear about friendship from the start.

"I'm sorry," I muttered. "I'm an idiot."

"You're a bloody oaf." She turned her face away. "A lovable bloody oaf."

I knew when to keep my mouth shut, so I casted my eyes downward while she collected herself. Brooke was important to me. But that was all there was to it, nothing more.

She dropped her arms after a while and took a deep breath. Brooke's head was high when she began to make her way to the door behind me. But the thing with her was she wasn't as good as hiding her feelings like me or Talia. The pain she wore like a badge on her face demanded respect. "Let's rescue the damsel in distress," she said. "I'm in the mood to kill some wankers."

Riding the car after discussing our true feelings was one of the hardest things I had to do with Brooke. We didn't speak. Some parts of me knew that it was easy to be with her, as easy as breathing. But that wasn't how it worked. Whoever I was with, however perfect she was, my heart would always belong to Talia. In one way or another, she was my paramour.

"We need to park the Beater off the road," Brooke said hours later. Her nose was red from crying, but her eyes were alive again, and that was more important. She'd returned to her smiling face when she looked at me. "No hard feelings, yeah?"

"Yeah," I said, a ghost of a smile on my lips.

The shipment of the most valuable cargo in the world would pass in a remote road at exactly three o'clock in the morning. We arrived there at two-thirty after following Viper's coordinates, and perfect timing too. Our car made too much noise as we bumped off road to hide it in the grassy patch.

I swatted a bug from my neck as Brooke and I left the car. The grass around us was too tall, but it provided good camouflage for the vehicle. I admired our handiwork before going to the trunk. "Twenty-five minutes, Brooke. Which gun do you want?"

I glanced over my shoulder to see her hand tighten on her machete. "I thought we're going to use the road spikes to blow up their tires?" she questioned.

I put my hand on the car's hood. "Yeah. But you know how I am with back-up plans. In case the spikes fail, we need to shoot." The trunk popped open, and my mouth widened into an unsettling grin. My favorite rifle, the AMW sniper, was resting inside. Pestering my adoptive parents to enroll me in different types of self-defense and weapons training was the right choice. I took the Glock beside it and offered it to Brooke. "Arm up and get the spikes."

Buying all kinds of equipment's while I was planning Talia's kidnapping had proven to be handy, if only I didn't have to use some of them today. After laying the trap, Brooke and I hurried to the side of the road near the camouflaged car, then knelt low between the grass to hide ourselves. Brooke's shiver was strong enough to make me stare. It was two months shy of Winter, but already, our breaths were fogging.

"Are you scared?" I asked, keeping an eye on Brooke. Tucking the stray hair behind her ear might not be a good idea, so I kept my hands on the rifle, one finger on the trigger.

"Y-yes," she answered, teeth chattering. "You?"

"No."

Angry? Yes. Cold? Definitely. But scared? Uh-uh. Whoever those hoodlums were, they would die tonight. Even Wang, for attempting to take Talia away from me. After I get the throne back, every illegal activity of his would be put to a stop.

Brooke and I halted the conversation as soon as we heard something in the distance. The delivery came earlier than the call time, but we were ready for them when the truck emerged in our line of sight.

My plan came into play when the vehicle careened out of control after running on the spike. Screeching to a stop only meters from us, tires flattened, anyone riding inside had nowhere to go but out. I shot the driver first.

Brooke stared at me in horror when she realized what happened, but I didn't bat a lash when I scoped out the rest of the targets. There were three left. All of them got out cautiously following the curdling scream of the driver, who, thanks to the bullet I've put on his knee, wouldn't walk right again.

Birds flew from the nearby trees when another shot penetrated the air. The two remaining uninjured men ran to the fields in the opposite way, leaving their crew behind. They were useless, selfish, but I wasn't celebrating yet. Talia wasn't with any of them. Where was she?

My question was answered when the blonde got off the car. She wasn't alone. With a gun pointed to the Princess 'temple, Talia was pushed out, used as a shield, and laughed at. Vanessa's gaze drifted in our direction. "Come out, come out, wherever you are," she taunted.

Brooke tugged at my arm to stop me, but I was already standing. "Don't hurt her." My voice was loud and clear. The rifle was lowered by my side, as pointless as the men who came with them. "I'll give you the money. How much do you need?"

The road was dark, but I could see how menacing Vanessa's grin was. My heart skipped a beat when she thrust the barrel on Talia's head. "I already have money," the blonde said. "Mr. Wang will give it to me."

"I'll double the offer."

"Will you now?" The psychopath's laughter made me want to slit her throat. Even more when she moved closer to Talia so her lips were next to the Princess 'ear. "She must be Cybele," Van said. "Man, she's obnoxious!" The gun was pointed to me. "Bye, bye!"

I was down on the ground before I realized what happened. Brooke was screaming something. My shoulder was getting hot, painful, but I was more concerned about the Princess being dragged to the side of the road where the two men escaped.

Brooke's words began to make sense. "Iris, you're bleeding!"

I pressed a hand on my wound and nodded to her. Damn, it hurt!

"I'll be all right," I lied through gritted teeth. "Follow them!"

" But you're hurt!"

"I don't care! Just go!"

Murder was loud and clear in my head as I ripped a portion of my shirt to patch myself up. No one could take the Princess and get away from me that easily. Vanessa was going down.

Chapter 20
Cybele

"Brooke," I whispered. "Where are you?"

Dead silence answered me. It hadn't been ten minutes since things went to shite, and already, things were headed for so much worse. The wound I've applied pressure to continue to bleed. Brooke was nowhere to be seen in the dark field. And counting the chilly wind that had swept my hair in disarray, I was ready to bludgeon someone, specifically a woman named Vanessa.

"Brooke," I whispered again.

The grass a few paces from me ruffled. Everything was higher than my head, which made it easier to lose each other. "Iris," came Brooke's low reply. "I'm here."

Mastering the art of silence had never been difficult for me, so I made it behind her without making a sound. She relaxed when I touched the small of her back but continued glancing in front where I spotted a break in the grassland. There was a clearing before a forest in the distance. "Why did you stop?" I said. "Why haven't you followed them?"

Brooke glanced at me over her shoulder, eyes narrowing in concern. "First thing's first," she said. "Are you okay?"

"Why wouldn't I be? It's just a scratch."

Brooke faced forward again. Meanwhile, I gripped my rifle tighter and tried not to groan out loud as she pointed to a tree in the clearing. It stood by itself right before the forest. "There," she said. "Do you see that? A man?"

I squinted and tried to see past the darkness. It was the glint of silver on his rifle that gave him away. "Is it one of the escapees?"

Brooke's breath fogged as she exhaled. "Dead on. I couldn't risk running to the forest because of him. What should we do?"

I considered the options while ignoring the numbness creeping in my shoulder. There was no time to circle the field just so we could get to the forest. I knelt and rested my cheek on the rifle where the scope gave me a good view of the target.

"The wind is strong," I informed Brooke. "There's a high chance that I'll miss, but I want you to run to the other side as soon as I shoot."

An anguished gasp came from her. "What about you? I can't just leave you here, Iris!"

"You can, and you will." My finger closed on the trigger. "Get ready."

Brooke was just preparing for her counter argument when I fired. A bewildered look passed on her face before she sprinted towards the clearing, and immediately, another man ran after her. We've forgotten that there were two of them.

"Iris!" Her bloodcurdling scream echoed when she got to the forest.

I tried not to think of it as I readied for another attack. The shooter on the tree was still a problem.

Bang!

There was a split, a crack, but I didn't linger to check if he survived the fall from the branch. I jumped from my hiding place and dashed towards the forest. Big mistake.

Someone yanked my hair, jerking me to a stop. Swiveling behind me, I caught the first fist aimed at my face, but not the second going to my stomach. I doubled over and coughed.

"Think you can outsmart Mr. Wang?" The mercenary sounded like he had a personal grudge as he took out a knife. "Well you can't! Mr. Wang had a high GPA!"

I gave him an incredulous stare through my dizziness. Was he crazy?

The man swung his knife downward, fast, but I had recovered then. With one fluid motion, I kneed his groin, caught the knife he dropped, then skewered his throat before he could retaliate.

I let go and stepped back as he collapsed and wheezed his final breaths. I had just killed a man.

An emptiness I couldn't understand echoed in my chest when I'd made it to the forest. What was this feeling? Was I scared?

I shook my head and concentrated on the path. I've promised myself never to be weak again, never to submit to my conscience. My real parents were dead, and Talia would soon be if I didn't get to her quick. A Queen had to be strong even when the world was against her. That was my duty. My curse.

A kilometer or so into my journey, the strangest sight beheld me. Some of Harland's forest were dangerous, especially in isolated areas, but this was hair-raising as much as it was a tragedy. I paused to inspect.

The man impaled on the spiky thorns sticking out from the tree was no longer breathing. Clutched in his hand was a piece of cloth: remarkably like mine and someone else's. My nose wrinkled as I ran to the direction where the dead man's eyes remained focused on. Remind me never to get on my best friend's bad side again.

" Ugh!" A faint groan in the distance made me stop. It was followed by wails, rasping, before I recognized who it belonged to. I ran again and almost missed my cue. Brooke was on the ground, moaning, clasping her leg.

"Dang, it hurts!" she cried.

Her eyes closed when I knelt to her side to examine the damage. The trap buried in the grass was digging into her ankle. "We need to release it," I said. "Hold on to my waist."

"No!" Brooke's terror was justified, but so was my insistence. The thing that caught her wasn't a bear trap. It was easier to pry open without a tool, but it would take her cooperation to do it.

I took her hands and pressed it against my leg as I stood. She started to scream when I tinkered with the release lever. "It's over! You're free!" I moved her foot out of the way before letting go of the trap. It remained opened but dangerous. Only a heartless person would put it there. A person like me.

Brooke sniffled while I ripped my already torn shirt and unbuckled my belt to put it all together against her ankle. She would survive this.

~ 207 ~

I knew she would. But I couldn't help but coddle her while I worked.

"No more modeling gigs for us," I chirped. "Now what will we do with all that spare time?"

Her attempted smile came out as a grimace. Brooke inhaled and wiped her tears. "I seriously doubt they're letting us go," she said. "We're hot as hell, Iris. A scar from a trap is nothing."

Atta girl. I ruffled her hair and leaned back when I was done. "Thought you'd go dramatic on me again."

"Again?"

I shrugged. "Remember that time when they didn't have salad at the party in Greece? You went diva on everyone."

She smirked at the memory. "I also had a runway show the next day. Cut me some slack." Brooke sighed and winced at her ankle, but her eyes were steadier when she stared at me. "Come back in one piece," she said. "I don't want to track your missing pieces using my computer."

"Right."

Brooke was leaning against a tree far from the trap when I hurried away. Her weapons were by her side. She'd be all right. As for me, it took a few more minutes of going in circles in the dark woods until I happened upon a meadow. My insides protested when I spotted Talia, moonlight shining where she sat, bound, gagged, and alone.

Her eyes enlarged when she noticed me draw nearer, but it was too late. A snap sounded on my foot, followed by a tug. No sooner had I seen her did I notice that she was upside down, or

I was upside down. Someone approached Talia from behind.

"What do we have here?" Vanessa removed the gag from the Princess 'mouth. "Live bait."

Talia squirmed against her binds. "Let go of Cybele, Van! I beg you!"

"And miss the opportunity to see you suffer?" The woman chuckled. "No way." Vanessa paid no attention to the Princess 'pleads, headed to me, and fished out something from her pocket. The Swiss knife made a snapping sound as the blade was popped free. Vanessa grinned. "How does your shoulder feel, Cybele? Can't get out of my trap because of it?"

I tilted my head to glance at my wound. It had stopped bleeding. But she was right, even if I could normally get out of being dangled upside down from a rope, the wound prevented me from reaching to my foot.

Vanessa continued approaching. "There's no getting out of here anyway," she said. "This forest is my home. I have a cabin a few kilometers back where my father used to take me for hunting." She grabbed my rope before I could reach her and swung me backward. The motion made me dizzy. "Sweet dreams, puppet." Her waiting fist knocked me unconscious.

"Cybele! Wake up! Wake up, Cybele!" Talia's voice was oddly far, muddled. I groaned.

The Princess 'face was contorted with worry when my eyes finally focused on her. Droplets of tears started to stream down her cheek. "I thought you were dead!" she whimpered. "Thank God you're alive!"

The need to comfort Talia prevailed despite the vomit building in my throat. I ignored the dizziness and slid closer to her. "Princess. . ." I licked my dry lips. "Don't cry. It doesn't suit you."

The urge to wrap my arms around her was so strong I could hurt someone. But while I'd been taken down from the trap while I was asleep, my hands had been tied behind me. My legs were bound together too.

Talia nuzzled her cheek against mine to offer comfort. "I didn't know what I would do if you never opened your eyes," she whispered. "You can't leave me alone again. I swear I'll burn your coffin if you send me back to Lance."

I couldn't help but grin. Trust the Princess to threaten me, even in the most dreadful situation.

"No one is coming back to Lance," I said. *And no one is going to marry you but me.*" We need to get out of here."

"How?"

"Wait." Talia and I broke apart to examine our surroundings. The rifle, my gun, even the knife I've attached to my leg for the rescue mission were gone. But I wasn't losing hope. "There must be something," I reasoned.

"There's nothing," Vanessa denied.

I whipped my head back and saw her emerging to the clearing, a stack of branches in her arms. The woods dropped noisily on the grass when she stopped.

"You made me miss the delivery," she said. "Now Mr. Wang will think I double-crossed him." Vanessa retrieved a lighter from her pocket and switched it open. Her face was strangely pale as she bent over and set the branches on fire. "I'll correct that mistake." She stood. "The deal is still on."

My teeth clenched at her. "I said I'll give you the money. What more do you want?"

"It was never about the money."

"Then what is it about?"

The flames in front of her danced when she pointed to Talia. "The bitch of a Queen needs to learn a lesson," Vanessa said. "Too bad for her, I caught the Princess."

I stared at Vanessa for what seemed like the first time. The kidnapping, the immorality, the psychopath tendencies were not new to me. I had done the same. We were just like each other.

Talia met my eyes with a fresh wave of fear in them, especially when Vanessa went to my side and started to drag me away. "No!" the Princess yelled. "Leave Cybele alone! What are you doing?"

Vanessa let go of my arms but didn't step away. Laughing, she moved the opened lighter closer to my shoulder. "I want to hear you scream now," she told Talia. "Scream for Cybele! Scream!"

But it was my cries that penetrated the woods. I bit down on my tongue when the flame licked my wound. It was agony.

"Stop it!" Talia begged. "We've done nothing to you! Just kill me instead!"

Vanessa stopped her assault and twisted to the Princess. "Kill you?" She lowered her lighter. "Do you think we went all this way just to kill you? Do you think I like what I'm doing?" Her face contorted in rage. "I hate to break it to you, Princess, but I hate this! I'm not like this! You motherfuckers did this to me!" She took a deep breath. "Your mother took away something important to me, so now I'm doing the same to you."

The Swiss knife from earlier was pressed against my throat. Ouch! Talia, before I realized what was happening, out of nowhere leaped to the fire that Vanessa had created.

"No, Princess!" I cried.

I watched in horror as a portion of Talia's clothes were set ablaze. Smoke came from everywhere, but eventually, Talia tugged her binds away. Vanessa was so surprised that she barely moved when the Princess ran and brought her arms down for a crushing blow. Before long, the psychopath slumped on the ground. But not dead.

"Talia!" The Princess didn't answer me as she took the knife from Vanessa's hand and cut through my binds. In seconds I was free, glaring at her. "Why did you do that?" My heart was ready to burst. "It was so stupid of you! You could have been seriously—"

Talia wrapped her arms around my neck and crushed our lips together before I could continue.

My knees weakened to oblivion as her tongue slipped inside my mouth, searching, playing, trying to convey words she couldn't have said over the years.

~ 212 ~

I cradled her cheek and surrendered to her touch. She was my Princess. My deity. The happy ending to my fairytale. I closed my eyes. For the first time ever, I didn't think of anything but how good she made me feel.

Chapter 21
Cybele

"Wake up, you asshole!"

Vanessa sputtered and blinked while I lowered the now empty bucket. It took a while before she figured out where she was, but when her eyes met mine, the insane girl had a huge smile on her face, as if she wasn't tied to a chair in a spare bedroom.

"Who are you again?" she asked, her hair sprinkling water everywhere as she shook it like a dog. She paused and stared at me again, her blue eyes gleaming. "Sorry, I didn't catch your name. I was too busy shooting you back there."

I returned her smile. "That's understandable. You can call me Cybele, or master—if you're into that sort of thing. As my new pet, I'm requiring you to follow my every order or else."

"Or else what?"

"You die." My strides were long and quick as I crossed the room to her. "Now where were we?" I snapped my fingers. "Oh, yeah! I was going to get back at you for everything you've done." Vanessa's eyes narrowed when I fished a lighter from my pocket, much like the one she'd used to torture me a few hours ago. It flickered open. "This is for shooting me, hurting Talia, and injuring Brooke."

Vanessa leaned her head back. She wasn't the least bit ashamed of the crimes I'd listed, but had looked proud of what she'd done.

Her mouth smacked together before she chuckled. "You have to do better than a lighter though. I recommend using gasoline if you plan to set me on fire."

"I'm not going to kill you." Her eyes turned suspicious. "But you and I are going to have so much fun." I moved the lighter closer, until the tip of the flame was almost touching her nose. It was my turn to beam. "Tell me, Vanessa. How much do you love your hair? From what I've gathered, your deceased mother had the same blonde. I wonder what you'll do if I burn it."

Her hands tightened on the armchair. "Fuck you!"

Finally. A reaction.

She breathed a sigh of relief when I closed the lighter, but I wasn't done yet. Tucking the thing in my pocket, I took the next item of interest: a utility knife that matched the one she'd used in the forest.

To her credit, Vanessa didn't flinch when I pressed it against her throat, but she did move closer. "Do it!" she challenged. "What are you waiting for?"

The knife lowered. "You're in such a hurry to die." I knelt in front of her. Vanessa's jeans were rolled, raised, until it came to her knees. "You were the one who set-up the trap, weren't you?"

"So?"

I shrugged. "My best friend will limp for the next few weeks. I think she'd understand if I make a little payback." Vanessa's shrieks filled the air, but I continued piercing her ankles with the knife, digging hard enough to hurt her, though not too deep to disable. She bucked against the chair, trying to throw me off. "Where's the tough girl now,

Vanessa?" I smirked. "Stop whining. You're still going to walk, you know."

Tears from pain and anger flowed down her cheek. "What are you doing to me!" she shrieked. "You crazy fuck!"

"Speak for yourself." The knife was placed on the floor. And out came my next toy.

"A water gun?" She disguised her pain with a contemptuous smile. "I expected better from you, Cybele."

I aimed on her wound and fired. The howl she made was fantastic. "What better to clean a cut than alcohol?" A deep laugh bubbled from my chest.

In front of me, Vanessa was beginning to exhibit signs of terror in her eyes, exactly what I was going for. Nothing made humans obey more than pain.

"Now tell me, Van," I said again. "Wait, that's what they call you, right? Van?" I groaned as I straightened and leveled my eyes with hers. Even when Brooke had patched me up, my shoulder still ached. "Why do you want to take revenge on the Queen?"

She answered by spitting on my face. I squirted the gun on her wound again.

"Don't make me repeat the question," I hissed, wiping my face. "Your hair is going next."

Vanessa started to shake. I didn't know whether it was from the torture of putting alcohol on her, or the threats of setting her hair on fire, but she suddenly broke into an uncontrollable sob. It started with a wail and ended into whimpers. "The Queen killed my mother!" she cried. "Happy?"

I stepped back to give her space. My stomach tightened into knots.

"Months ago," Vanessa continued. "Queen Esmeralda summoned my dad and his team for a project. The bitch fell in love with him." Van's eyes trailed to my face. "He didn't want to be romantically involved with her. That's why she murdered them."

"How did you find out?"

The muscles in Van's throat bobbed up and down. "Dad told me days after Mom died that he saw the Queen's men in the site of the accident. They found him dead soon too." Her eyes squeezed shut. When she opened them again, renewed anger gleamed like sharpened knives. "I hate Esmeralda!" she screamed. "The Queen needs to die! Because of her I lost everything!"

"Talia is innocent though," I murmured. "We shouldn't drag her in this." I realize that now. I was wrong.

"Don't you think I know that?" Van's laugh was humorless. "But what can I do? It was the only way."

I stared at her patiently. She was just like me, a victim.

"There is another way," I murmured. "Join me. Be my ally."

"What do you mean?"

I gestured to the door where our future was waiting to be opened. "Let's bring the Queen down together."

The lengthy tale of my past was spoken for the first time. Even Talia and Brooke didn't know how it truly happened, but this stranger, this girl who had suffered as much as I did was brought into light about my identity. Our shared tragedy made me empathize, and by the time my recollection was finished, she too had looked like we'd gone into battle together.

"Unbelievable!" The awestruck expression on her didn't leave. "To think that you're the real princess. But wait. . ." Van squirmed in her seat. "Why didn't you just show up when you turned into an adult and exposed the truth? People would have marched behind you. I know I would."

" It's not that simple." I sighed. "Over the years, the Queen had garnered supporters of her own. If I do what you've suggested, the country will be torn in two. Not only will the stock market plummet down, chaos will reign over as well. My ancestors had worked so hard to make this country into what it is now. I can't let that happen."

"Why did you kidnap the Princess then?"

I gave her a patronizing look. "Because months after, everyone would think Talia is dead. And when that happens, they will willingly give me the throne back because Esmeralda doesn't have a successor. It's a peaceful solution brought by initial mayhem."

Van shook her head. "I still don't understand. Aren't you and Talia lovers? What about your own successor?"

"That's the least of my worries." My smile was cheeky. "The Princess and I can use modern procedures to have a baby. Her mother doesn't have that opportunity because she's old." Besides, I was more worried about telling Talia the whole story. But that was a problem for another day. "So are you in, Vanessa?"

~ 218 ~

"Hell yeah, I'm in!" She winced. "But, uhm, can you remove this rope now? It itches, and I want to move around." The knife was used to cut Van free from the binds, then handed to her without second thoughts. She raised her brows at me. "What do you want me to do with this, Your Highness?" she asked.

"You don't have to call me that."

"Yeah, but I want to."

"Suit yourself." I gestured to the knife, now clasped uncertainly around her fingers. One wrong move and I'd kill her, but we needed to do this. "I want you to swear an oath of fealty to me," I said. "Make me trust you. Erase all my doubts."

Her eyes trailed to the blade, and in a moment of pure confidence, she cut her hair off in one swift motion. "I swear an oath of fealty to you, Your Majesty," she said while the locks of blonde fell on the floor. It was messy, jagged, but the shorter hair that came just about her chin suited her better. She smiled. "My life is yours to command. Your life is mine to protect. I pledge on my mother and father's memories."

"Very well, Van." I crossed my arms. "But just to be clear, Talia is also my life. Serving me means doing the same for her. Are we good?"

"Yes." She dropped the knife before reaching to her stomach. A growl as loud as a lion's purr came out. "Ugh!" she whined. "Can we eat now?"

Now that Vanessa was on my team, I could see that she wasn't menacing after all. A little rough on the edges, but then so was I. "Let's have that wound cleaned first," I said.

The two of us hobbled to the door after getting her up from the chair. Outside the room,

Brooke who was leaning on the opposite wall, straightened to attention. She breathed a sigh of relief upon seeing me, then frowned at the person I was helping.

I ignored her and glanced at Van. "Welcome to my house, Vanessa. We're located in a farm miles from the town. Brooke here will give you a tour after she tends to your wounds."

My best friend placed a hand over her waist. "Why the hell would I treat her?" she snapped. "She's our enemy, remember?"

"Not anymore." I gave Van a little push to Brooke, causing the blonde to almost trip. She clung to my best friend, earning me a curse from the latter.

Van's eyes went to Brooke's cleavage. "Well hello there, sexy."

"Iris," my best friend hissed.

I raised my hands and started to walk in the hallway. "Have fun, you two." The beginnings of their bickering died down when I rounded the corner. My room was just a few ways ahead.

Talia was exhausted when we arrived here hours earlier, so I let her be in the bedroom. I stopped upon reaching the door, my heart hammering unusually fast. What was I going to say to her?

I relaxed. *Don't be such a coward, Cybele. So what if she kissed you? There was no need to be nervous.* I reached a hand to the knob and twisted it open. The Princess was sleeping in the bed.

My breaths were uneven when I went inside and closed the door behind me. Talia was wearing a black nightgown she'd probably borrowed from the walk-in closet. Going closer, I could see the serenity on her face, the way her lips were partly opened like frozen in a mid-sentence. My gaze trailed lower. I swallowed involuntarily.

The Princess 'clothes left nothing to the imagination, especially at the chest part. Her shallow breaths made her breasts move up and down, and looking at them, sweat trickled down my neck, down to the areas I wanted her to touch.

What was I doing? I shook my head. A future Queen, slave to the daughter of her parent's murderers? But I already got down this part, right? Right?

"Cybele?" Talia's eyes opened as she stirred groggily. "What's happening?"

It seemed that I've developed the power to fly, because one moment I was hovering over her, the next I was standing all the way across the room. "N-nothing, Talia. Go back to sleep."

"Are you all right?"

"Yes." I lied. The Princess, as pure as she was, couldn't possibly know. The fantasies she'd given me didn't stop with a kiss.

Chapter 22
Cybele

"You're a naughty woman." Talia's purrs sent goosebumps on my flesh. I stared at her, confused. There was a glimmer in her eyes as she peeled her nightgown off, then let it drop on the floor silently. Only then did I notice that I was sitting in the middle of our bed—hands behind, legs spread apart, mouth agape as the Princess began to grind against me. I reared my head back and moaned.

"Like that?" She smirked when she pushed me down, then began to lift the shirt over my head. I was a mere spectator as she removed my top, twirled it above her head three times, before tossing it somewhere we couldn't reach.

My breaths were ragged. "What are you doing, Talia?"

"Shh."

My eyes darted to her breasts. She'd removed her nightgown but there was still the lacy bra to contend with. Her skin was coated with a fine sheen of sweat.

I cursed under my breath when she cupped my jaw and tilted my face to her. "Don't you want this?" she purred. "Because believe me, baby, I've dreamt of getting inside you for so long."

I fell apart when she bit her lip, but caught the hand that had made its way southward. "Wait."

"What is it?"

It took a moment before I found my voice. Talia was smothering me with her stare. "We have so much to do," I whispered. "There's a Palace to take and bad monarchs to overthrow. And this." I motioned between us. "Is for later. Much later."

"Whatever you say, love."

I couldn't do much when Talia's tongue found my neck. And when her hands glided between my legs, a different kind of flame set me on fire, sending me in ruins, licking me to ashes. I rolled on top of her before we could begin.

"What's going on?" she murmured.

I grinned. "I'm enjoying the royal goods, just like you wanted."

"Yes, but. . ."

The apprehension in her tone made me stop and look at her. The realization was a bucket of ice water on my face.

The Princess and I were sprawled on the floor instead of the bed, one of my hands pushing her shoulder down. Her nightgown was ripped in the middle as if something or someone had torn a Christmas present in a hurry. My other hand that had hovered over her breast was dropped to the side.

The Princess swallowed and said in a small voice. "I heard you moaning and thought you were having a bad dream. You attacked me when I touched your face."

"Oh." I was dreaming.

"But we can continue if you want!" She reddened under the glare of the lamp. "I mean, we could try. . . I mean. . ." She resigned and exhaled. "What do you want to do?"

I pulled myself from her with a heavy breath and stood. The Princess 'eyes narrowed before she took the hand I offered and went to the bed.

"Talia. . ."

"Never mind. Are you coming?" The hurt from my rejection reflected on her face as she draped the comforter over her chest and folded her arms. How could I tell her that we needed to settle down before we progress to the next level though? And furthermore, how do I even do that without my libido stopping me every few seconds? She was temptation!

The bed creaked when I climbed in after the Princess and stayed by her side. And to my delight, the argument in her was lost by the time my head hit the pillow. "What were you dreaming of anyway?" Her tone was gentler.

"Not you," I blurted.

She stilled and slowly turned her head to me.

"Don't tell me you were dreaming about another woman then?" Talia sounded like she'd murder me. "Because clearly, with you moaning, you wanted to have sex."

I flinched and shook my head. "Okay, I lied. I was dreaming about you." She smiled. "But the dream was innocent. We were children, playing. It had nothing to do with sex."

The smile was gone, followed by a roll of her eyes. "Whatever, Cybele," she muttered as she put her back to me. "Don't take me for a fool."

Talia reached over to the one lamp opened in the room, and with a draw of the string, submerged the place into darkness. I couldn't see her anymore, but the tension in her breaths were loud.

My hand hovered to her and stopped. "Can I. . . Can I touch you?" I asked.

I buried my face in my hands when she didn't respond. What the hell was wrong with me?

Talia, despite my shortcomings as a person, had offered herself to me. And what did I do? Nothing. Absolutely nothing but become a scaredy-cat. When it came to her, I was a plate of mashed potatoes. A weakling.

Teasing her when we were in the abandoned castle was one thing, but here? I face-palmed myself. She had the upper-hand, the winning streak. It was as if the role was reversed and she had kidnapped me. The Princess had taken my heart and imprisoned it inside a cage.

"Are you still awake?" Her sudden question almost made me jump. "Cybele?"

I tried to relax. It was just her. "Yes?"

"Please embrace me." Her voice was low now, fragile, all the irritation from earlier gone. "I keep thinking that someone will take me away again," she whispered.

My arms were wrapped around her in a second. "That won't happen. I won't let it. I swear."

"But if it does—if it does, will you come rescue me again?"

"Without a doubt." I tightened my grip over her waist and cocooned her in an embrace that would make her feel safe. "Talia?"

~ 225 ~

"Hmm?"

"Would you. . . Would you like to go out with me one of these days?"

"Like on a date?"

My groans were muffled when I buried my face in her hair. Talia's lavender scent slowed my heart rate a little bit. "Yes," I murmured. "Yes, on a date."

I used to think that things like that were trivial, a waste of time. But now that she was with me again, it felt like I needed to build something between us, catch up on lost time. And then I'd decide how to proceed telling her about Esmeralda. That might be the best solution for now.

"Sure."

One word. One word and I was the happiest ex-Princess, slash ex-kidnapper, slash future Queen in the world. "Goodnight, Princess," I said giddily.

"Dream of me again, My Queen."

A squabble awoke me the next day. The wristwatch I placed on the bedside table said it was already two in the afternoon. I groaned.

Beside me, the Princess was still enveloped in the comforter, a small smile on her lips. And though I wanted to stay there and look at her all afternoon, the shouting match increasing outside the door made me get out of the covers and hurriedly wear my boots. Someone would pay for this.

Brooke and Van ran past the hallway the moment I opened the door. To be more precise, Brooke was limping, while Van was dragging her feet, a dopey smile on her face. I closed the door behind me and followed them to the kitchen. "What's this?" I raised my voice. "Why are you acting like children?"

Brooke grabbed her hair. "Iris!" she shrieked. "Look at what this chav did!" My eyes squinted as I took her in. Only then did I notice the weird gooey mess on her black locks.

On the other side of the room, Van guffawed and raised a squirt gun. *My* squirt gun. "It's only honey." She snickered like a hyena. "It will come off as soon as you wash it. Isn't that right, Your Highness?" She gave me a respectful bow. "Status report. Your best friend and I are playing."

"We're not playing, you freak!" Brooke took out her dagger. "I'm going to slit your throat for ruining my hair!"

"You're so uptight, Brookey."

"I'm not uptight! Cybele's the one who's uptight!"

"That's complete rubbish." Talia looked like a Goddess who'd just rolled out of bed when she stepped into the kitchen too. She crossed her arms and frowned at Brooke. "Cybele is not uptight. She's just sexually frustrated with me."

Brooke flinched and covered her ears. "I don't want to hear that!"

"Jealous much?" Van butted in. She looked from Brooke to the Princess, then back to Brooke again. "Ooh, someone has a crush on Her Majesty."

I scowled. Shit!

Raising my hands, I stepped in the middle of the kitchen before things got out of hand. Talia frowned when I turned to her first. "Please go back to our room and prepare for later," I said. "I'll show you around the farm."

"But—"

"You're in your bathrobe." I cut my eyes at her. Talia's shoulder hunched before she nodded and left.

One down, two to go. I faced Brooke next. "Clean yourself up, eh mate? Van is right. The honey will come off if you wash it with shampoo."

"Iri—"

"I'll talk to her for you."

Brooke pursed her lips and stormed out the other way, leaving me with the prankster. Vanessa was staring at the floor when I finally turned to her.

I shook my head and sighed. "You really shouldn't have done that, Van. Brooke gets commercials because of her hair, aside from the obvious."

"The obvious?"

"Her good looks."

Vanessa scratched her head. The hair that she'd cut yesterday was still unkempt. But it looked good on her, so maybe we should leave it alone. "Do you find her beautiful?" she asked.

"Who? Brooke?" I tilted my head. "I just stated a fact. And you know I'm in love with Talia, right? Where's this conversation going?"

Van stared at the place where my best friend disappeared to, then wiggled her eyebrows at me. "So if I say dibs on Brooke, you won't feel bad about it? I mean, if you want to go for both women. . ." The rest of her sentence trailed into a question mark.

I shuddered at the suggestion. "Look, Vanessa." I gave her a deadpan stare. "There is possibly no way in hell that I'd want to bed both women at the same time. Brooke is like a sister to me." I pointed a thumb to the direction of my room. "Now if you're planning to pursue Talia, then we're going to have a problem. I know it's wrong to brand a person like a cattle, but she's mine. I'm claiming her. And if you step between us, you're going to find your head in the gutter. Clear?"

"Crystal." Van tucked the squirt gun in her pocket like a surrender to war. "Talia is too pretty for me anyhow, and besides, I can smell you all over her."

I raised an eyebrow. "What do you mean?"

"It's just animal talk for she's in heat for you," Van explained. "You can't brand her like cattle, but you can sure leave your mark. I can teach you if you haven't done it."

I turned away from Van before she could search my face. "There's no need for this kind of discussion," I said. "But remember, Brooke is important to me too. I'll skin you alive and have you eat your own flesh if you hurt her in any way." They had no idea what I was capable of.

After ensuring that Van was properly warned and everything was under control, I went to Brooke's room and knocked on the door. It was my duty to know if she was fine.

"Come in. The door is open." I stepped inside and gaped. Brooke was naked from head to foot. Close to the door, she shut it behind me before I could leave. "It's not like you haven't seen it before," she whispered.

I turned my head away. "I'll visit you later," I said evenly. "When you're decent."

Her arm didn't leave my side. It was still barring the door on my back, forcing me to look anywhere but her. "I thought I could give you up," she murmured. Brooke shook her head when I met her stare. "But I was wrong. Iris, it hurts to know that you've slept in the same room, in the same bed with another woman." Her lower lip quivered. "D-did something happen already? With you and Princess Talia?"

My shoulders sagged. I wanted to be honest. "No. Nothing happened." A relieved sigh from her. "But I can't give what you want either, Brooke. I'm sorry."

I lowered her arm before turning around. A knock sounded when I was about to reach the knob. "Brooke?" Talia's voice was loud. "Can we talk?" My eyes were wide with panic as I glanced at Brooke over my shoulder. I quickly locked the door when the knob started to twist. "Hey!" Talia sounded insulted. "What gives? I just wanted to talk."

Brooke hadn't budged an inch when I swiveled around. "Get dressed!" I hissed. "Move!"

Like a puppet tugged on a string, Brooke stared around the room and ran to the bathroom. Her face was white as a sheet when it didn't open to her will. "Oh for God's sake!" She turned to me. "I locked it by accident. My clothes are inside." The walk-in closet could only be accessed through there too, not to mention the windows were barred so I couldn't make my escape.

An idea crossed my mind. "Let's just wait for her to leave."

"I'm not leaving until you come out," Talia said. "I'll wait here all night if I have to. It's time we have a talk, woman to woman."

The Princess would know that something was up if Brooke came out with a blanket wrapped around her. We were quickly heading to a collision course, and there was no way out but honesty. I grasped the knob and inhaled.

Chapter 23
Cybele

"Princess?"

My hand froze before I could open the door. On my back, sweat began to trickle like blood, warm and disturbing. Behind me, Brooke managed a little squeak.

"Yes?" the Princess answered from behind the door. I detected the faint shuffling of feet so she could turn to Van who had called her.

"Erm. . . Her Majesty, Cybele, asked me to offer you food while she attends to important stuff," Vanessa said. "I may not look like it, but I'm a great cook. Why don't you follow me to the kitchen so we can eat?"

I edged closer to the door. What was Van planning?

"Seriously?" Talia said. I could imagine the kind of expression she made: a squint of her eyes with a hint of distrust. While I was glad that she wasn't the type to go with every stranger out there, I wish she'd reconsider just this once. "Do you expect me to just go with you to the kitchen after all you've put me through?"

"Yes."

A chuckle. "Look, Cybele might have trusted you for some weird reason," Talia said. "And Brooke? Well, I don't know what Brooke thinks. But me? Uh-uh. You've locked me up like a psycho for days pretending to be my friend. I'm not surprised if you're a molester too."

"Hey, that's not fair!" Van sounded hurt. "I was only doing what I thought was right."

"Your actions were crap." Talia paused. "In fact, if I can slap you right now, I'll do so without getting guilty."

"Well go right ahead," Van challenged. "I can see now why Cybele gets this look on her face whenever your name is mentioned. You must like it a little rough, don't you, sweet Princess?"

Talia made an incomprehensible sound, following the question. I leaned closer to the door to hear what she'd say. But it was too muffled. Low. I ran a hand through my hair when Van spoke again. "Tell you what, if you go to the kitchen right now, I might be able to remedy that. . . itch. I'm not only good at cooking, Princess. I've picked up a couple of things along the way. I'm sure you'll enjoy it."

Talia's laugh was surprisingly shaky. "R-really? Okay, but only because you look like a lost puppy." Their footsteps faded in the hallway.

"Whew!" Brooke exhaled behind me. "That was close."

I relaxed. But looking at my hands, I noticed that they were pressed firmly on the door, knuckles white as sheet. I let go and shook my head. Blondie had saved me this time. She had perfect timing too. But what were they talking about before they left?

I shook away the odd feeling in my stomach and tilted my head to Brooke. "We won't talk about this incident again." I clutched the knob. "Ever."

After making sure that Talia wasn't just waiting outside the door, ready to tackle me for leaving Brooke's room, I hurried straight to our bedroom and changed into a new top. My hands were still shaking, but I didn't let it get to me as I headed to the kitchen next.

"I'm telling you, Princess, the barn is the perfect place for those kinds of things." Van's voice was awfully low.

I stopped outside the door and frowned.

"The barn?" Talia sounded dubious. "But doesn't it smell there? I've been in enough smelly places to last me a lifetime, including your hideout. And might I ask what happened to your friends?"

"They're not my friends." Van sighed. "They're more of this stupid group I came across with while figuring out what to do with my life. Besides, that's not the issue. Don't you know it's a huge turn on when—Your Highness!" Vanessa knocked over the empty glass on the table when she saw me approach. "I didn't hear you come in."

Neither did Talia, apparently. The Princess went from the counter to the table where scrambled eggs, butter, and slices of bread were already prepared. Van had raided the pantry that Brooke and I had restocked after coming here.

"Where were you?" Talia and I took a seat. On the opposite side of the table, Van smirked. "You didn't follow me to the room earlier," the Princess continued. "And I didn't see you around when I searched."

I hardly spared Talia a glance as I took a bread and a butter knife. She had changed from the silk bathrobe from earlier into a simple white dress. Her hair was tied into a half-crown braid again.

I scowled and buttered the bread. There was the strangest urge to free her hair and curl my hands around it, all while asking what they were whispering about when I wasn't there. "I was in the barn." My face was poker. "The farmer I've previously paid to take care of everything won't drop by in the next few days for our privacy. I fed the animals to keep them healthy."

At the mention of the barn, Van and Talia exchanged excited looks. I dumped more bread onto my plate, then reached for the jar of strawberry jam I hadn't noticed before.

Talia dropped her fork on the table when I stood. "Where are you going?" she asked, face all innocent.

"To Brooke." I lifted the plate and balanced it with the strawberry jar. "We haven't talked in a while. I think I'll go to her and start now." Talia's face soured before I turned around and walked to the door. But I didn't care. If she was keeping secrets, then so was I. Tsk!

Brooke was in the living room when I went in, computer on her lap, checking out the messages in her inbox. I placed the plate on the coffee table in front of her and collapsed in the sofa. It was just like when we were searching for the Princess the other day, except now it was remarkably calm, save for my thoughts.

"I was under the impression that you were mad at me." Brooke glanced at the food that I offered. "No offense, but is that poisoned?"

I rolled my eyes at her. Women could be so melodramatic sometimes, not that I displayed those traits. All right, all right, maybe in moments of weakness.

"You know I can't stay mad at you for long." I nudged my chin at the screen. A picture of us was on the screensaver: Brooke and I on a semi-hug, wearing tight jeans and white t-shirts, smiling at the camera for a modeling campaign years back. "What are you doing?" I asked.

"Messaging our parents." Brooke turned back to the laptop. The screensaver vanished to return to her inbox, and I was left with a severe feeling of unease. "They're okay," she assured. "Your mom was even asking if you've been taking your vitamins. Are you?"

"You mean the vagitamins?"

Brooke's mouth fell open. "Did you just say that?"

"What?"

She burst out laughing and pinched my cheek. "You seriously don't know? Here, let me show you." She glowered. "I'm Iris Prescott, you twats. I'm studying, bugger off!" The accent she used was so off I had to snicker. She scowled and puffed her cheek in another failed attempt to copy me. "I'm going to kidnap the Princess. I'm going to be the bad guy. Ooh, I'm so evil."

I caught the hand she meant to pinch me with again and smirked. "One, I don't sound like that," I said. "Two, is that how you see me? A pudgy criminal with a broken accent?"

"No. But you still like me, right?" She sounded too hopeful for my taste. I had to let go of

~ 236 ~

her. "I'm sorry!" she rushed, then shook her head. "I completely ruined the conversation, didn't I?"

I leaned my head against the cushion and sighed. Here we were again, back to square one.

"I don't want to lose you, Brooke. Not over this."

"Me neither." She mustered a smile. "But I don't know how to move on. You're all I've wanted from the start, Iris. Isn't that pathetic?" I was about to answer again when someone cleared her throat. Turning behind me, I was surprised to see Van staring at us, a silent Talia standing beside her.

"Having a heart to heart talk?" Van folded her arms. I winced but not because of her. Talia had turned to the main door and was leaving faster than I could catch her.

"Wait!" The door slammed closed. Bollocks!

Outside, what little of the afternoon sunlight glared on my face as I walked the grounds. Our location was isolated like my other hideout. With nothing but the forest beyond and the grassland that made up most of the fields, Talia couldn't have gone anywhere but the barn. I hurried towards it.

"Princess?"

The barn door gave at my slightest push. It was one of those red doors that had big letter X's in front. I stepped in and closed it behind me— to be immediately greeted by darkness and shuffling of animal paws.

"Talia?"

I continued onward. The square windows above were the only source of light. But from what little I could see, the barn's interior had been remade, so everything was clean and well-kept even when the slightest smell of animal dung lingered in the air.

Where could she be though? The place was large enough to separate horses, chickens. I stepped back when something blinked. Jesus, it was just a cow.

"Just looking for someone," I murmured under my breath. The surprise from seeing the animal was replaced by a thrill in my spine as I moved along. If I think about it, wasn't this what the Princess and I used to do when we were younger? Play hide and seek?

I frowned and shook my head. Talia looked angry when she left. The prize wouldn't be good.

Rounding the corner, I stopped and stared at the stack of hays unceremoniously dumped at the backmost corner of the barn. But that wasn't what made my jaw hit the floor. It was courtesy of the Princess, standing there amidst the bed of hay, staring at me with the weirdest expression in her eyes.

A gurgle sounded at the back of my throat when her white dress fluttered down. Was I dreaming? Again?

"This is real," she said, answering my unspoken question. A semi-undressed Talia put her hand behind her, and with a tug, showed me everything there was to see up there. She began to slide her panties down, and I was gasping, choking, but unable to take my eyes off her. Every single part. "I'm not going to wait for you anymore." Her voice was husky. "Make love to me, Cybele. Now."

My heart threatened to explode when she spread her arms wide and fell onto the hay. But she didn't stop there. Like a Goddess commanding her servant, she curled a finger and beckoned to me.

"I'm going to count to three," she said, tone businesslike. "If you're not by my side at the end of the count, I'm going to leave."

"Talia—"

"One."

My legs weakened. The Princess knew how to get what she wanted, and I must admit, it was driving me insane how she could easily get in control.

"Two."

My desires were dampened with desperation. She needed to know everything about me first—why I decided to kidnap her and my plans to get the throne back. But would she forgive me knowing what I'd do to her mother? Would she believe me? Or would she push me away, and like a good daughter, extract her own revenge?

"Three."

I forgot everything there was to think about and lunged. The Princess moaned when my tongue slipped into her mouth, the hay around us scattering apart at my descent.

The kiss progressed into a dance while she unbuckled my belt and unbuttoned my jeans. I took her in my arms, pressed onto her, and bit her lip while I straddled her hips.

"Cybele. . ." My name in her mouth was a turn-on, an ignition. Those few seconds of removing my clothes were torture, but after they were gone, I moved my hips so they were grinding onto her pelvis. She met me thrust after thrust, hard. "I thought you didn't want this." She panted. Her neck was shiny with sweat. "That you didn't want me."

I pressed myself to her and gasped. She was fondling my breast now. It drove me crazy. I moaned. "How could I not want you, Talia?" I whimpered. "I've fantasized about this moment every single night since. . ." Since seeing her almost naked in the surveillance camera.

Talia tilted my chin to her, eyes clouded with lust but worried. "Why did you stop?" she asked. "Are you thinking of someone else?"

"No, there's only you."

"Prove it."

She knew I had a thing about challenges. But as I lowered my hand to the wetness between her legs, I knew it was inconsequential in the grander scheme of things. Especially when Talia, even before I touched her, was already writhing with pleasure.

"You want this?" I whispered. "Tell me you do."

"Cybele. . . I can't take it anymore."

"Say please."

"Oh, for the love of!" She gritted her teeth and glared at me. "Please! Fuck me."

That was more like it. But instead of sinking inside her, I shimmied downward, southward, until her arousal hit my nose like a perfume. She grasped my hair when I inched my head closer between her legs. I was about to lick her and taste her when she scratched my back.

That's when I froze.

"Cybele?" Her voice was small, disjointed, no longer there. I clapped my hands on my ears when screams began to sound. Of my mother. My father. Myself.

Talia's eyes were wide and confused when I jumped up and stared down at her. My mouth was still opened. I snapped it close.

Maybe I screamed. I didn't really know. All I understood was the scar on my back was burning. I couldn't look the Princess in the eyes anymore.

"I'm sorry!" I choked back a sob. "I. . . I don't think I can."

Talia gasped when I grabbed my clothes and ran away. The shame in my chest was too much, but it was insignificant compared to seeing a replay of my parents' death, triggered by the only person I knew could heal me.

Chapter 24
Talia

Three days have gone by since Cybele had refused to talk to me. No apologies have been made. No attempts at explanations. Just her leaving me confused and wanting at the barn, the ache between my legs contending with the one she ripped in my chest.

But why? I had to ask myself that.

Over the days, I've run through the possible things that could have turned her off, made her react that way. Was I not sexy enough? Beautiful enough? Did my breath smell bad? What was it? Damn it!

Beside me, Van spoke, "We're going to play a game." Her voice was a gunshot in the kitchen. Everyone stopped eating to glance at her, including Cybele. "The game is called, let's talk to each other before I lose my freaking mind. How about that?" Van smiled wolfishly.

Meanwhile, an encouraged Brooke let go of her knife and placed it on her plate. Her steak was half-eaten, and normally I would do a better job at finishing mine, but for once I had no appetite. "I agree with Van," she said. "This is getting out of hand."

"And fingers. Don't forget the fingers."

Brooke ignored Van's smart attempt to gain her favor, and turned her attention to Cybele. "Iris?" she said. "Do you have anything to say?"

My stomach clenched when Cybele raised her eyes and stared at space. She'd been like that for three days, more or less dead to the world. Dead, frighteningly so, even to me. "Everything is fine," Cybele murmured, turning back to her food. Like mine, her steak was barely touched. Even the wine glass beside her plate was still full. "The food will get cold." She gestured to the table. "Let's eat."

It hadn't been five minutes when Cybele pushed her chair back and suddenly stood. "I'm done," she said, though there was no improvement on her plate. "I need to go out. There are still chores to be finished." And just like the days before, she was already heading out, leaving me and the others to fend for ourselves.

Van grabbed my arm. "It's a great day for a walk, Princess. Excuse us, Brooke." I was dragged outside against my will, too disgruntled to even argue, when I saw Cybele heading towards the forest. But instead of going the other way, Van steered us in the same direction. "Hey!" Van's voice carried far. "Your Majesty! Just wait a second!"

Cybele, now aware that we'd followed her, stopped and turned around. The more we got closer, the more I could see that her eyebrow was up, and her lips, the lips I wanted to crush my mouth to, was parted.

She gasped and reached for me when I lurched out of balance. "What the bloody hell is your problem?" Cybele put a firm grip on my shoulder before whirling to Van. "Why did you push her? Talia could have hit her head!"

"Exactly." Van crossed her arms, no guilt whatsoever. I mean, I could have smashed my face on a rock, but I guess it came with the territory. "I'm glad to know that you still care about the Princess," she said. "You've been ignoring her for the past few days."

Cybele withdrew her hand from me and stared the other woman up and down. "What do you want, Vanessa?" Her eyes narrowed. "Don't you have chores to do? People to bother? Go play with Brooke. I'm busy." After waving us away, Cybele was back to her original intent of going to the forest, but Van I assumed, wasn't done.

"Wait!" Van said.

I glared at her. "What are you doing? Can't you see she wants to go?" I asked.

Van winked at me. "Trust me, Princess. I'm on your side."

Cybele had made it back to us with her nostrils flaring, and had shoved her hands in her pockets in annoyance. I caught the briefest glance of what could be a bookmark. But it was gone before I was sure. She scowled at Van. "I said I was busy, didn't I? What do you want?"

"Princess Talia."

"What did you say?"

Van didn't hide her smile. She stepped forward and wore it like a badge even when Cybele looked like she was about to hit someone. "You're ditching the Princess, aren't you?" Van asked. "I mean, that's the only explanation. You changed your mind."

"Changed her mind about what?" I stared between the two of them. They were locked in this stare-off that only Van seemed to be winning. "Did you hear me?" I said. "What are you talking about?"

"Nothing!"

But Van turned to me at the same time. "I'd like to be your girlfriend," she said.

The field was so silent, I thought I'd gone deaf. But then my heart started to pound. My hands became so clammy that they slipped on Van's shoulder when she pulled me to her. "W-what?" I stammered. "Is this a joke?" I glanced at Cybele and saw that though her jaw had clenched and her hands were balled by her side, she made no attempts to move. I felt my face contort. "Are you serious right now?"

Cybele looked away. But not before I saw the grief and remorse battling in her face. "Talia, I. . ." The muscles in her throat moved as she swallowed. "Maybe it's best if you go with Van. I'm so broken I can't. . . I can't love you the way you're supposed to be loved."

"So, what? You're. . . You're just going to dispose me like a rag doll?" My voice was too high. I couldn't help it. Neither could I help the bitterness in me. Cybele was so willing to give me away even after all we'd been through. "All right, if that's what you want." I grabbed Vanessa's collar and yanked her to me. The woman's blue eyes were stormy as the sea, but her mouth was ready. I gritted my teeth and squeezed my eyes shut.

A roar like thunder sounded just when our lips had brushed together. Opening my eyes, I was aghast to see that Cybele had pounced on Van, was strangling the woman on the ground. "She's mine!" Cybele screamed. "You don't get to touch her! I'm going to kill you!"

My body moved on its own to pull them apart. "Stop it!" I yelled. "Let go of Van! She's choking!"

"No!"

"What in blazes is going on?" A new voice, a sane voice, had called and was rushing to us before I could help it. Brooke pushed Cybele out of the way and knelt beside Van. The blonde was gasping, coughing, but otherwise alive. Brooke helped her up and gave Cybele a dirty look. "Sort yourself out, mate! You're becoming a menace!" She helped Van hobble back to the barn.

Cybele and I spent minutes just standing there, gazing everywhere but at each other. An invisible wall separated us again. I though nothing would come between us after she rescued me.

"Hey. . ."

As always, I was the first one to crack. Damn her and her prideful royal blood.

Cybele didn't answer, but I knew she was listening, so I just continued telling her how I felt, or what I could say while my lips trembled anyway. "I thought you cared for me. Was that all a lie?"

Her expression closed up. Like earlier, her hand went to her pocket, and what I could have sworn to be some kind of paper was touched then slipped away. Cybele took a sharp breath before staring at me. Her eyes, a forest green, made me feel untamed, free, but bothered. "I care for you." Her voice was thick. "But I'm so damaged, I don't want to give you broken goods."

I exhaled, long and hard. Was that how she thought of herself? Something to be discarded away?

No sooner had she made the confession did I reach her side and cradled her cheek. She surrendered to me and sighed. "I'll fix you," I whispered. "Whatever this is, I'll fix you."

Cybele didn't shy away when I drew her to me, nor did she stop my face from going closer to hers. And when our lips met for the third time, her hands enveloped me in an embrace. Her tongue, playing with mine, made me want something more. But then she stepped away, with a smirk this time. "You're getting good," she said, eyes going to my lips.

I snorted. "Was that really a compliment, darling? I thought I was already good the first time?"

An awestruck look flashed on her face. Whether the cause be the term of endearment or our kiss, I wouldn't really know. She shook her head as if waking up from a good dream and pointed towards the forest. "I wasn't lying when I said I wanted to go. Would you like to come with me, Princess?"

"Is it a date?"

Her nose pinked. "W-well, yeah. And consider it a tour too." I chuckled when she turned around. More so when she stumbled forward. What I would do to see that every day. "Give me five minutes," she said.

Cybele returned with a lovely black mare that was saddled and ready to be ridden. "Woah!" I gushed, my hands moving up to pet the horse. It whinnied and made low noises, but didn't buckle up to turn me away.

Cybele gestured to it. "Did they let you ride on your own?" she asked.

"In the Palace?"

Her nod was hesitant.

Cybele and I haven't broached the subject since my rescue, but I didn't want to ruin the moment by saying something that could set her off again. We'd just gotten back to talking.

I shrugged. "Sure, one or two times. I even have my own steed named Jessie."

Her eyes widened. "Jessie?"

"Yeah, after that song." My own heart galloped when Cybele suddenly scooped me up and chuckled. Sometimes it was great that she was taller than me. "Why are you so happy?" I asked. "Did I say something?"

She lowered me down. "Nothing in particular, Talia. Come on. Let's ride together."

The difference between the Stableman in the Palace and Cybele was night and day. First, the Stableman wasn't allowed to touch me while he was riding behind. Second, every breath of his didn't send me tingles. Cybele, in the meantime, had given me a heart attack when she sat behind and took over the reins. With me in front, I was sheltered between her arms, tucked away in the softness and the scent of green tea.

"Enjoying yourself?" Her question was a tickle on my ears.

"Yeah." I leaned to her. "Any particular destination in mind?"

"You'll see." She tugged the reins, commanding the steed to go faster.

After a while, the makings of a tree presented itself in the distance. It was no ordinary tree. It was huge. The kind that you'd only read about in a wonderful fairytale, or perhaps see in a documentary. It looked to be fifty years old.

"Wow!"

"I know." Cybele commanded the horse to slow until the strong gallops that whipped my hair back earlier, were no more but trots. "I found the tree the other day," she explained. "I was hoping we could go back together."

I smiled to myself when Cybele made the horse stop and jumped down, then offered me a hand for help. She hadn't spoken to me in three days, but she still thought of bringing me here.

I took her hand and got down. "It looks magical."

"It is." Cybele guided me to the tree. It was bigger up front, with a trunk that was possibly longer than a car, and a height that reached to the sky. My lips opened when she parted the curtain of vines that surrounded it. There was a hollow inside, a compartment. Cybele motioned to it. "The place is safe. There aren't any snakes inside. I checked yesterday if they had a nest nearby."

I wasn't worried about snakes or animals hiding there, but was more excited to explore. Cybele let me go in first, let me feel the cool space on my own, let me glance up and see the holes that made way for the light, so there was still brightness even when we were inside.

"I like it," I said, turning to her. Cybele wasn't listening though. She was slowly unbuttoning her blue shirt.

"Don't be scared," she murmured, as her bare shoulders began to make an appearance. Cybele shook her head as if willing me to think of other thoughts. To not concentrate on her sizable chest, or how the lace covering it could be torn apart by a simple tug.

I swallowed. "Are you making up for the barn?"

The shirt fell down. "No." She turned around. "Look at me."

I wanted to say that it was impossible not to look at her. To ignore her skin. To refrain from fantasizing. But then something else caught my eyes, a scar so discreet I only noticed it because of the light.

"What's this?" Cybele's shoulder blades rose and fell as I traced the scar on her back. She made no answer, and I assumed. "Did you hurt yourself? An accident perhaps?" Would that explain the foul behavior she displayed? The hatred she lashed out? My stomach twisted. My mother's words found its way into my memory. The tragedy. The fire. Cybele's disappearance. My head was suddenly spinning.

"I didn't know how to tell you." Cybele's voice was barely above a whisper. "But you need to know everything about me. After this, I will never lie or keep secrets from you again. I swear."

Her assurances calmed me, but the ramifications of them did not. I gasped when she turned to me, squeaked when she clutched my arms. "Wha—"

A gunshot cut me off. Not one, but three succeeding sounds. Cybele and I stared wide-eyed at each other. "Get dressed!"

Two minutes later, she was pulling me out of the tree, fully dressed but a mess. She was reluctant to let go, but I yanked my arm away, so she couldn't do anything but give me a frustrated sigh.

"S-sorry," I said. "I don't like being restrained."

She nodded. "All right, but here's the plan. We ride the horse and get out of here as fast as we can. I have another—"

"Wait a minute." I stopped her. "What do you mean get out of here? That sound came from the farmhouse. We need to go back."

Cybele forked a hand through her hair, as I knew she would. But her next statement came out as a surprise. "We won't go back," she said. "I need to keep you safe."

"But our friends are there!"

"They know how to defend themselves."

"No!" I couldn't believe this. She'd just leave them there? "If you're not coming back, then you have to watch my ass from out here because I will," I said. "You can't stop me."

A frightening look passed her face. "Don't say that, Princess. You know I can."

"Oh get over yourself for one second!" She gasped when I pinched her nose. "This is no time to argue. Let's just ride the horse and go back."

Cybele's eyes narrowed while she rubbed her reddening nose. There was something suspicious in the way she looked at me, but then she had taken my hand again and was guiding me to the steed. "I steer," she said. "You sit there and look pretty."

I snorted at her. "As if."

The mare galloped in the forest for the second time today, but faster and more harried with me on command. Behind me, Cybele's breaths were strained and fast, reflecting what I felt inside.

What happened back there? Was it just an accident? And for the love of God, were our friends all right?

Chapter 25
Cybele

Talia and I have been riding the horse—five, maybe ten minutes of torture. It wasn't because I hated having her steer. The Princess was a good rider. She was better in me in some ways, but when it came to her own safety, I was seriously having second thoughts. We were supposed to go the other way, not towards disaster.

"Faster!" Talia said, her boot nudging the horse. How was I supposed to tell her to turn around now? She was too set on going back.

"Talia."

"Yes?"

"We don't know what's waiting for us out there," I said. "And frankly, I don't want to find out."

The Princess 'back turned rigid, ice-like almost, before she sighed and glanced at me over her shoulder. The woman I loved displayed nothing but strength. But that was how she almost burned herself alive because of Van. I would not risk the same mistake.

"Brooke is your best friend, Cybele. How can you say that?"

"It's exactly because she's my best friend that I know she can take care of herself."

Talia scowled. "And I can't?"

"I'm not saying that, Princess. All I'm saying is—watch out!"

It was too late when I saw a rope being pulled, taut and strong in front of the horse. I tried to grab onto Talia, any part of her, but I was thrown upward, forward, then downward.

"Ugh!" Every part of me screamed in pain. My back, my neck, and with my eyes still closed, I didn't know what the damage was, but someone was nice enough to lift me up.

Whoever it was gripped the back of my shirt, dragged me on the grass, and continued while I remained dizzy. Questions started piling in my head. *Where was I? What happened? And more importantly.* My eyes snapped open when I thought of the Princess. The man behind me looked nothing like her.

Not waiting to find out who, I grabbed the man's arm and twisted it so he was forced to kneel beside me. The tell-tale uniform made my blood boil. How did they find us? Where was the Princess?

Something struck the back of my head.

It was twilight when I came about. The sky was a fiery red. But something was off, maybe it was the smell. The disturbingly familiar scent of something burning made me cry out, sit, and stare around. The farm and barn were on fire. "Your Majesty!" Van's voice lured me to the right. Three soldiers were tying her up, two of them gripping her arms and legs so she couldn't get away. "They shot Brooke!" she yelled. "She's badly hurt!"

My teeth snapped in anger, but I wasn't given time to do something about it. Four people immediately surrounded me, grabbed my feet, and clutched my hands. I was about to kick them away when a knife was placed over my throat. But that wasn't what made me stop. It was the deep, hateful voice that followed. "Talia will be in our possession soon." A throaty chuckle. "Her mother will be most pleased to see her."

The demon who said it went to Van and pointed a gun on the blonde's head. And just like that, I couldn't do a thing about Ronaldo.

Older but viler, his chuckle progressed to a full-blown laugh. "Well, well, if it isn't the fallen one. Who would have guessed?" My hands were pulled behind me to be tied. My legs were brought together for the same fate. Beside Ronaldo, Vanessa's mouth was being gagged. The monster laughed again. "I see you've made some friends, Cybele. What else have you been up to these past few. . ." He shrugged. "Forget it. Who's counting?"

Who's counting? Who's—I squeezed my eyes shut. This was exactly what he wanted, for me to lose control. I wouldn't give him the satisfaction. Not to this murderer. Certainly not to his false Queen.

I was relatively calm when I was gagged: like a statue with no feelings left. Van, meanwhile, continued to strain against her captors, giving them a hard time, trying to escape.

My thoughts raced for a plan. Anything that could help us right now would be magnificent. Brooke?

My stomach lurched.

In the heat of things, I've almost forgotten.

Ronaldo didn't lower the gun when I was completely subdued. Instead, he pointed it to me.

~ 255 ~

"Can't blame me, right?" His cold eyes gleamed. Wherever he went, there was fire and destruction, and the structures behind him were beginning to fall apart due to the flames. He smiled. "You really had me fooled back there. I thought I'd gotten rid of you back in the villa."

The other guards had no idea of the abomination he was talking about. But Van did. She struggled some more.

Ronaldo gave her a look of disgust. "The people you consider friends these days, Cybele. Your mother and father would be very disappointed."

I concentrated on his face. At the lines on his forehead, the sharp angle of his jaw. Even the stars on his uniform became a distraction. Anything to keep my mind from doing irrational things.

"Can you imagine what they would say if they see you right now?" Ronaldo walked back and forth, one hand to his side. The gun on the other hand never left my face. "Kidnapper. Traitor. Who knows what else?"

His speech was paused only when footsteps sounded in the field, followed by the emergence of a guard wearing the same uniform as them. The guard saluted at Ronaldo and came forward. The two of them talked in hushed tones while Vanessa and I communicated with our eyes. There was nothing but anger in hers.

After a few seconds, Ronaldo had turned to us again, and with a signal of his hand, issued a command. Vanessa and I were brought to our feet, and would be carried to a truck from the looks of it.

"You there. Guards." Ronaldo wasn't even kind enough to know his subordinates names. He would rid of them in a heartbeat. And he had the galls to call me a traitor. "Bring the blonde to the truck. The rest of you, ready the other car for the Princess." He glanced at me. "Leave the girl. I will escort her myself."

A sinking feeling in the pit of my stomach made my legs weak, especially when they began to drag a struggling Vanessa, and having the prospect of the Princess being captured weighted on my shoulders. Still, I straightened my back and held my head high when Ronaldo came to me.

"Still stubborn like your mother." He looked at me from head to foot. "But I doubt you'll last after I'm done with you. Believe me." He turned around, and as if remembering something, snapped his fingers and stared at me again. "Oh, and I won't hesitate to blow your head, or that blonde's head for that matter, just in case you're thinking of escape."

Ronaldo made it his personal mission to guard us while traveling. Van and I had been forced to sit at the back of the pickup truck while he looked over us, gun in his hand.

The convoy came to a full stop after hours of discomfort. And even though I could barely see where we were from the back, my other senses told me everything I needed to know. We were back in Harland's Palace. Back to my stolen home.

"Up!" Ronaldo motioned the gun to us while barking his order. Immediately after that, the truck's door opened, followed by the salute of a waiting soldier.

"Sir, Queen Esmeralda has been informed that you're here." The soldier glanced at us. "What would you have us do to the others?"

Ronaldo jumped down. But he didn't lower his gun as if he took great joy in wagging it to our noses. "I'll show them to their accommodations," he said. "Tell the Queen I'll follow in a minute."

"Yes, sir."

Ronaldo turned to us when the guard disappeared. "I almost forgot." The corner of his mouth curled up into a gloat. "Welcome home, Cybele. Harland sends its regard."

Vanessa gnawed on her gag while Ronaldo pushed and prodded us to move forward. All those times, I kept my gaze at my feet, dread and shame washing over me as we walked down the grounds.

What could I say? I've failed my parents. I've failed myself. Heck, I've failed Talia and everyone who was counting on me.

"In there," Ronaldo yapped, then shoved Vanessa to a door. It was the only time I glanced up. We were facing a narrow hallway.

I blocked Van's path the next time she was pushed, to Ronaldo's utter chagrin. "What do you think you're doing?" He stepped towards me. But Vanessa, eyes blazing, turned to him and shielded me. Ronaldo sneered. "Is that how it is? Do you honestly think the two of you can protect each other?" A laugh bubbled from his throat. "Nothing you say or do will change the outcome, Cybele. Now walk."

"Ugh. . ." Van's wails filtered the dungeon cell where we were put in. There wasn't even a bed. Only a small mat was on the floor and a basin to pee in. She turned to me. "I thought this was your Palace? How come there's a dungeon? How barbaric is that?"

I settled my head on the wall and sighed. Everything was cold and musty: from the floor, to the wall, to the frozen organ beating in my chest. "This building initially started as a monastery in the 7th century," I explained. "It was in the 13th century, during the crusades, that it was converted into a Palace for our family. Of course, there would be a dungeon."

"Is that so?"

"Uh-huh."

"I want to know something else." Van grinned when I raised an eyebrow. "Have you ever personally brought a girl here to be paddled?"

"Van. . ."

Her nervous laugh echoed around us. "I'm sorry," she murmured, dropping beside me. "This is me trying to cover my guilt. You should have left me in the farm while you had the chance."

"I was planning to." My head lowered. "If it wasn't for Talia—" Goodness, I was just like her mother after all.

"The Princess wasn't there when Waldo was threatening to blow my head off," Van said, as if reading my thoughts. "So yes, Your Highness, you're still a better Queen than Esmeralda will ever be. Raise your head and be proud."

She was about to say more when a screech from the cell gates made us look. Ronaldo, a guard accompanying him, swung the bars open and made his way inside. He lifted a familiar black choker before I could move.

"Where's Talia?" I tried to calm myself when he leaned on the door. To pretend as always that I wasn't affected. But damn it was hard.

"I'll tell you in a while," Ronaldo said. "But first, you will tell me how you managed to kidnap her from this Palace, right under my nose."

Van rose from the floor, fist waving at him. "Go to hell, Waldo! We tell you nothing!"

He barely paid any attention to her. "Cybele, Cybele, you know what's going to happen, right?" He turned to the man beside him and clapped a beefy paw on the soldier's shoulder. "Leave us for a while. I will question the prisoners."

"But, sir. Harland's rules states that—"

"Yes, I am well-aware that interrogations should be done in the presence of the Queen and a guard." Ronaldo's smile was quick. "But this woman and I go way back. We're just catching up."

The guard, while looking doubtful, nodded to him and retreated to the gate. The moment he left, Ronaldo brandished his gun for the hundredth time and waved it to us like a bully. "As I was saying, Cybele, you know what will happen."

"And what is that, fatso?" Van had either not seen the gun or was doing a good job at pretending she wasn't scared. Whichever it was, I pulled her down so she was squatting beside me.

"Easy," I whispered. "You know what he did to my parents."

"All the more reason to stick that gun in his farty hole."

"Just let me talk first." I glared at Ronaldo. The choker in his other hand was proof that he was trying to bait me with Talia. See what other interest I had with her. But I had no intention of them ever finding out. "One of your soldiers let me in," I said to him. "You can check the records. A man named Johnny Stinson was kind enough to be bribed, so I can slip inside the Palace and do what I want back then. Question him yourself if you want, but I doubt he'll say he knows me."

Van squeezed my hand. She sensed that I was lying. But it was a well-crafted alibi that only came to mind. As I was checking the records a few months back to infiltrate this place, I realized that a few of the guards were doing illegal activities too. Johnny was one of them, and this was my punishment to him.

Ronaldo's head tilted to the side while he considered my statement. "I'll double-check that claim," he said eventually. "But you wouldn't lie about this. You're too honorable like your father."

Wrong. Whatever honor I had died with my real parents. I was a woman of revenge. He shouldn't expect more.

Ronaldo's eyes flickered. "You really surprised me when I saw your face earlier. To think you were alive all this time, Cybele." He shook his head, impressed or disgusted; I didn't care. "But none of that matters today," he went on. "Guards!"

At his sharp call, six guards clambered down the hallway, towards the cell bars where we could see them. Van's hands trembled when she stood, but her eyes were alert when she looked at me. "Where are they taking us?"

"To execution," I answered.

My brain worked double-time while we marched up the winding stairs, all the way to a brightly lit corridor that almost blinded me. Van and I could probably fight our way through the guards, but what about Talia? Would they have left her in the bedroom or was she taken somewhere else?

"Your Highness!" Van's terrified voice followed me from behind.

What could I do to save us? Why was it so hard to think when a gun was pointed at my temple?

"Go inside." Ronaldo pressed the gun to my head so I was forced to enter the throne room. This one gave me déjà vu, and an overwhelming rush of anger. "My Queen." Ronaldo bowed at the presence of the woman in the throne. *My* throne. "I have found the defendant to be guilty. She is ready to receive the punishment as given by Her Majesty."

"Very well." The voice that spoke wasn't Esmeralda's though, nor any of the female guards who stood to watch. It was from the double doors that opened to admit yet another person. A woman who should have been by my side but had walked past us to bow at her mother. "Good evening everyone." Talia turned with a wicked smile on her face. "I, Princess Talia of Harland, is sentencing this traitor to work as my personal maid. You never should have kidnapped me, Cybele."

Chapter 26
Cybele

Anyone who had been inside Harland's Palace would testify how long of a stretch its hallways could get. It was hard to clean, especially when only two people were up for the task.

"I can't believe we're scrubbing the floor right now." Van groaned beside me. She dipped her brush in the bucket, made sure it was foamy enough, then began to attack the marble like we'd been doing for the past hour. "Ugh! I hate this! Why couldn't they have just sent us back to the dungeon?" She took a disinfectant spray and spritzed the floor. "I'm down for it if it was me. But Esmeralda has no right to do this to you. Poser!"

I followed Van's lead and made my own sponge foam. It was the first time in my life that I had to clean something as massive as this. Even the former hideouts weren't hard to tidy. But I guess there was a first to anything.

"Aren't you even going to say something?" Van made a face.

"Like what?"

"I don't know." Bubbles popped in the air when she threw her hands up. "Aren't you mad? Doesn't this make you feel disgusted?"

"I am mad and disgusted." Her forehead creased when I dumped the sponge in the bucket. "But I'm not doing this for Esmeralda."

"Who are you doing it for then? The almighty Princess Talia?" Van batted her lashes before folding her arms. She'd soil her uniform that way. We'd only been given two sets of black and white, as the standard for whoever had to work here. "FYI," she continued. "Princess Talia was the one who got us into this mess."

"She has her reasons." Van still didn't look convinced. "Listen," I said, pointing to the floor. "This? This isn't Talia."

"Of course it's not, Your Highness. It's a good ol 'floor."

Van was still snickering when I looked at her. "The point is, she's probably doing this to save our hides. Or Esmeralda could have said some things. Manipulated her in some way. What we need to do is. . ." Van and I paused. Someone was coming towards us, walking at a brisk pace. Van and I busied ourselves with the floor, until someone kicked the bucket down.

"Oops." Talia was covering her mouth when I raised my eyes. She shrugged. "Guess you missed that spot. Do it again."

"Wait!" I said when she turned around. My skirt was getting soaked with dirty water, but I drew closer in an attempt to talk. We hadn't been given the chance since last night.

"Yes?" Talia glanced at me over her shoulder. Her eyes took me in before she smirked. "What do you need, maid?"

I stopped Van before she grabbed the Princess 'leg. The woman could be an animal sometimes. "Get a grip, Van." I turned to Talia. "What's your plan?"

"Yes, Princess. Do tell." Ronaldo's footsteps were heavy and deliberate, but I didn't notice him until he was standing beside Talia, leering at us. "What's the grand plan?"

"I don't know." The Princess met his stare. "Is there supposed to be one?"

An awkward silence fell over us, with just the constant ticking of someone's watch, a reminder that time was moving. Finally, Ronaldo leaned back. "You may have your mother fooled, but I'm not convinced," he said. "Cybele was your best friend, was she not?"

"*Ex* best friend." Talia stood to full height. "And what right do you have to question me? Hmm?" The Princess stared him up and down. "You're just a guard here. Know your place, servant."

"Yeah," Van butted in. "You hear that, Waldo? Burn!"

His venomous smile could kill someone, especially when he turned to me. "You and your friend shouldn't be complacent, Cybele. The Palace has eyes and walls. Do something out of place, and your head is up for the guillotine."

"You old fart!" Van said.

"That's enough!" Talia motioned to the hallway. "I believe you have your own duties to attend to, Ronaldo. My maids are no different. They still have to clean."

"I'll leave them to it then." Ronaldo made a sweeping bow to the Princess. "But I still wonder what happened while you were kidnapped that made you a changed woman. Did she torture you that much?"

"I told my mother this. Who said I have to do the same with you? You're nothing." Talia stuck her nose in the air. "You may leave us now. Tell my mother I will be studying in the library. In peace."

Ronaldo had vanished in the distance when I rose from the floor and took the Princess by the arms. "Talia."

"Don't touch me!" My mouth fell open when she pushed me back. Even more when she produced a handkerchief from her pocket and wiped the arm where my hand used to be. "You're filthy. I don't want to be associated with you."

"Princess, you are one insult away from being choked slammed." Van stood up too. "Because I swear to God I'll go WrestleMania on you if you say that one more time."

Normally, I would be all over them right now, reprimanding them for acting like children. But not this time. Because this time, Talia had done it on her own. "Do you think I consider you my friends?" she said. "Do you think I really loved you, Cybele?" Talia dropped the handkerchief and kicked it to me. "Well tough luck. I lied to myself to survive." She gestured to the floor. "Clean that mess. I have an important guest I don't want to disappoint."

"Important guest, she said. Don't want to disappoint, she said." Van peeked behind the tree and scowled. "It's just a rich cocky boy. Are you seeing this?"

How could I not? The whole Palace was abuzz today, especially when a tall, curly-haired guy stepped into the hallway. And if that wasn't a red flag, the moment he took Talia to the garden sent a kettle blowing in my head.

~ 267 ~

"Who is he?"

"I believe his name is Lancelot," someone answered Van. The two of us turned to a striking brunette with wide chocolate brown eyes. She was wearing a green dress, but more than that, she was wearing a smile. Her hand went between us for a shake. "Alessandra. Nice to meet your acquaintance," she said.

Van took one good look at the woman and swiveled around. "No more pretty girls," she murmured to herself. "Brooke is not dead. She's just waiting for me."

Alessandra frowned when Van left us, before finally facing me. "What's up with her?" she asked.

I shrugged. But my mood was on a steady decline, if not for the situation, then the worries that were brought up with the mention of Brooke.

Alessandra, to my surprise, took my hand and shook it. "It's rude to keep a woman waiting." She winked. "Isn't that right, Queen Cybele?" Alessandra put a finger on my lips and smirked. "Shh. Call me Alex. And you may not remember me because I'm three years older. But I guarantee. You've grown hot as hell."

She giggled when she finally released me, then stepped back so I could take a better look at her. *Alex. Alessandra. Where had I heard that name before?*

"Exactly," she said first. "We were playmates. Don't you recall?"

The corner of my mouth tugged up. "Alessandra Bernini? Only daughter of the Earl in the next county. Smart but a resident flirt. To what do I owe the pleasure?"

Her bejeweled hand went to my face. Alessandra had always made the adults uncomfortable, especially when she'd tease and laugh at men twice her age. But they couldn't do a thing as the Earl was fond of her.

She looked disappointed when I stepped away. "You don't seem thrilled to see my face again."

"And you don't seem surprised to see mine." I watched her reaction. "Wasn't I supposed to be dead? The small Princess, burned in the fire?"

She paused for a while. Let's see how she could worm her way out of this. Was her family involved with the murder of mine? I could kill her with my bare hands if need be. She sighed. "Don't look at me like that. Truth is, I was shocked out of my wits when Esmeralda called me today. If I'd known you were alive, I would have been the first to search for you. I swear."

Her words were meaningless. So were the promises of each and every nobility in this land. They couldn't protect me. I had no one to trust but myself. "Who else knows?" I asked.

"About you?" Alessandra shook her head. "None, as far as I know. And Lancelot, if you remember him, was too young when your parents were around. He's the oldest son of the Marquis. But he lived so far from here, they could only go once a year to your parties."

"I see." But I still didn't believe her. Esmeralda wouldn't allow Alessandra to see me unless there was an ulterior motive. And sad as it was, everyone always had ulterior motives. "I have duties to attend to," I excused. "I'll see you around."

Alessandra was quick to catch my hand. She tugged me to her. "Your duties are with me, Cybele. Come and I'll explain."

Alessandra dragged me away from the tree, straight to the place that I wanted to avoid. Talia's eyes flickered to us when got there, but it was Lancelot who addressed us. "Is it time for tea?"

"Nope." Alessandra pushed me down, then took the seat next to mine. "We're here for the Queen's orders."

I took the opportunity to examine the man just as he turned to study me. His face wasn't bad. So were his stormy blue eyes. But everything about him would look more remarkable when stabbed with a fork. Where was Van when I needed her?

"Pleased to meet you," Lance said. "What's your name again?"

"Cybele," Talia answered. "My maid."

"My fiancé too," Alessandra chimed in. "Or has the Queen forgotten to tell you?"

The silence that ensued was broken only by a cough. Lance's. "Your what?" He openly gaped at Alessandra. It wasn't even funny. "When were you planning to tell me this? We're supposed to be friends."

Alessandra shrugged and shifted to Talia. The Princess had not said anything. "Won't you offer your congratulations to us, Princess? It's because of your mother that I'm marrying Cybele. I'm sure you were informed of this."

"No." Talia's gaze flitted to me. "Were you?"

"No," I said.

Alessandra put a hand on top of mine. We all glanced at her when she began to chuckle. "It seems like I'm not going to have a congratulation after all. But regardless, I will still give you mine. Congratulations, Princess, I heard your wedding with Lance is pushing through next month. Your mother told me you insisted it yourself."

"You what?" My voice was so loud that Talia flinched when I shouted at her. But that didn't stop me. My chair toppled on the grass as I pushed it away to stand. "What did you do?"

Alessandra rose and touched my arm. "Calm down," she said. "Guards are nearby."

"I don't care about the guards!" I yelled. "Tell me this isn't true, Princess!"

Talia's head was low so I couldn't see her eyes. But when she raised it, nothing but bitterness was in her. She even had the galls to stand up to meet me. "Every moment I spent in that rotten castle you called your home was a nightmare," she whispered. "You made me clean. You made me weak. You even tried to rape me."

"Talia!"

"Wasn't it true, Cybele? Tell them you didn't make me close my eyes in your room, lay on the bed, and ask me to touch you. Tell them that's not true."

"You wanted that!"

~ 271 ~

"No. *You* wanted that." Talia sat down. "You kidnapped me in hopes to demean my mother, and now I'm going to do the same to you. Congratulations with your engagement. Consider it a punishment."

Chapter 27
Cybele

If there was one thing, I was thankful for in this whole ordeal, it was that most of them left me alone in my misery. To wallow in my despair over the last few days, with the exception of one.

Van placed a tray beside me by the pond and began to unpack the food. She'd brought me a sandwich, an apple, and a bottle of water, which she had now fully uncapped before offering to me. I shook my head. "It's clean, I swear to God." She sniffed the water and offered it to me again. "Ronaldo didn't pee on it."

Her silly attempts to make me smile worked a little. She beamed when I took the bottle and sipped, then she started to work on the sandwich.

"Mama chicken will feed you now," she said to me. "Say ahh!"

"Vanessa."

"I'm not emotionally equipped for rejections. Just say ah."

There was ham in the sandwich. A bit of bacon and cheese too. Van and I were silent while she fed me. From an heir of the throne to an incompetent fool. How easily I had fallen.

"Sometimes I'm still wondering why you haven't killed the Queen yet." Van was unblinking when she crumpled the tissue. It was tossed to the tray before the apple was retrieved. "Slash her throat or something. That would solve our problems."

"Don't you think I haven't thought of that?" I pushed her hand away. The color of the fruit was making me nauseous. "Why'd you think I kidnapped Talia instead of stabbing Esmeralda? Because she's always surrounded by guards. That's why. And we won't be able to get into her room at night. Apart from the CCTV, Ronaldo sleeps there."

"Eew!" Van covered her ears. "Can we not talk about that?"

"What else is there to discuss?"

"Escape." Van wiped the apple on her uniform and took a bite. She continued to talk while chewing. "I don't think the Princess is going to cancel her engagement anytime soon. So, what are we still doing here? You're not planning to marry that Alex girl, are you?"

" No. But I'm not planning on escaping either. Talia is. . ." I sighed. Talia was my one and only chance to secure the throne, and with her marrying Lancelot, she not only squashed my chances, she delivered my execution too. I turned away from Van to stare at the pond. "Everything I've worked for has failed. Go home, Vanessa. You still have your chance."

"And break my oath by leaving you here? Nah-uh." She grasped my shoulder and squeezed. "Look at you. You're letting this whole thing weigh you down. Talia is just a woman. There are loads more out there."

But none of them was *her*. That was the point. None of them could make my heart run and slow down, almost like music.

~ 274 ~

Van chucked the core of the apple to the tray and wiped her mouth. "Listen to me saying that," she mumbled. "I can't even take my mind off Brookey. Do you think she's all right?"

A different kind of worry stabbed my chest. A week of being here and I have neither talked to Brooke nor knew her whereabouts. The last thing we heard of was her getting shot in the barn. What if the bleeding was severe?

I shook the awful thoughts away and faked a smile to Van. "Brooke is a smart girl. She's probably out there right now, recovering from this mess. Don't worry too much."

"If you say so." Van took the tray and stood. "By the way, Your Highness, we need to go to the garden in fifteen minutes. Princess Talia has requested us to serve her tea. And I personally do not want to miss the chance to make her angry."

Fifteen minutes later, and a teapot in both our hands, Vanessa and I stood next to the table where Talia and Lance were having their afternoon biscuits. The Princess ignored me, as she'd been doing since the confrontation with her engagement.

If only I could talk to her for just a second, single her out. But every time I tried, something or someone would come between us. There was never a moment when she wasn't watched by guards.

"More water please," Lance drawled with a bored tone. He and Talia weren't speaking at all. They were just there eating biscuits.

"Didn't you hear him?" Talia snapped her fingers to me. "Serve him tea. What are you waiting for?"

~ 275 ~

Van came forward and began serving in my stead. Lance cried out after a second. "Ow! Ow! Hot!"

Van snickered while she righted the teapot. "Sorry. My bad."

"Your bad?" Lance pulled the soaked shirt from him. "What kind of maid are you? You could have burned me alive!"

"It's a freaking water, not the gates to hell, you pipsqueak."

I turned to Talia while the two continued to argue. Her gaze was far away. Her lips were pressed together. She might have felt me looking because her eyes flickered to me. "Cybele?"

"Y-yes?"

It was the first time she spoke my name in days. She'd barely given me a second glance. "You're blocking my sunlight. Get out of my sight."

Van and Lance stopped whatever they were saying and turned to us. Meanwhile, my hands curled beside me. Talia could be planning something. My heart wished she did. But these insults were uncalled for.

"Is that what you wish? For me to get out of here?" I asked.

Her grey eyes went to the distance. A wave and a nod later, and I realized what she'd done.

Van snarled at the Princess. "You're calling the guards on us? How original." The woman grabbed my hand. "Let's go, Your Highness. It's obvious we're not needed here. And

I'm sick and tired of talking to these jerks. They don't see us for what we are. Superstars."

Vanessa eventually left me alone after I've insisted for the millionth time that I was all right. It was the biggest lie I've ever told. After ensuring that she wouldn't follow me, I snuck to the library—one of the largest rooms in the Palace or maybe even the whole of Harland. Few people went there. But I was no stranger to the high ceiling and walls upon walls of bookshelves that filled the space.

"Why didn't I come here sooner?" I murmured.

Simple. Because I was too preoccupied of the Princess, revenge, and her mother, that I've almost forgotten my real self, traded my passion for retaliation. Would my dead parents be proud?

My footsteps echoed on the floor as I went further inside the library. The place smelled of wax, paper, and memories. The balcony on the second floor called out to me.

"Books again?" Six-year-old Talia glanced up. She was standing beside me, looking up. "Cybele, can't we just play in the garden?"

"In a moment. I want to show you something." Ten-year-old Cybele took something from the shelves, came running down the stairs, and had an excited gleam in her eyes as she placed the large book on the table. "I found this yesterday. Look." The book was opened, flipped through, until it stopped on a page where two women were locked in a passionate embrace.

"I thought I might find you here." The memory faded in the wake of someone's voice. Alex. She beckoned to me from the second floor. "Join me." More books were arranged neatly in the shelf of the floor above, and Alex, sitting beside one, already had novels on her lap when I got there. "You used to hate it when people touch these books," she said. "Don't you remember, Cybele?"

"Did I?" I sat beside her. The book she was browsing was one of my favorites.

She handed it to me. "I thought it was unfair that you only allowed Talia in here when we were kids. You were very protective of the library. And these walls. Harland." She traced the cover of the book with her finger. "But now you're just watching everything like a ghost. What happened to you?"

I was captured. And Talia was getting married. My throne was going to be given away.

Alex squeezed my knee before the thoughts drowned me. "I heard you kidnapped the Princess."

My eyebrows raised at her. "Are you mocking me?"

"I'm doing anything but that." She glanced down when the doors whined open. Someone was coming in.

I breathed deeply when Talia marched inside, followed quickly by Lancelot. The Princess' expression, at this distance, couldn't be more than just a blur. But I saw with great clarity when she pushed Lance against the wall and leaned closer to kiss him. Alessandra at the last moment, stood, pulled me up with her, and began to attack me with kisses on the neck too.

Bang!

Her kisses ended, but so did whatever Talia and Lance were doing because the four of us stared wide-eyed at each other, shocked. Alex kissed me one more time on the neck and giggled before letting go. She went to the railing of the balcony and leaned forward. "I dropped the book by accident." Her voice was loud enough to be heard. "Fancy seeing the two of you here, by the way. Came in the library to play?" Alex swiveled to me when Lance and Talia didn't answer. "Looks like we've been found, Cybele. Let's continue this in my room."

My mind screamed of betrayal when Alessandra dragged me down the stairs. She didn't even pick the fallen book down. But she did curtsy in front of the Princess whose eyes were locked on my face. I couldn't bear to look at her. How could she?

"We'll give you some space." Alex was cheerful. "Later, Princess."

Alessandra's room had the fragrance of black licorice, almost like she wanted to seduce anyone who'd come inside. She pulled me in and guided me to the bed. After which, she pushed me down and started to remove her dress.

My eyes took in her red lingerie. "What are you doing?"

"Taking your mind off things. Why?" She climbed on the bed and straddled me. "Still a virgin?"

"That's none of your business." I tried to roll off, but her legs held me firmly between her.

She smirked. "We're going to get married. What's the big deal?"

"Harland doesn't even permit two women to be wed."

"So?" She leaned her torso to me. "The Queen can bend the rules. I thought you're aware of that?"

I was. As much as I was aware that her breasts were almost on my face, and her hand was gliding down my legs inside my uniform. "Alessandra."

"I told you to call me Alex." Her lips broadened into a smile when her hand went to my inner thigh. "You're hot down here," she murmured. "What position do you usually like?" Her chocolate brown eyes widened in surprise when I flipped us over. She licked her lips. "The Queen is aroused."

"Don't call me that."

"Then what do you prefer?" Her fingers climbed up. "Your Highness? Master?" She gasped when I nipped her neck. "Yes, right there, baby."

"Here?" I pecked lower. "Or here." My mouth hovered over her bra. "Should I remove this?"

"As you please." Alessandra watched me with clouded eyes as my teeth grazed the flimsy lingerie, then tugged it down torturously slow. She groaned when I stopped. "Cybele?"

"I'm not a rapist."

Her eyes flickered. "I know that," she said. "Why are you bringing this up?"

I pushed myself to sit and stared down. Alex seemed confused. "I didn't molest Talia," I said. "And I don't make the habit of fucking a woman who doesn't want me. Even if it's as beautiful as you."

Alessandra tried to grab my hand, but I was too fast for her. She followed me to the edge of the bed. "I don't understand," she complained. "Did I say something?"

"Look at me." Her head turned my way at the command, her lips parted in surprise at her own reaction. I brushed a hand on her cheek. "You were trembling the whole time, Alex. Don't pretend you're not scared." My hand lowered to her lips. "Reserve those for someone you truly love. And thank you."

"For what?"

My back was straight when I stood. "You've been trying to help me all this time, and I was too depressed to even see it." I smiled at her. She was right. I've stood by and watched while the rest of them walked all over my Palace. Well not anymore. "Can I borrow your clothes? There's something I must do."

Chapter 28
Cybele

My newly acquired blue dress was ankle-long and chic, but it was this or the red one, so I grabbed what I could and thanked Alex for her support.

After waiting for hours, I finally emerged in the hallway. Everything was up to fate now, and I was relieved to see that the guard on duty was beginning to leave his post. There was only minutes left. Alex couldn't have stalled the next one that long.

The room I entered was dim, with only a single lamp lighting it, plus the moonlight shining through the window, illuminating the silhouette of the loveliest woman I'd ever laid eyes on.

Talia gaped at me the moment I locked the door. "What are you doing here?" She glanced at the windows. "I'll call the guards. Leave."

"No. Not until we've talked this through." She stood but I was quicker. In seconds, I was by the window, drawing the curtains close. "Sit down," I said. "I'm not going to hurt you."

My own words left a bitter taste in my tongue, yet I knew they needed to be spoken. Talia had been uncooperative the last few days. I didn't know what to make of it.

The Princess sat back on the bed and folded her arms. "A guard could be standing outside the door at this very moment," she said. "One scream and he comes breaking through my door. Why should I listen to you?"

"Because you love me."

"Yet your face is full of doubts." Her head tilted. Only then did I see that her hair was down for the night, free and flowing like honey. I wanted to run my fingers through them, pull her to me for a kiss. "Cybele," she said, drawing my attention back to her. "Stop wasting my time."

"I'm sorry." I shook my head and paced the room. "I'm sorry for a lot of things, Talia. But I would never be sorry for kidnapping you."

"Are you saying you're here to do it again?"

"No."

"Then what did you come here for?"

I stopped and stared at her. It was time to dig the skeletons.

"I'm here to tell you how Esmeralda murdered my parents to secure the throne for herself."

The laughter that burst from Talia's mouth was loud enough to wake the Palace. She'd reared her head back, touched her stomach, and began to shake like she'd heard the best joke. I glanced warily at the door. "Relax," she said, wiping her eyes. What did she find so funny?

"Do you think my parents 'deaths are a cause for laughter?" I asked.

"I'm not laughing about that." She glanced at my balled fist and leaned back. "I'm just amused at how different your statement is from my mother's. She said *your* parents tried to kill us."

"That's a lie!"

"But why should I believe you?" She crossed her legs and propped her elbows up. Resting her chin on her hands, she stared at me with pure distrust. This was what I was afraid of. The day I was unwilling to live through. It was her mother or me. Who would she choose?

I went to the bookshelf with a snail's pace to bid my time. Up close, I saw that the books were different. The biographies were traded for long-length stories. The children's tales were no more. We weren't kids, she and I.

Talia was still looking at me when I turned to her. "I saw the whole thing," I whispered. "The head guard even tried to kill me." My stomach lurched with every step I took until the Princess was in front of me and I was kneeling. The memories were starting to stir again, but I fought the nausea it brought, just so my voice wouldn't shake. I failed. "That night in the villa, Ronaldo told us everything after he'd stabbed my father."

Talia flinched. "But what he did had nothing to do with my mother."

"But he wasn't working alone. You know this, Princess."

Talia pulled her hand away before I could touch it. "Do you have proof other than Ronaldo's words? Why are you doing this to me, Cybele? The Queen you're accusing of is my flesh and blood."

"Because it's the truth." I swallowed the desperation in me. It was crawling, climbing, trying to get out. "And you recognize this in your heart. Your mother is evil."

"She is still *my* mother." Talia stood up. "And what you're saying is treason. I could have you hanged for these lies. I could have you killed!"

"Be my guest, Princess. But hear out my last plea." I pushed past her and went to the bed. Then to her complete shock, started to remove my dress right in front of her very eyes.

Talia's gaze flickered to my chest when the last of my clothing dropped beside me. "I'm not sure I understand," she murmured, her anger dissipating away.

My hand stretched to her. "I've given the truth, and now it's time for my sentence. Kill me now with your own hands, or claim me as your lover and sleep with me."

She balked. "That's insane!"

"Isn't this all?" I shook my head. Her mother had done this. And now I was finishing it. "Death or love. That's all you can choose, Princess. And should you turn me away or ask the guards to dispose of me, before they do that, I will find a way to your mother's room and murder her tonight."

Talia glowered. "That's fruitless," she chastised. "The whole Palace will be onto you."

"I don't care. If you truly hate me as you say, then you will take my life yourself. Either way, you cannot stand by and be indifferent anymore. You must choose sides."

It took an eternity before Talia climbed onto the bed, straddled me, and stared me down. My chest rose and fell as her lips moved. Even as my executioner, she'd never been more beautiful.

"Don't look at me." That was her wish.

I've resigned myself to her judgement as I turned my head away. A few seconds more and something silky and soft went around my neck. And then the choking began.

I gripped the bedsheet beside me and struggled not to free myself. I've wanted this. Wished for it. My airway became constricted. I couldn't breathe.

"Princess. . ." I choked. It was so hard to speak, but I had to try. "I'm. . . I'm glad it was you."

Something wet fell on my cheek. "You're an idiot! The biggest one there is!"

I wheezed when the choker was removed from my neck, then I reached out to catch the rest of her tears. Why was Talia crying? She shouldn't have. It was a fate worse than death, seeing that I caused her sadness.

"I'm sorry," I rasped. "You may continue my punishment."

"And what? Lose the only person I ever loved?" Talia pushed my hand away and wiped her own tears. "I'm so mad at you for thinking I am capable of that. How you believe my lies so easily is a crime. "

"You. . ."

"My mother was onto me!" Her voice hardened. "I had to protect us in some way. If I had to marry Lance just to keep you alive, then so be it."

"Talia—"

"I'll punish you for this, not for anything else." Her hand went to the hem of her dress, then started to pull it over her head. "You will not move

~ 286 ~

until I tell you so," she said. "I will do bad things, and you will not stop me even once. Do you understand?"

The sight of her lingerie-clad breast made me gulp. "I'm supposed to be your Queen," I said.

"Not tonight, you aren't." Talia unclasped her bra and dangled it on my face. Her eyes became vibrant. More alive than I've ever seen them. "Tonight, you're my servant. Please me, and we shall see if I'll treat you like royalty. Hands above your head."

"Princess."

"Stop growling and do it."

She sounded more commanding. But there was huskiness in her voice that made me raise my arms to follow. "Now what?" I said.

Talia lowered her face to mine and stared me in the eyes. Simultaneously, her finger went to my chest and squeezed the tip of of my nipples. "Just enjoy," she said.

I couldn't keep my hands still while she began to kiss my neck. And when her mouth moved to suck my lips, I knew I was going to go crazy. She started slow and gentle, progressing to play with my tongue while she rubbed her pelvis to my thighs.

The wetness between her legs aroused me more. She yearned for this. Craved for it as much as I did. I groaned when her fingers moved down. "This is so hard!" I complained. "Why can't I touch you?"

" Because you doubted me," she said, fingers going to my inner thigh. "Hold on."

To what?

But soon, those thoughts were replaced by a different feeling. An increasing pleasure that only climbed some more when she broke inside me. I was lost in a sea of sensations. I could hardly keep my eyes open.

"Talia. . ." I moaned.

"I know." Her voice was gentler now. Tender. But she rubbed herself to me harder. "You feel so good!" Her legs quivered and bucked. "I'm coming. . . I love you, Cybele!"

That was the only thing we were waiting for. I clutched onto her. Embraced her. Until her cries became mine, and the two of us couldn't figure which was which anymore.

Talia was still shaking against me after seconds. Her low breaths panted against my ear. "My heart is yours, My Queen." Her smile was nothing but satisfied as she pulled herself from me. "Now give me my punishment for disobeying you."

We didn't stop at one. We did it the second time my way. And by the fourth, I could proudly say that I've explored every crevasse of her body, every contour of her skin. But Talia wasn't done. Even while sweat-soaked and panting, with a messy bed of hair from rolling, she traced circles on my stomach, as if ready for another round.

My lower stomach tightened. "What are the servants feeding you down here?" I murmured.

Her giggles were musical. "Why? Giving up?"

"Definitely not." I took her hand and placed it against my lips. She shivered when I kissed it. "You're one hell of a woman, Talia. I'm proud to call you mine."

"I feel the same way with you." Her eyes fluttered close. "Cybele?"

"Hmm?" It was disappointing to have her move instead of answering me. Talia crawled to the edge of the bed, head bowed down, in deep contemplation. The absence of her warmth made me lonely, so I sat up and enfolded her from behind. "What's wrong?" I murmured. "Why did you turn away from me?"

The Princess took a deep breath before glancing over her shoulder. "I'm tired of this," she whispered.

"Me?"

"No, silly." She cradled my cheek. "I'm so lovesick with you, it will put Juliet Capulet to shame."

"Romeo might not agree."

"Well I don't care what he thinks." Talia tilted her head. "I have my own Cybele. Romeo who?"

"Good one," I said, though I didn't laugh. Even while her words were light, the tone behind it was anything but. "Tell me what's on your mind, Princess."

Talia's face was grim as she moved from my touch and walked to the window. That's why it surprised me so much to see the fire in her eyes when she turned around. It's been ignited out of nowhere. A torch that was suddenly lit. "You asked me to choose earlier, Cybele, and now I want you

to do the same." She leaned back and studied me.
"The right for the throne, or happiness with me."

Chapter 29
Cybele

I spent the next couple of minutes just staring at the Princess, at the nakedness that ensnared my rabid heart. Yet even though nothing stood between us anymore, I still didn't understand.

"Pardon?" I said, taking my eyes off her breast. They were beautiful but too distracting. I concentrated on the flames in her eyes instead. "What did you say again?"

Rather than answering outright, Talia walked to the bookshelf, plucked a novel from the selection, and opened it to a page. She spoke to the paper as if she was speaking to me. "I think it's time to create our fairy tale, my love. But that will only happen if you choose me over the throne."

"That throne is my birthright."

"And the Queen sitting in it is my mother. We've been through this." The book snapped shut, and Talia, expression hardened, placed it back where she found it. "There can only be one choice," she continued. "Should you pick the throne, I will go to my mother's room, murder her myself, then commit suicide right after. It's the only punishment fitting for such a monstrous crime, but that will give you the throne back."

I could feel my jaw tighten. This was not my idea of an after-sex talk.

"Listen to yourself, Princess. You're asking me to turn my back on something I was born to do."

"And I'm sorry." Her words were so sincere I could not speak out of my turn. "I'm sorry that Esmeralda is my mother. I'm sorry she did that to you and your parents. I'm sorry. I'm—" She paused and looked me in the eyes. "I know I'm a poor substitute to the throne. But if you choose me, I'm going to run away with you. We'll never look back."

"How is that different from when I kidnapped you?"

Esmeralda would double her efforts to search for us, especially after she discovered that I was alive. They'd hunt us down until we had nowhere to run.

Yet Talia was insistent. And with every step she took to get back to me, the walls I had fortified all my life crumbled at her feet. "Cybele," she whispered, a breath away from me now. "The choice is in your hands. I'll do what you want. I always had." She knelt so she was lower than me. "You'll always be my Queen. Just give me the order."

I looked at her face, not knowing what to say. My parents deaths should be avenged. I should be sitting in that throne.

And yet.

How could I live without her? Every moment spent away from Talia was torture. Would I ever find someone to replace her?

"Get dressed," I whispered, rising up from the bed. I was the Queen of Harland, and a ruler answers to her duty.

The decision had been made.

Twenty minutes later in the maid's quarters, I knelt beside Van's bed, trying to shake her awake. "Wha—Brooke, is that you?" She covered her face and groaned. "Argh! It's too bright. Did I die in my sleep and go to heaven?"

"Get up and you'll know the answer to that."

I switched the flashlight off and tossed the clothes to her. Van caught them just in time as she was sitting up. "I really thought you were Brooke," she grumbled. "I've had a nice dream of her. We were in this warm jacuzzi and. . ." She stopped and squinted behind me. "Is that Princess Talia? What is she doing here?"

I glanced behind me and smirked. The Princess was in the middle of tying her hair in a half-crown braid.

I turned to Van again. "We had a talk."

"And by talk you meant moan, right?" Van's lips quirked in the dark. Only the moonlight illuminated us in the room, but I could see how impressed she was with me. "You little bean," she whispered. "What holes were you cleaning?"

"None of your business. Get dressed."

"Where are we going?" She glanced at the clothes in her hands, then looked back to us. "Black shirt. Black jeans. Don't tell me." She snapped her fingers. "We're joining a sorority?"

Talia went beside me and rolled her eyes. Even so, I could see the smile forming on her lips. Van was hard to hate. "We want you to get dressed so we can escape the Palace together," the Princess said. "Then we'll take shelter and live happily ever after."

~ 293 ~

"Well you should have said so in the first place!" Van complained. "We're wasting time here. What's wrong with you people?"

Another ten minutes after, and a flashlight in the middle of us, Talia, Van, and I huddled on the floor, ready to discuss the plan. "Here's the thing," I whispered. "The Palace grounds is big, intricate. And with guards watching the surveillance camera, there's little to no chance of escape. But thankfully, I know a way out."

"Hold up," Van said. "You mentioned a surveillance camera. How come we haven't been caught yet?"

"Good question." I took the bookmark from my pocket, then sighed when Talia snatched it from my hand. That was expected.

" Sorry," she murmured, "but I'm really curious about this." Talia turned the bookmark over and studied the flower in the laminate. "It looks familiar."

"I'm sure it is." I plucked the bookmark from her hand again and kept it close to my chest. "You used to give me flowers when we were young, Princess. Do you recall?" A smile flitted to her lips before she nodded. "Well I preserved one of those flowers and turned it into this bookmark. Somehow, keeping it with me always calmed me down."

"Sorry to interrupt." Van flailed her arms. "I'm not being bitter here because I'm single. I'm totally not. But what's the relationship of the bookmark to my question?"

"Brooke." I gestured to the paper in my hand. "Brooke knows how important this is to me. After leaving Alessandra's room earlier, I held the

~ 294 ~

bookmark up knowing that if Brooke is alive, she's probably watching the CCTV from her laptop and would know I needed her help. Hacking the surveillance was up to her. Alex helped me distract the guard."

"Oh really?" Talia folded her arms. "And what exactly were you doing in Alessandra Bernini's room prior to that?"

"They were talking too," Van chirped.

I glared at the blonde. Was she on my side or not?

"Alex was a good friend of mine," I explained. "If it weren't for her help, going to your room would be impossible, Princess."

Talia pursed her lips but motioned for me to continue.

I cleared my throat. "Now that you're both up to speed with the security cameras, let me tell you about the secret passageways."

"Shut up!" Van exclaimed, before clapping a hand over her mouth. In a lower voice, she said, "I'm sorry but this is good. Secret what?"

"Passageways," I repeated. "The Palace grounds is full of them." I turned to Talia whose expression showed that she was beginning to understand.

"You used that to kidnap me," she murmured, eyes snapping to mine. "You spied on me using the camera too, didn't you, Cybele? What did you see?"

"Nothing," I said while Van snickered. Nothing I didn't want. Talia had begun to giggle too when I rose from the floor. These two would be good friends. But we had so much to do before we could come close to that. "Let's make our escape."

The walk from the hallway to one of the hidden tunnels was easy. The guards were either too drowsy or lax to notice us slip in and out of the walls. And for that, I was glad they were Esmeralda's, not mine.

"Well that was anticlimactic," Van said soon as we emerged to the garden. Only the woods stood in our way now. After going through it, we could make our way to the tunnel leading out, and then to total freedom. "I thought I could at least fight a guard or two, but all of them were zombified." Vanessa made a disgusted face.

I clapped a hand on her back. "Don't wish for such things, Van. I for one don't want to encounter anyone." It would be much harder to keep my promise to Talia if that's the case. "The tunnel is a five-minute walk from here," I continued. "Don't make noises, keep your head down, and kill anyone that stands in the way. Clear?"

"Copy that, commander."

A loud wail rang when we were about to move away from the bushes. Turning to the two, I saw that Van and Talia echoed the same surprise. "What's happening?" I said, beginning to hear movement from every direction. The wails have stopped, following three sharp whistles. Was that what I thought it was?

"Someone must have checked my room and didn't see me there!" Talia grabbed my hand. "I think we should go!"

That was the only explanation I needed. Holding onto Talia's hand, we made a mad dash from bush to bush, stopping every time someone ran by. The tunnel was just around the bend, ready and waiting for us to enter. But I guess we'd run out of luck soon, because just as we turned the corner, someone who wasn't supposed to be there was standing by the entrance.

"Princess?" Lance took a step forward. Behind him, the bushes hiding the entrance was undisturbed. He was there by coincidence. "I was taking a stroll when the alarm rang," he said. "What's going on?"

"Go away, Lance. This is none of your business." Talia had none of the politeness she'd showered him over the last days. It satisfied me, but I scowled when he shook his head.

"You're not making any sense."

"It doesn't matter, lover boy." Van cracked her knuckles. "When the Princess tells you to go away, you go away or else!"

She lunged at him before any of us could react. One moment Van was beside me tilting her head side to side, the next she was clawing, scratching, kneeing Lance everywhere.

" Stop it!" Alessandra came out of nowhere and tried to pry the two apart. "Cybele, help me!"

"Why should I?"

"He's my boyfriend!"

Even Vanessa stared at her. "He's your what now?"

"He's my boyfriend! He's innocent!" Alessandra's face was red when she yanked

Van's collar one more time. Vanessa, astonished, had to let go.

Lance was breathing hard when he finally stood from the grass and straightened his white shirt. He didn't look like a proper noble now. It was like he was dragged in a dog kennel and what was left of him was all torn and mangled up. I glanced at a frustrated Alessandra and tilted my head. "Explain now or I'll set the animal loose again," I said.

Alex gritted her teeth but nodded. "Lance and I had liked each other since we were young. But his family was pressured by the Queen, so he had no choice but to get engaged with Talia." She glanced at the Princess and frowned. "I'm sorry, Talia, but my Lancelot is not in love with you."

"Neither am I with him," Talia said.

Alex sighed and continued. "The Queen eventually found out about our relationship. And I know her revenge had been coming for years, but I was really surprised when she told me to marry, Cybele. We all thought she was dead."

Lance wiped his bleeding lips and nodded. Van's attacks were beginning to show on his face. "We're sorry for all of this," he mumbled. "We were victims of circumstances."

"More like victims of my mother." Talia's head bowed low. Before she could say anything, I was reaching out for her chin, tilting it to me.

"Don't do this," I murmured. "Don't apologize for anyone. It's not your fault your mother's an. . . erm. . ."

"A bitch?" Talia cracked a smile.

"Something like that." I turned to the others. "If someone should apologize here, it should be Vanessa, for attacking Lance out of the blue."

Van responded with a snort. "I love you, Your Majesty, but there's absolutely no way I'll apologize to this douche." She scowled. "Tea this! Tea that! Get your own tea, you freak!"

The conversation was cut short when shuffling of feet were heard nearby. I hurried to Alessandra and leaned closer to whisper. "Thanks for helping me earlier. Talia and I agreed to escape."

"But the throne!"

"I'm not interested in it anymore." I took hold of her shoulders and squeezed. "With us gone, Esmeralda won't have an heir. That means you'll get the throne when the time comes. I want you to take care of it."

"Cybele. . ."

"Search for the Princess that way!"

Lance squared his shoulders upon hearing the guards. "It looks like you need a diversion." He glanced at me and smiled. "I always knew that Talia had fallen hard for someone. I just didn't realize it was with a woman. Marvelous." He bowed to the Princess. "It was a pleasure being engaged with you, Princess. I enjoyed our afternoon tea together."

"Oh for the love of!" Van palmed her face. "Just quit it with your tea. Ever heard of coffee?"

Lance laughed and slipped away. He'd just bought us a few more minutes.

I signaled to Vanessa and pointed to the tunnel. "Go inside and wait for us."

"Yes, ma'am!"

Talia was heading to Alessandra when I turned back to them. The Princess held out her hand and smiled. "This is probably the last time we'll see each other again," the Princess said. "Let's part as friends, shall we?"

Alex shook the Princess 'hand. "Take care of our Cybele."

"My Cybele." Talia let go and stepped to me. "Be quick or I'll miss you."

"I will." Talia was slipping inside the secret entrance too when I breathed in and focused on Alex. It was my turn to say goodbye. "About the throne. . ."

"I'll take care of it for you," she cut off. "But only until you get back. Only you deserve that seat. Not me. Not Talia. And certainly not her mother."

I gave Alex a look of gratitude before swiveling to the entrance and began making my way inside. The tunnel was dark and cold. There was barely anything to see, much less hold onto to support myself.

"Talia?"

"I'm here."

A sigh of relief was released from my mouth when her hand found its way to mine. She was safe. We were together.

I made a quick apology while we walked the length of the tunnel on our way out to freedom.

~ 300 ~

Mother, father, if you're watching us, please keep me safe, especially Talia. I left the throne to be with her. I left the throne to be happy.

Chapter 30
Cybele

The house on top of the hill was decrepit. And the more we got nearer, the more I could see the spaces where the missing shingles used to be. The white paint covering its outside walls had turned to grey over the years of neglect. But if it had one good thing about it, the place would buy us time.

Van sneezed the moment I opened the door. "Urk." She wiped her nose and turned to me. She'd been the first one inside, with Talia not far behind.

"What do you think?" I said, before closing the door behind me.

Van took a wary glance at the peeling wallpaper. "You want the truth from me, Your Highness?"

"Yes."

Her stare was deadpan. "I think someone was murdered here. And I'd like to say it was my hopes and dreams, but I swear I just felt Thelma. She was the ex-girlfriend I locked in the cabinet a long time ago."

"You're crazy," Talia murmured.

"Good crazy? Or bad crazy?"

The Princess shrugged and turned to me. "Van has a point though. Not that I'm complaining, but. . ." She shifted her attention to the space. Everything was covered with white sheet, with layers of dust on top. "I won't be surprised if Thelma does spring up somewhere, especially in that dark hallway. What is this place?"

I didn't answer the Princess just yet. Going further inside the room, I grabbed a sheet, yanked it upward, and waited for the cloud of dust to settle before gesturing to the sofa. "This," I said, "is the back up to my back up. I didn't think I'd ever need this house, so I just left it alone."

"That explains the odor." Van pinched her nose. "I thought it was the Princess."

"Excuse me?"

Van sneered at the payback. "Until when are we staying here, Your Highness?"

"Until we're sure that it's safe to go back to England," I answered. "But don't worry. It's safe here. The house sits on top of the hill so we can see intruders approaching. And with thirty minutes from the town, we can gather supplies while trying to contact Brooke." I motioned upstairs. "You're free to choose a room, Van. There's three available, each with their own bathroom. We'll sleep in shifts."

"Fine with me." Van headed to the sofa, collapsed, and sighed. "But I suggest we look for Brooke soon. I miss how she glares at me. And her scowl. And her knife-throwing skills." Van hugged herself. "God, I wish she skewers me."

I clapped my hands to my ears. "Can we please not talk about my best friend that way?"

"What? I'm just saying she's really good with knives."

"Enough already."

Talia, who'd been watching us with a bemused expression on her face, chuckled at the last part. "Don't worry," she assured me. "I'll make sure to keep you busy while Van does her thing. In fact, we can start now if you want, Cybele. Keeping busy, I mean."

Warmth rose to my neck. And Vanessa, waiting for an opportunity to tease anyone, started to guffaw. "I knew it!" she said. "Her Highness is a bottom!"

I ignored her last statement and closed the distance between me and Talia. "Let's go to our room before I lose my patience, Princess. Van, you stay here and guard."

"Do you want me to serve you bottomless iced tea?" She zipped her lips when I glared at her. "On second thought, I'll go on watch duty. Enjoy."

The Princess and I chose the farthest room in the second floor, equipped with a lumpy bed, a dresser, and two shutter windows that overlooked the town below. Night had begun to fall, causing the lights of the homes and establishments to glimmer like stars.

"It's beautiful, isn't it?" Talia's footsteps echoed behind me.

"It is," I said. "But we can't relax too much. The guards are going to be after us tenfold."

"That's expected." The bed creaked. "But we can't be worried forever. Come here, Cybele."

I sighed and left the window for the bed, but stopped mid-stride when I caught a glance of her. Talia had stripped down to her underwear, and was poised and seducing in the mattress.

"Told you I'll keep you busy."

"Princess."

"You don't want to?"

I licked my lips as I took in the contour of her waist. This sight would never get old. And frankly, I could feel something building in me, shifting downward, outward. Talia smiled triumphantly as I headed to her.

"We're going to sleep," I said.

"But I thought. . ." Disappointment crossed her features. "It will be quick."

"Not tonight." I tried to keep my expression as neutral as possible as I settled beside her and took her in my arms. But it was hard. With Talia looking like that and my own needs rising to the surface, I had to keep the desires from wreaking havoc in my brain. Tonight, of all nights would be tricky. Everyone in the Palace would be on high alert. "Were you always thinking of thoughts like this?" I segued.

"Weren't you?"

The memory of the past made my breaths uneven. "Nope."

"Liar." She threw her leg over mine. "You fantasized about me, didn't you? Come on, just say it."

"Will you sleep if I do?"

She grinned and winked at me, the muted light of the lamp making her face glow. "Can't promise."

I drew out a breath. Talia had never been a follower of rules, while I? I was strict to reinforce them.

She gasped when I rolled us over, so she was pinned under me. "I've imagined this every day, Princess." My lips set on a smirk. "Happy?" Talia still looked surprised, but she bit her lip and nodded. I leaned my head on her chest. "Let's stay like this for a while. Van's shift will be over before you know it."

The Princess was fast asleep when I crept out of the room and headed downstairs. Van was wide awake in the sofa, eyes steely on the door, only budging when she heard me descend.

"Where'd you get the candle?" I asked. There was one in the middle of the room that I didn't recognize buying. This house had been an afterthought following its transition to my alias.

Van waved her hand dismissively. "Found it in the cupboard." She made room for me in the sofa. "Can't sleep?"

"No." My hand automatically when to the bookmark in my pocket. Talia might be safe, but another person important to me wasn't. "I'm thinking about Brooke," I admitted. "Now that we're out of the Palace, I can't help but wonder where she is. We need to get to a computer or phone to contact her."

"I'll take care of that." Van hugged her knees to her chest. "I'll run to the town soon as the shops open tomorrow. You don't have to worry about me."

" Who said I was?" My hand slipped out of my pocket. "You're like a cat, Van. You can scamper out of the way or hide when the occasion calls for it."

"Or scratch someone's face, but I don't want to brag." Both of us turned to the candle when it flickered. The windows were closed, so it must have been Thelma again. "On a serious note, Your Highness. Why are we going to England again?"

"It's where my adoptive parents live," I reminded. "Don't you remember the story I told you? After staying in Augustine Center, these two billionaires found and brought me to England."

"Holy moly! Billionaires?" Van rubbed her hand excitedly. "When are you going to adopt me?" She shook my arm persistently when I didn't answer. "I'll be good! I swear on Brooke's ooh-lala body!"

The seriousness on her face made me chuckle. It was so contradicting to what she was. "I was right about you, Vanessa. You're a good person." She stopped shaking me long enough to listen. "And even though we haven't been acquainted long, I feel like you're the little sister I never had."

"No kidding?"

"I'm not the kind to kid."

Van yawned before curling on my lap. "Remember that when I'm courting Brooke," she mumbled. "Now pat my head, sissy."

I tried pushing her away, but she'd locked her fingers around my legs. "Get off me," I ordered. "Now."

"But I like it here." She buried her face on my lap. "And besides, I feel safe for the first time since my parents died. Just let me rest."

My hands fell to the sofa, unable to move, following her confession. We'd been orphaned because of circumstances, and while I was lucky to have been secured by the Prescott's, she had nothing but one misfortune after another.

My fingers found their way through her hair. That's where it stayed the rest of the night.

I was awoken the next day with a kiss on the forehead. Talia, smelling like lavender and fresh morning dew, leaned back with a vibrant smile. "Good morning," she greeted.

"Good morning." I was given mere seconds before yesterday's experience and our grand escape jolted me awake. Van wasn't anywhere in the sofa when I checked.

"She left early," Talia said, as if reading my mind. "She said she'll run to a store for groceries and steal a computer after. I'm not sure if she's joking about the stealing part, but I can definitely use food." The Princess 'stomach growled on cue. "Any chance we can have something to eat?"

"Does porridge count?" I clutched her waist and pulled her to me before she could walk out. The Princess wouldn't get away from me anymore. "We'll scavenge the kitchen for food," I said. "No porridge."

"No porridge," she agreed.

Thirty minutes later and even porridge sounded appealing. There was nothing in the kitchen aside for two more candles. Talia slammed the last cupboard shut before swiveling to me, her stomach growling for the umpteenth time. "God, I'm so hungry."

So was I. But I pressed my palms on the counter and hauled myself to sit instead of saying so. "How long has it been since you've eaten a proper meal?" I asked.

"Before or after you?" I waited for her self-satisfied grin to disappear, so she could answer properly. "Actually," Talia said, "I haven't eaten in two days."

"That long?"

She shrugged. "I was worried when we were in the Palace. My appetite was gone."

This could be problematic. If guards come breaking the door, the Princess wouldn't be able to defend herself. We need all the strength we could get.

I hopped down from the counter. "Van will be here soon," I said. "Drink water in the meantime. That will relieve some of the hunger."

But Van wasn't here by noon. Neither did she make it back when it was close to sunset. I rose from the sofa after seeing the sun on the east, then hurried to the stairs to talk to Talia. I happened upon her in the room next to the one we'd chosen, holding a plastic bag in one hand, a cream-colored stocking in the other.

"I think the previous owners of this house belonged to the theatre." The plastic rustled as Talia took a blonde, puffy wig. "Should we go after Van with these?"

"I will."

Her eyes narrowed. "And me?"

"You stay here."

I took the last steps to get in front of her, but Talia moved the wig out of the way. "Not fair!" she said. "I found this!"

"Yes, and your reward is by staying here and being safe."

Talia ducked from my reach and ran to other side of the room. "You don't get to leave me here," she complained. "What if the guards appear and I'm alone?"

"What if the guards see us together outside?"

"We slap them and run."

What kind of solution was that?

I forked my fingers through my hair before reaching my hand out. "Princess, give me the wig."

She hugged it to her. "No, Cybele. If you want it, you have to win it. On a bet."

Like last time? Like the part where she tricked me? My lips curled at the memory. We loved each other. That was clear. But damn it if I could get the Princess to follow everything I wanted.

"What kind of bet?" I finally said. "Not that I'm agreeing with anything."

She relaxed her guard only after she'd hid the wig behind her. "Why, My Queen? Are you scared to lose? Again?"

My shoulder went up for a shrug, but already I could feel myself rising to the challenge.

~ 310 ~

Talia's smile said she knew that too. "Just tell me the bet," I murmured.

"We're going to do a *how well do you know me game*," she said. "If I win, we go after Van together and maybe have a date."

"That's prepost—"

"I'm not done yet." The Princess 'hands went to her waist. "If you win, I'll hide under the bed until you come back. Agreed?"

My thumb brushed my chin. The game was rubbish for someone like us. Talia knew we'd been close since before this, and everything she said recently was carefully stored in my mind for safekeeping. What's the point?

"All right," I said regardless. "You won't win this time."

Chapter 31
Cybele

The Princess and I exchanged challenging stares that would have put the gladiators to shame. She startled to circle the room. And what was I to do but circle too? She wouldn't intimidate me.

"Are you ready for my question?" Talia continued circling.

"Anytime you're ready to lose, love."

Twilight hit the side of her faces when she stopped beside the window. But she didn't look out. She tilted her head to me and said, "Who is my father?"

I took a sharp breath. Oh dear.

The Princess and I were young when we were introduced to each other. But aside from Esmeralda and the guards, no one had accompanied Talia when visiting the Palace. Her father could be anyone: a duke, a guard, even Santa Clause.

Talia twirled the wig in her fingers. "You don't know because you've never asked."

"You. . . You're right. That was foolish of me."

The twirling stopped. "No, it wasn't," she said. "I didn't talk about it because the subject was taboo. Mother had kept my father's identity from me for years. Even now she doesn't know that I'm aware."

Who was it then? The suspense was killing me.

I froze. *Was it perhaps?*

"It's not Ronaldo if that's what you're thinking." She smiled when I released the breath through my mouth. "It's a businessman Mother blackmailed into bedding. I didn't believe the journal entry I came upon as a child. But last night it got me thinking. Mother never saw the man again."

The words were stuck in my lips. How awful it must have been to find out that you were the product of blackmail.

Talia, though, didn't look the least bit concerned. A flash of gold hit the sun's rays as she tossed the wig to me. I caught it and studied the costume.

"I believe you owe me a date in town, Cybele."

I was a dunce for agreeing with her. I had to be. Because so many things could go wrong: guards finding us, people recognizing her, or someone somewhere tipping something to anyone.

"We should go back!" I whispered; throat scratchy from thirst. The thirty minutes it took us to walk from the hideout to the town had depleted my energy. And it didn't help that a few meters from us, a café door was open, causing the whole street to smell like croissant.

But who cared about thirst or hunger when Talia could be in danger? I looked behind me and frowned. The second wig she'd found in the house was big, brown, and curly. It clashed with her eye color.

"You worry too much," she said, though in a louder voice than mine. Talia fixed her wig when I scowled. "No one will know it's us."

"I'm not taking any chances." I was about to touch her wrist when she darted from the truck we'd been hiding behind and ran straight for a man in a tweed jacket.

Oh no!

My heart made a nosedive when she tapped the man's shoulder.

"Princess!" My legs started moving. "I mean, woman!"

The two of them glanced at me when I came to their side, the man in particular giving me a second look. Talia stretched her hand to him. "Thanks for your time, Jim. See you later."

The man was out of earshot when I swiveled to her. She'd kill me one of these days with her antics. I just knew it.

"What were you thinking, Talia? He could have recognized you!"

"Well he didn't, did he?" She took my hand and pressed a paper on my palm. It was surprising to find myself looking at a twenty. "We need to pay him back later. I promised him that," she said. "And I also realized why Van was taking too long. She wasn't kidding about stealing something."

I blinked at her a few times before the realization hit me. "Shite! I forgot to give her money."

"It's not your fault." Talia adjusted her wig again. "We'd escaped in the middle of the night

~ 314 ~

with nothing but our clothes. I know you're a person with plans, but you must forgive yourself from time to time when you overlook things like this. Our life is not exactly a book with a plot."

I'd love it to be one though. It would be outrageous.

I tucked the bill in my pocket and glanced around. The town was quaint, with structures going back to the early centuries. Few shops had been modernized, and even the cafe nearby was straight out of a story-book with its brick walls and Hungarian-inspired architecture.

"We need to find a payphone." I gave in. "That's the only way we can pay off this debt."

After we'd located a shop that allowed us to call, Talia and I lingered in the back alley and waited for our contact. At first, I didn't think much of a guy wearing a Manchester cap. But then he dropped a brown paper bag in front of me, tipped his hat, and didn't look anywhere in my direction again. Viper and his network operated in mysterious ways.

"I'm not even going to ask," Talia said when I picked up the bag. There was a hefty amount of money bundled inside. She turned away when I tried to show her.

"It's not bad money," I said.

" Still not going to ask." Talia was poker-faced when she straightened away from the wall. The back street was grimy. And a few paces from us a trash bin was attracting flies. But she hadn't spoken once, only now. "I'll forgive whatever secrets you had or is still having," she said. "But once we've found some footing in our life, I hope we can start from scratch. Deal?"

I have her a weary nod. That was probably for the best.

The rest of the day wasn't as serious as when we were in the back alley, or as troubling as our first foray into town. In fact, Talia had managed to coax me into heading to one of the diners. I didn't have the heart to say no.

"Aren't you forgetting something?" The Princess was all smiles when we left our booth.

My stomach was still full from all the smoked bacon, cabbage rolls, and to cap it off, a banana split she insisted on sharing with me. I was light-headed when I shook my head. "No. What is it?"

"Guess."

"I hate guessing."

She pouted when she opened the door leading out.

I racked my brain for anything I might have forgotten. If what we suspect about Van was true, the woman would probably be back in the house, grocery and computer with her. It made me a little guilty that we were out here having fun, but then this kind of opportunity did not happen every day.

Talia threw her hands in the air. "It's our first date," she revealed. "We've never had one."

Another wave of guilt mingled with the bacon and rolls in my stomach. It *was* our first date. If you didn't count the one in the forest where were captured right after.

I grasped Talia's hand and pulled her to an alley. But it was a different back street. Not the one with the trashcan. And instead of a rotting smell there was the sweet scent of ice cream scones, the flowery fragrance of a lily. All of them came from the shops in front.

I pressed Talia to the wall, my mouth stopping just before it reached hers. "How do I make it up to you?" I whispered.

Tingles ran down my spine as she traced her fingers on my back. But before we could kiss, a trumpet sounded, followed by the banging of a drum.

Talia and I were beside ourselves with shock as the first of the marchers came invading the alley. There were women and children, men and old people too. But I wasn't too sure if they were humans altogether. All of them were wearing a costume, if not as lovely as a fairy, then as creepy as a clown.

I turned my back to Talia and hurriedly hid her behind me. My height made it easy, but with this many people, I couldn't be too sure that one or two wouldn't notice her.

"Keep your head down," I instructed.

"Cybele!"

"I know!"

The passing crowd didn't stop to acknowledge us, nor asked for anything, to my relief. One of them did hand us a flyer though.

Peek-a-boo! It's Halloween, boo. Join the celebration in the Square tonight. Be there, or Dracula will find you and bite.

Talia and I waited for the procession to disappear before speaking. But I didn't understand a word she said because both of us prattled at the same time.

"We need to leave!" I said.

"Let's check it out!" she blurted.

"What?" I could feel my shoulders tensing. "You want to go to a celebration full of people that have grown up seeing your face in the news? How irresponsible is that?"

Talia kept her eyes on her shoes. Kept her eyes there until she had the courage to look at me. But tears threatened to spill. "I've never seen anything like that," she said. "I've been trapped in the Palace. By my own mother."

"I know that."

"But you don't understand."

Maybe I should have turned away. Maybe I shouldn't have listened. But the Princess, as always, knew my weakest spots.

"Five minutes," I growled. "Then we're going home."

Luckily, we found a proper costume shop before heading to the town square. The Princess and I ditched our wigs and changed into something more appropriate before stepping out.

Staring at Talia made me smile despite the possible consequences. She was going as a ghost for the Halloween celebration but ended up looking like a pixie in white. The makeup hid her face so well that no one would recognize her if they didn't take a closer look. And with her dressed like that? Wow.

"I think I changed my mind about tonight," I said. "Maybe we should go home."

"But you promised!" Talia was all pouts.

My eyes trailed to her legs. Yes, I did promise to celebrate, but she didn't tell me anything about looking sexy.

She noticed where my eyes were straying and placed a hand on my face. "No way, Cybele. Uh-uh. We're going to the square."

Lost at my own game, Talia and I made our way to the plaza. The town square was bustling with people, all in different costumes, trading conversations as if there was nothing better to do.

Seeing this many locals made me wary but feel alive. They were my people. My land. Was I right in giving them up?

Talia tugged at my cape. "Hey, Dracula? Why the long face?"

The overwhelming sense of sadness was quickly replaced by serenity when I glanced at her. "Nothing," I murmured. "There's a group dancing over there. Want to join?"

"Do I!"

The group was comprised of people of all ages, ranging from children to the undead. Talia and I were admitted in the big circle at once, shuffled along with the swaying, while trying to pick-up our own rhythm.

The Princess had the widest grin when I twirled her around. We should go to parties like this more often in England. That smile was something I'd love to see.

"That was magnificent!" Talia's forehead shone with sweat. We'd just finished our third song but most of the original group was still preparing for the fourth. I pulled her away. "Where are we going?" she asked, looking over her shoulder longingly.

"We're just—"

"Look, Cybele! Do you see that?"

My brows knitted with the interruption, but I couldn't help but turn at the spot where she was pointing to. In the distance was a wooden stage with a large white canopy. In our eagerness to dance, Talia and I hadn't paid attention to it.

"We agreed on five minutes," I reminded.

"Yeah, but. . ." She twiddled her fingers. "Can that be our last stop? I'll just take a glimpse."

It was difficult to go near the stage as a crowd had staked their claim and was attracting more people as seconds passed by. Still, we pushed through until we couldn't anymore. Beside me, Talia was standing on tiptoes, trying to take a peek.

"Do you want me to carry you over my shoulder?" I asked.

"Is that a simple jab at my height?" She grinned at me. "I'm heavy."

"Nothing I can't handle."

I was beginning to kneel when the crowd became more active and started pushing. Changing my mind for fear of being trampled, I glanced at the stage and saw that two individuals with grotesque masks were pulling a struggling woman up there.

"It's starting!" a man close by said. "I've waited for this play all year!"

Talia and I exchanged quizzical looks before I stared at the stage again. The face of the woman there was worryingly familiar. Something clicked. And all of a sudden, it felt that someone had splashed a bucketful of ice water on me.

"Talia!" I gasped. "I think the woman on stage is Vanessa!"

Chapter 32
Cybele

The people around us began to clap. It started like a drizzle that progressed to pouring rain, then to a raging storm that was so loud it rendered me deaf for seconds. All of this was when the masked performers tied Vanessa to a large wooden pole in the middle of the stage. But that wasn't all. They've ignited a torch, lowered it down, and created a circle of fire around our friend too.

"A-are you sure it's her?" Talia yelled, trying to be heard above the clapping.

My senses didn't lie. Even at this distance, I could see the outline of Van's features: the clothes she was wearing, the way she struggled against the rope. It was our friend, and she wasn't acting.

"I'm positive it's her," I said. "We need to get to Van before it's too late. Hold my hand."

Talia and I didn't waste time making assertions and started pushing through the crowd together. But they pushed us back. With everyone trying to make their way to the stage, we were just one of the sea of hopeful viewers.

"Oh no!"

Talia's cry made me look back at the stage, to one of the stocky performers that brought Van to such horrid conditions. The man was handed a microphone, and after tapping on it several times, he brought it to close to his mask and announced, "Ladies and gentlemen! Welcome!"

The crowd cheered once again, louder, wilder. Beside me, Talia stuttered. "M-Muscles! It's definitely Muscles!"

"Who?"

"He was a part of Van's original group!" Talia rushed. "He's awful! Malicious! I hated him the most!"

My teeth were bared when she was done explaining. I've heard enough. From the looks of it, Muscles wasn't horsing around too. And no matter what his motives were, this foolery couldn't continue.

Seconds before we could get a move on, the audio feedback made the microphone screech. With it came the sound of cat's nails being dragged on chalkboards. We all covered our ears to block the noise.

It took a while before it subsided, and when it did, everyone around us were confused. "Do we have your full attention now?" Muscles said from the stage. Several groans made him chuckle. Despising. "Tonight," he said, "is a night unlike any other. We will show you something different. A magical performance." He flourished his hand like a magician. "What do you think happens to people who betray their friends? Any guesses?"

A person from the front spoke, but she was too far away to be heard by the people at the back. Us included.

"That's right," Muscles said regardless. "You stop being friends. You stop respecting and liking them. Why? Because basic bitches don't deserve that from you! They deserve to be punished!"

The whole plaza had hushed followed by his outburst. No one had laughed at the high pitch of his voice, or dared question why he was so angry. All of them related it to acting, and he did a fine job by sweeping his hand to the stage once more.

"This play is called burned alive," he spoke. "Without further ado, enjoy!"

The thunderous clapping was only broken by the protest of my lungs and the jerking pull Talia had made. "Hurry!" she cried. "If the fire doesn't get to her, the smoke will!"

The Princess and I battled through the throng harder—pushing away, uncaring who we might hurt. A little step on the foot was nothing compared to being set in flames. These people wouldn't know what they were watching. They'd think it was nothing but a show even if we screamed it to their faces.

Seconds into the ordeal, what I thought couldn't get worse just made a turn hell bound. A great number of police were edging to the stage, guns still holstered, no doubt to prevent a stampede from exploding. They must have caught wind of the false performance and was there to intervene.

" This is bad!" Talia said. "If the police manage to stop the show, one of them will recognize Van. She's a fugitive."

She was also my responsibility. My newly acquired family.

I didn't take my eyes off the stage as Talia and I resumed pushing. Muscles and his companion had noticed the approach of the police and had begun to light the edge of the stage with fire.

It was a clever way to bid them some time. Van would be long dead before the police reached her. Muscles would have made his escape too. But they hadn't factored us in.

" Oof!" a man groaned when I elbowed his rib. He was probably cursing me, but I had moved on to my next victim. And the third. Fourth.

On the stage, another development was unfolding. Aside from the previous police who'd reached the stairs, another group of security had appeared with buckets of water. They tried to splash the edge of the stage with it, to the total delight of the audience who thought it was still part of the show.

"We're almost there!" Talia said. "I think Van saw us too. We just made eye contact."

Hope bloomed in my chest like flowers in a field. Talia was right. Van was closer than before. But all flowers were born to die. A rumbling sound made us look up. The canopy on top of the stage had caught fire.

There was a hiss, a rumble, as the flimsy wires that supported the canopy snapped one by one. And before long, with a horrible groan, the structure caved in.

For a few seconds, the whole stage and its surrounding areas were filled with smoke, dust, and commotion. Muscles and his group were trapped under the canopy. But so was Vanessa.

"Clear the stage!" the commander of the police yelled. "I want them arrested, now!"

Muscles was able to scramble out of the rubble while the police threaded closer. He was filthy, clothes torn. The accident gave him fresh cuts all over, but he wasn't giving up. "Where's the bitch?" His head turned side to side. "Find her!"

Another of his cohorts, a man who was equally big but on a lumpy sort of way, removed his mask and groaned. "The guards are coming, Snookiebear," he said. "Maybe we should scram."

"Scram, sham! Shut up and just follow my lead!" Muscles said. "Where's your knife?"

The other guy unsheathed a six-inch blade then handed it to Muscles. "What are you going to do?"

"Simple." Muscles kicked fallen debris out of his way. "I'm getting rid of a pest."

My eyes widened when I realized where he was heading and why he picked that location. A short distance from them, someone was struggling under the fallen canopy, waving, calling attention, asking for help.

"Vanessa!" I shouted. "I think I see her. Stay here, Talia!"

The Princess grasped my cape. "You're not going anywhere without me!"

Talia and I pushed the crowd as one, most of them too shaken by what was taking place to complain. Everything was happening too much too soon. Half of the police had made it to the stage before we could.

"Snookiebear," the lumpy man said nervously. "The guards are coming."

"Let them come." Muscles tore off his mask. "This will be over soon."

It was at the last second that I figured that Muscles had reached his destination and had raised his knife for the kill. My heart pummeled like a rocket ship out of control. Van. . . We were almost there. We—

Talia grabbed my collar as Muscles 'knife swung down to the figure in the stage. Talia pulled me to her and swallowed my sobs by kissing me hard. But it was too late. Waves of pain swept over me like a tsunami.

The Princess 'lips were still quivering when she let me go. "We need to leave," she whispered. "The police will arrest Muscles and start ushering the crowd. They'll recognize us."

Everything about me was numb as I nodded and followed her to the back. The scene I was walking away from was devastatingly familiar. Someone close to me had died again, and I was too powerless to stop it.

The thirty minutes it would take us to go back to the hideout was shortened to fifteen. Inside the house, Talia sat beside me in the sofa. I turned away soon as she tried to touch my cheek.

"Cybele. . ." She sighed. "Don't do this."

"Do what?"

Her jaw had hardened when I stared at her. "You're blaming yourself."

"Well maybe I should." The candle in front of us flickered when I stood. We couldn't even open the lights for fear of being spotted by the police. "Are you regretting this?" I said to her. "Running away with me?"

Talia shook her head. "We chose this together."

"Yeah, but I'm the only one who failed."

My footsteps were heavy and dragging. But I couldn't seem to stop from pacing because if I did then everything would catch up to me. Van was dead. So, I continued walking, and walking, until Talia had gotten up to block my way.

"You know that's not true," she convinced. "You know you're not a failure."

Oh really?

"Then how come Van left this morning, huh? How come Brooke is missing?" I thumped my chest with my fist in anger. "It's my fault your mother still has the throne, my fault everyone is dying, my fucking fault if you get hurt!"

"So, what?" she argued. "You're just going to give up?"

"What else do you want me to do?"

Talia's lips pressed together in frustration. She was disappointed at me, I know. But her eyes—her eyes told of a different story. They were mad, yes, but there was longing in them too.

" I want you to be as fierce as the day you kidnapped me," she said. "That determined

~ 327 ~

Cybele? I want her back." The Princess 'shoulders hunched as she turned to the stairs. But before I could do or say anything, she raised a hand to stop me. "You need time to mourn alone." She exhaled. "So do I."

My head fell to the cushion following her ascend to the second floor. This bad luck that had plagued us shouldn't continue. And it was up to me to fix it no matter what the cost.

I didn't know what time I'd fallen asleep in the evening, or how I could have lowered my guard in such circumstances. But I knew exactly how I was awoken: with something sharp and cold pressing on my neck, and an unknown person breathing behind me.

"Who are you?" I said, adrenaline coursing through my veins.

Whoever it was leaned closer, his cologne reeking like sewer water. "People around these parts call me Muscles," he murmured. "I'm here to take what's promised to me."

"And what might that be?" I asked. But I knew the answer to my question even before the scream sounded upstairs.

"Uh-uh." Muscles pressed the knife to my neck firmly. "We both know what will happen. Don't make this hard for us, girl."

The desire to break free intensified when I heard a scuffle from the stairs. Before long, the huge accomplice from before dragged Talia into the living room.

"Let go of her," I hissed. "If it's money you want, I'll give it to you."

The breath got caught in my throat when Talia was pushed down and shoved against the floor. Even so, she raised her head defiantly to look at us. "Leave Cybele alone, Muscles! Whatever happened to us, she had nothing to do with it!"

"Shut up, bitch!"

The tip of the knife dug onto my neck until blood trickled down my skin. Yet I didn't flinch. My eyes were on the Princess.

"Tell me," I insisted. "How much do you need? One million? Two million?" *How much for the life of the person I valued most in the world?*

The man holding Talia smiled toothily at me. But whatever he was going to say, whatever bargain he came up with, had suddenly disappeared when his eyes rolled back, his knees buckled as he collapsed.

And if that wasn't enough to surprise me, a person emerging from the kitchen did.

Brooke, bruises fading, black hair long and shiny, blew on the tip of her gun before grinning at me. "Hey, Iris. Sorry I'm late," she said.

Muscles yanked my hair before I could celebrate. "Snookiebear!" He growled. "You're going to pay for this! You—"

I heard him fall before I even turned around, just in time for another figure to emerge from the shadow. "What, Your Highness?" Van looked like a Cheshire cat when she smiled. "You really thought I was dead?"

Chapter 33
Vanessa

It wasn't hard to bury Muscles and his boyfriend at the back of the house. We weren't best friends or anything. They also tried to burn me alive last night.

That's why when Her Majesty, Cybele, suggested to get rid of their corpses, I was the one who volunteered. I mean, no one else would do it, right? And besides, burying them was cleaning out my past. From now on, Vanessa Krieger was free.

"Are you finished yet, Van?" Princess Talia's voice called out to me from inside the house.

I grunted instead of answering, then topped the grave with the last bit of soil I've collected from digging.

There. They were all covered up.

The shutter windows from the kitchen opened at the same time, only to reveal Princess Talia's bewildered face. Like me and everyone else, the dark circles around her eyes were pronounced. None of us got much sleep after the murder spree the other day.

"Didn't you hear me calling?" she asked, elbows propping on the window sill.

I let go of the shovel and shrugged. "Sorry, Princess. Muscles was making a lot of noises." I chuckled when her eyes grew wider. "Psych!"

"Har-har." She rolled her eyes before beckoning to me. "Come inside. We're having a meeting."

The meeting was done in the kitchen while the four of us were seated around the table. Because Brooke was beside the window, the sunlight made a spotlight on the side of her face. I've never seen anyone look better.

My old man used to say that I was a sucker for anything pretty. And though it might seem like that with Brooke, the reason why I liked her went beyond the physical. It was intergalactic. The big bang. Those geeky reasons, plus the fact that she'd saved me twice now: first, in the barn. Second, from the fire on the stage. If it weren't for her, I would be buried beside Muscles. No questions asked.

"Before our meeting comes to order," Cybele started, "Is everyone all right?" Her Majesty's eyes went to each one in our group, eventually leading to me and Brooke. She beamed at her best friend. "I'm glad you could join us again, Brooke."

"Me too." But Brooke wasn't smiling. Her eyes were focused on Cybele's hand, interlocked with the Princess 'on the table. It seemed like someone was not over her crush. "So. . . What do you want to discuss about, Iris?" she asked.

"Food." Cybele dropped Talia's hand and focused on Brooke too. "Were you able to bring any?"

"Sadly, no." Brooke shifted in her seat. "After I calculated what town you're going to, I collected my things and figured we could buy stuff easily." She nudged her head to me. "What I wasn't counting on was seeing Van tied to a pole

~ 331 ~

at the plaza last night. Every plan I had disappeared in trying to rescue her, including my bag and personal supplies."

"Damn it!" I cringed when Cybele scowled. But she shook her head as if to dismiss the issue, then nudged her chin to Brooke. "How exactly did you calculate my location? It wasn't like I had a pattern."

"Yeah?" A glimmer of a smile flashed on Brooke's lips. "But you're my best friend, Iris. I have a sense of these things."

"Great," Talia chimed in. "Hooray for you two. What about food again?"

The Princess 'jealousy made me snicker under my breath. Sometimes I wondered who was more into who.

Brooke sighed and leaned back on her chair. The morning sunlight was on her skin now, tanned and beautiful, just like the rest of her.

She noticed me looking and frowned. "Is there something on my face?"

"Nothing," I said.

Her frown deepened. See the thing with Brooke was she was mad at me whether I say something or not. It kinda makes me think that she hates me. But that was one of the reasons I liked her too. She'd say one thing and do another.

"Whatever," Brooke murmured, before turning to Cybele again. "It looks like we have no choice, Iris. I need to go back to town and get supplies. At least then we'll have a longer time hiding here."

"I'm sorry, but I don't agree." Her Majesty crossed her arms. "You know it's unsafe to go back now. I can't risk you again. Ever."

"So we all starve," I said. "Unless. . ."

"Unless?"

I glanced at the Princess, the knots on her forehead making me smile. "I heard humans taste good."

" Eew! No!" she said.

"But you weren't against eating Her Majest—"

"Can we just get back to the topic?" Brooke placed a dagger on the table. Boy, she wasn't kidding. Should I test to see how far she'd go?

A kick from under the table made me groan and stare at Her Highness. Cybele shook her head at me, then motioned to Brooke. "I'm open to any suggestions," she said.

Brooke exhaled through her nose. "There's a forest at the back," she said. "If we can't go to town, maybe we can hunt for food."

"I like that idea." Cybele straightened. "You and I can search this afternoon, Brooke. And with two guns we can—"

"You're not going." Brooke took her dagger and shrugged. "I'm sorry, but if you can't risk me, then I can't risk you too. You have to stay here with the Princess. Van and I will go."

I pointed to myself. "Me? Vanessa?"

Brooke rolled her eyes. "Who else?"

"But you hate me."

She brushed off my statement and stared at Cybele, as if no one else was in the kitchen but them. In turn, Her Majesty beamed at us. "You know what? This is a great opportunity to reconcile your differences," she said. The green-eyed royal stood, effectively ending the meeting. Afterward, she leaned to me and whispered, "Go get em ' tiger."

"I wish."

Her Highness clapped a hand on my shoulder. "What are you nervous for, mate? I thought you had this all figured out?"

I glanced at Brooke and made a mental cringe. With other girls maybe. With this one and her dagger? I'd be lucky to be stabbed in the right place.

After ransacking the house that noon, our group had an impressive collection of water bottles, old jeans, ropes, and other junk. Princess Talia also conveniently discovered a sewing kit in one of the drawers, which she used to create a bag by transforming a pair of jeans.

"Are you sure you're leaving one of the guns behind?" Her Majesty, Cybele, looked at the revolver that Brooke had given her, then stared back at us. "You might need both when out."

I stepped away from the door with a wink. "One gun is more than enough, Your Highness. And besides, we have other weapons. Right, Brooke?"

She shrugged. "If you're talking about the one you stole from your bandmate, then yes."

"Muscles wasn't my bandmate!" I complained.

"I don't care." Brooke smiled briefly to Talia, then at Cybele, before motioning to me. "Let's get to work."

The forest, like the town in the opposite way, was a few walks from the house on the hill. Brooke hadn't talked to me once since our hike. But she was particularly attached to her dagger, tossing it in the air every now and then, only to catch it by the handle before it cut her fingers off.

I reckoned that there was no better time than at present to talk to her, so I opened my big mouth. "Brooke?"

"Yes?"

"What's your favorite music?"

The dagger twirled in the air before it dropped to her waiting hand. Meanwhile, I swallowed the lump in my throat. No other woman had made me this nervous.

"Why do you want to know?" she asked.

"Because I'm going to murder you in your sleep by singing the songs you listen to." I clapped a hand over my mouth when I realized what I said. Vanessa, what the Frick Frack kitty cat is wrong with you?

My heart was doing the loop de loop when I stared at her, but Brooke didn't look irritated at my answer. A ghost of a smile even haunted on her lips. "Dead Syrens," she said. "You know them?"

"Nope." I touched the knife I borrowed from Muscles. "Sadly, the tribe I came from don't listen to those kinds of music. We're only allowed to chant and repeat spells, especially when making a virgin sacrifice at full moons."

She gaped at me. "Are you serious?"

Her eyes narrowed when I laughed. "Sorry to disappoint," I said, "but I'm a normal person despite what you think. Of course, I listen to their songs."

"You're not funny."

It was my turn to frown as we went on our way. In the near distance, the forest was looming. "What do you mean I'm not funny?" I said. "Everyone loves my humor. Just ask every woman I've dated, and they'd say that's my winning quality."

"That's probably the reason why they broke up with you too." Brooke gave me a sidelong glance. "Listen, Van. I'm different, okay? Your jokes don't amuse me. Not a bit."

Our conversation discontinued when the forest edge swallowed us like an alligator's mouth. Below us, the grounds were rocky like teeth. The two of us concentrated on the path until we came upon a river.

"This is a good spot," she said. "Hand me the trap."

"Do you want me to teach you how to set it?"

"No."

Brooke surveyed the surroundings while I shuffled through the jean-bag. The forest was humid even when the sun was about to rest, and though I was familiar with this scene, I knew that

Brooke was a city girl like Her Majesty. So how come she wasn't bothered by it?

"There." I retrieved the trap. "Found it."

Brooke came to me and held out her hand to get the trap, and in doing so, exposed her sweat-matted shirt. I glanced away when I realized that she'd somehow removed her bra. The outline underneath wasn't helping.

"I th-thought rich girls didn't know how to do these sort of s-stuff?" I stammered.

Vanessa, chill the frick out!

Brooke went to a bushy spot and began to work on the wires. I was confident that we'd catch something with the trap. It was my handiwork after all.

"Cybele might not look it," she said after seconds, "but the nerd likes to learn stuff. I had to adapt to ride with her quirks."

"Her Majesty does look like the nerdy type." I kicked an imaginary ball. "If you don't count the gun slinging, ass kicking, sexy smirk she's hiding in all that hot royalty body." I turned to Brooke. "Do you have any other interest that doesn't involve her?"

"What do you mean?" she asked.

"I meant it as I said it. You're too caught up with your best friend."

Lines appeared on Brooke's forehead. "Am I?"

"It's kind of obvious."

She didn't answer immediately and stood to loop the wire on a nearby tree. I watched

~ 337 ~

transfixed at her for minutes, until she murmured to no one in particular. "I think I'll end up alone."

My stomach protested. "Why is that?"

"I don't know." She sighed. "I can't imagine myself with someone other than Iris. Even when. . ." Brooke's fingers fumbled on the rope. "Even when I've seen everything from the CCTV in Talia's room," she finished.

I lowered my eyes to the grass and swallowed. I had a feeling I knew exactly what she was referring to. "So you know?"

"Everything." Her voice had thickened. "I still can't believe it."

Neither could I, and the fact that she saw Cybele and Talia doing things. It must have hurt her.

I found myself going closer to Brooke, to the point where my hands were touching her shoulders, my face inches from her. She and I were the same height. And it wasn't hard to stare at her dark eyes, to see that she needed care too.

"Love someone else," I said. "You deserve it."

She glanced away. "Who do you want me love? You?"

"You won't regret it. I'll make you forget."

Brooke gave a small laugh before moving away from my grip. "Don't promise something like that," she whispered. "I might make the mistake of believing in you."

Chapter 34
Vanessa

It's been several days since Brooke had suggested hunting to the others. Since then, the two of us would leave the house in the afternoon, fresh water and supplies ready, to have an adventure of our own. I've never felt so alive.

Maybe it was because we were in the forest—nature has been close to my heart after my old man bought a cabin. Or maybe because I felt useful to Cybele and the Princess by getting food to tide us by. But the main reason, I figured, was because of all the time I'd been spending with Brooke. I'd learned so much about her in the past few days.

Half of her family originated from Australia. The other half were British. After her parents established a business, they moved from sunny Whitehaven Beach to chillier England and had settled there ever since. All these she told me one day while we were setting up new traps. And I think my little crush was not so little anymore. Especially after I saw the look on her face.

Brooke got this gleam in her eyes when she talked about her parents. Not just a simple gleam too. It was brighter compared to the one she'd get when holding her dagger or typing on her computer. Brighter, even, when speaking to Cybele.

That's why I wanted to meet her parents someday. Correction, Mom and Mad. Ha-ha-ha!

"Shh!" Brooke shushed, head turning to me. Uh-oh. She didn't look happy.

"What?" I asked. "I didn't say anything."

The muscles on her jaw twitched. "You were standing there and laughing. Have you gone mad?" A fleeting sound made her look forward and groan. The game we were tracking a while ago had disappeared from sight, not even a trace in the bushes. She turned to me fully. "You're such a freaking maniac, you know that?"

My shoulders slumped. This was why she wouldn't take me seriously compared to Her Majesty. I had to explain myself. "It's okay, Brookey baby. It's just a bunny anyway. You don't want to eat that." She raised an eyebrow. Okay, maybe this was the reason why she didn't take me seriously. But what could I do? Even my mom used to tell me that I couldn't keep my trap shut. "It's momma might miss it," I continued. "Did you think of that? No? How selfish of you."

I might be mistaken. I really didn't know. But for a second, the trace of a smile flitted on Brooke's lips before she turned away. "Unbelievable," she murmured. "And to think you were a hunter before you met us. Was that all an act?"

"Hey, I'm good at catching things, not killing them," I said. "Stop judging me."

She pocketed her dagger. "Do you know who Charles is?"

"Xavier?" I pumped my fist in the air. "Who doesn't? He's bald, but man, his powers are the best."

"I was talking about Darwin." Brooke started walking. "Theory of evolution? Natural selection? Does any of that ring a bell?" She stepped over a small branch and sighed. "Blimey, Van, your mind is always in the clouds. Did you listen to any of your lessons at school?"

I lagged behind her but took the branch instead of stepping over it. My grades were great, if that's what she was asking. Dad said I had a talent with contraptions too. But I guess I was more of an expert in messing things up than building them, if you didn't count the traps.

"I thought we were talking about mutants," I muttered.

"It figures."

My lips quirked up. She sounded annoyed but that wouldn't stop me. "I did learn a thing or two," I said. "From school, I mean."

"Oh yeah? And what's that?"

I caught up with her and grinned. "My favorite professor said that all women have a sensitive side, Brookey. Mind showing me yours?" The statement got me another scowl from her, so I raised my hands in surrender. "Okay, let's talk about Darwin instead since you love the dude so much. What was it you were trying to tell me again?"

She stopped walking and took the knife out. Its pointed edge glimmered when it came in contact with the sunlight. "Like I said," she murmured. "Survival of the fittest, Van. If we let go of every cute thing we see like we've been doing for the past few days because of you, we'll starve to death. All of us. I'd rather them be dead than me. Do you get what I'm saying?"

~ 341 ~

"Yeah." I glanced warily at the blade. "I take it back about your sensitive side though. You're savage like your best friend."

"Correct. And if you ever get in the way of my catch again?" The knife went to my throat. "This goes inside you in the most painful way imaginable."

I gulped. "Y-yes, Ma'am."

The next afternoon, we were back in the forest doing our usual hunt. The sun was prickly hot today, and what could have been an enjoyable walk through nature has become unbearably tiring for us. Even Brooke's shirt was drenched in sweat.

I took out a canister of water and bounced to her. The outline of her breasts was obvious again, so I looked away while handing the container to her. "You must be thirsty," I said. "Drink up."

But Brooke kept on walking, eyes trained forward, forehead lined with sweat. Earlier, Princess Talia had been kind enough to give me a handkerchief that she'd fashioned from unused bed sheet. I took that out too and made a move to wipe Brooke's face.

She grabbed my wrist before I could. "Stop," she whispered. "Do you hear that?"

Hear what? I wanted to ask. But my old man had taught me to listen first when hunting, which was hard considering how talkative I was. Yet I followed.

Brooke's head tilted to the direction as I it dawned on me that a small, almost indistinct sound was coming from the west. "That's an animal's cry," I said. "It's big, about a few feet tall. It sounds like it's in pain."

Brooke looked impressed before she closed her eyes to listen better. "I think you're right," she said. "Let's check it out."

The two of us went to the path with an unspoken agreement to go on stealth. We haven't encountered anyone since we'd hunted in the woods, but you could never be too sure with these things. An animal getting hurt might mean that other hunters were around. That, or there was a larger predator. My old man would be proud.

The path lead us to a steep cliff about two-story high. But if I was right about the injured animal, my assumption about the hunters or predator was a miss. The bear had obviously fallen from the cliff. It wasn't dead yet, but with all the blood it was losing, recovery was fifty-fifty.

"Wow, that's large." Brooke motioned down.

I scratched my neck and continued focusing on the bear. It was rare on these parts and must have hidden deep in the woods for us to miss it.

"You're not thinking of eating that are you?" I asked.

Brooke glanced around and beamed. Not far from us was a steady path leading down, the foothold looking stable enough for support. "Remember what I told you about Charles?" she said.

"Yeah, but my Charles is better than yours." I followed her to the path. "Yours may not be bald, but mine has super powers. Does yours have telepathic abilities? No, because Darwin sucks."

Brooke tested the first foothold before descending. "You talk too much," she said. "How did the girls you date stand it?"

"Stand it?" I snorted. "They loved it. And so will you."

Minutes later, the two of us had safely made it down, all the while keeping a safe distance from the bear. I looked up from the place where it fell from, down to the bloody state where it arrived at. The bear should have been dead, but its eyes were still alive.

My stomach turned as I stepped closer to Brooke. "Maybe we should leave it alone," I whispered. "Find a smaller catch. There could be an antelope here or something. Or maybe a squirrel."

My begs were met with a firm shake of her head. "No. We're looking at 400 kilos of protein," Brooke said. "And it's hot in these woods, but colder on the hill. If the snow finally falls, we can use the fur to keep us warm. We can take turns with its coat."

Brooke sounded a lot like Her Highness while she explained the bear's uses. But I couldn't see its benefits to us. All I could see was a living, breathing being that needed help. Maybe I was failing my old man with hunting, but animals were purer than humans. Humans killed my parents.

My eyes widened when Brooke took her dagger out and stepped forward to the paralyzed bear. "W-What are you doing?" I stammered.

She raised the knife. "Killing it, bringing it, cooking it, eating it." Brooke stopped in her tracks when I moved between her and the bear. "What do you think *you're* doing?" She'd returned the question to me.

"I. . . I don't know." It was an impulsive move. A split-second decision.

Irritation flashed on her face. "Move, Van. Remember what I told you yesterday."

Yes, I did remember. But that didn't mean I was going anywhere.

"No," I said. "I don't care if you stab me with that dagger. Leave Pooh bear alone!"

Brooke merely side-stepped me and continued going to her target. What was I supposed to do? Tackle her? Stab her? I couldn't lift a finger to hurt her, but the way this was going, she was going to kill the bear. And I was partly to blame.

"Stop," I begged. "Please!"

Brooke had almost made it there. Her fingers tightened around the hilt of her dagger, no indication of ever stopping her attacks. My eyes squeezed shut. But quickly opened again when I heard her gasp.

"W-what?"

"Oh!"

Three cubs had mysteriously found their way back to their momma, small fluffy things that looked too cute too pass. All of them circled around Brooke, one of the cubs sniffing her boots.

Helplessness was written all over her face when she gaped at me. "V-Van!"

"What?" I couldn't help the smirk from breaking out. "Survival of the fittest, right? Looks like they're stronger than you."

It took a minute for Brooke to look down, clench her jaw, and process what was happening. In such a short time, one of the cubs had settled on her boot, looking like it would fall asleep on the spot.

"Aww," I gushed. "It likes you."

"Shut up!" Brooke tried shaking the cub away. "Will you just help me and grab it?"

"Why? So you can kill their mom?"

"Exactly."

My heart was crushed by that. How could she be so heartless? "Oh, come on," I said. "Can't you just leave it alone? There are lots of animals here."

" You need to be practical." Brooke successfully got rid of one, but there were two left. "Do you think the bear is having a wonderful time?" She gritted her teeth. "It's hurt. Dying. You're just prolonging its suffering by refusing to kill it. If Cybele was here, she'd do the right thing."

"But she's not," I reasoned. "And I'm not her."

Brooke had managed to shoo away two cubs before she looked at me again. "For someone who has no problem hurting humans, you seem to be strangely fascinated with animals. And don't deny it either," she said. "Cybele had told me all about you and Lance."

The reminder made me snort. Good times.

"Can we not bring out my past and just start from here, baby?" Brooke was not amused by what I called her, but that was beside the point. "Please don't kill the bear anymore," I said. "For me?"

My begging had no effect anymore as the last cub had moved away. And despite my convincing, Brooke started for Pooh again, her knife raised higher than before.

"Suit yourself," I called. "Her death is on you. Not on me."

I turned away to wash my hands from the killing, but it didn't take away the nasty feeling in my chest. After a few seconds, I heard the dagger digging into something. I had no other choice but to look.

Brooke was grabbing her hair to my surprise, the dagger she loved pierced in the ground next to the target. She stooped over to snatch it, then swiveled to me with rage in her eyes. "Don't!" she warned. "Not a word from you, Vanessa." I closed my mouth and followed her under the tree.

We stayed under the shade for a while, not saying anything while trying to cool down. But me being me, I couldn't keep it that way for long. Especially since hundreds of questions were burning in my head.

"Why didn't you kill it?" I asked.

"God. . ." She glanced at me for the first time. "Don't you ever shut up?"

"Err. . . No?"

~ 347 ~

She hugged her knees to her chest, her eyes going to the dagger she'd pinned on the ground. "Whatever. I don't want to talk about it," she said.

"You can tell me anything."

"As if that would help." Her sigh was long and sad. "But I guess. . . I guess you deserve to know." Brooke had the loneliest look in her eyes when she turned her head to me again. It made me want to cradle her cheek. Or see if her tanned skin was real because it looked surreal to me. But I knew now wasn't the time. She was just saying something. "The bear is innocent," she whispered. "Its cubs deserve a chance to be with their parent too."

"I know."

I couldn't help myself. I touched her cheek without her permission. But she didn't swat my hand away. She only stared at me.

"You know what?" I murmured. "Your parents must be good people to raise a daughter like you."

"They are." She closed her eyes. "They'd do everything for me. And I'd do everything for them too." The last of the sunlight played on her face. She was beautiful. Perfect. And just when I was leaning for a taste of her lips, she opened her eyes and flinched. "That's why I have to kill Iris, Van."

Chapter 35
Vanessa

I hadn't slept a wink last night. No, siree. And I could probably blame it on the bugs—there were a lot of them around the house. But I think Brooke was the problem. Her admission yesterday worried me a lot. Because of it, I felt like a zombie the next day.

"Ow!"

The Princess lowered her hand. Talia didn't look guilty as her eyes scanned the area above my head, before her palms clapped together again. "Sorry," she said sheepishly. "Mosquito."

"Oh." I rubbed my cheek. "I thought you didn't like me anymore, Princess. I thought you wanted to hurt me."

She gave me a look. "Don't be dramatic, please. It really is the mosquito, Van." Talia slapped her leg for emphasis.

The two of us were supposed to be looking for things to do, just as Her Majesty had suggested at breakfast. But we'd given up after thirty minutes and just sat on the grass. There weren't much activities available out here.

Princess Talia stared questioningly at me. Looks like the mosquito she'd been fighting had finally buzzed away. "So," she said, now scratching her arm. "You haven't answered my question a while ago, Van. How's it going with you and Brooke?"

Me and her? We were great, thanks. Next question please.

The Princess waved her hand in front of my face. "Hello? Didn't you hear what I said? It's incredibly rude to ignore your Princess like this."

I knew that. And I also knew that it took her a lot to forgive me for what I've done before, and that if it weren't for her and Her Majesty, Cybele, I'd still be wasting my life. But the view below was so good. The town, whether at night or day, was just intriguing. Like a snow globe that's beautiful but a million miles away. That, and I wanted to avoid answering her. But I had to.

"Sorry, Princess. It's just. . . I'm spacing out because I didn't get enough sleep last night."

"Why, did something happen?" She plucked a grass from the ground. "You and Brooke were quiet after you've returned from the hunt yesterday. Cybele and I think something must be up."

My gosh. The intuition of these two.

"No, Princess. Nothing happened," I said. Which was a big fat lie! And I hated myself for having to say that to her, especially after they'd welcomed me like family.

This was all Brooke's fault. If she hadn't confessed her secret last night, I wouldn't have to betray the Princess—which I had pinky promised never to do again. Why did it have to be this way?

Talia nudged me with her elbow. "Hey. . . You sure nothing is bothering you?"

"Yup." I faked a smile and motioned to the horizon. "I'm just astounded by the great sun. Oh, such beauty! Oh, such splendor!"

"Oh, such bull crap," Talia chimed in. "Can you cut the nonsense and tell me? You know we can solve this together."

Ooh, Princess, stop tempting me to spill the beans.

I pressed a finger to my lips instead. "Shh. Be quiet. The spirit of your dead mother can hear you cursing like a pirate. She's not going to like it."

The Princess leaned back and exposed her neck to the sun. With the choker gone since our escape from the Palace, and her skin laid bare like that, an old scar on her throat called my attention.

I looked away and didn't ask about it though. We all had secrets to keep.

"Unfortunately," Talia picked up the conversation, "My mother is still very much alive and looking for us. And you're not telling me something, Van. You can't hide these things from me."

"Maybe you're right." I stood and dusted my jeans. "Maybe I am keeping something from you, Princess."

Her eyes flashed when I had finished getting rid of the dirt. Talia had taken the bait.

"What is it?" she asked.

I started to jog away; my voice shaky as I giggled. "I've always had a crush on your girlfriend," I said. "Someday, I'm going to steal her from you."

"Why, you!" Talia scrambled to get up, but I was faster. Her mildly irritated face was the last thing I saw before I ran to the house and closed the door behind me.

~ 351 ~

Victory!

I pumped my fist in the air. Taking a look through the window, I saw that Princess Talia had settled back on the grass and was now staring at the sky, her arms spread on either side of her. So much for a round of chase. But this was probably better. Now if I—

Thud!

What's that?

I glanced to the stairs following another louder noise, before my own heart blasted in my chest. Something felt off. My Vancy senses were tingling.

Thud!

Dang! Her Majesty could be in trouble! Where was she?

I dashed to the stairs without thinking and took two steps at a time. The noises were getting louder now: grunting, snarling, people were fighting.

Opening the first door to the left, I was greeted with the picture of Brooke on top of Cybele, a dagger pressed on Her Majesty's throat. And here I was thinking that the guards have somehow entered the house through the back. But the snake was with us all along.

"Not on my watch!" I yelled.

There were a few seconds of commotion. Brooke had elbowed my stomach following my own pounce. "Get off me!" she screamed. "What are you doing?"

I tightened my embrace on her, even when the pain in my tummy was screaming for me to let go. "This is how I love people, Brookey! I crush them to my heart!" It probably wasn't the best time to joke, but the whole thing had left me blubbering in panic.

What would happen now? Would Her Majesty forgive Brooke for trying to kill her?

I turned to Cybele to search for her reaction. Her Highness had sat up and was staring at us with a blank expression. "What is going on, Vanessa?" Cybele asked.

"Just hear me out!" I begged. "Brooke didn't mean it, okay?"

"Of course, I meant it!" She struggled against my arms. "You're so sweaty! Let go of me before I punch you!"

Cybele shrugged when I turned to her. "What she said, mate. You shouldn't harass a woman like that."

Harass? I wasn't harassing anyone.

"I don't know what's gotten into you," Cybele continued. "But you're getting in the way of our training, so please release my best friend before she does something we'll all regret."

My hands unclasped Brooke. They should have told me that in the first place. Now I. . . They. . .

I jumped up and hurried to the door. "E-Excuse me," I said. "I need to catch a unicorn."

There was nothing like a good ol 'nap to make me calm down after the disaster this morning. So, I made a mistake. Big deal. Nobody was perfect.

~ 353 ~

"Not even Her Highness."

I stretched my arms and yawned, the midday sunlight was getting too hot on my face. Maybe I should go back inside and ask them what the plan for lunch was. Cybele was surprisingly good at cooking.

Getting up from the grass, I made my way to the corner of the house and stopped. A few meters from me, Her Highness was standing rigidly, back turned to me, all by herself.

Should I call out to her?

Cybele would sometimes get this look on her face that told everyone to back off. It didn't happen too often lately, but when it did, I got the feeling that she would rather be alone to think. Was this one of those moments?

A subtle movement on the left made me look. My palms became sweaty. Brooke was watching Her Majesty not far from me, an intent look on her own face. The knife in her hand gleamed. Yikes!

My legs acted on their own accord. I was running to Brooke before I've decided anything, tackled her to the grass, and pinned her underneath me. If this wasn't an assassination attempt, I'd probably be thanking my lucky stars that we were in this position. But she'd tried to kill Her Highness, and I was breathing hard.

"How could you?" I said.

"How could I what?" Brooke tried to buck me off. "You gormless twit!"

"Oh, so now you're calling me names?" I moved my knee against her leg. "You look like Tweety bird too!"

Harried footsteps sounded to our right until another person was squeezing my shoulder. "Vanessa, this is getting ridiculous." I turned to Her Majesty, Cybele. She didn't look so happy that I'd nailed her best friend a second time.

Realization hit me like a hammer. "Still training?" I asked.

"Still training," she said.

Brooke gave out an anguished cry as I finally let go and rolled off her. I didn't speak or apologize and simply stood and rushed to the house.

Talia was leaning on the wall beside the door when I passed. "Having a rough day?" she asked.

"Super." I entered the house and didn't look back.

What was wrong with me? Was this the guilt of knowing something I shouldn't have? Maybe. Because under different circumstances, I wouldn't risk embarrassing myself, and not just once, but twice in a day.

Afternoon couldn't have come any sooner. By that time, I was more than ready to apologize for my mistakes. Wipe the slate clean. I headed down the stairs and saw the Princess writing on an old notebook in the kitchen.

"Where'd you get that?" I asked.

"Under the bed." There was a scratching sound as she continued to write. Her brows were pulled together in concentration. "There's nothing to do out here," she murmured. "I might as well be productive."

"I agree. . ." More scratching. "Are you making a diary entry?"

"Nope. I'm writing a story about an alien. My mother would be so disturbed if she finds out."

"Let's hope she doesn't find out. Ever." I looked around the kitchen. We hadn't eaten lunch yet, and the monster in my stomach would start chomping me if I didn't feed it soon. "Where's Her Highness at?" My eyes fell back to Talia. "Did you see her?" The Princess 'pen pointed to the window. "Thanks."

I was feeling better about myself when I went through the door. Except for the growling stomach, there was nothing to be ashamed of. Everything was under control.

Her Majesty was talking to Brooke when I finally spotted them. From the look on her face, she was fascinated with whatever conversation they were having. And Brooke was sweet enough to pass Cybele a glass of water. My heartbeat quickened. A glass of pure, clean—no Van. Stop what you're thinking!

"Whoops!"

The three of us glanced down. I had slapped the glass from Her Majesty's hand so hard it toppled on the grass.

Cybele took a deep shaky breath before her eyes returned to me, but I was already rambling. "When are you going to get your period, Your Highness?" I asked.

From the corner of my eye, I saw Brooke's mouth slacken. Even Her Majesty looked disturbed by my question. But she was a pro for answering with a straight face. "I don't know. Who cares?"

"I do!" My hands moved with my explanation. "If you want to impregnate the Princess, you have to stay away from cold water."

"Huh?" Cybele stared worriedly at Brooke. "Is it just me or did the heat get to her head? What should we do? I've never encountered anything like this."

Because her best friend had never tried to murder her before! That was what I was trying to say!

I took in a gulp of air before speaking again. "If you want your baby to be nice and juicy, Your Highness, you have to stay away from your best friend." I shook my head. "No! I made a mistake! Not nice and juicy, because that's for chicken. And your daughter will be human. A bouncing baby girl."

Cybele reached out and squeezed my shoulders. "Vanessa," she said. "I think you need to sit down, mate."

I shook her hands away. "No, Your Majesty! Vanessa will not rest. Vanessa will protect you!"

The two of them exchanged glances before Brooke started for me. "Van, are you okay?"

The muscles on my face tightened. Okay? Okay? "No, I'm not okay!" I yelled. "Are you?" I started to circle them. "Cause you known damn well why I'm acting this way, Brooke!"

She froze. That's right, woman, cower before me.

"Wait a minute," she hissed. "We should talk about this."

"Talk about what?" Her Majesty had a bewildered look about her as she swiveled to Brooke. "What happened last night?"

"I'd like to know that too." Princess Talia had obviously heard the racket and had made it to us without anyone noticing. She folded her arms and pursed her lips at me. "Tell us what's going on, Van. I know for a fact that you lied about having a crush on Cybele."

"Wait. Who has a crush on me?"

Brooke yanked my hand. "You have a crush on Cybele?"

Their questions and accusations were making me dizzy. First with Brooke. And then with Cybele and Talia.

None of this would have happened if Brooke didn't say what she'd said or if she'd just answered my questions last night instead of pretending nothing was spoken. Now things were a mess, and I didn't know which was worse: keeping a secret while hoping no one would end up dead, or telling them about it and having Brooke punished.

"Screw this!" I screamed.

Without waiting to see their reactions, I grabbed Brooke's arms, hauled her to my back, and carried her fireman style before jogging away.

"You didn't tell us what's going on!" Talia's voice echoed to me.

I fixed my gaze on the forest in the distance. "Brooke and I became a couple last night!" I hollered. "We're having our first date."

Brooke's hand missed my face by inches. "The nerve!" she said, struggling to break free.

~ 358 ~

I smacked her ass. "Just stay still, woman! I'm trying to save you."

Chapter 36
Vanessa

My old man had showed me that being loyal to a woman had its benefit: forever. Those sappy movies where the guy meets the girl and they ride off to the sunset with a horse? Exactly my parents tale. Except maybe it wasn't a horse but a car. And my mom stole it when dad was trying to load in his gas at the station—she said she always had a crush on him at school.

Law-breaking and craziness aside, yup, that was how my parents got together. That was how I, Vanessa Krieger, came to be. That was how I believed in forever.

But! There was a big but here. Every time I see beautiful women with kissable lips and to-die for body, the concept of forever just vanishes. Kaput! And eventually, I become a serial flirt.

It was easy too. Can't lie about that. Women had always eaten up my sense of humor. And I ate them right after. Cannibalism alert!

So, you see, it had never been hard for me to hook up with someone, move on to another person when the going gets rough, and start the process all over again. But I think all of that was about to end. Because the moment Brooke rescued me? I hadn't thought once about ditching her like I did with so many other girls. She was my Neo. She was the one.

"Can you just put me down?" Brooke grumbled for the tenth time. "I can walk perfectly fine. Don't act like I'm injured."

I stepped over a tree root and ignored her. The forest was the kind of place where you needed to concentrate if you didn't want a broken neck. Besides, she'd just run to Cybele the moment I released her.

"Ow!" I yelped. She'd pinched my butt out of nowhere.

Brooke was grinning when I finally squatted to put her down. "You made me do it," she said. "You should have known better than to carry me in the forest against my will."

And she should have known better than to pretend that she wasn't going to kill Cybele. But I guess we were even now.

I folded my arms and smirked. "Why are you acting like this, baby? You know I would have carried you straight to our wedding reception."

"Ha!" she said. "You wish!"

Her inability to tolerate my jokes made me scratch my chin. "How do you do it?" I murmured.

"Do what?"

"Resist me."

Amusement flashed on her face before the corner of her eyes crinkled. She found this funnier than all my jokes put together. "First of all, you're not my type. You're blonde, but I like dark hair. You always have a silly smile on your face, and the brooding type appeals to me more." Brooke stared at me from head to foot. "Plus, I'm sensing something from you."

"What?" I asked. "Superstar qualities?"

The corner of her mouth twitched. "Psychopathic tendencies," she said.

Ouch. That would have burned big time if it wasn't really true.

I stared upward nonetheless to the yellowing leaves that had heard every insult that came from her mouth. But the thing was, insults weren't the only ones that they'd heard or seen. Over the last few days, the forest had witnessed the constant push and pull of Brooke. How there was a good side to her even when she tended to be mean.

I looked at her again. "Tell me the truth, here and now," I said. "Why do you want to kill Cybele?"

The muscles in her jaw hardened. "I refuse to answer."

"Then we have no choice but to stay here."

She rolled her eyes at me. "As if you can make me do that."

Brooke had stepped forward to take the path back home when I blocked her way. She swerved to the right. But I blocked her again. "Let me pass," she growled, taking her dagger out.

I leaned forward until the darkness of her eyes sucked me in like a black hole. "Nope!" I said, then jumped back when her dagger swung my way. I knew she'd attack me eventually.

Brooke tried to make a go for it to the left, but stopped her tracks and veered to the right. I saw everything a mile away and was on her face before she could make the escape. "Bugger off!" she hissed.

"Till divorce do us part," I claimed, before avoiding another deadly attack from her dagger.

Brooke was working up a sweat now. Her shirt was clinging to her chest. She was graceful, fast, and all of that got me smitten. I've never encountered a woman who was as beautiful but spirited like her.

"Why are you staring at me like that?" she demanded. "Are you stoned?"

I avoided a punch on the face and pulled her to me. "No, I'm not stoned, but dang you're cute. Want to be my girlfriend?"

Her mouth dropped in surprise.

"Is that a yes?" I said.

"No!"

"Well then." I stole a kiss on her cheek before dodging another punch. She froze.

"Did you just?" Brooke touched her cheek, and I could see that she was pissed off by what I've done. And I mean really, really pissed off. Her face was scarlet.

Before I knew it, Brooke had grabbed me, twisted me around, and in seconds, I was staring up at her, the grass scratching my back.

Even while dizzy, I wrapped my legs around her. "You couldn't have waited until we got home, huh?" I said. "You wanted to do it here?"

"You're such a pervert!" she growled.

"Only for you, baby." I was about to say more when my ears picked up something. Noises. Coming from humans. I rolled us over and covered Brooke's mouth.

"Mff!"

"Shh!"

The drumming of her heart against my own chest made me calm down and listen. Brooke's eyes were wide open below me, but she hadn't struggled like earlier, or told me to get lost. She listened too.

We both flinched when a scream rang through the air. It was fleeting, low, but there.

I removed my hands from Brooke's mouth slowly. "Someone's in trouble."

Both of us had quickly gotten to our feet, not about to be caught in such a vulnerable position. Whoever or whatever that was, a scream meant there was danger.

Brooke pressed a hand on my chest before I could move past her. "The scream came from that way." She pointed a finger behind me. "Where are you going?"

"Back to our house." I pushed her hand away. "Her Majesty needs to be warned."

"I don't think it has anything to do with the Palace guards though." Brooke leaned down to pick up her dagger. What was up with her? She didn't look too thrilled that I wanted to go back home, even when she was the one who kept insisting earlier. Her face was decided when she straightened. "Go back if you want," she said. "But I want to see what's going on. You don't have to come with me."

Brooke didn't wait for my response. She gripped her knife, walked away, and had made it a few steps from me when I bounced beside her.

"Relationship tip," I said. "Don't make your girlfriend feel alone."

She gave me a sideward glance. "Who said you're my girlfriend?"

"I thought we've agreed?"

Finding the location of the scream hadn't been too difficult considering all we had to do was follow the tracks. My old man had taught me how to observe the forest. Every slant of the grass, every blade that was out of place indicated where humans had been. And Brooke was such a great help. Eventually, she'd found footprints leading to the thicker part of the forest.

I motioned to slow down when I heard voices beyond the thicket. More than two people were talking, and from the sound of it, not everyone was having fun. I quietly took the borrowed knife from my pocket and crouched. Glancing behind me, I saw that Brooke had silently followed my lead.

"I told ya, Smith! I told ya we ain't stealin' from that shop. But what did ya do, ya numbskull? Ya pushed right through when I wasn't lookin'. Ya'll get us rottin 'back to jail!"

"Sorry, Finky!"

"Don't call me that. My mom calls me that!"

"Sorry, Bruno!"

Bruno and Smith, two stupid-looking people, were standing in the clearing arguing. My eyes narrowed at their outfits. Everything was ill-fitting, like they'd grabbed whatever they could and got away before the real owners noticed they were gone. They reminded me of Muscles 'and his boyfriend.

"What if the owner has a camera, huh?" Bruno, the bigger guy of the two, spoke. "He'll report us to the police! Ya want your ass to be poked again?"

"No, boss. No poking." Smith scratched his head. "But what about the shopkeeper's daughter, boss? What will we do with her?"

"Ya should have asked yourself that before ya dragged her in this." Bruno jabbed a finger on Smith's chest. "We have no choice but to kill her."

Both of them turned to the right, to a struggling girl that I've only noticed at that point. She was several feet away from us, but I could see that she was only years younger. And from the look on her face, she know what was going to happen to her. She wrestled against her duct tape.

Smith started to unbutton his jeans. "No use leavin 'this girl to waste, boss. Just a quick one before we dump her."

Brooke clasped my arm. "I can't take this," she whispered. "Wait here."

Was she out of her mind? As if I could stand here and watch while she put herself in danger. But Brooke had leaped out of the bushes already.

I watched mesmerized as she raised her hand and release the dagger in the air. My stomach clenched when the blade found its target.

~ 366 ~

Smith crumpled to the ground, head bleeding from the attack.

"What the?" Bruno turned to them, saw what happened to Smith, and took a gun from under his shirt. It was my turn to jump out of the hiding place.

"No, you don't!"

Something smacked on the back of my head. For a few seconds, I found myself coughing on the ground, while another pair of legs made their way towards me.

There was a third goon. There weren't just Bruno and Smith. And the other guy kicked me on the stomach, making me roll on the ground, gasping for air.

"You're. . ."

He bent over and grabbed my hair. "I'm what?" he said.

I sneered before I reared my head. Time to make a comeback. "You're ugleh!" I yelled, then head-butted him so hard, I thought my own skull was going to crack. But that did the trick. He removed his hand from me, crouched in pain, and I took that opportunity to stand and kick him in the balls. My eyes widened. "Heck, dude! Why aren't you hurt?" I asked.

He straightened his back and moved his head side to side. "That won't work. I'm a woman."

"Really?" I stepped towards her and grabbed her chest. "How about this?"

She shrieked in pain when I twisted her nips, then smacked me on the face that I fell on the ground. "Die!" she screamed, and took out something from her jeans. Was that a gun?

My head was still spinning from the punch, so I couldn't get away in time. The woman put her finger on the trigger, sneered at me, then suddenly fell forward. Brooke, eyes blazing, lowered her own weapon from behind. Where'd she got that?

"Idiot!" she yelled. "You're such a blundering mass of stupidity!" She picked a stone and threw it to me.

I tried to dodge, but it still hit my leg. "Hey. . ."

"Shut it! Put a sock in your mouth for once, Vanessa!" Her face was the reddest I've seen it—even redder when I'd teased her this morning.

Brooke turned on her heels and marched to the girl. Bruno, from what I could see, was dead and had a stab wound on his neck.

It was dark when Brooke and I came to a hot spring. After having a conversation with the girl, she'd agreed to help us get supplies as thank you for saving her life. We were told to meet after two hours, and was pointed to the spring to wait.

Brooke still hadn't talked to me even after we'd walked there. She was mad at me for some reason, and what that reason was, I didn't understand. But I did understand this; she was removing her clothes a few feet in front of me.

"Woah!" I said, unable to help myself. "Wh-What are you getting nakey for?"

She didn't speak and continued getting her clothes off. Afterward, she dipped her toes into the water.

~ 368 ~

"Oh. . ." My laugh was shaky. "Bath time. Right."

I caught a small glimpse of her back before I looked the other way and sat on the grass. If Brooke was beautiful clothed, she made me imagine dirty things like this. I swallowed and hugged my knees.

A few minutes passed without us talking. A few minutes spent feeling ants crawling in my boot, and me picking them away. Until one of them got me.

I jumped up and screeched. "Ant! Ant!" I hopped on one foot while trying to remove the little sheeks from me. And that was when it happened. I slipped, right into the spring.

Splash!

I gasped and swallowed water. Now I was going to die because it was malaria-infested. Halp!

Someone hauled me upward. "You are such a migraine-inducing woman. Do you realize that?" Brooke was pursing her lips at me when I wiped my face.

"S-Sorry!" I said. "I. . ." My throat swallowed on its own when I looked down. Brooke was not only inches from me, she was naked and beautiful too.

"You were saying?"

"I. . ." The words got caught in my throat. "I. . . I want to kiss you."

She slapped me on the cheek. "Try it."

I didn't. But I did trail my finger on her back, and celebrated quietly when she closed her eyes.

Realization swept over me. "You like me," I whispered. "You want me too."

"I don't." But her breaths were quickening. And below the water, the rest of her was gravitating towards me, as if being pulled by a magnet.

She groaned when I leaned forward and kissed her neck. "I'll treat you right," I murmured. "You'll be my only one."

"Van. . ."

"You'll never work for my attention because you'll always have it." I bit her skin.

The moan she made was music to my ears. But it was when she slapped me again, followed by the grabbing of my hair, that made me forget how to breathe. Her eyes were cloudy under the moonlight. "I do like you," she whispered. "Damn you for making me admit it."

My eyes closed when she started to remove my shirt. Maybe forever wasn't such a bad thing after all.

Chapter 37
Cybele

It was at the wake of dawn when Talia and I met in the living room. With Van and Brooke gone for the night, I've taken it upon myself to stay on guard. But the Princess, too, appeared like she had slipped in and out of sleep herself. On top of that, she looked worriedly to the window.

"They haven't returned yet," she murmured, eyes traveling back to me. "Do you think something happened?"

The old couch creaked when I stood. "Brooke is a smart girl."

"I understand that." Talia studied my face. "But I also understand that something is bothering her. She did try to kill you before Van stepped in."

I gasped. "Really?"

The Princess gave a mirthless laugh. "Don't play the innocent game with me, Cybele. You're not blind. You know what I'm talking about."

I braced myself when Talia went to me, a gleam in her eyes. What she'd do was slap me for covering up for Brooke, and I deserved the sting of it, even more.

My lips parted open when her palm raised and headed towards me. But the pain didn't come, only a caress.

"Relax," she murmured, stroking my cheek. "If I want to punish you, I'll do it where I'll benefit most—the bedroom." She had moved away before I could reciprocate the gesture. Talia had total ownership of my heart now, and the woman knew how to play her strengths.

"You're such a tease," I said, voice gruff.

"Precisely." The Princess 'face turned serious. "But really, now. Why do you think Brooke would want to harm you? Is it because of our relationship?"

The shake of my head was firm. "No," I said. "She wouldn't sink that low."

"Then there's only one explanation left." Talia's eyes closed briefly when she sighed. Upon opening them again, she looked apologetic. "I should have turned a blind eye when you wanted to kill my mother," she whispered. "I'm sorry."

The usual torment whenever Esmeralda's name was mentioned came like a sweeping wave. But my feelings for Talia overpowered it— overshadowed the hate. And even though I knew that the Princess still loved her mother, a small part of me was reassured too. Because Talia feeling like that proved that she was different. The monster gene didn't get to her.

"It's not your fault," I found myself saying. "And instead of blaming yourself, why don't we just figure things out? All right?"

Her nod was meek. "Sure."

Both of us headed to the sofa. The sun hadn't fully risen outside yet, and with the candle almost gone on its holder, darkness threatened to consume us. But it was all right. Everything would be fine as long as Talia was with me. We just had to figure things out.

"Let's think of possible scenarios about their delayed return," I offered. My pointer finger came up. "One, they went so deep into the forest and got lost."

"Impossible." Talia was quick to dismiss it. "I don't know about Brooke, but Van knows her way into the woods. Remember what she told us the other day? She grew up in this kind of environment, so I doubt that she wouldn't find her way back."

I remembered. But at least we got that out of the way.

"Number two," I said, ticking off another finger. "They had an accident."

"Likely." A shadow crossed Talia's face. "But I can derive an argument from that. Say Brooke fell and broke her ankle." The Princess cringed when I made noises at the back of my throat. "Just for the sake of argument," she reminded. "In that scenario, Van would be able to lift Brooke, or vice versa, correct? And the probability of both of them experiencing the same fall would be low. Which only leads us to one other thing. . ."

The bad feeling clawing inside me finally made its way out when I kicked the candle beside us onto the floor. But it didn't make any difference. The candle had long been extinguished. And Van and Brooke were probably being marched back to the Palace as we speak.

"I need to get them," I said.

"What about me?"

Yes, dummy. What about her?

"I have to leave you somewhere safe," I said, my legs springing up on their own. The lack of sleep wasn't a problem. The thought of my friends was enough to make me feel like I've swallowed ten cups of coffee.

But Talia wasn't the type to just get left behind. "I'm coming with you," she declared.

"No."

She crossed her arms. "Why not? They're my friends too."

"I know that, but we've been through this before. You go to the Palace, the guards get you. Where does that leave us?"

I tried to pull her away from the sofa. It was under the couch where we'd hidden the guns. Brooke and Van left both of them by accident before going to the woods last night. I thought they'd just make a quick trip to talk and come home.

"I'm not budging from here," the Princess said when I pulled her again.

"Talia." My tone was all the warning she would get. Next time, I would lift her without telling, and I wouldn't care if she slapped me left and right.

The Princess pinched her eyes at me. "Don't you dare," she murmured. "I know what you're thinking, you sneaky little lesbian."

"No, you don't." I readied my hands. "And haven't we come to an agreement that we're both lesbians? Don't bring a conversation that had been resolved eons ago."

She squealed when I attacked. But then, so did the door. It groaned when someone knocked on it three times.

Talia and I stopped in the middle of grabbing each other. "That's not our secret code." She pushed me from her gently.

I reciprocated by pulling her up. But this time, she didn't make a fuss and gave me a concerned look. "I'll check on the window," I whispered.

As usual, Talia couldn't stop herself from trailing behind me. Her breaths were warm and bothersome on my nape, but I tried to keep my focus as I parted the curtains and peeked outside.

"It's a teenager," I whispered. "A girl."

The stranger was standing a few steps from the door, unassuming in jeans and a jacket. She turned to the window just before I pulled Talia downward. "You don't happen to have a friend near here, do you, Princess?"

Talia glanced up to the window, to the curtains hiding us inside, before looking at me again and shaking her head. "You know the answer to that."

Yes. But I still wanted to make sure. It meant the girl was either a stray or a spy.

"Wait here," I whispered. Dashing to the kitchen, I rummaged through the sack we'd found from one of the rooms upstairs and grabbed what I was looking for.

Talia was still crouched by the window when I ran back to the living room. She gave me a questioning stare as I tossed her a scarf, then wrapped a second one over my nose and mouth, on the pretense that I was just a bit cold because of the morning temperature. "What are you planning?" she asked.

"Just watch."

The knocks repeated when I was taking the guns from the couch. I handed one to Talia before I hooked the other behind my jeans. And then I finally opened the door.

"Hello," I greeted. "Isn't it a bit too early to be bothering other people?"

The teenager straightened. She was wearing a backpack from what I could see. And on each side of her were duffel bags. But she was alone. That, I was sure of.

"Hello?" I repeated. "What do you want?"

"Are you Cybele?" She didn't beat around the bush. Nor did she shy away from looking straight into my eyes. "Brooke told me that you'll have an unmissable face. But since you've done a fab job of covering it up, I'll have to rely on those gorgeous wide green eyes. Her descriptions are pretty accurate."

All right, I've heard enough.

Taking the gun from behind me, I pointed it between her eyes and demanded, "Raise your hands. Slowly."

The girl did as I told her, though not without a curse under her breath.

Talia looked to be the only one surprised as I walked backward to the house with the teenager in tow. "I thought you had a sound plan?" she said. The Princess quickly covered her face with the scarf I gave her earlier. "Why are we keeping her hostage?"

"She knows about me." I grabbed the girl by the neck as soon as she walked inside the house, then kicked the door shut behind me. "Walk straight," I instructed. "There. To the kitchen."

Talia followed behind us while I directed the girl to the chair. The Princess looked shaken by the whole thing, though I could see that if push comes to shove, she wouldn't hesitate to do what I say. Which I took advantage of.

"Love, please take the ropes from the sack." I pointed the gun to the girl again. "You, there. Talk."

For a few seconds, the teenager looked like she would hold back. But her eyes widened when I removed the scarf. "Holy cow!" she exclaimed. "You're hella cute!"

"Isn't she?" Talia made it to the girl and started wrapping the rope around the chair even though I haven't told her what to do with it yet. The sun had begun to rise now, and the light through the window made the Princess 'eyes gleam. "I know Cybele is cute," she whispered. "But she's mine. Back off."

"Okay, sister. You don't have to be batshit about it." The girl rolled her eyes before she glanced at me. "I'm straight, by the way, so no homo."

I removed the safety switch from the gun. Every second this kid talked irritated me more and more. "Where are Brooke and Van?" I demanded. "Who are you?"

"I'm you," she answered. "Only cooler." The teenager rocked back and forth on the chair when I put my finger on the trigger. "I was kidding!" she protested. "Why are you all so serious? Van and Brooke sent me here to bring you the goods. And I ain't talking about my sexy body either. Just look inside the duffel bags."

Talia was about to move when I stopped her. "No," I said. "Let me do it. Take out your gun while I check."

Talia had pointed the revolver to the tied-up teenager and was patting down her pockets when I slipped away. The air was still chilly when I opened the door a crack. But as I've inspected earlier, no guards had followed the girl up the hill. But we could never be too sure.

My heartbeat raced a notch when I stooped down and unzipped the duffel an inch. Nothing exploded on my face. But when I finally opened the whole thing, I was so surprised that I immediately took it with me inside and put it on the kitchen table.

Talia also looked shocked when she saw the over spilling contents. "Hey," she murmured. "Why did she bring guns?"

"I don't know," I said, before turning to girl. "You're going to tell me now or I'll use one of that on your face. Where are our friends?"

The girl gave a disconcerting half shrug. "Beats me," she admitted. "I barely even know them. But they've helped me escape yesterday from the thugs that took me to the woods, so I offered them anything they wanted. My dad's a businessman in town. I hate to brag, but I'm kinda rich."

Talia couldn't help but snort. But I wasn't relaxed yet. Van and Brooke should be here, not the duffels, and I had a feeling there was more.

The teenager shifted on her seat, a knowing look on her smug face. "They told me that if you really want to know, you'll check the thing in my backpack. All the answers are there."

Chapter 38
Cybele

Whether the girl was telling the truth or not was subject to debate. Unfortunately, the luxury of time was not on our side. Our friends could be in danger, and it was up to me to save them however I could. Coincidentally, Talia was thinking the same.

"Look at me," she commanded. But before either the girl or I could ask why, the Princess had taken off the shawl covering her face. "Do you recognize me?"

My knuckles whitened. "You didn't have to do that," I said. People knowing that she was here was not a good idea. But Talia ignored me.

For her part, the gangly teenager gaped at the Princess, the signs of recognition dawning on her eyes. "You're. . ."

Talia moved forward so the light was shining on her. "Yes?"

The teenager smirked. "You look fatter in person," she remarked.

I seized Talia's hand before she could do something we'd both regret, and pushed her behind me. To the girl who was now laughing merrily, I said, "Enough small talks. You appeared surprised when you saw the Princess. That's good. But didn't the Palace say anything in the news?"

The teenager stopped laughing. "Like what?" she asked. "Last I heard, the Princess was getting married to what's-his-face."

I turned to Talia who was still simpering behind me. "We should let her go," I murmured. "She's innocent."

The Princess stared heavenward. "For goodness sake, Cybele, let your jealousy for Lancelot go."

"Who said I was jealous?" I was smiling when I stared at the teenager again. A moment ago, she looked conceited. But now I could also see the awe in her. Meeting the Princess in person must have been thrilling. "You look nothing but a small-town girl who got caught up in this," I said to the girl. "Will you tell a soul what you've just witnessed here?"

I waited for her to lie. But the look on her face as she muttered no was earnest. Talia must have hoped the same when she revealed herself. I wasn't done though.

"What's in the backpack?" I prodded.

"A laptop." The girl nudged her chin to the direction of the door. "The other duffel that you didn't bring inside has canned goods," she said. "Van and Brooke told me to bring you stock that will last for weeks, but they didn't tell me why."

Talia bit her lip before turning to me. The worry in her face had doubled since this morning. "Can you check the laptop while I talk to the girl, Cybele?" It wasn't a question. She was requesting it from me.

"Sure," I said.

The two of them remained in the kitchen after the girl was untied. I could see them in the corner of my eye, hear them whispering about the news in town. I tried to concentrate on my own task by retrieving the laptop from the backpack. It looked innocent enough, but a file named '*Iris*' told me that it really came from Brooke. More so when it refused to open.

I was running a program to unlock it when Talia came behind me and peered over my shoulder. Her scent immediately relaxed me. If we were any other people living any other life, this would have been a lovely picture: us together in a house, looking over each other's shoulders, waiting for our children to wake-up upstairs.

I sighed when she wrapped her arms around me. "I sent the girl home," she murmured. "There's no use keeping her here."

The password-protected file took me a few minutes to crack. It was not enough time to savor the Princess 'warmth, though it helped that she was there. Huddled together, we stared at the screen as I opened the folder and clicked the file. It brought out a video.

My eyebrows raised when I realized who had made it.

"Iris," Brooke greeted. "And Princess Talia. . ."

"Your Majesty's," Van supplied.

The two of them were seated near a small fire, and what looked to be a body of water in the background. The darkness told me that it was nighttime, though how and why they did this worried me as much as the thought of the guards catching them.

"You must be boggled," Brooke continued. "I would be too. I mean, what we're planning is bloody crazy." She followed it with a humorless laugh, shook her head in disbelief, then looked straight at the camera again as if talking directly to me. "The bag contains supplies, Iris. Use them to survive for however long you can. That's my parting gift to you." She nudged Vanessa with her knee. "Your turn."

"That's it?" Van looked disappointed. "When were you planning to tell them that we're running away because I got you pregnant?"

"Van. . ."

"They know I'm joking." The blonde stared at the camera. "Okay, I'm serious now. What do you want me to say, Brookey?"

"Just like what we practiced."

Van looked at her. "Seriously? You want me to scream their names like you did with mine?" She laughed and immediately shielded her face. She knew what was coming after the bold statement.

But surprisingly, Brooke didn't make a move to scold her. My best friend leaned her head on Van's shoulder and closed her eyes. "Come on," she said in a small voice. "Say goodbye."

"D-Do I have to?"

"Yes."

It took a few seconds for Van to pick up where they left off. And when she did, the look in her eyes made me want run to them. "I guess there's no helping it." Her voice was shaky. "I. . . I can't join your adventures anymore, Your Highness. I'm sorry."

~ 383 ~

"Huh?" Talia moved closer to the laptop. "What's going on?"

On the screen, Brooke was trying to console a sniffing Vanessa. "We agreed not to cry," my best friend said.

"Yeah, but I'm so sad for them." Van wiped her eyes. "Imagine losing someone like me. I can't think of a bigger tragedy."

Brooke laughed and stared at the camera. But like Vanessa, she had begun to cry too. "We should make this quick then," she said. "There's no use prolonging the inevitable." Brooke took a shaky breath and continued. "Iris. . . The Queen had my parents captured and asked me to kill you in exchange for their freedom. I thought. . . I thought if I pretended to harm you then I could finally go through with it. But I couldn't. You're too important to me."

A silence hung in the air. A silence so thick it could only be broken by her.

"Don't look for us," she whispered. "We're going to try and track down my parents. We think the guards have brought them to a separate safe house."

"Don't call us, we'll call you," Van said before the video concluded.

The blank screen was as much a message as the one we'd watched seconds ago. Beside me, I could feel Talia's eyes boring down my face. It was time to make a decision.

The Princess and I stayed in separate rooms while I figured out what to do. The sun had fully risen now, but inside the house it was still cold.

Finally, after what seemed like minutes, I called her back to the kitchen where we'd left the bags and laptop untouched, and gestured to the chair. "Please," I invited.

Talia was more than happy to comply, albeit with a poker face. I studied her for a while. The choice I made could backfire somehow, and years from now, I could be somewhere alone, regretting what I've done. But this was how it should be.

"I'm not your mother," I started, earning a mild look of surprise from Talia. "The decision whether to go with me should come from you. I can't hold you back anymore."

Her fingers twitched, but she didn't say anything. Briefly, I wondered if it was too late to recant my statement.

"Do you still wish to go with me to the rescue mission?"

"Yes." She sounded sure of herself. It was one of the many things I've admired about her, but coincidentally one of the many we fought about too. The Princess, when decided, could be hardheaded.

My own chair scraped on the floor when I stood. I couldn't do anything about her lack of self-preservation, but I was going to make sure that she was prepared.

"Cybele?" Talia said when I had passed her chair. She didn't touch my arm nor reached for my hand. She simply looked up at me, grey eyes on fire, pink lips moving. "Thank you for respecting me," she said. "I know you're not my mother—God forbid you become as evil as her." Talia's eyes twinkled. "But you're my girl. And maybe after we'd rescued our maid of honors, my wife too."

My breath came out short. She had snatched my lungs in just a few words.

Talia laughed and covered her ears when I was about to answer. "Not yet," she said. "Tell me when we've gotten them. Only after that."

"Y-You sure?"

"Yes." She lowered her hands while I tried to compose myself. The Princess saying that out of nowhere unhinged me. "So. . ." she continued, jumping from her chair. "Where do we begin?"

The bags had everything we'd need just like Brooke promised: food, untraceable phones, clothes, money, and more importantly, guns and ammos of different calibers. I asked Talia to change while I determined what to bring for the mission. She looked fresh in tight jeans and a long-sleeved t-shirt when she came back. Her hair was also secured in a ponytail.

"Follow me outside," I said.

The Princess 'brows furrowed as I handed her a gun with a suppressor once we were under the sun.

"How much do you know about it?"

She inspected it every inch, as if seeing it for the first time. "Not much," she admitted. "My mother didn't allow me to go anywhere near the shooting range, even when I insisted."

As expected of the false Queen. She wanted to leave her daughter feeling defenseless, on the pretense that Talia was well-protected with the guards. A big mistake.

I went closer to the Princess and took her hand that was holding the gun, then raised the tip of the barrel so it was pointing at my chest. She clammed up. "Is this a good idea?"

"It's okay," I assured. "The safety switch is on and the magazine is in my pocket." She still looked uncomfortable, so I added. "We have four tasks today before we leave for the mission. One, you will know how to handle the gun. Two, I'll teach you the basics of self-defense. Three, we'll do a mini-course. And four. . . You'll find out about the fourth if you pass my test."

We skipped the small talk. Since we only had a day to practice everything, and we still had to figure out where Brooke and Van went, Talia and I dove straight to handling the gun, how to reload, and how to shoot. She was a fast learner, but I was still worried each time she missed a target. The guards we'd be going against had been trained for years.

By midday, both of us were drenched in sweat, breathing hard, and dog-tired. We'd just sparred for a straight hour.

"We should stop here," I said, wiping my face with my sleeves.

Talia stooped over and placed her hands on her knees, though her head made a firm shake. "No," she panted. "I can still do this. I want this."

I know she did. Talia made me proud by not giving up. But there were still two tasks left, and there was the issue of resting. We needed that too if we wanted to be strong enough to infiltrate any building tonight.

"I'm not letting you off the hook easily, Princess. I just need you to prepare for my third task."

Curiosity filled her eyes as she straightened. "What is it?"

"A challenge." I motioned to the house behind me. "Your goal is to get to our bedroom in the second floor without me catching you. If you manage to do that, then I'll know you're ready. Fail, and we're both dead tonight."

"I see. Can you give me time to think of a strategy?"

The corner of my mouth pulled-up. The Princess hadn't backed down. "Just inform me when you're done," I said. "I'll cook some brunch in the meantime."

A pot of chicken soup was boiling on the stove when I finally tinkered with the laptop. The food gave the kitchen such a great smell that my stomach rumbled every few minutes, but I directed my efforts on trying to pinpoint Brooke's last know location.

Knowing her, she'd probably obtain another computer for her own needs. Brooke had become close to my Mum and Dad over the years. And even though it looked like she was with Vanessa now, she would definitely try to contact my parents to give some sort of goodbye. It was through it that I'd find her.

"Cybele?" Talia's voice sounded behind me. "I think I'm ready."

I glanced at her over my shoulder. She had washed her face and was sniffing like I did when I first made the soup. "Don't you want to have lunch first?" I said.

"Maybe later."

The soup was left to simmer when Talia and I went to the main door. Her hair was in a bun now, and she looked especially excited as she skipped outside. "I'll remain here," I said. "You can enter the house at any time, but make sure I can't see you."

She smiled. "Like our hide and seek?"

I smiled too. The carelessness of our youth was a long time ago. I closed the door and walked backwards to the living room. "Begin."

Nothing happened for the next five minutes. Then ten. Fifteen.

I went to the kitchen to close the stove, but something made me stop as soon as I clicked the switch. There was the sound of running on grass. Talia was waiting for me to get distracted, so she could get inside and bolt up the stairs. It was her plan all along.

Leaving the kitchen, I jogged back into the living room and waited for the door to slam open. It didn't. Instead I heard something back in the kitchen. She had lured me out of there, so she could enter through the window.

"Aha!" I said, jumping back there. My eyes narrowed at the empty space. Apart from the vapor created by the soup, nothing else was moving.

"Cybele," Talia whispered. "I'm here."

Huh? No she wasn't. Both the kitchen and the living room were vacated apart from me. I could see everything while standing in the middle of the hallway.

"Above you," her voice came again.

I was gullible enough to check the ceiling, which made her laugh.

"Talia," I growled, then realized where the voice was coming from when she laughed again.

Going back to the kitchen, I snatched the cellphone from the counter and turned it off. It was clever of the Princess to plant it when she came to get me earlier, but I needed to teach her a lesson.

A sound in the hallway leading to the back made me freeze. Of course! Why didn't I remember that? There was also a window in there.

"I got you now," I murmured under my breath.

The window was wide open when I rounded the corner, and Talia, caught red-handed, was in the middle of entering, her hair covering her pretty face. I ran to her with a triumphant smile, only to realize that I'd been played as I got closer. "What?" My stomach lurched as I examined her trickery. She had used extra set of clothes and propped it up with branches, then topped it off with a wig. This woman!

I was panting when I finally entered our bedroom on the second floor. Talia was sprawled in the mattress, looking like she'd been there for a while.

I shook my head in amusement as she took a peach from a half-open can and put it in her mouth. "You know what I think?" she said while chewing. "I think your fourth challenge involves us getting naked. Am I right?"

The door creaked as I nudged it behind me. We had the whole afternoon to kill before our mission commenced. "Maybe," I said, unbuttoning my jeans.

Chapter 39
Cybele

Rain clouds loomed in the sky as Talia entered the Toyota pickup. It was the only car I could barter in such short notice.

Handing her the laptop, I stepped on the gas and made way for the road. Only when we were outside the town did I remove the shawl from my face. Talia was still concentrated on the computer, one finger scrolling.

"Any improvements?" I asked.

"Barely." Her lips twitched. "The coordinates you pulled up isn't making much sense. There's nothing on the map."

Of course, there wasn't. She should know her mother by now.

"The coordinates are Brooke's and Van's last known location, so they must be heading somewhere near there," I said. "As for the map, your mother could have easily redone it."

"You mean erased things?" Unsettledness crossed Talia's face. Only now was she beginning to understand the extent of her mother's lunacy. She closed the laptop and stared out the window. With the way her lips were curled downward, and how white her knuckles were, I reached for her hand and gave it a soft squeeze.

"Focus on the mission," I said.

The coordinates brought us to a secluded place west of the town where we came from.

Soon, the road itself was replaced by a dirt path. The trees thickened, and we found ourselves in the heart of a forest until there was no more room for the car to maneuver. I pulled over and glanced at Talia.

"Hey. You okay?"

Her cheeks puffed before she looked at me. Slowly, she blew the air out. "I love you," she whispered.

"Are you saying goodbye?"

"No." She gave me a lovely smile. "It feels like I don't say it enough though."

I took her hand and placed it on my face. Talia had always been warm, even when the rest around us were frozen. "I love you too," I murmured.

The gravity of what we were going to do only sprung up on me when both of us left the car. But my heart refused to race. There had been many times when I was caught in similar situations. Somehow, sometime, I didn't realize that I had gotten used to it.

"How many guns are we supposed to take?" Talia opened the duffel bag.

"One each. One knife in your back pocket. Three magazines. Can you carry them all?"

"You sure you're talking to me?"

I gave her a small smile as we armed ourselves to the teeth. If it were up to me, we wouldn't be using these weapons and should be in and out before they noticed us. But better safe than sorry.

"Take this too," I said, handing her a small flashlight. "Point it to the ground so you don't attract attention. Hear one noise and you close it. Clear?"

"Yes."

Talia and I exchanged one long kiss before heading out. She was trembling everywhere, but had learned to be still, maybe after feeling that I was relaxed enough.

It wasn't clear where we were supposed to go, only that there was some sort of building nearby. Talia and I spent minutes walking to find it, stumbling quite a few times because of how dark everything was, and stopping every now then when something made a noise. It didn't help that the forest was chillier than the house on the hill. It smelled like rain too.

Talia's flashlight suddenly flickered close. "I see lights ahead," she whispered. "I think that's it."

The two of us ducked and walked, careful not to make excessive noises, until only tall shrubs got in the way of the view. Looking at each other once, we parted them together.

I froze. It was like seeing a mirage.

But the thing with mirages was they were usually positive, like a spring of water in a scorching hot desert. This mirage was different. It was nightmare relieved over and over again. It felt like someone punched a hole in my gut. And with it a screw was inserted, turned, deepened into the gaping wound. Beside me, I had the faint feeling of Talia shaking my shoulder.

"Cybele," she whispered, tone urgent. "Are you all right?"

No.

She shook me some more. "Please tell me what's wrong. I'm getting nervous."

I would have bolted from there if her hand wasn't connected to my skin, telling me that everything was going to be fine. Yet I forced myself to suck in my breath. To be calm. But my voice was all wrong. It was shaking. "The v-villa." I stared at Talia whose eyes had enlarged. All the while the invisible noose tightened around my neck. "That's the villa where my parents died. It should have burned down!"

Talia made incoherent noises at the back of her throat. She was stuck between looking like she wanted to tell me it was all right, and asking me more questions. But thankfully she didn't. Talia gave me a few seconds to think. To analyze. To talk myself against leaving and abandoning the mission.

"We need to look for Brooke and Van," I finally said.

"How? Do you think they've made it inside?"

I swiveled backward. Now that I knew our location, a plan had begun to form. "Every place built for my family had a secret passageway just like the Palace. The entrance is nearby. We can go through there and enter the villa undetected."

The entryway was nestled between two big boulders, hidden by thorny shrubs, like what I was shown when I was young. By the time I hacked away the plants, I was breathing hard, ready to collapse. Talia crept to the mesh gate and shone the light inside. "Are you sure you can do this?" she asked. "There's still time to back out."

And leave our friends? I took my gun, the trigger feeling comfortable against my finger. I felt sorry for the fools who would get in my way.

"Open the gate, Princess. I'm stronger than I look."

My words backfired as soon as we got to the dark, narrow tunnel. I was not strong at all. My bones were rattled. If there was one good thing though, no one had attacked us inside. It only meant that the tunnel was clear. Esmeralda and her men did not discover its secrets, though how it was still standing after what it had been through was a mystery to me. I could have sworn it was engulfed in the fire.

"It's a dead end." Talia's voice was ghostly behind me.

"No. Look closer." I shone the light to the dirt wall where a metal ladder was attached. It crawled upward and lead to a circular seal. Very much like a manhole cover on a sewer. "Ready your gun," I whispered.

Clouds of debris showered on my face as I pried the cover open. I pinched my nose and clamped my mouth shut. But it was the noise I was wary of. Someone could be using the room above us, or worse, it could be in the middle of a crowded hallway.

I waited for the cloud to settle before hauling myself up. Below me, Talia made a small squeak as my legs disappeared from her view. I surveyed the room. There were taters everywhere, with carrots coming a close second in sacks. We had stumbled inside the pantry.

I poked my head back to the tunnel and shone my light on the Princess. She gave a sigh of relief when she saw me. "Is it safe?"

"Yes," I said. "Let me help you up."

Talia and I huddled together near a table minutes later. She was looking around trying to familiarize herself with the place, while I was busy tinkering with my cellphone. She tapped my leg after a while. "Shouldn't we get going?"

"Just a second." I was trying to check for a wireless connection that could hopefully allow me to enter their system. But nothing was coming. Like the villa itself, one wouldn't know about it unless he had been there. With a frustrated shake of my head, I placed the phone back in my pocket. "There could be a CCTV here like in the Palace," I whispered. "Let's just hope that they placed everything outside."

A few minutes more and Talia and I were creeping along the corridor, eyes peeled for a sign of life. So far there had been none. Though I didn't think my soul could take a minute more of the torture. The layout was exactly as I remembered it.

"Maybe they're all sleeping," the Princess suggested. "It's the middle of the night."

Maybe. Or maybe they were lying in wait for us, ready to slit our throats.

A light beneath a door in one of the rooms made me halt. I glanced behind me to see Talia's hands tightening on her gun. She was ready as I was.

One. I counted with my finger. *Two.*

I pried the door open and ran inside. Only one guard. I slammed the handle of my gun on his head before he had the chance to see me.

Behind me, the door clicked close. "Is he dead?"

"I'm not sure." My eyes didn't go to Talia. I was concentrated on the panels of screens greeting me left and right. "We hit the jackpot, Princess. Take care of the guard while I rewind the footage."

Both of us went to work. Fiddling with the buttons did the trick for me.

"Found it," I said, my tone matching the sinking feeling in my stomach. The video on the screen was taken just a few minutes ago. It wasn't good. Van and Brooke were here all right, but the guards had gotten to them first.

"Forward it," Talia instructed. I did, then gasped. The footage showed our friends being dragged outside. The two of them were kicking, shouting, trying to hold on to each other while the guards forced them inside a water well.

My hands crushed the keyboard. I knew that stone well. Had visited it, even. The former King and Queen had told me about it when I was young. It had been built a long time ago to collect rain water for miscellaneous uses. In more recent times, they had installed a faucet just inside it for extended use in the summer season. In the video starring Van and Brooke, the same faucet was being opened when they got inside. The guards were trying to drown them.

"We can still rescue them!" Talia said. "It's just a few minutes ago! The well couldn't be full."

She couldn't have been more wrong. The well was over-spilling when we got there later, its stone cover trapping our friends below.

"We have visitors!" Talia alarmed.

"Go on. I'll handle them." I turned to the guards. The three had not noticed us yet. And from the way they strolled about, heads turned to each other, I had the bigger advantage as I rushed to attack.

"Intruder!"

The bigger oaf tried to draw his gun, but I was quicker. My knife slit his throat, withdrew, before I faced the last two remaining. Behind me, I could hear Talia moving to the well. It only took a second of missed concentration before something slammed on the side of my face.

"Like that?" The second guard sneered. "There's more where that came from!"

I shook my head from the dizziness and stepped back when he moved for another punch. Almost simultaneously, I kicked the third guard who was trying to target me with his knife.

"Princess! Help! Brooke isn't moving!"

My ears picked up on the cries. Vanessa's.

Turning back to my enemies, I avoided a punch on the rib, then did a roundhouse kick. But the guard had been waiting for it. He caught my leg, twisted it around, until I found myself looking at the sky.

"Please do something about it!" Van's cries had become stronger. "We only found each other! Please!"

I rolled around to deflect a kick on my face. I had to finish this. My friends needed me.

I got to my feet just in time for one of the guards to pounce on me. But I didn't move away. Pressing my gun on his stomach, I twisted us around and shot my gun twice. Both he and the other guard fell on the grass.

"Brooke!"

Van's screams had me abandoning the corpses and running to them. I pushed away Talia who was trying to pump life into Brooke's chest, leaned down, and began to breathe air through my best friend's mouth.

"Ulk!"

It was on the third try that Brooke sputtered water out. The third try that I collapsed next to her, the sting on my face numbing, my whole-body aching. "You're all right," I assured. "You're all right, Brooke."

I wanted to cry as Vanessa and Talia helped her lie on her side to collect herself. For a second there I thought I'd lost her. It seemed like everything I do, everything I was, always lead to people around me dying.

"We should go," Talia said after a while. She looked at the recovering Brooke, to the shaken Vanessa, until her worried eyes fell on me. She flinched when she saw my face. "You're hurt."

"I'll survive," I said.

I was beginning to stand up when Vanessa grabbed my sleeves. "Thank you!" she rasped. "I owe you so much, Your Highness. I don't know how to begin to repay you." Her hand tightened on me still. "But we can't go yet. We need to rescue her."

"Who? Brooke's parents?" Talia looked as curious as I felt. She helped Brooke sit while I glanced at Van again.

"Not her parents," the blonde said. "They're not here anymore. I'm talking about the woman we met in the cell. She can't stay here."

Woman? Cell? What was she talking about?

Brooke, still pale and weak, stretched her hand to me on my other side. "Iris," she said, "no one deserves to be in that place. If you don't rescue her then we will. I swear to God, there's something about that woman."

Chapter 40
Cybele

Droplets of water sprinkled on my face. The rain that had been threatening since this afternoon had finally fallen, increasing in volume every second, cold against my skin. Brooke, Vanessa, and Talia waited for my decision. A decision I didn't know how to issue given the nature of their request.

"Let me get this straight." I had to shout over the din. "You're asking me to go back, risk our lives, all for the sake of someone you've become mushy with in your jail time?"

Brooke's wet hair fell over her face. "You should have seen her, Iris. She's incapable to defend herself!"

So? The clock was ticking. If we didn't get out of here, we'd end up in the same cot as their friend.

I almost slipped while trying to stand. But none of them had moved to follow me. Even Talia was still on the ground, letting the rain wash away her clothes. "I agree with them," she murmured. "We shouldn't leave anyone here."

"She might be a criminal."

"They wouldn't put her here if that was so." The Princess gave me a tired smile. "You of all people know what this place stands for."

She didn't have to remind me. And I didn't need to feel so guilty, so dirty.

"Okay," I said reluctantly. "I'll go back inside in one condition. It only has to be me. The rest of you should go back to the car and wait. Any sign of danger and you leave."

Talia opened her mouth to argue. Van and Brooke did too. But the steely determination in my eyes told them everything they needed to know. There would be no going back if the condition wasn't met.

"You respected me." The Princess was the first to speak. "I'll respect you too, Cybele, but come back to me alive or I swear I'll find you and murder you again."

It was a threat I wasn't willing to go through. Gripping my gun, I said, "Don't worry about me dying, Princess. I still need to introduce you to my mum."

The villa was silent as a tomb when I re-entered. There probably weren't that many guards stationed here. Or perhaps they were too lax knowing that nobody knew its location. Whatever it was, I threaded down the hall.

Brooke informed me that the holding cells were located further back where a single guard stood. I was more concerned about its existence though. The last time I was here, the villa never had a prison. It made more sense in the Palace. But here? Highly unlikely.

I paused.

Around the corner, I could hear shuffling. Someone was moving.

Peering carefully behind the wall, I saw the guard stationed outside the cell doors. He was alone, seated in a chair, his head tipping as he unsuccessfully tried to fend off sleep. I took my knife out—and with a steady precision, released.

My breaths were uneven when I finally reached the dead man. The keys were hooked in his belt, brought together by a small ring. Taking that, I faced the cells that held our most valuable prisoner. She was lurking further inside her unit, face hidden by a lock of long hair.

"Miss," I whispered, hurrying to the door. The keys made a jiggly sound as I put one in the hole. "Miss, I'm here to set you free."

The door whined when I finally pulled it open. But I was disappointed to see that the prisoner had not moved.

"Miss?" I repeated. "Other guards could be lurking nearby and I'm in no mood for another fight."

So much for trying to help. She was still unresponsive.

"I'm leaving," I warned. "No one will come look for you." But even that elicited no reaction from her. I pinched the bridge of my nose. Couldn't Brooke and Van have befriended someone more reasonable? Tsk!

Going inside a cell out of my own volition gave me a strange feeling. So was rescuing a complete stranger. She was dirty from head to foot. But as I loomed nearer, got the chance to examine her closely, the annoyance turned to pity, the pity to distress. Not only was her white dress soiled and hadn't been changed for a while, the woman was barefoot too. What had been going on behind these walls?

"Miss. . ." My breaths had become sharp. Perhaps they were right. Perhaps there was something about this woman. I felt a tug deep in my stomach when I stopped in front of her. And my hands, my hands were shaking as I raised them to her face, to part them from the curtain of her hair.

The world stopped when she looked at me. Staring at me were the brightest green eyes, even brighter than my own.

I gave a small squeak. "M-Mother?"

She pushed me and bolted. She ran out of my reach, exited the cell, rounded the corner before disappearing.

How? Why?

I stumbled after her, flashes of the past lingering with my every step: Ronaldo stabbing my father. Ronaldo going after Mother. Mother's white nightgown soiled with blood.

"Wait!"

The door to the kitchen was slamming shut when I made it there. I jammed my foot between the crack. The pain that shot at my limbs was a wake-up call.

"Open the door!" I growled. "Don't you remember? It's me! Your daughter!"

The door continued to play tug-of-war between us. I couldn't wait any longer. Bracing myself, I slammed my shoulder on the door, heard her stumbling inside, waited for her to fall.

"Mother?"

I limped inside and looked around. Where was she?

"Daughter?"

I swiveled around and saw Mother there, breathing hard, staring at me. It was at the last moment when I realized that she was holding a pan. She slammed it at the side of my head.

"Want to play hide and seek?" six-year-old Talia invited. Her pink frilly dress was especially made for today. Her hair was worn loose, unlike the many times she'd kept them on a half crown braid. And with a naughty smile that could put anyone to shame, she was easily the cutest in the party.

"Unfortunately, I have to say no." My answer made her frown. "It's my mother's birthday today, remember? Important people will be here. I doubt they'd like to see us running around."

"But we won't be running. We'll be hiding." Talia's cheeks puffed. "You also pwomised to play with me last week."

Did I? Maybe. But how could I resist this kid? She would throw a fit and I'd have no one to talk to in the party aside from Alex. The rest of the noble children weren't here yet.

I took Talia's hand and pulled her to the side of the buffet table. They'd put up several of them earlier in the Palace garden where the party was being held. The one beside us was decorated with a chocolate fountain in the middle. Talia was looking at it longingly before I shook her gently, so she'd focus back to me. "Sorry," she said. "It looks so yummy."

"I thought you wanted to play first?" I asked.

"I do!" She rubbed her small hands together. "Where though?"

"Inside. I don't want to mess around here. Father would be furious."

Talia's throat moved as she swallowed. Both of us knew that my parents were the most patient lot, but this was the Queen's, my mothers, celebration. Even the King would have his limit. "Let's do it inside," she agreed.

"Okay, Talia, if I don't find you after fifteen minutes, we should meet back here and end the game."

Her brows furrowed. Rather than saying she understood, she scuffed her pink shoes on the grass. "Sorry," she mumbled shyly. "But what's fifteen minutes?"

Her unexpected question made me smile. Sometimes I tend to forget that we were years apart. I removed my wristwatch and handed it to her. "See that long one?" My finger tapped on the face. "If it reaches the number twelve, it means fifteen minutes have passed. You would have won by then if I haven't found you."

She nodded to herself. "All righty. But don't cheat on me."

"Of course, I won't. I'm the future Queen." I stuck my tongue out at her before turning around. If I were her, I would have already started running.

Twenty seconds later, the celebration was in full pace when I swiveled. The guests in the garden had doubled in so little time. It made me rethink whether to stop and greet them all or to continue to the Palace like I hadn't seen them. I chose the latter and decided to perform my duties after finding Talia. The adults could handle themselves.

The sweet smell from the buffet, plus the orchestrated music from the party, lingered in my senses even when I made it inside. The Palace proper was eerily quiet. Everyone, including most of the servants and staff, were outside attending to the needs of the guests.

"Talia?" I called.

My footsteps echoed as I entered the throne room. It was the fourth I went to after searching in my bedroom, the library, and the kitchen where all the cooks were too busy shouting instructions. I continued inside and froze. The throne room, with its lights off, and the impressive golden chair vacated, was not empty as I thought. Voices were whispering.

"Are you sure no one saw you?"

"Yes, don't worry. I slipped away when no one was looking and let my husband entertain the guests." The sound of something shuffling. "Here, we both have something for you."

I bit my bottom lip and ducked as I crept closer to the throne. It was Mother's voice I was hearing. But who was she talking to?

"You shouldn't have given me this." The receiver sounded bothered. "It's your birthday."

"I know, Lizzie. But if it wasn't for your sacrifice, none of this would be possible. This is just a small thank you for all the—Cybele? Is that you?"

I'd reach the back of the throne. Talia was nowhere in sight, but the game was the last thing on my mind now. Mother had sounded suspicious, secretive. What was more was the person she was talking to was wearing a cloak. Whoever it was under it turned her face away before I could catch a glimpse.

"Ugh!" My eyes fluttered open. *What happened?*

A few seconds had passed before I became fully aware of the time, the place, and what I was doing there. Mother had run to the kitchen following our short chase from the prison cell, lured me in, and almost bludgeoned me with a bloody pan. My skull felt like it was fractured in a million pieces, though that was a big exaggeration.

Standing up, I tried to shake away the dizziness and looked around to check. The door leading to the villa's pantry was still open. It was highly possible that Mother had gone through the secret passageway to escape. I staggered towards it.

The rain had stopped when I resurfaced outside, with calls of birds coming from somewhere above me. I considered what to do. Should I go to Talia and our group first and ask them to help search? Or should I do it by myself even when knowing the chances of finding Mother in the woods alone might be slim?

Something snapped to my left.

"Mother," I whispered. "Mother!"

I ran blindly to the forest, following only the flash of dark hair. Where was she going? Why was she running away? Did she not recognize me?

The familiar shape of a car shone under the moonlight. I had made it to our meeting point without realizing it.

"Get back!" someone screamed. "Cybele, it's a trap!"

But the warning was too late. My reflex was too slow. In front of me, gripping the Princess, Ronaldo stepped away from the guards, from my tied-up friends, and from my mother who seemed equally shocked as I was to see them there, and pointed a gun at me. "Welcome to hell, Cybele." Ronaldo grinned. "This is where it all ends."

The devil pulled the trigger.

Chapter 41
Cybele

Pain. There wasn't any of it as I awoke, sit up, and saw the white sheet draped over my legs. Where was I?

The tick-tick of the clock somewhere drew my attention from myself to the room. It was unreasonably neat, with books listed in alphabetical order, first by author, then genre, and series on the shelf. The sturdy oak desk facing the bay windows was dust-free. The pillows in the huge purple couch were fluff. I knew all this because it was mine—my bedroom in the Prescott's mansion. My semi-sanctuary in England.

"Welcome." A voice made me jump. I hadn't been expecting anyone to be here, much less standing by the second bay windows in the room, hands behind her back. Vanessa was wearing a white cotton t-shirt and pants, the sunlight making her glow. "To the afterlife," she said.

I stared at her blankly for seconds until one word made sense, then another. They rearranged themselves in my head lazily until I was gaping at her serious face, the breath knocked out from my chest. "C-Come again?" My voice had sounded grated, unused.

Vanessa stepped away from the light and went to me. Her pants were long. I couldn't see whether she had floated, but was it important? She said I was dead.

~ 411 ~

"Ronaldo had killed you, Cybele. This place," she gestured at the room, "is your last stop before you go where you're supposed to. Feel free to ask me questions."

Questions, she said. I had a lot of them. A million. Now that I'd been shocked to awareness, or whatever this state was called, I could faintly remember pieces of what happened. Flashes. But it was too dark that night. Too confusing. I wasn't sure if they were nightmares or reality. It unsettled me.

"Breathe," Vanessa reminded.

My brows were drawn together when I looked at her again. "Do I have to?"

"You're used to it. And it will help calm you down."

She was right. I opened my mouth wide and vacuumed air in, and could almost imagine my lung expanding. After which, I asked, "Why you? Why not my dead parents?"

"I was the one you conjured, and both of them had passed to the light."

"Does that mean you're dead too?"

"Oh, no, no, no." Vanessa sat on the edge of the bed. "The real Vanessa Krieger is alive on the other side. In fact, most of them are." She shifted, causing the mattress to shift too. I wonder if the movement, her weight, the feeling in my own hands as I clasped them together were just something I conjured as well. "You've been dead for quite some time in human years," she continued. "Everyone had moved on, including Talia."

"Wh-what do you mean?"

"She found another woman. She's married now and is living off-coast with two children."

The pain that struck me couldn't be real, yet it felt like it—it felt like a rod had been put under fire, and finally when it was hotter than hell, was impaled in my chest repeatedly like a broken torture machine.

My hands bundled the sheets in front of me. My head tilted down. "Is she happy?"

"Yes."

There were tears in my eyes as I raised them. "That's good enough for me."

Vanessa's touch over the sheets felt real, substantial. Yet she moved her hand away and stood, then headed to the shelf taking interest in my books. In college they were my lifeline, along with the thoughts that someday I could get back the throne. It should have been mine.

"Ronaldo was the one who killed you." Her voice was matter-of-fact. "Your friends tried everything to save you; Brooke was stabbed on the back. Talia was punched on the side of her face." Vanessa plucked a book from the shelf and opened it to a page I had bookmarked. "But it was too late," she went on. "You bled to death before they could get—"

The door on the left opened. A woman, dressed in staff clothes, was staring at us, surprise and question on her face.

I turned to Van just in time to see her expression change from serene to afraid. "Call everyone quick before your mistress murders me!" she said.

The door was shutting when I had made it to her, hooked my arm around her neck, and choked her underneath me. "Dead? What the hell, Van! I almost believed you!"

"Ack! I'm just kidding! Ack!"

Lucky her, the door opened for the second time. The butler of the Prescott's household gave me a small smile. Chandra. "We have a lot to discuss," she said.

No one else had come inside the room, much to my disappointment. There were only the three of us—two of them making a beeline for the couch as I paced. I couldn't go back to sit, to rest, or to sleep in my eternal slumber as Vanessa had joked. Speaking of which, damn that woman and her sense of humor. One of these days I'd get her back.

"Tell me everything from the start," I snapped, "and this time, don't leave anything out."

So they did. But it wasn't pretty.

"After you went back inside the villa, Ronaldo and his men showed up and rounded us." Vanessa squeezed her eyes shut, as if remembering also pained her. "You came back, he shot you, and things went crazy after that. The Princess went shakalaka."

I paused and stared at her. "In human terms please."

"Talia went berserk, you normie." Van opened her eyes. "Then Brooke got stabbed in the back. I bit off a guard's ear—it didn't taste great by the way—then we got rescued."

~ 414 ~

I stopped in the middle of the room, unwilling to address the fact that both my girl and best friend weren't here, so my voice was shaking when I finally did. "A-are they okay?"

"Oh, yeah. They're fine." Vanessa jutted her thumb to the butler. "Thanks to her."

Chandra? I turned my attention to the woman. Our middle-aged butler who'd been creeping me out since I got here in the Prescott's mansion?

Her off-kilter smile told me that she knew what I was thinking. "No need to thank me," she said in her nasally voice. "It is not me trying to save the day. It is me atoning for my sins."

"Sins?"

Her nod was brief, but her shoulders, at least to me, seemed like they were unburdened from a heavy weight as she stood. The woman was taller than I'd ever seen her. Happier. "It began twelve years ago," she said.

"On a galaxy, far, far—" Vanessa zipped her lips when I gave her a warning look.

Chandra hugged herself, continuing. "I wasn't always a staff of the Prescott's. In fact, my first employer was. . ." She dragged the word and sighed. "Esmeralda."

I thought nothing could faze me. But this. This was news to me.

"You're from Harland?"

"Yes. I was a staff there before Esmeralda became the Queen. I overheard her and Ronaldo talking about bad things, evil things. Had I known that they were planning it for your mother and father, I would have put a stop to it even at the cost of my own life." Chandra's next words were rapid. "I tried to escape after they murdered the rulers. Esmeralda found out I knew the truth and had me hunted, so I went here in England seeking a new life."

My hands shook beside me. "But I was adopted by the Prescott's. Was that a coincidence?"

"Yes, Your Majesty. But everything I did after that was not. I convinced the Prescott's to have me trained so I would be well-equipped to guard you. They agreed even though they didn't know the truth." She fished something out of her pocket, then without a second thought tossed it to me.

"A cellphone?" I said, catching it swiftly.

"7292014. Phoenix."

The cellphone dropped from my hand. "Viper? Are you him?"

She nodded. She was the assassin.

I couldn't believe it. It was like I'd been blind all my life. My bloody butler was a resident of Harland, had known about my past, and had pretended to be a hacker to help me. She must have tracked Brooke the same way I did, leading her to the villa to rescue us. And Brooke's parents too.

Vanessa fanned her face. "I am so shook, you guys," she said. "I don't know what's really going on, but I'm shook."

The door opened again before any of us could proceed. The Princess searched the room until she saw me. "You're awake!" Before long

Talia was in my arms, lips forming against mine, fingers tugging at my hair.

The shock. The forming dizziness. The uncertainty all vanished as I scooped her from the floor and pressed her to me. But then a shooting pain on my chest made me recoil.

"Easy," she said, nose against mine. "Your wound hasn't healed yet."

"Wound?"

"Yes, you've been shot." Talia's feet landed on the floor, but her fingers sought out my face. "Didn't they tell you?"

Vanessa coughed from the couch.

I pulled Talia to me again. The Princess ' worries became moans against my mouth. Desire tugged in my abdomen as our tongue met each others.

"Get a room, you two!" Van sounded bewildered. "Okay, my bad. Chandra, dear, we should leave." The two moved away from the couch. "On second thought." She considered. "I can stay if you want me to watch. I'm not picky with—" Chandra forced her out of the door before it slammed shut.

Talia was breathing hard when she finally stopped the kiss. Her lips were wet, her eyes cloudy. Her face, though, was guilt-ridden. "I'm sorry I wasn't here when you woke up," she panted.

"It's okay." My hands brushed against her chin, her neck, going down to her chest. I wanted her now. All of her. The animalistic side of me was yearning to rip her dress apart, throw her to the bed. Van's jokes about my Princess getting

~ 417 ~

married to another person made me want to claim Talia, to assure myself that it wasn't real. The rational side won though, and I guided her to the bed like a Queen.

"Cybele," she whispered as I crawled on top of her. "This is hardly the time."

"When is the right time?" I asked.

"Your parents will come soon."

I stopped. My hand was positioned on her inner thigh. "You've met them?"

Talia swallowed and tried to compose herself. "I wasn't sure how to tell them about me. But Brooke, Van, and I. . ." She cringed. "I hope you don't mind that we explained the situation without you. You've been asleep for days."

Was that so?

I moved to a sitting position and hugged myself. Talia crawled behind me, so she could embrace my back. "I'm sorry," I murmured to her. "You must have been scared."

"I was." Her head leaned on me. "Don't do that again. Don't close your eyes so long I thought you'd never wake up. How will I survive?"

By marrying another woman, living offshore, and having two kids. Vanessa had really gotten to me. God.

"What did you do while I was asleep?" I said to get rid of the thoughts.

Talia didn't answer at once. But when she did she sounded guilty. Guilty, even, than when she told me about informing my parents about my identity. "I checked around your room," she said. "I read your books. I went to your walk-in closet, trying to piece together the person you were before we met again as adults. I was trying to catch up for the lost time."

"What did you find?"

"That. . ." She took a shaky breath. "That you loved me when you said you didn't. My favorite books, the ones you used to read me when we were children, were in your shelves. A potted lavender was in your bathroom. And your notes. . ." She gave of an incredulous laugh. "You wrote my name backwards until the notebook was filled. That wasn't hate. Not when it was done in such an elaborate script, it came out beautiful."

I guess the jig was up. For me. For her. Even for Chandra who had lain in the dark waiting to be absolved from the past. One more mystery was meant to be solved, but for here, for now, I was content in my bed, with Talia embracing me, safe from all the horrors outside.

Chapter 42
Cybele

A day after I woke up, I was aware of two things. The first one being about my adoptive parents. They weren't mad that I've kept my real identity a secret. They were saddened by it. Shattered. Mum said it explained a lot about my behavior when she first saw me in Saint Augustine. I was hateful, reserved. And even after years, some part of me was closed off from them. Now she knew why.

"Talia?"

"Yes?"

"Can you join me for a second?"

It was early afternoon, and I had just finished speaking to my parents in the study. After that, I went in search for Talia. She was lurking in the kitchen, watching the house-helps whip dessert for later.

"Hi," she said upon reaching my side. "Need anything?"

"Yes, your company." I drew her away from the curious staff who'd all turned to us and had whispered excitedly. It's been a while since I've seen them. I didn't think I'd ever say this, but for once I was really grateful for the services they've rendered to the Prescott's. I should probably throw a party in their honor.

"Where are we going?" Talia said, getting my thoughts back to the topic.

"On a tour."

"A tour? Is it all right to leave the house?"

I veered to the left and opened a door. The room was bathed in light when I flipped the switch. "It's actually a house tour, Princess. I thought I'd show you some of my favorite places here in the mansion while growing up."

"Oh." She poked her head inside the room with a touch of curiosity. There was a billiards table, a bar, and a dart board that had one too many holes in it. She sniffed the rich scent of mahogany before turning to me again. "Do you play any of those?"

"Yes. Brooke bugged me to learn so she could have someone to play with. I also thought it would come in handy for developing my socialization skills. Sometimes assassins, informants, and all kinds of people looking for unique jobs are found in bars playing billiards. I wanted to widen my network."

Talia's eyebrows raised before it met together in the middle of her forehead. "I hope you're kidding," she said.

Why would I? I closed the door behind us and continued to the hallway. "This path leads to the court." I pointed to a glass door. "There, you'll find a tennis court, a gym, and a pool. I used them for strengthening my body when I wasn't doing martial arts. That way, my enemies can't drown me easily, and I'll be able to defend myself by being quick. Want to check the training facilities?"

Talia's mouth opened and closed. "That's a very. . . err. . . interesting fact. But no. I think I have to pass."

"Suit yourself." I shrugged and moved forward.

The second floor was a network of rooms and big spaces. I took Talia to the small art gallery that was circular in nature and had a glass for a ceiling. The afternoon light shafted through them and created natural illumination. I still opened the lights to accentuate the paintings though. I wanted her to see them in their full glory.

" Fun fact," I said. "I was the one who picked most of these paintings. Aren't they beautiful?"

Talia stared around, her eyes landing on the artwork in the leftmost first. I followed her as she went closer to it. The painting was nothing sort of exquisite—with muted colors, a great scene, and emotions that would disturb the feelings of the most hardened criminal.

She frowned. "That's. . . a guillotine."

"Yes." I shifted excitedly. "What else do you see?"

"A decapitated head on the floor."

She shivered and hugged herself while I smiled widely. "Isn't it pretty accurate?" I said. "That's how they punish people before. It's quite amazing, really."

Talia looked around for a couple of minutes—to the painting of the hanging man on the tree, to the woman stoned in the plaza, to the man who was being dragged by a horse to his death. All of them were my proud collection.

"Should we go?" I asked.

"To where?"

I pushed my hand in my pocket and found the comforting shape of the bookmark. It had been with me when Viper—Chandra the butler—rescued us, though out of shape and damaged on the edges.

"Just follow me," I said.

Our shoes were crunching on the gravel pathway leading to the garden when Talia hurried so she could match me step by step. She didn't speak for a while and gave me time to appreciate the way her yellow dress fluttered to her knees, or how her hand went to her mouth as she tried to pull together a coherent thought.

Finally, she spoke, "I appreciate you giving me the tour, but. . ." She hesitated. In front, I could spot the big oak tree—the same kind as the one in the Palace in Harland, though not quite as memorable. Talia took and squeezed my hand. "I'm bothered by it."

"Which part?"

"All of it." We stopped beneath the oak tree; our faces shaded by the leaves. "Everything you did in the past was a preparation for battle, Cybele. Do you think you can ever move on from that?"

"I don't know." Perhaps I should try to make peace with my demons. Maybe that was the reason why I took us to those places too. I wanted her to see and understand. "Does this tree remind you of something?"

Talia looked up and caught a leaf just in time before it touched her forehead. She cradled it between her thumb and forefinger and faced me again. "It looks remarkably like our favorite tree."

"And do you remember what you said before we rescued Brooke and Van?"

She considered. "Yes?"

"Great then. This wouldn't be so hard." My leg gave way for a kneel. In front of me, Talia gave a small gasp. "If you do me the honors, Princess, I would like to say my piece." My throat started to clam up on me, to betray me like the little coward they were. But I continued nonetheless. "If you wed me, Talia, I would read you a story every night for the rest of our lives. You would never get cold again because I would stay by your side. The porridge—"

"Cybele!"

My heart thrummed as I raised the diamond ring. "It was my mum's. I got both of my parents blessing this morning. Now I only need your answer, Princess."

Talia had frozen like an ice sculpture, her hands still by her side. Her grey eyes were glassy, seeing nothing but the ring, as if entranced by sorcery.

Pink and white petals begin to fall from above. "Can you please say yes?" Someone said. "My girlfriend and I didn't snoop all the way up here to hear a no." Van was smirking when I raised my eyes. In her hand was a bucketful of petals. Brooke was sitting beside her on the branch, giggling.

I glanced at Talia again to see her nodding vigorously. She— my Queen—had made the suffering all those years worth it.

A toast and countless congratulations and thank you's later, I made my way to the second floor alone. Someone was waiting for me in one of the rooms: the second thing I was aware of after I had woken yesterday.

Knock. Knock.

"Who is it?"

"It's me," I answered. "Cybele."

After an invitation to come in, I opened the door and stepped inside. The calming scent of chamomile drifted to my nose as my eyes trailed to the queen-sized bed, the drawn curtains. Near that, a smaller circular table with a teapot, a milk jug, and two set of teacups—one of which was held by a long-fingered hand. "Join me," the woman who owned it said.

I let the door close behind me and allowed myself to gravitate where I should. Every inch of me studied every inch of her. "You. . ." My heart skipped a beat. "You look so much like her," I said.

"And you look so much like me," she answered back.

Touché. I pulled a chair and seated myself, not once taking my eyes from her face. She was cleaner now compared to when I'd last seen her in the prison cell. Her tattered clothes had been replaced by a flowery silk dress, the best that money could buy. But the most remarkable thing was her eyes. The green in them were bright as ever, coherent.

She gave me a small, wistful smile before offering her cup. "Tea? Thanks to the Prescott's, I've discovered that the English makes a mean batch."

"I know." My head shook. "But ironically I still prefer coffee even after living here in England all these years."

The answer elicited a sigh from her. A heavy, forlorn sound that made a ripple in my own chest. "You're just like your mother," she said. "I miss her. I don't think I'll be whole again without the Queen."

"But you're the Queen too, are you not?"

It was time for the answers. My mother had died in the villa years before, I was sure of it now. So if that was the truth, then where did this woman come from? How could they have possibly hidden such a big secret from everyone? Even me?

The betrayal that had sprouted in my eyes must have been obvious to her. The woman's longing smile became gentler, guilty, begging me to understand. "What do you think will happen if twins are born to succeed the throne?" she started.

"An outrage," I said, ready for the answer. "It will be difficult to decide who should get the seat. The minutes born apart would not matter."

"Exactly. Which was why our parents kept us a closely guarded secret."

"Us?"

"Your mother and me, and that we were twins." she said. "After the announcement that the successor to the throne was born, the King and Queen, your grandfather and grandmother, kept us sheltered in the Palace where only a few people had known the truth. It wasn't until our seventh birthday, when I agreed to stay in the shadow, did they introduce your mother to everyone as the successor. The only successor."

"Jesus!" I said. "Why would you do that?"

"For a simpler life? To make my sister happy? There are many reasons for giving up a throne, Cybele. You, yourself, should be familiar with this."

The warmth in my neck had turned to a burning fire. She must have noted my discomfort and continued.

"Shortly after your mother's introduction to the people of Harland, our parents had a villa constructed for me. Some servants were sworn to secrecy to keep me company. As for my twin and I, living apart did not stop us. We sent each other letters to stay in touch."

I shifted in my chair. "What kind of letters?"

"All of them." Her eyes lit up. "Stupid letters. Clever poetry. We had always been close, your mother and I. It was through those letters that we remained so."

The fondness of the way she said it, the yearning in her voice—all of this told me that she was telling the truth. You couldn't hide a love like this, not when it was so palpable you could almost reach out and touch it.

"The letters. . ." she trailed. "Had continued only to be about us until our eight birthday. That's when she began to tell me of a boy. A very special boy."

"My father?"

She took a spoon and began stirring her tea with it. I was at the edge of my seat waiting for her to continue, but I let her be until she was finished. "Yes," she finally said. "Your father. They had always been childhood friends; my sister, your father, and Esmeralda."

"That's bullshit!" I found myself leaving the chair, the table— the stirring of anger stealing my patience. I knew that mother and the snake had been best friends. But since they were eight? What could possibly have happened to make it end that way? I turned to Lizzie who I knew now to be the mysterious guest in my mother's birthday celebration back then. She, too, was unsettled. But it wasn't anger in her. More of a crestfallen acceptance.

"Sit," she urged, motioning back to my vacated chair. "Let me tell you the whole story."

I didn't know how I remained calm after getting back to my chair. Neither did I know how I kept from trashing the table. But throwing a tantrum in front of my long-lost aunt would not be good, especially since she was ready to supply the missing puzzle pieces.

"That night," Lizzie picked on, "the night my sister died? We'd been planning to tell you about me. That I was her sister."

I took an involuntary sharp breath.

"But everyone was so tired from the long trip. We decided to postpone it until the next day." The teacup rattled against the saucer as she lifted it up to her lips. After a sip, she placed it down, though not until she'd wiped her mouth and twisted the napkin repeatedly did she continue. "That night," she whispered, dread closing in her voice. "I was awoken by the smell of something

~ 428 ~

burning. Tiptoeing in the hallway, I was surprised to see that everything was on fire. My sister and her husband, they. . . It was too late when I got to their room."

"I wasn't there," I said. "Why didn't you look for me?"

"I did." Her voice was as grim as mine. "I searched everywhere for you, Cybele, but they said on the news that you had died too." Her shoulders hunched. "After that, I went to the Palace to secure the throne. I was caught before I reached the gates. Esmeralda, she. . . She didn't know about me like your father did. She thought my twin, you mother, had survived."

I kept my eyes on the table not uttering a thing. Lizzie had suffered as much as I did.

"Esmeralda had the villa rebuilt and imprisoned me there, thinking I was your mother. She thought it was better than killing me after all. Every few weeks, she would visit me, get inside my head, telling me about how she won, how my supposed husband should have been hers. How she'd been in love with him first, but I ruined it for her. It was a pity."

"Pity?" A sarcastic laugh burst from my mouth. "How could you pity such a monster, Lizzie? She had our whole family killed! She had treated you like dirt!"

Lizzie's sympathetic face didn't change. Her eyes remained at me, steady, studying, calm. "Love and hate could do a lot of things," she said, "like kidnapping the daughter of your enemy even when you're in love with her."

"How did you know that?"

"Chandra and I had a long talk after she brought me here." Lizzie tossed the napkin to the table. "She told me what you've done, and I can't say I approved of it, but I understand your reasons.

A long silence settled between us. We had all been victims of Esmeralda's lunacy. And even when we were safe in here under my adoptive parents care, we would always look over our shoulders. Always wondering when Satan and her demons would strike.

"You should retrieve the throne," I finally said. "You deserve it better than me."

Her laughter was startling. "Who would believe me? My parents had kept me a secret, and all my personal servants have died." A quiet determination settled over her. "Besides, I am tired of living my sisters life to pretend that I'm her. If someone should get the throne back, it's you."

Me? But I had promised Talia, given her my oath.

"Running is no use anymore," Lizzie convinced. "You have done that and look where it got you. I think even Talia, even the Princess, can understand. It's not about revenge anymore." She took the teapot and gave herself another serving. Afterwards, she poured some in my own cup. "Be ready, Cybele. Because like it or not? Esmeralda will find you."

Chapter 43
Cybele

Lizzie's warning kept me on edge, anxious. It was as if any moment now, Esmeralda and Ronaldo would come barreling down the door, steal Talia away from me, and slaughter my friends and family. I needed to prepare.

Three days was selfish considering I had just suffered from comatose, but three days was what I told all of them to give me. Three days to lock myself in the room with zero disturbance, even from the Princess and my parents, just so I could be given time to think.

I emerged one day, thirsty, weak-kneed from having stayed in one place too long, blinking from the excessive light coming from everywhere.

"I suppose I can't tell you that you've died again, can I?" Van was sitting crossed-legged outside my bedroom door. "Are you good now?"

Funny she had asked. I felt great. Maybe because the solution to our problems was just around the corner. We just had to bring things in motion.

I looked around and didn't find Talia. Or even house helps scurrying around from one place to another, usually with extra bedsheets in their hands.

"They're preparing like what you've instructed before being in lock-down, Your Majesty." Van answered my unspoken question. She placed her palm on the floor, pushed herself up, and with a grunt stretched her arms to the ceiling. "I would have helped them," she added, sounding bored. "But they shooed me away like I was some kind of troublemaker. I told them I'd happily prepare your daily meals, but they didn't trust me enough with the royal stomach."

I couldn't help but smirk. The head cook didn't trust anyone with our stomachs, royal or otherwise.

"Iris?" The call made me glance to the long corridor. Brooke, alive and okay, was carrying a tray of food, heading towards us.

Van crossed her arms. "Well, well, if it isn't the betrayer." The blonde pointed an accusing finger at my best friend. "Everyone trusts you but not me," she said. "I see a pattern here."

Brooke placed the tray on the floor and stepped closer to a fuming Van. With a pull of the blonde's collar, she planted a big kiss on the woman's lips.

I turned away and shielded my eyes. "Is that really necessary in my presence?"

"You did it with the Princess in your room too," Van said, though she sounded happy for someone defending herself.

Brooke slapped Van's ass and smiled lazily. "You're wanted in the living room, by the way, Van. Talia wishes to get your help regarding the gathering tonight. She said—and I'm just repeating this—only Van can figure out what to do."

"Did she now?" Van puffed out her chest. "Finally! Someone who knows my worth in this household. I knew the Princess makes the most sense around here." She winked at us. "See you non-important people later. I have a job to do."

Brooke was shaking her head when Vanessa rushed to the hallway. I, in the meantime, gave her an inquiring look. "You and her, huh? How exactly did that happen?"

A blush crept over Brooke's face. She almost never blushed, except with matters concerning me. I was ecstatic for her. Brooke only deserved the best.

"It's a long story," she brushed off. "It would take us one whole chapter to say it."

"Ha!" I tilted my head to the corridor to make her follow. "Tell it to me in the study anyway. I want to know everything about you in these past few days, even how you were stabbed while struggling with the guards."

Brooke and I caught up with each other: our adventures, the things we discovered, her watered-down version of how she and Van pestered each other until the attraction was accepted. I had always been honest with her about the limitation of our relationship, though this time, for as long as we had been friends, did I only truly feel that we'd opened up to each other. It was through that well-meaning and open nature did I tell her about my plan.

"Do you think this will work?" she said, eyes assessing me. "Not that I'm doubting you, Iris. It's just that I'm beginning to understand why you were such a hermit in college. People are hard to trust in your position."

I leaned back on the leather chair and brought my fingertips together. No one had gone in the study room while we were here. Even my parents were knee-deep in the preparation for tonight's gathering, with Talia on top of everything. I should be with her right now, overseeing the smallest details. But me being here with Brooke was the biggest help I could give. This was for our future after all.

"It will work," I assured. "When had my plans never worked?"

"Uhm?" Brooke raised a finger. "There was that time in college—"

"Really, Brooke? You're bringing up the past now?"

She gave a low chuckle. "Hey, you're the one who started it."

"I'm ending it too." My eyes went to the phone on the desk, an antique like everything in the room. Dad had always been drawn to those. I was glad because I had been pretty much stuck in the past myself. "We should probably start," I said. "There's so much to do, and I want to finish them all before twilight."

Brooke fished out her cellphone, looking like she was just waiting for me to give a signal. "I'll give them a ring."

The venue for the most awaited celebration was done in a secluded property by a lake. The theme was fairytale, and it couldn't have been truer with the lanterns bobbing in the water, the lights meticulously hung over the trees, so it would create a net above us, and the long tables, draped in white cloth, adorned with candlelight's, stretched out to seat the guests.

My favorite thing about the design was the bridge. Made of stone, arched over the lake, it was where we had stood as God repainted the sky from sunset to the night sky, while I introduced Talia to everyone me and my family had ever known. It was precious.

"Are you enjoying yourself, Iris?" Mum, who was seated directly on my right, touched my hand and squeezed.

I nodded and gave her a smile. "Yes, Mum. Thank you."

"I didn't go overboard with the invites, did I?"

"Not at all."

A white lie. She had invited their colleagues, all the people I had become acquainted to over the years, and had made them promise not to tell a soul that they were coming to this party. But this was my parent's moment as much as it was mine and Talia's. Let them have their fun.

Mum exhaled in relief before squeezing my hand again. "I'm glad you think that," she said. "You're our source of happiness, Iris. We want you to have the best in everything." She paused to take a sip of her wine. I knew the things she'd say when the next thing she did was to take the napkin and dab her eyes with it. "You were so small then. Defenseless. You should have let us help you."

"Mum. . ." I swallowed the tears threatening to choke me. "Cheer up! This is supposed to be a bloody party."

"I know." She sniffled. "But I just can't help but think about the pain you went through. While

~ 435 ~

your daddy and I fawned over you, you must have dark thoughts. Nightmares. If we had known about Esmeralda, we would have done everything to stop her."

"That's exactly why I didn't say a word," I admitted. "Look at Brooke, Mum, they used her parents against her. I don't want you as their leverage. It would kill me."

Talia broke the conversation with whoever she was talking to, so she could offer her help to us. "Are you all right?" she said, looking directly at Mum. "Can I get you anything?"

"Yes, dearest." Mum wiped her nose with the napkin. "Give me lots of grandchildren. I want twelve of them running in my house. Bonnie, Lucas, Samantha, Peter, Ingrid. The rest of the names would come later."

Talia looked slightly mortified. "S-sure," she stammered. "Will the adoption center allow us to get so many though?"

"Who said anything about adoption?" Mum tapped Daddy's shoulder. "There are modern ways to conceive your own child now. Aren't you working on that, sweetheart?"

Dad was sipping his wine when he turned to her. "Can you repeat that again, dear? Lizzie was just telling me about Harland."

"I was informing Talia here about your research," Mum said. "How you and your colleagues are intending to help couples like them?"

"Oh yes!" Dad put down his wine glass excitedly. "Our latest project involves the embryonic development. Once we're done,

~ 436 ~

millions of people will benefit stupendously. You'll be the first to try it once the experiments become a success."

"That's. . ." Talia hugged herself and shivered. "That sounds amazing, but twelve children?"

"I guess you better start now, huh?" Van was passing by and had heard the statement. She winked at Talia, leaned down, and whispered something against the Princess 'ears.

Talia suddenly stood. "I'll be checking for the desserts." She smiled quickly at me and my parents. "I'll be back in a while."

Mum turned back to me after the Princess had walked away from our table. "I'm curious about something," Mum said. "You told me how you met Talia. But this woman." She tugged Vanessa's hand fondly. "You, or anyone else, had not given me the whole picture."

"Eep. . ." Van laughed nervously. "Do you really have to know?"

"Of course." Mum was expecting the answer from me. "Well?"

I shrugged. I guess there was no helping it. "It's nothing special, really," I said. "To make the story short, Van was from a gang."

"A gang?"

"Yes. The international girl group she came from was called, The Gang. They're performers. Like K-pop idols."

"Oh. . ." Mum's shoulders relaxed. "So how did you cross paths with her?"

"Let's see. First, she kidnapped—"

"Pardon?"

"*Recruited* Talia," I corrected. "But the Princess didn't want to join their group, so I was pushed to meet Van. We became good friends after that."

"Hmm." Mum gave both me and Van a look. "A friendship born of unusual circumstances. Keep this forever, Iris. I can see that you're happier with these girls around."

"Speaking of girls!" Van jumped up and down. "My surprise is here. Everyone, please prepare."

The lights above us closed. What was supposed to be a lively chatter died down, turned into confusion, until the lights opened again. To my surprise, girls, dozens of them, were lined not far from our table wearing black skimpy dresses. An energetic music began to play.

"Introducing. . ." I didn't know where Van had gotten the wireless microphone. But she was holding one as she gestured to the women. "The main entertainment for tonight. Feast your eyes, my good sirs and ladies."

Everyone clapped when the fashion show started. I recognized most of them, having worked with the girls at some point in my modeling career.

"Here comes my girlfriend," Van said over the mic. "Mine, you all hear?"

Brooke was leading the line now, went to me, and took my hand. I glanced helplessly to my parents over my shoulder, but my mum was just clapping, my dad shaking his head. The girls took me to the bridge.

"And now, to give you a short performance, Your Majesty. Here's Talia!"

The models parted to give way for my Queen. Outfitted in a white, sexy dress, she was not only set apart by the color of clothes, but by the way her eyes sought mine, her hips shaking as she made her way in front of me, and how the rest of her seemed more regal, even while her dance was anything but decent.

My eyes widened when she put her fingers through my hair and tugged it back. "I'm so embarrassed right now," she purred. "But I'm cuter than these girls. Don't you agree?"

"With my whole heart." I licked my lips. "How did Van make you agree to do this?"

The other models slowly ambled away while Talia and I caught our breaths. "A bet," she said. "I guess I'm a sucker for it as much as you are."

That one was true. I took the Princess ' hands and intertwined them through my own. This was our moment, our time.

I was about to comment on how beautiful she was, when out of place noises made us look back to the guests. The dinner I have eaten threatened to spill from my mouth. Police, so many of them, had mingled with the crowd.

"This is an outrage!" Mum had gotten up from her chair. "Who gave you permission to do this? It's a private event!"

The police told her the answer in a barely audible voice. Some of them grabbed Van and Brooke. I was stepping away from Talia to help them when someone grabbed my own arm. "Not so fast." Ronaldo's grin broadened when I swiveled to him. "It was a matter of time before we figured out where you were," he said. "We've already informed the government of this country. You are under arrest for kidnapping the Princess of Harland." He glanced at Talia and sneered. "I'm sorry for ruining someone's birthday party. I really am."

Talia stood to full height, looking every bit like the Princess he claimed her to be. "You are not interrupting a birthday celebration, you dimwit. This is my wedding reception." Her eyes gleamed. "I demand you to let go of my wife right now, or else."

Chapter 44
Cybele

The protests in the background seized when Talia addressed Ronaldo. It seemed like no one had breathed—watching, waiting, anxious for what was about to transpire.

Ronaldo, still in disbelief over what the Princess said, tilted his head and gave us a disparaging smile. "Wife?" His tone mocking. "You haven't been here for months, Princess. How can you be her wife?"

Talia forced my arm away from the man and held her head high. "You have your connections, we have ours. Let's leave it at that." She turned to me. "Are you hurt?"

"Not at all," I said. "If anything, his ugly mug is more painful to my eyes." I smirked at Ronaldo. "Talia is right though. There's no reason to act like monkeys in front of our guests. They're citizens of this country and can have you arrested for their own grounds."

Ronaldo stared at the reception. Every eye was on us, from my parents, the models, to the influential people that all occupied the tables. His eyes strayed to the police who were manhandling Brooke and Van. "Make sure to take them to the car. Appropriately," he added before facing me. "As for you. . . You're coming with me. You've committed a crime in Harland, and as such, the parliament of this country agreed to hand you over to us for trial." His eyes flashed in triumph. "You're going home."

"And what of the Princess?" I said, holding my ground. "Will she get punished with me knowing that she married her kidnapper?"

"That is for the Queen to decide, not me. But mark my word, your marriage will not protect you."

"I didn't expect it to." My fingers interlaced with the Princess'. "We got married out of love—something you wouldn't understand because the woman you're bedding feels nothing for you." I leaned to Talia and whispered. "Sorry you have to hear that, love."

"No matter. The truth can't hurt me anymore." Talia's face set with determination, overflowing with spirit that I had always admired. "You," she said to Ronaldo. "I take it that my mother had arranged a ride back to our country. How will I know that you won't hurt or harass my wife and our friends while in transit?" Her question was loud, carrying.

Ronaldo answered in kind. "The police of this country will escort you. Rest assured that no one will be harmed." His voice lowered right after, his fingers curling as if he wanted to choke me. "But once they leave, you're mine, Cybele. Mine!"

"I doubt that." I glanced at my parents. They looked scared for me, outraged. I should assure them before leaving that everything would be all right. "Let me say goodbye to them first," I told Ronaldo. "Don't worry. None of us will escape. We're way past that point, don't you think?"

"I'm giving you twenty seconds."

"Thanks, man." I squeezed his shoulder with as much force as I could muster, all the while keeping my mouth in a rigid smile. My hate for him burned to the core. On top of what he did to us in the past, he had the guts to come here, ruin my party, threaten me and my wife in front of our guests. There would be a time for his judgment, and it would be long, painful, and severe. "Let's go, Talia."

Mum and Dad took us in a fierce embrace soon as we got back to the table. "My baby!" Mum cried. "Let me help you! Both of you!"

"No, Mum. Don't drag yourself into this." I squeezed my eyes tight. For years I've lied to them, used their influence, and made it dangerous for them behind their backs. No more. I slipped from their embrace. "Trust me," I begged.

Dad stroked my head. He was a big man. A strong man. But tonight, everyone could see what his weakness was. It had always been me. "I'll take care of your Mum," he promised, the quiver in his voice betraying him. "Now go and do your duty, Iris. Protect yourself and Talia." He pinched Talia's cheek. "Don't forget my twelve grandchildren. I'll be expecting them."

A sharp whistle came from behind us. Ronaldo, it seemed, couldn't wait a second more. "Time is up," he said. "The Queen of Harland awaits."

The flight back to my homeland was an uneasy and a short ride. Ronaldo had stayed by my side the whole time and prevented me talk to the others.

The exchange of authority occurred right outside the plane when we landed. Papers were signed, instructions were told, until we were handcuffed and dragged away, straight to the airport.

"Queen Esmeralda will be so delighted to see you." Ronaldo and I were leading the procession. His face was set into the brightest smile as he turned to me, teeth showing and all. "She's been dreaming of this moment for a long time, do you know that?"

"Why? Is she in love with me?" I asked.

His teeth mashed together. "Why you, you do not talk about the Queen in that manner! I cannot wait until the guillotine strikes down your neck and make your head roll!"

"Guillotine?" My shoulders shrugged. "It's not the 18th century anymore, Ronaldo. But from the smell coming from you, it appears like you haven't showered since then."

"Burn!" Vanessa piped up behind us. She had listened to the whole exchange and was now laughing like a hyena. "Her Majesty roasted you. Admit it."

The hulking man stopped and swiveled to her. All the other guards halted as a result. "Majesty?" Ronaldo's eyebrow twitched. "That title only belongs to the Queen. Call Cybele that one more time and I cut off your tongue!"

Brooke was quick to leap in Van's defense. "She didn't mean that!"

"Of course, I did!" Van wasn't one to be hampered. Even at the face of execution, her outlook in life remained solidly happy. She had a touch of madness I could relate to in so many levels. "Cut my tongue off. Do it, Ronaldi! I still have fingers. Fingers are all I need in my relationship."

"Maybe I'll cut those off too." Ronaldo's foot moved forward. "And maybe I. . . Huh?" He glanced over his shoulder and gasped. A great number of people were rushing to us all at once.

The mob came swiftly, out of nowhere, alarming. But it wasn't just one type of crowd. People from all walks of life swarmed around us, even reporters.

"We heard from a reliable source that the Princess got married to a model named Iris overseas," one said. "Is that true?"

"Princess Talia is wearing boots, jeans, and a simple white t-shirt following her marriage. . ." Rambled another.

"The Princess was reported missing a few months ago, but here she is now married to her kidnapper. Did she suffer from the Stockholm syndrome? Or did they run away together in the first place because they were in love? More of this scoop on our channel."

"Okaerinasai, Hime-san!" shouted a foreigner.

That was the last straw. Ronaldo turned to the guards, shock written all over his face, and barked. "Secure Talia! Guard the others!"

As one, the guards who had accompanied us from the plane surrounded us in a tight formation. Before someone pushed my head down to shield me from the cameras, I caught sight of someone incredibly familiar. Alessandra. She was leaning beside a vending machine, smirking at me, making do with the promise she swore over the phone before my wedding.

~ 445 ~

"You're welcome," she mouthed.

More reporters were waiting for us at the lobby. They weren't alone. The citizens of Harland who dropped by were carrying banners of greetings and support, happy that the Princess had defied expectations to marry her true love. The extreme ones were wearing t-shirts. I couldn't help but read the colorful printed words.

You kidnapped my heart too, Iris.

Van is my bae.

Brooke can ramp all over me.

They were absurd, comical, but the look on Ronaldo's face as he saw them was absolutely priceless. This was all Alessandra's doing. She'd been a friend to me no matter the consequence.

Van waved to a group of teenage girls who was waving a banner with her name. "I love you all!" she said. "I have a girlfriend now, but I love you!"

The press and the people had outnumbered us. The guards were using their walkie-talkies to call for back-up, but it still didn't dampen the spirit of many news hounds. Some of them had breached the circle of security to get close to my wife.

"Princess Talia!" A reporter who managed to veer close shoved her recorder to us. "We heard you got married behind your mother's back. Aren't you afraid to be disowned because you can't carry the next successor for Harland?"

Talia was all smiles. "That shouldn't be a problem anymore," she said. "There are modern ways to let me have Cybele's child. Even her adoptive father is working on it as we speak." Her charming smile slowly dissolved into a frown. And everyone, transfixed, listened closely to what she had to say, wondering perhaps why she suddenly got sad. "I doubt my mother will allow it though. My wife has been her enemy for a long time."

"Stop this at once, Princess!" Ronaldo pushed the reporters away in anger. The reporters pushed him back. They weren't done asking questions.

"Care to elaborate on that, Princess?" a reporter asked.

Talia, who was in the thick of it all, wiped the edge of her eyes like a well-practiced actress. Around us, people murmured their sympathy. The Princess had always been sweet. Innocent. If only they knew.

"My mother had always been afraid to get the throne stolen from her," Talia whispered. "After all. . ." She paused for full effect. "My mother stole it herself."

A collective gasp.

Ronaldo had enough of it. "Don't you dare speak another word, Princess! Guards!" He signaled to the ones closest to Talia. "Make sure she doesn't talk again! She's wreaking havoc to the image of the kingdom!"

Talia turned to the security. "Stand down, soldiers!" Her order was sharp. "Have you no respect for your Princess?" The hardness made way for softness as she met my eyes. Talia was nailing it through and through. "Cybele and I have known each other since we were children," she continued. "Her father and mother, the former King and Queen, were kind enough to invite us all the time."

~ 447 ~

A baffled reporter shouldered a guard, so he could interview the Princess too. "Are you talking about the deceased rulers of the throne?"

I took a sharp breath as Talia nodded. "Yes," she revealed. "I'm talking about them." A short silence ensued. But for me it felt like eternity before she raised her eyes again and motioned my way. "Cybele here, my wife, is the Princess that supposedly died in the fire. She's the rightful heir to the throne, a born leader, and what's more, a victim of my mother's act of treason!"

"P-Princess!" Ronaldo cried.

But Talia continued. "Once we leave here, my mother is going to execute my wife, force me to marry a man I do not love, all so she can cover her brutal acts of murder. I demand a public trial. Let those she has wronged unjustly come forward and band together to end this lunacy. I call on you!"

The speech was going so smoothly that none of us had noticed the back-up guards arriving. They rounded us up, separated us from the crowd, and put us in a vehicle, until we were delivered to the Palace.

My fingers gripped the cold, iron rail of the dungeon gate minutes later. From a wedding reception to this. And here I was, expecting a honeymoon.

"Good thing they let us change before coming here, eh?" Van collapsed on the floor and leaned on the wall. "Imagine being stuck here in your wedding gown, Your Highness. Now that would be a sight."

"Leave her alone." Brooke made her way to me. "Can't you see Iris is worried as it is?

Besides, you're adding stress by opening your mouth. You almost got your tongue cut off for that."

"Heh!" Van stuck out the said tongue. "That's what the braille is for, Brookey!"

"The braille is for blind people, smart-arse." Brooke had reached my side and was gently prying my hands from the iron bars. "Don't worry too much," she murmured. "Wherever they put Talia, I know she's safe. Just believe in your own plan."

I did believe in it. But Talia being separated from us was still bothersome. Ronaldo couldn't be trusted. Neither was her mother.

Especially her mother.

"Let's hope everything is fine," I said. "The two of you get some rest. We have a long night ahead of us."

Chapter 45
Cybele

I fought off sleep the whole night, worried about the Princess 'whereabouts. Where was she? What were they doing to my wife?

It was in the wee hours of the morning when my body gave in due to exhaustion. But minutes after I closed my eyes, someone was shaking my shoulder again, with a firm command to wake up. "The three of you." I blinked my eyes open to see a guard standing over us. "You need to come with me. The Queen commands your presence."

"In the early morning?" Van had a crisscross mark on her cheek as she sat. "Why? Does she want to hookup or something?"

"Move!"

The three of us huddled together while six armed guards accompanied us. They didn't say where we would go, but I knew the Palace by heart to know that we were headed to the throne room. Thus, I was able to prepare myself when the double doors opened to admit us. Esmeralda lay in wait on the other side.

"Still stubborn as ever I see." Her words rang true and solid. She sounded amused. She must have thought it was funny.

"You're sitting in my throne," I remarked.

"Your throne?" She leaned back in the gilded chair as if to confirm that it was still there.

Afterwards, she gave a satisfied smile. "It's not your throne, Cybele. You've never had it."

"Thanks to you?"

"Thanks to me."

I crossed my arms. It was to my unfortunate luck that my mother-in-law was deranged.

"You're quite proud of your achievement," I said. "But what do you think will happen once you die? Talia will never touch that seat. She hates you."

"She's weak." Esmeralda shrugged. "It doesn't matter if she hates me or not. I raised her to follow my rules."

Revulsion and contempt made their way into my veins, spreading out into my system. To hear her talking about her daughter—my wife like that. "No wonder my father chose my mother." The words spilled out of nowhere. And even if Esmeralda's eyes had started to bulge, her lips beginning to tremble, I pressed on just to feel the satisfaction. "I knew you were in love with my father. But no matter what you did, he would have never loved you back. You're a worm compared to my mom!"

"Ronaldo!" Esmeralda's following shriek was appalling. "Ronaldo!"

"I guess he left you too," I said.

She decided to take matters into her own hands and stood from the throne, and walk to a guard. "Knife!" she said, holding her palm out. Automatically, four other guards subdued my hands and legs. Esmeralda shot me a contemptuous look and headed towards me. "It's funny when you think about it, Cybele. You've worked this hard for what? To end up executed? Failing your parents? Losing?"

"She's not the loser. You are!" Van rushed across the room defiantly, only to be stopped by more guards on standby. Behind us, Brooke was being restrained too. "Let go of me!" Van yelled. "Your Queen is spreading gonorrhea!"

Esmeralda gave her an amused glanced before continuing to me. "The company you keep, Cybele. . . is atrocious."

"They're better than you in every way." I held my head high. Even if she killed me now, slit my throat and spilled my blood, I was proud to do it here. The throne was a witness to how much we fought. How much I stood up for love.

Esmeralda's knife gleamed under the light. She had made it to me now, and was raising the weapon that would end my life.

The door burst open.

Lance, Alex, Chandra, and two more people I didn't recognize stormed into the throne room, all armed to the teeth. Esmeralda had looked taken aback by the sheer number of them, prompting her to call again. "Ronaldo! Who are these people? Where are you?"

Talia entered the throne room, looking like she'd just went to hell and back to see me. "The swine escaped," she said. A banging echo from the southwestern part of the Palace made us all halt. But my eyes were set on her. There was no terror in her face now, only punishment. Her eyes glinted when she glared at Esmeralda. "Didn't I tell you earlier to lay the fuck off my wife, Mother?"

Esmeralda had looked shocked with the appearance of my friends, but it was Talia's statement that made her face contort in fury. With a stretch of her hand, her fingers wrapped around my neck and began to choke me.

"You think you can just barge in here and tell me those things?" Esmeralda's squeeze tightened. "There are consequences to this, Talia! It's about time you learn discipline!"

A gun pointed to the Queen. "Let go of Cybele or I shoot." Talia was not kidding. But then, so was her mother.

"Do it!" Esmeralda taunted. "Kill me!"

Bang!

One of the guards holding me dropped to ground and screeched.

"I missed!" Talia declared. "But I might not miss again, Mother. Next time, that will be you."

The Queen laughed. A low disturbing sound that came from nothing. It increased in pitch until she let go of me, brought her hands to her stomach, and barked like she was howling at the moon. "You've grown!" she said in glee. "I didn't foresee that. You're just like me!"

"I'm nothing like you!" Talia yelled.

Esmeralda stopped laughing. "You're saying that now, but when you've had power, you relish it until it drives you mad." The knife made a clanging sound as she released it. Her hands, trembling with excitement, spread wide at her sides. "Join me," she invited, eyes manic with happiness. "If you marry Cybele, you're nothing but a sidekick. A second person. But if you pledge your loyalty to me, the throne will be yours. Oh, Talia, you'll love how it feels! You can have anything, anyone!"

Talia's hand lowered. Her head shook in disbelief. "Cybele is everything I've ever wanted. How can you ask a thing from me?"

"Uhh, because she's freaking insane?" Van's loud voice demanded to be heard. "And excuse me to butt in your family drama, but I'm getting tired here!"

All of us looked in Van's direction, to the guards that have jerked her head back and restrained her hands. I knew I made a mistake by taking my eyes off the enemy. Esmeralda and some of her personal guards were running behind the throne when I glanced back. They were heading straight for the wall.

"Mother!" Talia screamed.

Esmeralda wasn't listening anymore. She was focused on the opening walls—something I wasn't aware of until today.

"She must have had her own secret passageway installed," I rasped. "She's going to escape!"

Chandra and her crew ran to the Queen but was immediately stopped by the guards who had subdued me. They were more intent on protecting Esmeralda than killing me now.

Talia rushed to my side. "A-are you okay?" she said, arms looping around my waist. "Can you breathe normally?"

"I'm fine." I kissed her forehead and leaned away. Our team was regrouping, but so was theirs. In front, Esmeralda was entering the tunnel through the walls.

"Kill them," Esmeralda said before disappearing. As a result, the remaining guards in the room drew out their guns.

"Okay," Chandra said, eyes on the approaching guards. Our numbers were uneven, them more than us. But no one seemed to start the bloodbath yet. The throne room was too open. There was barely any room to duck behind. If anyone open fired now, no one would win. "Your Majesty, you and the other girls follow Esmeralda. Me, Alessandra, and our small group here will try to fend them off."

"Are you sure?" I waited for her confirmation. She'd always been punishing when she pretended to be Viper on the phone, but I didn't know how good her skills were in real life.

Chandra nodded and tossed me a gun. Lance and Alex tossed two more to Brooke and Van. "We can handle ourselves," she said. "Just go and do your duty."

My duty. I gave Chandra a grateful look. "I will forever owe you," I said. "You too, Alessandra and Lance."

Lance rolled his shoulders and grinned. "I can't believe I'm doing this."

"Believe it because it's happening, tea boy." Van threw him a smile. "Nice to see you again."

"You too."

The two of them had finished exchanging high-fives when I took Talia's hand and braced myself. "They won't open fire," I whispered. "On three, we run to the left. Brooke and Van, you run to the right. The rest, cover us. One." I tightened my grip on the gun. "Two—"

I had barely finished the count when Talia and I dashed to the target. The guards immediately began to split off. Chandra and the others were prepared for it, waiting. A fight broke behind us when we made it to the opened wall.

"Hurry!" I said to Van and Brooke. "Get inside!"

"What about them?" Talia hesitated by the entrance.

I gave Alessandra and the others one last look behind. "They will make it," I said.

The passageway was so narrow, only one of us could fit in the space at a time. Electric torches lined the wall above us, though I was guessing that the power in the Palace was having problems what with its flickering lights.

"You guys okay over there?"

"Yes, Your Majesty." Van was in the lead. "But it feels like Thelma's in here."

"Thelma?" Brooke sounded bewildered.

"Long story."

We followed the path, feeling along the wall while at it. There could be some sort of door or hidden exit. But unfortunately, we found a different type.

"Watch out!" Talia yelled, as something gleamed above Brooke's head.

Brooke ducked at the perfect time, then Talia, then me. A swinging axe trap had come out from nowhere. Vanessa must have activated it without knowing.

"Everyone all right?" I said, as the axe disappeared from sight. My heart still raced from the surprise. The place was as evil as the mistress who had made it.

"I. . . I'm good," Talia assured. "B-Brooke? Van?"

"I'm okay."

"I'm lesbian." Van chuckled nervously from in front. "Should I get going?"

"Yes. But be more careful," I said.

We crept along the passageway, taking extra measures not to activate anything this time. It slowed us down by a few extra seconds, though neither of us knew how long this tunnel was or where it lead. Finally, after minutes of walking, Van proclaimed. "I think I see the path forking. Which way should I take, Your Majesty?"

Left, my head scream. No, *right*.

"Let's meet in the middle first," I said. "It will be easier to decide there."

The three of them shuffled to the left to give me space, so all of us could stand in the middle. But before I could tell them to stop, something rumbled like an earthquake. Made me lean on the shaking wall. Made me cover my ears. The ceiling on top of us collapsed.

"Cybele!"

"Iris!"

I coughed instead of answering them. My nose was clogged. Everywhere around me was smoke. I spit dust from my mouth and groaned. "I'm alive. . ."

"Thank God!"

"Where are you guys?" I waved my arms. "I can't see you, Talia! Brooke? Van?"

The smoke settled to explain my predicament. Rocks—a great number of them in different sizes, were blocking my way.

"I think we're separated!" Talia sounded far. "What should we do?"

The rocks in front of me were solid and unmoving. It could collapse on us if we tried to crawl our way through.

"Continue taking the path there," I yelled. "I'll see where mine leads. They might converge at some point." I looked around to see if my gun was nearby, but no such luck. It must have been thrown away when I tried to shield my face, then got crushed by the rocks by accident. "Van?"

"Yes, Your Highness?" she called.

My tongue felt papery dry as I dragged it to my lips. "Take care of the girls for me. I'm counting on you."

"Cybele!" Talia had a warning tone.

"I'll be okay," I said. "I'll see you in a bit." I moved away from the rubble to start my journey. The quicker I walked, the faster we'd catch up.

My wrist watch had been taken away before they put us in the dungeon cells this evening. Or was it yesterday? I couldn't really say. Either way, my ring was still in my finger. I toyed with it as I walked, remembering how Talia had giggled when I slipped hers on. How her cheeks tinted red when Mum and Dad welcomed her to the family. How I wish the king and Queen had been there too, looking at us.

My footsteps stopped.

At the end of my path was not the exit nor a converging of tunnels. It was a door. An unsettlingly familiar one. It swung open even before I put my hand on the knob.

Chapter 46
Cybele

The creak of the door ignited goosebumps in my flesh. I hesitated. What would I find on the other side?

You've never been scared before, a voice said at the back of my head. *Why here? Why now?*

Why, you say? Because. . . I didn't know.

Steeling myself, I shouldered the door and was greeted by a strong light, enough to make me blink for a few seconds and close my eyes. The room beyond began to take form as I stepped inside.

I gasped.

"Isn't it amazing how you should end up here?" A deep, victorious voice said.

My eyes traveled to the room, but he wasn't anywhere in sight. Instead, there was a four-poster bed with its silk sheets prepared, a burning fireplace that made the space feel like inferno, a room that had should have been left in memory in the villa, yet here it was after twelve years, looking like an exact copy of the old one, making me shake.

I took an involuntary step back, but the door had slammed shut behind me.

"There's no use," Ronaldo's voice echoed. "There is only one way for you to get out of here, Cybele—inside a body bag."

I wanted to tell him he was wrong. I wanted to retort a smart comeback. Yet it seemed that all energy had been drained from me. It was only sheer will that made me stand up. Made me lean on the wall. But even that was closing in on me.

"Cybele, Cybele." Ronaldo sounded impatient. "Come to the bed. I have something to show you."

"N-No!"

He laughed. "Aren't you a bit curious? You hadn't been back here for a long time. It's fitting that you investigate."

What did he take me for? A fool? Where was he hiding? Through the walls? In the cabinetry?

I marched to the latter on my right and flung it open. There was nothing.

"Wasn't hide-and seek your favorite game with Talia?" Ronaldo's question lingered as I went to the walls next and felt for a secret compartment. There was no hollowed sound. We were surrounded by thicker bricks, probably due to the tunnel. "Give it up," he said, sounding amused. "You won't find anything here that can help you. Even the door is sealed shut. There's only me and you."

I swiveled to the bed, feeling dread, nausea, and the emergence of panic.

Calm down, Cybele. This was just a ruse, so I wouldn't be able to fight him. Because that's what snakes do. They poison before they choke.

"Come closer," Ronaldo whispered. "Closer to the bed, young royal. Closer."

~ 461 ~

What should I do? There were neither means to escape nor weapons that could save me. A drop of sweat slid down my throat. And then my feet moved.

"That's right," Ronaldo encouraged. "My surprise is just waiting. See it for yourself."

I was almost to the bed when my shoes crunched on something. Before I could wonder what it was, a snapping sounded, a compartment opened, and two blackish forms dangled from the ceiling.

"Aaaah!" My shrieks filled the room. But it wasn't the sheer terror that clouded my eyes. The tears had come automatically, rushing out like a wave, when I realized what those were.

"Say hello to Mother and Father!" Ronaldo's sadistic laughter echoed. "Or should I say, just Father?"

I blinked away the tears to stare at the corpses inches from me. They were charred, deformed, and smelled heavily of preservative chemicals, though the scent of death lingered.

My head moved to the side as the last of what I've eaten came out through my mouth.

"Aww. . . The young royal doesn't have a stomach for these things." Ronaldo's sympathy was as phony as his loyalty. "Tough luck, Cybele. If you want to sit in the throne, you can't be a bumbling, crying loser. You have to be tough. Like the Queen."

Something moved above me, followed by the groan of the bed.

"Remember this room because it will be the last thing you see." Ronaldo's voice sounded closer, hovering. "I commend your guts for starting an uprising against us. But that's all there is to it. Tomorrow when you're dead, the guards will round up the civilians who've entered the Palace tonight and hang them for treason. Talia, Brooke, and that runt you call your friend will come next. Esmeralda has no use for them. Not in the new world she's creating."

The floorboard behind me whined.

"Farewell," he said.

I turned around and kicked his leg before his knife crushed down. He was a conceited man. A hateful man. He thought he could kill me without using a gun, but that's where he was wrong.

Ronaldo fell to his knees following my attack. He let go of the knife in surprise, giving me the opportunity to snatch it from the floor and raise it above his head. But he wasn't done yet. He pounced on me like a raging bull.

"You're as stupid as your father!" Ronaldo punched my face, then wrestled the knife from my hand. "He's too trusting! Too soft! Esmeralda shouldn't have fallen for him!"

The knife was knocked from me, slid on the floor, away from my grip.

Ronaldo's fingers wrapped around my neck. "All of you," he spat, "Including Esmeralda, thought I didn't know!" He squeezed me tighter, harder, until black spots danced on my eyes. My lungs began to suffocate. "But I've always known she was in love with him. Your father deserved to die because of that!"

My vision blurred as I tried to pry his hands away. But he was too strong. Too big. And it was like I was ten again, helpless, alone, with only my dead parents to accompany me in my last moment.

Ronaldo leaned to me, his breath smelling of murder. "Don't worry about Talia," he whispered. "I'll make sure she enjoys me first before she follows you in death."

My foot came in contact with something hard, something swinging. I kicked it on a last strain of breath and hoped that it would do its job.

"Huh?" Ronaldo glanced over his shoulder. "What's—"

I used the distraction and tilted my head down. His fingers tasted salty as I gave it a hard bite.

"Aaaah!"

I kicked him away from me. My chest was heaving when I gulped in air, but I wasn't safe yet. Ronaldo was going to retaliate.

"Come here, you bitch!"

I rolled to the side before he could grab me, choke me again, and crawled next to my mother's legs. She'd been the one Ronaldo felt.

Turning away, I tugged mother's corpse free from the cord and let her fall to the ground. Ronaldo rushed to me. "You're joining her soon, Cybele! Ack!"

I looped the cord around his neck, over and over until it created a noose that he couldn't break free off. What Talia said about me was true. I was preparing for war, a war that I did not intend to lose.

Ronaldo clawed his arm on my face, struggled to punch me, all to no avail. His shoes skidded on the floor as his lungs gave way, his body defeated. He stilled. And I stilled too. Beyond the tunnel, explosions from the uprising sounded.

Epilogue

The blowing of horns signaled the end of the procession. On both my sides, positioned in a straight line, newly sworn Palace guards stilled and gave a salute, waiting for my next move.

I bent over and took soil from the earth. People of Harland had a saying; all that was born of the ground comes back to the ground. I showered my parent's coffins with soil. May they finally rest in peace.

A three-day silence had followed the uprising. It was for Mother and Father, and for me. For the people too. Harland had suffered with the disease of Esmeralda's cruelty for far too long. It was time to end it, to move forward, and though it might take some time, to recover what was lost and replace it with something better.

"This is a really cool place, Your Majesty." Vanessa looked around the Palace study. She gawked at the portraits of my dead parents on the wall—the King and Queen—marveled at the chandelier, before marching to the window and staring at the expanse of land outside. "What time did you say your shift will end?"

"It's not a shift, Van. I can go anytime I wish," I said to her.

"So why don't you go now?" she asked.

"Because I have work." I flattened the document on the table, took the seal, and stamped my signature. It read, *Her Royal Majesty, Cybele.*

Van's reflection on the window told me she had frowned. "Let me get this straight," she said. "You have work, but you don't call it a shift? Sounds fishy to me."

"For God's sake, Vanessa."

She turned to me and crossed her arms. "Am I bothering you?" she asked. "Do you feel personally attacked by these questions?"

I put the seal back on the holder and smirked at her. If anything, I had missed her. She and Brooke hadn't visited me for three months, though I knew they had a villa to run.

"How's my best friend?" I asked.

Van shrugged. "You'll know when you leave your office, Your Majesty." She smiled before skipping to my table. The woman smelled like the sun and mischief. "Are you ready for tonight?" she asked.

Now that was a question I was waiting for.

"Yes," I said. "Be thorough."

That night, while the moon was at its peak, Talia, now the Queen of Harland like me, struggled against her captors, her head covered by a black sack. "Let go of me!" she screamed. "I will sock your head! Cybele! Where are you? Cybele, help me!"

The culprits placed her on her feet, took a step back, allowing me to come forward to remove the cover from her face. Talia's lips moved for another scream, but when she saw that it was me, her terror turned to confusion.

"C-Cybele?" She looked around. Brooke and Van were on either side of her, my adoptive parents just ways after that. A few paces from us were Aunt Lizzie, Chandra, Alessandra, and even Lancelot. The pond beside us was a clear blue under the moonlight. "W-what?" Talia sounded amazed. "Why did you kidnap me?"

I reached for her hand and kissed her knuckles. "Forgive me, my Queen. It has become a habit."

A man came forward: Harland's head Judge. He hadn't been noticeable in the heat of the confusion, but the moment he was, he gave a sweeping bow. "My Queens," he said. "Everything is ready for your wedding."

Talia and I stared at one another. "Let's do it right," I whispered. "Is that okay with you?"

She smiled.

The ceremony was intimate compared to my coronation a few months before. Only people that we were close to, the ones who were with us from the beginning, witnessed our union in the Palace garden. I couldn't have it any other way.

"I'm so happy for you!" Brooke was among the last to greet me after the vows. She let my parents and the others talk to me first before coming for an embrace.

I rubbed her back before letting go. My best friend was the finest maid of honor there was. "Are you going straight back to the villa after this?" I asked.

"I guess so," she said. "Why? Would you prefer that we stay?"

"Only for a while. I know you're busy." My head shook on its own. "It must be hard to guard my mother-in-law. How's her health?"

Brooke gave me a knowing smile. Following the decision from the people of Harland, Esmeralda was sentenced to live the remainders of her life in a solitary room in the villa. The same place where she imprisoned my aunt. Brooke and Van resided in the cabin nearby that I had built for them. The forest was their home now. Guarding Esmeralda was their duty.

"She's healthy as a horse," Brooke answered. "You should visit her from time to time. See how she's doing."

"Perhaps."

Van walked to us. "Hey," she whispered. "Your Majesty? Don't look now, but that chick over there is checking you out. Total heartthrob."

My eyebrows raised as I glanced at the direction she was pointing to. From the distance, my wife seemed embarrassed and turned away.

"See?" Van elbowed me. "I bet she has a crush on you. Why don't you talk to her?"

"Wish me luck," I said.

"You don't need it," Brooke supplied.

Talia might have sensed that I was coming for her. She excused herself from my parents, nibbled on her lower lip, and strolled to me the same time I went to her. "Hi," I said.

"Hi. . ." My wife's cheeks were flushed with natural pink. It reddened when she took my hand.

The two of us left our own party to go to the oak tree. It was there that so many things were said, so many stories were exchanged. It was there where she invited me to sit, so she could lean her head on my chest and breathe me in.

"I still can't believe it's over," she murmured. "All these months felt like they flew by." Talia sighed and closed her eyes. "Cybele?"

"Yes, My Queen?"

"Please tell me a story. Something I won't forget."

I smiled to myself and stroked her head. I knew just the perfect tale for her.

The crazy tale of Kidnapping the Princess.

FIN

Acknowledgement

If you bought this book and had followed my journey throughout the years, thank you, thank you, thank you. Publishing this book has been a long time coming. People had been asking me for years, but I had to grow up just as much as the characters before I could finely tune everything to how I wanted.

To Regina, thank you as always. I hope the heartbreaks, the grouchiness, and all the time kept away from you because I was making this book was worth it. To my parents who, at first, didn't like the idea of me writing but soon warmed up to it, thank you too. To my longtime readers who'd been waiting so patiently for this, you now have Kidnapping the Princess in your hands. I hope the support doesn't stop there. I will continue writing over the years to come.

Made in United States
Troutdale, OR
12/13/2023

15778651R00289